# PAUL CROUCH
WITH CYNTHIA CIRILE

## Charisma®
## HOUSE
Books about Spirit-Led Living

MEGIDDO by Paul Crouch with Cynthia Cirile
Published by Charisma House
A part of Strang Communications Company
600 Rinehart Road
Lake Mary, Florida 32746
www.charismahouse.com

Unless otherwise noted, all Scripture quotations are from the
King James Version of the Bible.

Scripture quotations marked NLT are from the Holy Bible, New
Living Translation, copyright © 1996. Used by permission of
Tyndale House Publishers, Inc., Wheaton, IL 60189. All rights
reserved.

Cover design by P.O.V. Design

Novel based on original screenplay by John Fasano and Steven
Blinn

Library of Congress Catalog Card Number: 2001092857
International Standard Book Number: 0-88419-799-9


01 02 03 04 87654321
Printed in the United States of America

This book is dedicated to
All of you who have found The Faith;
And to all you who are still searching for it...

# Foreword

MEGIDDO! Just the sound of the name sends shudders through anyone familiar with its story in the Book of Revelation in the Holy Bible.

It is a vast valley in northern Israel, thirty miles long and twelve miles wide, that multitudes of armies have fought their way through on their way to Jerusalem. The kings of the Old Testament fought here; the Babylonians fought here; Alexander the Great fought here; the Roman Caesars fought here; Napoleon fought here. Even in modern times, wars and skirmishes, great and small, have been and continue to be fought here. If the blood of all the fallen could be resurrected from the rich earth of this valley, it would surely flow to the horses' bridles!

But there remains one last, great, titanic battle of the ages yet to be fought here:

> And he gathered them together into a place called in the Hebrew tongue Armageddon.
>
> —Revelation 16:16

In this novel, *Megiddo,* the Antichrist, in his lust for total control of Planet Earth, summons the kings and military leaders of the world to this great valley to do battle with God Almighty. He knows that he must seize and control Jerusalem if he is to achieve his goal. He also knows the time for Jesus Christ's return is imminent and that the prophecies declare Christ will rule and reign for a thousand years on the throne of David—from Jerusalem!

The best fiction writers of all time could not have conjured up a more breathtaking, hair-raising story than that recorded in St. John's apocalypse—THE REVELATION! In this fictionalized account, you will experience a vivid portrayal of End-Time Bible prophecy and the greatest drama of all time: the rise to power by Satan himself cloaked in the human flesh of Stone Alexander—the Antichrist.

Never has such a graphic depiction of this last great battle been told—until now! Go with us in spirit to this great climax of the ages—go with us to the valley of blood—see for yourself what millions will see, for the last time: **MEGIDDO.**

—Paul F. Crouch, President
Trinity Broadcasting Network

# PROLOGUE

Sleep, my child, and peace attend thee,
All through the night.
Guardian angels
God will send thee
All through the night.
Dark and drowsy hours are creeping
Hill and vale in slumber sleeping,
I my loving vigil keeping—
All through the night.
While the Moon her watch is keeping
All through the night
While the weary world is sleeping
All through the night.
Through your dreams you're softly stealing
Visions of delight revealing
God His loving vigil keeping—
All through the night.

—Traditional lullaby

On a chilly winter's night, a young boy lay tossing and turning in his bed. For some reason, he couldn't sleep at all. Part of the trouble was that he felt uncomfortable in his surroundings. This was his bed, yes, the very same bed he had slept in since he was just a young boy. Now, he had grown much bigger, he thought, and if he extended his toes out as far as he could, he found that they just about reached the foot of the bed. He supposed that very soon he would outgrow that bed entirely and would have to adjust to a new bed. A bigger bed. One for bigger boys. Or maybe even an adult-sized bed that he would sleep in until he was actually an adult. An adult, he mused. He was eight years old now. That meant—he counted carefully on his fingers as the moon illuminated his face through the window behind him—that in eight years he would be an adult. And then, his toes would probably reach the foot of even an adult-sized bed. A bed the size of his father's!

His father's bed was huge—and so was he! At least he certainly appeared so to the young boy. He felt it must be true, since he had heard people commenting on his father's size, how tall he was, for as long as he could remember. The boy's father often seemed almost larger than life—and that thought captivated him for some time. To be as large as his father would mean that he would grow up to be just like his father, didn't it? He wondered if, in growing up, in becoming as large as his father, he would also become as dour and taciturn as his father.

Of course, these were not the words the boy thought. These were grown-up words—not to be found in the limited vocabulary of even the brightest of eight-year-olds. No words at all came into the young boy's head. Instead, he just thought of his father's face and saw it in his mind's eye. That face was cold and sad. It seemed to him that his father never had much fun. He had never seen him laugh, and he certainly had never seen him play. The boy sighed heavily. *Would growing up mean becoming sad for always?* he thought.

The fair-haired youngster shivered. He pulled his down comforter up closer to his throat and hugged a stuffed bear for comfort. No, he thought, he would rather stay small, stay eight years old forever if growing up, getting big, meant that he would have to be sad for always.

At eight years old this child was no stranger to sadness, to loneliness. He felt sad and lonely right now, in this room that *was* his room, but felt like the room of a stranger. And it was little wonder he felt that way. Though this had been his room for many years—it had even been his nursery—he felt no connection to it, no warmth in it. For some reason he couldn't understand, it felt like the coldest place in the entire house. Perhaps that was why when he actually slept there—slept in that bed that was fast becoming too small for him—he slept only fitfully, drifting in and out of light slumber until finally, the sun rose and the day began anew.

He looked around at the sterile, virtually barren room. Most of his personal belongings had been left behind at school; he had brought with him only the few necessities he'd need for a short stay, such as this one was. He was only to be home for a quick Christmas visit, less than a week, and then it was back into the car for the two-hour drive to his school, which felt more like a home than this cold, forbidding place would ever seem to him.

At least at school he would be surrounded by his friends, sharing a dorm room with three other boisterous boarders who had become like family to him. And then there were the kindly masters, and even the headmaster himself, whom he supposed to be about his father's age, or at least, he thought, they were both "grown up." But the headmaster wasn't sad. Not like his father seemed to be. He was never angry or impatient, as his father often was.

But, he thought, his father wasn't angry with *him*. Just as his sadness didn't have anything to do with him either. At least he didn't *think* it did. His father seemed to care so little for him and seemed so utterly uninterested in him when he *was* around that the boy couldn't imagine that any of his father's feelings could have anything to do with him whatsoever. Just as his own sadness, the way he felt that night, had nothing to do with his father. How could it? His sadness was *his* alone, and somehow, the familiarity of these feelings blanketed him, comforting him in this big, cold, old house. He longed for the vacation to be over so that he could return to his friends and the smiling headmaster.

The door cracked open ever so slightly, a ray of light piercing the darkness of his den. The boy raised himself up on one elbow, desperately hoping to see his father at the door. A voice spoke to him from the hallway. A soft voice, with a lilting, Irish brogue. "Are you all right in there, little master?"

The boy bolted upright in his bed, recognizing the voice of his old nanny, now one of the housemaids since he had been sent off to boarding school. She was his only link, his only connection, to a time that seemed so long ago, a time when he actually lived in this house and went running to Stella for everything.

"Stella?" he called, hoping for a temporary reprieve, or at least a short break from this interminable loneliness.

The buxom, red-headed woman, clad in a dress that made music as she walked, crossed the room and sat down on his bed. "What on earth are you doing up this time of night, my little darling?" The little boy put his arms affectionately around the woman as if she were his only lifeline. "There, there, now, sweetheart, tell Stella what's the matter..."

"I...I just can't sleep," the boy lied, not wanting to bombard Stella with all his feelings. "This bed's getting too small for me, I guess."

The woman laughed, feeling love and sympathy for this boy who was once her charge. "Yes, yes, my darling. You are getting to be quite the big one, aren't you? Master Peter told me that you were the tallest boy in your grade! Imagine that!"

For some reason, the compliment failed to have the desired effect. Instead of cheering him up, the comment only seemed to agitate the boy further. Stella looked down at him, seeing his face clearly through the glimmer of light coming in from the hall.

"You're probably just getting excited about Christmas like all young boys do. I'll bet that's what this is all about—am I right?" Stella said mischievously, hoping once again to see some happiness in the boy's eyes. But she didn't. He continued to clutch at her. *This might be the only boy in America who is not thinking of Santa Claus this night,* she thought.

She knew very well what was troubling him. She had lived in that house for many years. She knew, perhaps better than anyone else, all that had happened there. This poor boy had plenty to stay up nights about.

"Now listen to me," Stella tried once again. "Would you like it if I told you a bedtime story—just like I used to do when you were a wee laddie and had trouble falling asleep?"

*A story,* he thought. *What a wonderful, luxurious notion.* He couldn't remember the last time he had had a bedtime story. He smiled up at Stella, giving her the answer she wanted.

"Very well, then. I'll tell you a lovely Christmas story..."

"No," the boy said, almost heatedly. "Not a Christmas story!"

Stella backed off, hearing the bitterness in his voice. Christmas obviously held no charms for this serious lad, old far beyond his years. "Fine, then, I'll tell you one of the Br'er Rabbit tales, like the one where Br'er Bear met Br'er Rabbit for the first time. Do you remember those old Uncle Remus stories I used to tell you?"

The boy smiled faintly. Yes, he remembered them. But it was something different he was looking for. Something he couldn't quite put his finger on. The truth was, he was looking for something inspirational, something that would give him, well, what grown-ups would call "the will to go on." The will to get up and face his father the next day. His father, the man with the sad face. But the boy

9

couldn't articulate any of that, so he merely said, "No, nothing with rabbits or anything like that, Stella. Tell me a *true* story, a story about a boy like myself!"

Stella thought for a long moment, running her fingers comfortingly through his hair. A boy like himself. Yes, she thought; she knew just the thing. "You mean a *real* story, a true-life story about a real boy?" The boy nodded his head excitedly. Yes, that was exactly what he wanted. She nodded to herself, trying to figure out where to begin.

"Well then," she said, "this is a true story about a boy just about your own age—though I doubt he was as tall as you yourself—you being so very tall. He would've been more like the size of some of your schoolmates, just the ordinary size. But—this was no ordinary boy, no, not at all. Does this story sound like it would appeal to you?"

The boy shook his head fervently. "Yes, yes. I want to hear it." He sank back into his bed, feeling more at home now, in his too small bed, than he had ever remembered.

"Well," Stella said, "It's been a long time since I've told a story, you know. So I might be a little rusty. Let me work up to it a bit, all right?" The boy didn't say a word, and Stella threw back her head, deep in thought. Finally she spoke.

"Well, this was all taking place some very long time ago..."

"Before I was born?" the boy piped up.

"Oh, my, well, yes—not only before *you* were born, but before your father was born, and his father before him. And long before that even! This story takes place earlier than anyone can remember, thousands of years ago, in the place that is now called Israel." The boy didn't interrupt, so she continued.

"This was a lovely little lad, much like yourself, but the main difference between you was, he had many brothers. Maybe seven or eight of them. I can't recall. So, he was never alone."

The boy merely whispered, "Wow," as if in awe of what that would be like.

"Yes, it certainly was a large family, that's for sure; but our boy, the hero of our story, was the youngest of all the brothers, the baby, you might say. And he had his work to do, just as you do. But instead of going to school and learning about reading and writing, this lad had to care for the sheep. That was his job, and he did it very well. His father and his brothers were very pleased with him."

The young boy looked up at her. "Didn't he have a mother?"

The woman paused for moment, unsure. "Well, everyone has a mother, darling; it's just that some of them cross over to the other

10

side to be with our Lord a little sooner than the others. I think that was the case with this boy; though I truly can't recall, since it's a long time since I heard this story myself—but I do think that this boy's mother, like your own, had gone to our Lord."

This explanation seemed clear enough and seemed to comfort the boy, so Stella continued. "But the boy was not only good at tending sheep. No indeed. In fact, he became known all over the land for his playing on the harp. I suppose he had a lot of time to practice while he was tending to his flock, and he became so good at it that even the king, whose name was Saul, called him to come for a visit. He, the king that is, wasn't feeling very well. He was troubled in the heart."

"You mean," the boy said, "like Father?"

Stella paused again, sighing deeply. This child *would* ask the most difficult questions. "Well, yes and no, darling. You see, this king was in the middle of a big war between his people, the Israelites, and these other people, not very nice at all, called the Philistines. And that was mostly what was bothering the king, because the Philistines were very powerful enemies, and he was worried whether he could defeat them. So the king called the boy's father, whose name was Jesse, and asked him if it would be all right if the boy came for a visit to play his harp for him."

The boy appeared confused.

"You see, music has a way of calming people down, even grown-up people, just like lullabies soothe babies to sleep—like the ones I used to sing to you when you were but a wee bairn. Anyway, the king thought that maybe listening to some of the boy's harp playing might calm him down and help him to relax. And naturally, the boy's father was very proud when the king himself asked if his son would come and play for him. This was a great honor, and the father was delighted to bring his son to see the king. And that's exactly what happened. And when the king heard the boy play, he was...it is difficult to describe, but he had never heard anything like it. It was like...like a chorus of angels was playing to him! The boy's music had such power over the king that it helped him to regain his confidence all at once, and he felt ready to do battle against his enemies."

The boy interrupted again. "So the king was no longer sad?"

"That's right," Stella said. "He now felt that he could do anything. So he gathered all his men together into a big army and went out to war. And everything looked as if it was going splendidly, and the king felt very encouraged, until one of the Philistines came forward on the battlefield. You see; this one was different from the rest. This was a huge giant of a man!"

"Like Father?" the boy asked, wide-eyed.

"No," Stella laughed. "He was much bigger than even your father! I can't even tell you how huge he was! He was truly a giant—grander maybe than five or six men put together. And he was wearing a big brass helmet, and he was covered from head to toe with mail."

"You mean, like envelopes?" the boy asked.

"No, silly," she said. "Mail is, mail was..." she fumbled for an answer. "It was just like a suit of armor. That's what it was. A gigantic suit of armor big enough to fit a giant of a man. And then, suddenly, this man, whose name was Goliath, spoke right to the king, as if giving him orders. 'All right, this is how it's going to be. You send out your best warrior, and I will fight him; and whoever is the victor,' that is, whoever wins, 'will become the servant of the other.'"

"You mean, they'd become *slaves?*" the boy asked in horror.

"Yes, exactly, that's what he was saying. That the side that lost would become the slaves of the other side. Well, now, as you can imagine, the king was very upset upon hearing this news. He knew that he didn't have one man in his army as big as this beast, and he wondered if there was one brave enough to even try to take him on. So the king just walked back over to his army, feeling very disheartened. When he told his men the request that the giant had made, all the soldiers started to flee, terrified at either being killed or at being made into slaves! At that moment, it seemed to the king that all was lost.

"And then, suddenly, he heard a familiar music in his ears. He'd recognize that music anywhere; it was the little boy with the harp! The king went to seek him out, and he found the boy sitting with his brothers. He had come all the way from home with cheese, olives and other such things that they liked to eat back in those days, to give his brothers strength for the battle. Now he was entertaining them while they all feasted.

"When the king came in, all the feasting stopped. The king told the boy and his brothers what had just happened. The boy's brothers had already seen Goliath, and they were terrified. Just as the other soldiers had done, they too began gathering up all their belongings and preparing to run off. The king just looked at them, wondering if anything could save them from this giant. Would no man be brave enough to stand up against him?

"Seeing his brothers hastily packing up their bags, the little boy looked puzzled. He asked them where they were going. 'Home,' they said, 'before we all get slaughtered by that monster!' The boy turned to the king, who now appeared very sad. 'Why are they all leaving you? I don't understand?' The king replied softly, 'Because none of them dare go up against Goliath. And unless someone does, everything we have is lost...'

"Now, the boy dropped his harp to the ground. Even though he was but a lad, he drew himself up as tall as he could and announced to the king that *he* would fight Goliath! Well, you can just imagine the reaction of all those men! His brothers scoffed at the boy; the other soldiers just fell to their knees, they were laughing so hard. 'This boy—go up against that...giant?' The thought was utterly ridiculous. Very silly indeed.

"The only ones who didn't think it was silly were the boy himself and the king. The king, who was very wise, as kings are meant to be, now sat down beside the young boy. He looked him right in the eyes. 'What makes you think that you can conquer this giant, when all my other soldiers—even your own brothers—don't dare to take him on?'

"And then the boy turned to the king, telling him the most remarkable story. He told him that one night while he was having a bit of a snooze, he was awakened by the sound of one of his lambs crying out in the dark. He looked over and saw both a bear and a lion—which you ordinarily wouldn't find in the land of Israel—and they were carrying away his favorite baby lamb! So up the boy jumped and ran after them, and found the lion just about to devour the little lamb. But the boy pulled the lamb right out of the lion's mouth and saved him. Then he killed the lion."

"How?" the boy asked, amazed.

"I don't actually recall how he did it, but I do know he did it," Stella replied animatedly, all caught up in her story. "And what's more, then the bear leaped up at him as he was carrying the lamb back to safety, and the boy promptly sent the bear back to meet his Maker as well!"

"You mean," the boy whispered, "that he killed the bear, too?"

"Yes, that's exactly right. And he risked his own life and fought off a lion and a bear, just for the sake of a baby lamb. So then, after telling this story, the boy turned back to the king. The king did not understand the boy's story. Of course, he thought it was wonderful, even miraculous, that the boy had fought off both a bear and a lion— he too had never heard of those animals existing in his land. He didn't even have a good idea of what a lion, or a bear, for that matter, looked like! This boy was brave, to be sure, and he didn't doubt the truth of what he said for a moment.

"He looked over at the wee lad. He liked him a great deal and didn't want to see him get hurt. So he told the boy, 'Look, this

Philistine is a man of war. You are but a wee laddie.' Or something like that, but in his own words. But the boy said something that really surprised him. He said, 'This giant will be just the same to me as if he were the bear or the lion. If my heavenly Father saved me from the jaws of those ferocious beasts, surely He will once again save me against this giant!'

"Well, I can't begin to describe the look on the king's face! He was so proud of the boy's courage, with his being such a young lad, too. Could he really send him up against the most ferocious villain in the land? You see, he was deathly afraid of accepting the responsibility." Stella saw that the word *responsibility* was clearly not in her young charge's vocabulary. She tried to boil it down.

"You see, the king had become like something of a father to the boy, and he would've felt awful inside if something happened to him. Just like, if something bad happened to the boy, it would be his fault, and he'd feel it on his conscience for the rest of his days."

The boy nodded thoughtfully. Yes, now he understood what she meant by responsibility. "But if the boy wanted to do it, if it was his own choice, then I think it would be his own fault if something bad happened to him. His own...responsibility."

Stella pondered for a moment. Was this a lad of eight, she thought, or a full-grown man in disguise? "Well, you know, that's exactly what the king thought. He felt that if the boy was willing to do this—wanted to do this of his own free will, that yes, it was his own responsibility, no matter what happened to him."

"What did happen?" the boy asked, completely absorbed in the tale.

Stella laughed at his earnestness. "I'm about to tell you, if you just quiet down. But don't worry, now—you don't think I'd tell you a bedtime story without a happy ending, do you?" She smiled down at the lovable child. The boy's head sank back down into his pillow, the plump Irish woman leaning over him, trying to remember where on earth she had been in the story.

"Yes," she started again. "So the king decided to take the boy at his word. He had always known, from the first moment the boy had played the harp for him, that there was something special about him. Something magical. And now, hearing the incredible story the boy had told him about the lion and the bear, he was even more taken with him, and thought that yes, the boy had been greatly blessed— he was being guided by a higher power and was being watched over by a force much stronger that his own. If the boy felt himself so blessed, the king felt, in his heart, that it must be so.

"So he decided to give him a chance. He had the boy all fit out in mail, well, armor, that is, and a helmet to protect his head, and a fine sword so heavy that the boy could hardly lift it. It turned out that the boy hated the armor and the sword. He asked the king to please let him take them off at once. The king didn't understand—didn't the boy want to be as protected as much as possible against this Goliath? But the boy just shook his head, telling the king that all these things weren't going to help him at all. He wasn't used to them, you see. He wasn't a trained soldier, like his brothers, so they would do him no good at all. Instead, the boy picked up five smooth stones off the ground and took a slingshot out of his pocket. The king looked at him as if to faint right there on the spot! Surely the boy didn't mean to take on the giant with a slingshot? Some of the soldiers, who had just been standing around waiting to see what was going to happen, started to laugh at the boy.

"But the boy paid them no mind. He was only looking at the king. He saw how worried the king was, and he tried to reassure him, to make him feel better. He told the king that he shouldn't worry about anything, that his faith in his God would protect him."

"What is faith?" the young boy interrupted.

Stella looked down at him, shaking her head. "You dear lad—faith is the feeling that we have deep inside, of believing in something greater than ourselves, of another plane of existence, where our Father dwells, looking after us and protecting us." She segued back into the story. "And it was faith that the young boy had more of than anyone else in the whole land, including the king himself! And it was that faith—knowing that he was protected by divine grace—that gave him the confidence to move away from the king, and all the other soldiers, and march as proudly as ever you could imagine, right onto the battlefield.

"Goliath stood there; big as the Empire State Building he looked as the young boy moved in closer and closer to him. The king and a few soldiers, some of them the boy's own brothers, waited nervously at the edge of the battlefield. They were very scared for the boy. But the boy himself wasn't scared at all, you see, because he was filled with faith in his God! That faith made him keep on moving closer and closer, until finally he could get a good look at the man he was going to fight."

"But," the boy asked, "I thought you said he was a giant?"

Stella acted exasperated, though she wasn't at all. "If you keep interrupting me like this, we're going to have to finish this story another night!"

The boy grabbed on to her arm. "No! I promise! Just finish it, please?"

15

"Well, all right," Stella chuckled. "As it happens, this Goliath was a man, but he was also a giant, or rather, this is hard to explain—he had become a beast, because he didn't have faith. Or, let me put this another way—he had faith in all the wrong things, in everything in this world that was terrible, and evil—and all this evil inside of him had turned him into a beast."

The boy paused for a moment, deep in thought. "Is this *really* a true story?" he asked.

"I thought you said there'd be no more questions, young man," Stella chided him good-naturedly.

"But is it? I have to know!" he demanded.

"Why, certainly it is a true story, as I told you before!"

*Well,* the boy thought, *if this is a true story, then evil is something to be avoided at all costs—if it has the power to turn you into a monster!* The side of good looked a whole lot more attractive to him, and the boy with the slingshot seemed like just about the bravest boy he had ever heard of. *He was nothing like me,* he thought, *lying here cowering in fear of the dark.*

"So anyway, the boy looked at Goliath—you *do* want to hear the ending, don't you?" The boy stared up at her in rapt attention, so she went on. "And Goliath was angry, insulted. He said, 'Is this your king's idea of a joke? I ask him to send out his strongest, bravest warrior—and he sends me a little boy?' And his voice was like thunder, it was.

"But don't you know that wee lad stared the beast down as cool as can be and said to him, 'Well, you may think you can win against me, since you're so strong and have so many weapons. But I have something much more powerful than your swords! I have faith in Jehovah, my God.' And Goliath just looked down at the boy, amazed as could be. But before the monster could even draw his sword, the boy had loaded his slingshot with one of those smooth stones; he pulled it back, and let it go. The stone found its mark right between the eyes! Well, the giant toppled backwards to the ground, and the earth trembled when he fell; that's how big he was. And that was the end of that. The Philistines went home that night beaten by a young boy with a slingshot."

Stella smiled down at the boy, who didn't seem to want the story to end. "And then what happened?" he asked eagerly.

"Well," she said patiently, "then the king took the boy home with him, and over the years, he shared all of his wisdom with the lad, so that, when he had become very tired of being king, he could take off his crown and give it to the boy—making *him* king over all the land! And the boy grew up to become the greatest king that anyone had ever known. He kept a tight hold on his faith in God for the rest of his life, and it kept him strong and wise. And that's the end of the story. I told you it had a happy ending!"

The boy just shook his head. "I just can't believe that story is true. It's so...amazing."

Stella smiled down at him. "Well, the power of faith is an amazing thing, laddie. Now, will you finally go to sleep?" The boy nodded, and Stella bent over him to kiss him on both cheeks. "You are a darling child. With the power of faith, you might grow up to be as strong and powerful as the lad in the story. You might even find your own Goliath to fight one day!"

With that, Stella got up from the bed, rearranging her wide skirt. The boy watched as she walked across the room, standing framed by the door.

"Stella," he called.

She turned back to him. "Yes, darling?"

"You never told me the name of the little boy in the story."

Stella moved back into the room now, her eyes glistening with tears. "I was wondering when you were going to ask me that! Since you must know, his name was David."

The boy was stunned. "David? Really?"

"Yes, really. Now will you go to sleep?"

"Yes," he murmured, his mind already a thousand miles away. "Thank you, Stella. I love you."

She smiled over at him, eyes still moist with tears. "And I love you too, little David."

# CHAPTER ONE

Behold, I stand at the door,
and knock: if any man hear my voice,
and open the door, I will come in to him ...

—Revelation 3:20

A string of shiny, valet-parked cars lined the mile-long driveway leading to Daniel Alexander's elegant Richmond, Virginia home. The mansion was one of the few original landmarks left unscathed by the ravages of the Civil War, now well over a hundred years ago. If it weren't for the squeaky-clean Jaguars, Mercedes Benz and the occasional Cadillac, it could have been an elaborate Southern ball—before the War Between the States had stopped all that frippery and reduced Richmond to rubble.

But tonight the house was aglow, not with candle-filled chandeliers carefully illuminated by servants, as in the 1850s, but with immense crystal chandeliers—yet somehow, the effect was much the same. The house itself was so bright that it almost seemed to have a life force of its own. In the blackness of the Virginia evening, it stood out like a beacon, and yet, it was somehow too bright, its ostentation like one constellation in the heavens that had the self-assurance to believe it could outshine and outlast all the others.

Whatever the occasion, it was a grand one. There was live music—not a quartet, mind you, but a full-string orchestra—and the sound of music, baroque, antiquated, far too heavy for the lilting summer night, filled not only the house but also the dense woods surrounding it.

There was an air of falseness to the whole picture. It didn't feel like a real house at all, but rather a movie set or an exhibit at Disneyland. There was the feeling that if one tried to go upstairs, there would be none—nothing but a false façade created entirely for the occasion, to be dismantled the very moment all the guests had left. It was clear that its owner wanted to create a distinct impression—but his intention was entirely up for grabs.

A red-jacketed valet helped an elegantly dressed lady out of her S-Class Mercedes, while her husband tipped the exceptionally obsequious black man. He nodded in thanks as the couple walked slowly into the house, as if on eggshells. From the expressions on their faces, they might as well have been entering Buckingham Palace. The valet turned to one of his cronies.

"You wouldn't catch me in there if you paid me."

"Yeah?" the other responded. "You'd eat dog crap if somebody paid you."

The valet, the look of false obsequiousness completely gone from his face, looked up at the illuminated mansion where his ancestors had worked as cooks and menservants—as slaves.

He shook his head, very happy to be outside. "Uh-uh. Not in this place. Something about it gives me the creeps. I can't wait to get home and take a shower." He shivered visibly.

The other valet laughed at him as he helped another couple out of their car.

The well-dressed couple moved to the front door, where a maid in a crisp black and white uniform took their wraps and curtsied in the old Southern manner. The couple barely nodded at her as they joined hands and entered the ballroom.

Everyone here at Daniel Alexander's country estate (yes, he had another home—less modest—in Richmond proper) was wearing a tuxedo. Except the ladies, of course, who vied with each other in the contest of how expensive, how mighty the designer, of the designer labels they sported. A host of exclusively black waiters distributed champagne in Waterford fluted crystal, while the orchestra, outside on the overlit lawn overlooking the river, supplied appropriate ambiance. The black "servants," the live music, the cool autumn air, all contributed to that feeling of somehow having been transported back in time, until just before the Yankees invaded Atlanta. It was a most curious effect indeed.

The ladies in their jewel-studded tiaras and satin night wraps moved as if one into the ballroom, while the men automatically sepa-rated, wordlessly filing into the smoke-filled den where their host held court. As the women filled the ballroom, their Parisian perfumes clashing frightfully, there was something missing—a *non-sequiter*, yes, but still, there was a palpable void in this house. There was no one to greet them. No hostess. No empress presiding over the affair. The women sensed this loss and clustered in groups, trying to find something to talk about.

But the men were not lacking a host. In fact, they jockeyed for position in the smoky, wood-paneled den off the main ballroom, desperately hoping to get within eye contact of the main attraction: Daniel Alexander. Though the room was literally packed as immi-grants had been at Ellis Island, Daniel Alexander, most certainly the host, stood out in the crowd.

Daniel Alexander was a man who would stand out in any crowd. He was taller than everyone else in the room, with the air of a Shakespearean tragic hero. This was the man whose self-confidence had created this whole peculiar scene. On him, the heroic figure he was, it was all very becoming—as if he had earned the right to his outrageous and overbearing pride. There was a pervasive sadness about him, a pathos that one couldn't put a finger on. His eyes were glassy, and his jaw clenched far too tightly to be comfortable. His air of sorrow was at distinct odds with the glitter, the glamour, of his sur-roundings. This charade, this house of wax, he had created for the express purpose of convincing the "outside world," his guests, of his success, and therefore, his supreme happiness.

This den of fools, all tripping over each other for entry into the den, was completely taken in by the charade. They ate out of Alexander's hand as if they were sparrows before St. Francis of Assisi. To this superficial lot, Daniel Alexander was a king. An invincible fortress of a man. They were incapable of seeing any deeper than the surface, which was exactly how Alexander wanted it. And it was true that at only forty-five years of age, Alexander had already reached the height of his personal power. He was a real tycoon, in every sense of the word, and if he wasn't exactly reveling in it, at least he wanted everyone else to believe it!

The tycoon stood in the center of a knot of his most powerful guests, a warm and inviting fire burning behind him. Among the tuxedoed throng were a handful of men in the formal dress of their native lands: one with the ornate sash of a foreign ambassador from the Middle East; another, an African general in full regalia, medals shining against the dangling crystals of the antique chandelier. They clustered around Alexander like a horde of jackals, currying favor with their illustrious host.

In the center of the group, the voice of an American army general now commanded Alexander's sole attention. "Nixon's gonna win it in a landslide. I guarantee it. America's not gonna vote for a Catholic."

Daniel Alexander stared into his fluted champagne glass, replying in monotone, "Dick Nixon will not be president."

The elderly general bristled. All around them were quiet—not wanting to disrupt this vital discussion. "What? How can you possibly know that, Daniel...?"

Alexander cut him off with a shake of his head. "Not this time, for sure."

The Middle Eastern ambassador fought to be let into the conversation. "Mr. Alexander, if you please, why not, sir?"

The room was silent, all awaiting Alexander's reply. Still staring blankly into his fluted glass, observing the dance of lights created by the reflection of the chandelier on the crystal, its effect made even more hypnotic by the crackling crimson fire behind him, Alexander replied with a knowing look. "Because he doesn't look good on television. That's why."

The cluster of officials stared at each other, not wanting to blunder before Alexander. The general bought time by clearing his throat. Finally, he choked out a tentative response. "He's not auditioning to replace Jim Arness on *Gunsmoke*, Daniel!"

Everyone chuckled. Alexander smiled, without once looking up from his glass. "Gentlemen, what you fail to grasp is that the world is television. It is what people see that will make them form their opinions and cast their votes. And people like myself...we'll help to shape those opinions."

The general appeared miffed by Alexander's self-aggrandizement and puffed himself out like a blowfish trying desperately to match Daniel's power and charisma. "It may be as you say, Daniel, as regards Nixon and the rest, but Southeast Asia has to be where we draw the line in the sand!"

You could hear a pin drop as the crowd waited for Daniel Alexander's view on this controversial foreign policy issue. Alexander stared the elderly general right in the eyes.

"You want a war, General? Well, that's dandy. But if you do, you'd better clear it with me first. Because if I don't support it, neither will the people—and then you'll have two wars: one abroad and one at home. I have more than a thousand television stations, radio stations and more daily and monthly journals than I care to count. Everyone who watches television—and that would be *everyone* in the world—will hear what *I* want them to hear!" Alexander lowered his voice for effect. "I think I've made myself perfectly clear."

He certainly had—as clear as the champagne glass he held up against the light, still absorbed in studying the little dancing rainbows on the ceiling. They seemed far more interesting to him than anyone in this room.

Before the general could stutter out a response, a faint wail drew their attention to the other side of the room. A sturdy, red-headed nanny, the map of Ireland etched on her face, carried a newborn infant wrapped in a powder blue blanket. Alexander drained his champagne in one gulp and handed the empty glass to a servant. Alexander managed to muster some expression on his face, though it was perhaps closer to a grimace than a smile.

"Ah—my new son is here."

He turned toward the enormous, circular stairway and called out authoritatively, "Stone!"

Slowly moving down the stairs, with an air that seemed at once both proud and tentative, was a sandy-haired little boy, dressed in formal wear identical to Daniel Alexander's. The flock of ambassadors, military men and other dignitaries parted like the Red Sea before Moses as the young boy made his way into the den. His was the face of an angel, yet his sense of composure, his cockiness, made him seem less an angel than a replica of Daniel Alexander in miniature.

Alexander commanded, calmly but firmly, "Stone, come here!"

Stone moved silently to his father's side as the nanny holding the baby moved toward them. Daniel awkwardly took the infant and held him up for his guests to see. He was a red-faced, premature infant, almost entirely hairless.

"Everyone, I'd like to introduce David Stanton Alexander." Alexander found himself almost choking on his own words. It seemed a struggle just getting them out. "And this is his first day home from the hospital."

Everyone in the room cheered, holding up their champagne glasses to toast the newborn. Yet, the atmosphere in the room was tense, unnerving and surreal. The look on the young boy's face, the one named Stone, was frightening. He was seemingly rooted to the ground, glaring at the baby. His eyes were riveted on the baby, and it was hardly a look of love on his face, not by far. Even the most superficial of partygoers couldn't miss it. But Daniel Alexander went on as if nothing were amiss. He had no choice. He looked down at the boy standing beside him, a tiny version of himself.

"Stone? I'd like you to meet your new brother."

The guests applauded formally now, gathering around the newest member of the Alexander clan. Stone was squeezed out of the way as the guests clustered around Alexander and the baby. Stone—choking from the smoke and claustrophobic—had to literally fight his way out of the room, trying to hold in his tears. The nanny noticed Stone's expression as he headed for the stairs. She called after him with concern in her voice, "Stone?" But the boy was gone. An upstairs door slammed shut with a thud.

Back in the den, Daniel Alexander held his new son, and the people surrounding them seemed at once joyful but sad. The American general moved closer to Alexander, who clearly had never held an infant before in his life. This holding of the baby was just a "photo opportunity" for him, a grandstanding opportunity. The general placed a tentative hand on his shoulder. "I'm terribly sorry for your loss, Daniel. To gain a son and lose a wife in the same day, I...I can't imagine how you feel."

This was the first time any real emotion had been expressed the entire evening. Alexander was clearly moved, but he didn't dare show it, especially before this group of piranha. His jaw remained set, his eyes glassy. He spoke like a robot, not even daring to look down at the mewing infant.

"Yes. Emily was a special woman." It seemed that there was a volume he could speak, but this was neither the time nor the place. For Daniel Alexander, whose whole life had become a media circus, there might never be a time or a place.

To Alexander's thinking, he'd already shown enough weakness this evening—weakness that could give his enemies, and there were plenty of them gathered in his den, drinking his best champagne—a tool to use against him. He would not give them that tool. He quickly handed the infant back to the nanny, fighting the emotions welling up inside him. He turned curtly to the nanny. "Take him back to the nursery. There's way too much smoke in here."

The general thought about hugging Daniel, but decided against it. He knew Daniel too well. Instead he cleared his throat, hoping to clear the air along with it. "Um, yes. Way too much smoke. You're quite right."

# CHAPTER TWO

The tree is known by his fruit.

—Matthew 12:33


For I am come to set a man at variance
against his father...And a man's foes
shall be they of his own household.

—Matthew 10:35–36

The party was long since over. The servants had gone to their sleeping quarters, having returned the house to its former pristine glory. The night was dark, only faintly illuminated by a waning moon as young Stone descended the creaky mahogany stairway and entered the den. Though the guests had gone home and his father to a lonely bedroom, embers in the old fireplace still burned. Stone advanced toward the fireplace, confused, bitter and enraged.

*Why? Why,* he thought, *has my mother been taken from me? What have I done to deserve being abandoned like this?*

The boy glared into the crackling fireplace, his blue eyes focused on the embers as they sought to consume the dry logs. A look of pathos suddenly turned to anger as he noticed the long box of matchsticks beside the hearth. His tiny eyes narrowed as fury and revenge filled his mind. It was his father's fault, and that puny little thing upstairs in the nursery, that "thing" they were all calling "his brother." *They* had taken his mother from him.

Stone was startled out of his reverie as suddenly the flames flared up, red and gold tendrils of fire—reaching out to him, calling him by name. He stood riveted before its majesty, enjoying a sense of oneness with the flames, a sense of being enveloped by them in a way that was both warm and intoxicating. Not warm in the way it felt when his mother had held him in her arms and called him sweet names, but comforting nonetheless. Mesmerizing.

The flames transported him to a place that few of the living had ever entered, and fewer still would want to visit—even for an afternoon. It was only prophets and clairvoyants on this side who sometimes found themselves in this situation, and when that happened, even they wanted to buy the first bus ticket they could taking them anywhere, just as long as it was *out.*

This place could be called the land that time forgot, but that would be not only glib, but also a pathetic understatement. Yes, there was nothing here—a paradox it would seem. Stone knew he was not caught in a colorless and tragic dream, for a persistent, guttural moaning convinced him—once and for all time—that this was most certainly *not* a dream. A nightmare, perhaps, but not a dream.

*Stone couldn't make out any words or identify any one language—but from somewhere that seemed very far away, and yet also very present, there were echoes, fragments, that haunted him to the depth of his being—even without words, he knew that these could only be the sounds of lamentation from another dimension, echoes that resonated throughout the eons of the bleakest, most irrevocable torment. It seemed to Stone that this was neither a dream nor a nightmare—but the world of the damned.*

*Stone tried desperately to see, to hear, something tangible, but he could only make out the faintest impressions. Without the help of his earthly senses, through his keenly intuitive mind, he clearly heard these words: "Satan has been released from prison, and has come out to deceive the nations."*

*He had no idea what this meant, but he would. He would...*

*Though this Stygian realm didn't exist anywhere on the globe Stone had so often examined in his father's den, his vision convinced him that it did exist. Though ordinary mortals were unable to penetrate the dark kingdom through their narrow telescope of existence, Stone's vision assured him that there was another dimension of existence—a dimension since the very beginning of time in which dwelt the souls of those who had come before him. They continued to live—if one could call such a miserable existence "living."*

*Imprisoned, wallowing in agony and up to their waists in a blanket of molten lava, Stone sensed that the good and the bad, like fertile and rotten eggs, had been separated by a vast, superior consciousness. Those who had allied themselves with the good and held tight to their faith throughout their earthly lives were not there. He knew beyond a shadow of a doubt that his mother was not there.*

*If he had been old enough to study history, Stone would probably have been able to make out some familiar faces in this dark realm. Cain, Judas Iscariot, Robespierre, Cardinal Richelieu, Adolph Hitler, to name but a few of the more illustrious of the brotherhood. Stone watched in fascination as the skin of the damned was burned away by plumes of flame. It seemed to him that their agony was destined to be eternal. All the known languages of the world—Aramaic, Arabic, the romance languages and even English—melded together into one grievous plea for deliverance. But there was none to be granted.*

*Only one seemed to take pleasure in the grotesquerie of this scene. The cacophony of wails was like Mozart to the ears of the Overseer of this place, a Beast whose features were obscured by a veil of fire. The Beast, the Overlord of Suffering, looked down upon his ripe harvest of writhing lost souls. He was far more than merely content—he was elated! As his silhouette shifted on his molten throne, Stone watched as the eyes of the Beast burned like two pinpoints of laser light—and in response, the flames of hell suddenly exploded in a blaze of crimson and gold—making the fire in Daniel Alexander's den virtually burst right out of the stone fireplace. Stone stood entranced, while in his vision the damned screamed on ceaselessly...eternally...*

# CHAPTER THREE

And the brother shall deliver up
the brother to death, and the father the child:
and the children shall rise up against their
parents, and cause them to be put to death.

—Matthew 10:21

The late Emily Alexander had exquisitely and expensively decorated the nursery for her new son. Sweet panoramas of dancing
angels, colorful balloons and nursery rhymes covered the walls.
Next to the white-netted crib was a comfortable rocking chair and
hand-embroidered footstool, from which Emily had planned to
spend days and nights nursing her newborn child. But that was
before an emergency cesarean section had abruptly changed her
plans.

The huge nursery was lined wall to wall with cellophane-wrapped
gift baskets from heads of state all over the world. All this extrava-
gance—for the tiny six-pound newborn with no mother.

The warm-hearted nanny wound up the colorful mobile hanging
over the crib, "Mary had a little lamb" sweetly playing as she swad-
dled the tiny David tightly in his blankets. The nanny sensed
something behind her and was startled to see young Stone at her
elbow.

"Stone, what are you doing up? Did you come to see the baby?"

Stone did not reply. His eyes, like his father's, were glassy, difficult to read. She moved aside and gently pushed Stone over so the
boy could get a good look at the baby. She noticed his brow knit
with tension. A good woman, her eyes welled up with tears, the first
signs of any real emotion anyone in the Alexander household had
dared to show. It was clear that she was very fond of her late mis-
tress, as well as her mysterious little charge.

"Yes, yes. I know how you must feel, Stone. But we mustn't
question the ways of our heavenly Father. He has a plan for all of us,
and He had a special plan for your mother. She's an angel now,
watching over you from heaven above. She'll never *really* leave
you..."

She looked over at Stone to see if her words were having any
effect. From the blank look in his eyes, she could tell that he hadn't
heard a word she said. She tried to gather him in her arms for a tight
hug, but he resisted. She shook her head. "You poor child. You
poor, poor darling."

She stared down into the crib at the beautiful newborn boy and
then turned back to Stone. "You're all each other has now, Stone.
You and your brother. You must always love each other. Take care of
each other for your mother's sake. The good Lord took away your
mother—He wanted her nearer to Him, but He gave you this new
baby brother in her place. You must love him and tell him all about
your mother and how she will always be with both of you."

The teary-eyed nanny looked Stone in the eyes, but saw
nothing—nothing but a fathomless depth. She sighed. It would take a

32

lot to get through to this child and bring him out of his grief.

Speaking to herself as much as to Stone, she said, "I must go get your brother a fresh bottle. Will you watch over him for me, Stone?"

Fighting back her tears, the nanny turned and left the room. Stone moved closer to David's head. He looked down at the helpless infant. Stared at him ominously. Then, reaching into his bathrobe, Stone pulled out the box of matches he had taken from above the fireplace. He struck a match and held it up to the edge of the white netting covering the crib.

"The Lord giveth..."

The flame erupted, instantly sweeping over the baby blue blanket in a blazing blue and gold inferno. Within seconds, the entire crib was devoured by flames. The infant David began to cry. Stone watched dispassionately as if over a funeral pyre.

"...and the Lord taketh away."

The nanny suddenly appeared in the door with the fresh bottle. She was momentarily frozen upon seeing the raging fire, but then she dropped the bottle and screamed, rushing over to the crib. Stone merely stood by, as if comatose, as the nanny frantically cried for help, covering the baby with blankets to extinguish the flames. Several household maids rushed into the room, dashing about, opening windows and trying desperately to put out the fire while Stone stood silently by. When the fire was all but extinguished, the room a haze of smoke and embers, Daniel Alexander finally appeared, eyes still clouded by sleep, in his bed jacket. The sight of the burned-out shell of what used to be a nursery immediately jolted him wide-awake.

"What in hell—?"

He stared at the nanny accusingly as she sat on the carpet crying hysterically, little David clutched to her bosom.

The servants slipped out of the room silently when Daniel appeared—not wanting to be caught in the crossfire. Through the haze of smoke, Daniel saw Stone still standing riveted before the remains of the crib, the box of matchsticks still clenched tightly in his hand. Slowly, Stone turned around to face his father. Their eyes met. The look they exchanged defied all earthly description.

33

# CHAPTER FOUR

The child is the father of the man.

—William Wordsworth

D aniel Alexander sat wordlessly beside his son in a burgundy stretch limousine the size of a double-length trailer. The doe-eyed Italian chauffeur whistled to himself as he proceeded farther and farther up into the densely wooded mountains. They were so high that both Stone and his father were almost gasping for oxygen—how much farther could the summit be?

Finally, against the dazzling backdrop of the countryside below, they came upon what appeared to be an old fortress of some sort, possibly dating back to ancient Roman times. A sign announced that they had entered the grounds of the Francini Military Academy.

The limousine glided through the elaborate front gates, elegant and ancient, beyond anything America had to offer, then past a lush, green parade ground where young, uniformed cadets—some as young as six years old—practiced a marching drill. A voice came through the speaker from the driver into the back seat.

"*Signore—Eccoci. All'Accademia Francini.*"

Daniel glanced over at Stone. There was no trace of expression on his face. Daniel sighed.

"*Grazie.* Pull up to the office. *Prego.*"

# CHAPTER FIVE

You may my glories and my state depose,
But not my griefs; still am I king of those.

—William Shakespeare, *Richard II*


The just man walketh in his integrity;
his children are blessed after him.

—Proverbs 19:7

Flanked by plaster busts of Julius Caesar, Alexander the Great and other notable military heroes, the office of Generale Vittorio Francini was warm, yet befitting the dignity of a military man. Francini, a vigorous man in his early fifties, rose from his desk as Daniel Alexander entered the room. Francini rushed over to Daniel and gave him a warm hug. The men smiled at each other like old friends, which they clearly were.

"Daniel. It is so good to see you again."

Alexander loosened up visibly before Francini. "Yes, it is good to see you, too, Vittorio." He appraised Francini's fine figure. "I see you are taking good care of yourself as always."

Francini laughed. "With Rosa's cooking, it is not always so easy. But once a military man, always a military man. And what would the students think if their *commandante* walked around with a big belly out to here?"

Daniel laughed, surveying the office as if he'd been there before many times. "Nothing else seems to have changed around here either."

Francini smiled. "Well, I try to stay as thin as my hair. But that gets more difficult every year."

Daniel grinned. "That sounds like a good policy. How is Rosa? And *la bambina?*"

Francini preened himself like a peacock. "Rosa is Rosa. But my Gabriella...*che belleza*...at this time of my life to have such a one..." Francini was transported into raptures by thoughts of his child. "What a blessing. I thank the Holy Mother every day."

Alexander smiled for Francini, but his sad eyes couldn't help but glance over at the fruit of his own loins, who did not transport him into raptures—and of whom he was now justly afraid. A son who might be condemned forever by the same Holy Mother Francini had just thanked for his own good fortune. How ironic it all seemed.

A persistent, malignant thought crossed Alexander's mind as he surveyed his old haunt. *What is this all about? Is this all some kind of a test? Could the Holy Mother—or somebody else on a highly elevated plane—have something against me? Why have I been robbed of the wife I loved and given a modern-day Cain for a son? What have I done in this—or any other life—to deserve this?* He simply could not imagine, and tried to push the thoughts out of his head.

Francini understood, more than anyone else did, Alexander's state of mind. Unlike the reluctant American army general, Francini placed both hands on Daniel's shoulders and stared at him with a love, an understanding, that bolstered him and, for the moment at least, made him feel that he was not completely alone in the world. Francini squeezed Daniel's shoulders tightly.

"The pain shall pass, Daniel. The pain shall pass. When my Carmella passed away, I thought my life was over. I wanted to jump right in the grave with her. But I didn't jump. Instead, I left the army and started the school. And soon, time and prayer eased my pain. Carmella spoke to me in my dreams. She told me she was with the Holy Mother, and I learned to accept it. And later on, Rosa came into my life, and then little Gabriella. And now, look at me, an old man, happy once again. Life is nothing but a circle, Daniel."

Alexander was shaken by Francini's frankness. There wasn't another man alive who would dare speak to him like this. But Daniel drank in every word that Francini said.

"I hope I can look back over the years as you do now, Vittorio, like the pain is just a burned-out volcano from long ago."

"You will, you will," Francini murmured reassuringly.

Standing a few scant feet away, Stone had not uttered a word, but had been thoroughly absorbed as the men talked. Outside the office window, he had noticed a young girl, barely five, feeding a white pony on the school's parade ground. She was adorable, with long, dark hair cascading in ringlets down her back. She somehow seemed to sense she was being watched and looked up, making eye contact with Stone. Neither of them turned away. It became a staring contest that neither would ever forget.

Francini showed Alexander a plush leather seat, and sat down behind his desk. Then he took his first serious look at Stone, his new charge. Something strange came over his face. Alexander noticed it and turned to see Stone virtually glued to the window. Francini took a moment to compose himself.

"This is, so to speak, 'a special dispensation,' my friend, since the academy term has already begun. But for you..."

Alexander couldn't help but notice Francini carefully eyeing Stone's every move. Stone had left his spot by the window, and was now contemplating a print of Hieronymus Bosch's painting "The Last Judgment," in which insectlike demons rode about a ravaged landscape, tormenting human slaves. Both men could not help but notice how absorbed Stone seemed to be with the painting, particularly disconcerting in light of its horrific theme. Francini tried to make light of Stone's unusual comportment.

"Your son has a keen appreciation for art, I see."

Alexander appreciated Francini's glossing over what was quite obvious to both of them: that it was not the quality of the art that Stone appreciated, but the *theme*.

"Yes," Alexander replied carefully. "I really appreciate you taking Stone—under the circumstances. And on such short notice. I didn't know where else to turn."

Alexander was as close to tears as anyone would ever see him, in public, at least. He tried to pull himself together. "Your kindness will not go unrewarded, Vittorio."

Daniel Alexander took his checkbook from the inside pocket of his jacket. He immediately felt on more comfortable ground getting down to business, doling out money. He slid the check across the desk to Francini. Francini's eyes widened at the amount.

"Daniel, this is far too much..." Francini rose from his desk and tried to hand the check back to Daniel. Alexander raised his hand to stop him.

"This is not tuition, Vittorio. This is a donation. Without this place, without you, I would never have become the man I am today. I owe you more than I could ever repay—in dollars or in lira."

The men exchanged a meaningful look and a long handshake. Francini knew without saying that no amount of money could possibly compensate for the responsibility of taking charge of Stone Alexander, who still stared at the Bosch painting with a look that could only be described as rapture. The sight made both men's stomachs sink.

"I will do my best with your son, Daniel. You know I will."

"I know that you will. That's why I'm here."

Their final handshake was like a blood pact. Francini stared at his old student and friend wistfully.

"Life brings with it many challenges and surprises that we can never anticipate, can we, my old friend?" Francini said, leading Alexander toward the door of his office.

"You're right about that, Vittorio. But at least, here, things seem to stay the same. There's something comforting in that."

Francini nodded. For the first time he addressed Stone. "Come, young Stone Alexander. Let us have a look around your new home."

Stone complied, moving slowly toward Francini.

"I believe you will grow to become a fine young man here, just like your father."

Stone stared daggers at his father, which made both men's hearts sink. Still, Francini remained upbeat, leading father and son out to the courtyard.

"I will give you now, how you say, the chef's tour..."

As the group walked out into the lovely courtyard, the snow-capped mountains in the distance, they caught the same little girl Stone noticed before sneaking a look at them through the old, wrought iron fence. Francini smiled at her proudly.

*"Gabriella! Veini qui!"*

Instead of following her father's wishes, the little girl dashed off with a tantalizing giggle. Francini roared with delight. "Now you see what I mean. That is my beautiful Gabriella. Just like her mama, she does nothing of what her father asks."

Daniel Alexander laughed for the first time since his wife's death.

# CHAPTER SIX

Here I disclaim all my paternal care,
Propinquity and property of blood,
And as a stranger to my heart and me
Hold thee, from this, for ever.

—William Shakespeare, *King Lear*


They shall say unto the elders of his city,
This our son is stubborn and rebellious,
he will not obey our voice.

—Deuteronomy 21:20

Stone and Francini stood beside Daniel Alexander's waiting limousine as Alexander glided into the back seat. Stone stared off at a fixed point in the distance, refusing to take official leave of his father. Neither Daniel nor Francini failed to notice the vast gap, the negative polarity, between father and son.

Francini leaned into the limo, looking at Alexander reassuringly as he took both of Daniel's hands. "Time, my son, time. Don't worry about the boy, Daniel. Be well. You take care of your new *bambino*."

Daniel was moved beyond his capacity to respond.

Francini lowered his voice. "As for *this* one, my old friend, you know I will do my best." Daniel nodded silently, grateful beyond description for having this burden—this stone—lifted from his shoulders, at least for the time being.

Francini and Alexander smiled at each other with their eyes, as only people who respect each other deeply can do. The unassuming chauffeur closed the door.

His back still turned, Stone visibly bristled at the sound of the slamming door. For a moment it seemed that he might do something, run toward his father, throw himself at the car—but no, after that first, slight upheaval, he dug his feet in the soil and stood firm, even stoic.

The chauffeur took off down the stone-covered driveway, some of the gravel ricocheting off of Stone and his suitcase. Before they could get too far away, Francini went over to Stone and leaned over him, speaking in a calming, caring voice. "There goes your papa. Don't you even want to wave him good-bye?"

But Stone simply would not budge. Francini felt the boy's shoulders, and they were almost knitted to his neck in a spasm of fury. Francini heaved a heavy sigh as he stood alone with Stone for the first time, suddenly sensing the tremendous burden he had just taken upon himself.

He put a tentative hand on the boy's back, leading him back toward the academy grounds. "Come, Stone, let's get your things." Stone came back as if from another space and time, looking down at the suitcase at his feet. He looked around as if noticing his surroundings for the first time. Francini noticed with some concern that his new charge appeared completely disoriented. Where on earth was he? Or was he on earth at all?

Stone lifted the bag with a mechanical precision and followed Francini up the long driveway. Only the hardest of hearts could remain unmoved by the sight of the slight boy, eyes glazed, lugging the huge suitcase as an enormous, black fog covered the snow-covered crags and enshrouded the lake.

# CHAPTER SEVEN

He will give the devil his due.

—William Shakespeare, *Henry IV*


Verily I say unto thee, That this night,
before the cock crow, thou shalt deny me thrice.

—Matthew 26:34

A storm raged outside as Stone, now dragging his suitcase, slowly made his way down the seemingly endless white corridor lined with narrow doorways. The sound of children's voices came at him from both sides of the hallway, the bright lights and noise disturbing his delicate sensibilities.

He shuddered as eyes glared at him from every doorway he passed. There were whispers and laughter in foreign tongues. Italian. Spanish. Arabic.

He stopped in front of the doorway to the empty cubicle that was to be his fortress. All laughter and giggling stopped as Stone entered the tiny room. He surveyed his quarters. Clean white walls. No decorations of any sort. A small footlocker and a simple wooden bed. His eyes moved over to the bed. They suddenly grew wide. On the bed was a plastic baby doll, naked, its head charred. Stone's face turned crimson as the silence turned into cruel and outrageous laughter from the children lining the halls to see his reaction to their prank.

Among all the taunting voices, Stone could make out only one phrase: "*Amazzate i bambini!*" Stone turned to see the doorway filled with his tormentors, chanting now, "*Amazzate i bambini! Amazzate i bambini!!*"

Enraged, Stone heaved his heavy suitcase at the accusers and darted out of the cubicle, running back down the narrow hallway and out into the rainy night.

# CHAPTER EIGHT

The father shall be divided against the son,
and the son against the father...

—Luke 12:53


Beneath is all the fiends':
There's hell, there's darkness,
There's the sulphurous pit,
Burning, scalding, stench, consumption.

—William Shakespeare, *King Lear*

Stone slammed the heavy wooden door of the dormitory and ran aimlessly, tears of rage pouring down his face. Away from the compound, with the pounding rain pelting him in seeming accusation, Stone raged against the agonies of his young life. Staring up at the heavens, he screamed out, "Why me? Why is this happening to me?"

Exhausted from running, Stone sank to his knees on the muddy ground, sobbing wildly. Suddenly, he felt a warm glow surrounding him. He lifted his head to see the clouds part and the rain stop, revealing a waxing moon before him. The shadow crossing the moon beguiled him. Enchanted, Stone wiped the rain and tears from his face, staring at what seemed to him to be an invitation of sorts. A beckoning. He turned to see the academy chapel in the near distance; it was the spire of its cross that had silhouetted the moon.

Stone was mysteriously compelled. He plodded on toward the ancient building, his feet now heavy with mud. But he didn't even notice. As he neared the chapel, he saw that the door was curiously ajar and lights burning faintly from within.

Stone stared at the old chapel. It was so old and dilapidated that it looked as if it could collapse at any moment. Like the rest of the academy, it was genuinely ancient, adding to its appeal, probably built over the ruins of a still older pagan temple.

*Something seemed to call to Stone from within. Voices? Music? Whatever it was, the effect was soothing and welcoming, not taunting. He squeezed his narrow frame easily through the slightly opened door. Suddenly, he began to shake involuntarily. He was soaked to the skin and freezing, and yet—that was not what made him shake. There was something terribly mysterious going on in there; something he longed to become a part of.*

*Though his body shook, he resolved to advance, and he stepped into the midst of the dank, ancient chapel, completely dark—except for a host of votive candles by the altar casting an eerie glow.*

*Still hearing the music, or were they voices—he didn't know or care—urging him to come nearer, Stone moved down the center of the church in a light trance, past the empty pews, past the time-worn paintings and statues depicting Christ's journey to the cross. The flickering candles made the statues cast strange, monstrous shadows. But strangely, Stone was not afraid.*

*As he reached the altar, the shadows congealed into a dark form. Stone stood riveted before the image. Was this Jesus Christ Himself come to save him? That seemed most unlikely. The figure first appeared to be a gaunt priest, robes covering all but his face. Stone rubbed his eyes—did the man just appear, take shape from the very shadows, or was he just imagining it?*

The gaunt specter spoke to him. "I know who you are."

Stone tried to get his bearings. The "priest's" mouth hadn't moved at all! The voice he heard seemed to be coming from inside his own head! Bewildered as he was, Stone somehow found the courage to reply. "How...do you know me?"

The robed figure moved closer, seeming to float on air rather than walk. "Because I have been here, waiting for you. For a very long time."

Finally, Stone broke down. This had been the longest day in his life. The longest, that is, since his mother...but he didn't want to think about that just now. He *wouldn't* think about her...Tears began streaming down the boy's face.

"I don't want to be here! My father sent me here to get rid of me! He hates me, so he sent me away. Everybody here hates me, too. They all hate me. And I hate them. I...I...hate everyone! Everyone!!"

The creature floated right before the hysterical boy, his voice soothing him into a state of enchantment. "Rest, child. You must sleep. Right here..."

*Stone felt as if he were losing consciousness. He felt drawn to this figure, felt a kinship with him he'd never experienced with anyone else. Unlike his father, this...being...really seemed to understand him. His voice caressed Stone like the voice of his own mother's.*

"You have nothing to worry about. I am your Guardian. I am here for no other reason but to protect you."

*Dazed and sleepy, Stone looked at his Guardian, who sometimes appeared very much a man, but at other times, like nothing more than a blur of colors and gasses. Whoever or whatever he was, Stone was intoxicated by him. He felt warmer than he'd felt since his mother suckled him at her breast. For the bereaved young child, this sense of envelopment was most welcome...most welcome.*

*Stone became used to the fact that his Guardian didn't speak, at least not in any way he had been trained to hear—but somehow, he knew Stone's thoughts, even before he had them! His voice was as soothing as an evening breeze, and the young boy gladly submitted to his embrace.*

"I will always protect you, Stone. I will be here for you as long as you need me. Here. Lie down here."

*The blurring mélange of images motioned toward the altar. Stone felt himself being lifted—transported through the air—but he was not afraid. The sensation was wonderful...weightless...like returning to the womb.*

"Sleep now, Stone. In the morning, the sun will return, the rain will be gone, and your new life will begin. Sleep, my darling son..."

Stone, in a deep, altered state of consciousness, lay before the altar like a human sacrifice. The Guardian swirled itself into a rainbow of colors over the sleeping boy, and when it finally dissolved into mist, Stone Alexander lay there, hair and clothes completely dry, shoes cleaned and the priest's thick cassock covering him against the chill of the night.

As Stone's breathing settled into a peaceful rhythm, the frightful horror of the night forgotten, the Guardian's voice caressed him as it entered Stone's dreams.

# CHAPTER NINE

We are never deceived; we deceive ourselves.

—Goethe

To every thing there is a season, and a time
to every purpose under the heaven...

—Ecclesiastes 3:1

The weather had cleared. In fact, the seasons had changed. It was a bright spring day, and all Francini Academy turned out for a critical soccer match. Local families from up on the mountain, the families of day students who lived close by and every student and teacher at the academy were there that Saturday afternoon. Soccer was serious business at the Francini Academy.

Off by himself in a corner of the field, waiting for the coach to blow the whistle, was a handsome young man. Slim, but broad shouldered, his sandy hair set off bright blue eyes, eager and yearning to fight. This was Stone Alexander.

Not only had the seasons changed, but many years had passed as well. Stone was now eighteen years old and chafing at the bit to enter the match. He paced in a small circle impatiently until he caught a glimpse of Gabriella Francini standing next to her mother in the bleachers.

His entire body froze. His blue eyes burned their way into her vision, forcing her to look over at him. As always when this happened, when he *willed* her to look at him, she did. She blushed crimson, acknowledging his remarkable power over her. Stone didn't smile, that wasn't his style, but his stare undressed her, unnerved her to the core. She stared at him with no defenses, like a deer caught in the headlights, until her mother noticed what was happening and smacked her on the arm, bringing Gabriella out of her reverie.

Two other cadets on the field also noticed the heated, nonverbal exchange between Stone and the general's daughter. They made it a point to take note of it every time it happened, because it was a subject of great curiosity to them.

The whistle blew, and it was finally Stone's turn to bound onto the field. An Italian boy called the play, nodding at two other cadets on the opposing team. Stone wasted no time. He darted forward— stealing the ball from an opposing player before he even saw him coming. Stone rushed across the field.

The two older cadets angled in from the bench, headed right for Stone. The look in their eyes was vicious. Watching the critical match attentively from the sidelines were Generale Francini, the schoolmasters and a priest in a simple cassock. No one else seemed to see the Guardian. Not even Generale Francini seemed to notice him kneel down and touch the sod.

On the field, the lithe and well-practiced Stone evaded a defender and had a clear line to the goal. The two larger cadets were closing on him. Suddenly, the grass beneath the boys' feet seemed to ripple—to move beneath them, tripping them viciously—as Stone continued on and took his shot on goal—a score! Stone threw up his hands in victory.

When he turned back to the field, he saw the two boys who had rushed him writhing and screaming in pain. Francini and the school doctor were already on the scene, examining what appeared to be compound fractures. The game was over.

Stone jogged past them wordlessly to his side of the field, his eyes riveted on Gabriella. She had been watching the accident with concern, but now that Stone was back in her immediate vicinity, she again fell under his spell. And if the truth be known—he fell under hers.

# CHAPTER TEN

The private wound is deepest.

—William Shakespeare,
*Two Gentlemen of Verona*


Behold, the hand of him that
betrayeth me is with me on the table.

—Luke 22:21

Almost two years later Gabriella Francini had blossomed from an adorable child into full-blown womanhood. At eighteen, she had become the unofficial "mascot," the Betty Grable of the Francini Academy. If pin-ups of her had been available to the cadets, you can believe there would have been one hanging in every young man's bunker.

Granted, being the only female under the age of sixty on the premises certainly increased her desirability, but had there been scores of women, even women cadets, Gabriella's presence would have been none the less potent. It was very difficult for the squad of young cadets running drills in the field as she looked on to keep their eyes on their instructor. But Gabriella herself had no trouble at all keeping her eyes pinned on their instructor.

Now almost twenty, strong and majestic, Stone stood before a squad of young cadets on a foggy fall day, running them through their paces, setting up a piece of field artillery. Of course, he was well aware of Gabriella's eyes upon him, and it made him act more proud, even crueler perhaps, than he would have otherwise. He bellowed at the squad, and the boys leaped as if scalded, rolling the cannon into position with precise movements. As they circled around Stone he turned, but it was to keep his eyes on Gabriella. She couldn't help but giggle when she caught him looking over at her, and it was enough to drive him wild.

"Double time!"

The hapless cadets panted as they circled the parade grounds. Their eyes pleaded with Stone to stop—but his eyes were on Gabriella, who finally jumped off the bleachers and dashed into her father's office. Stone sighed, but finally, the voices of the exhausted boys reached him. "Please, sir!"

Stone looked over at his squad, drenched to the skin with sweat. He smirked. They all looked like him when he first came to the academy. Thin. Pasty faced. Terrified of the squad leaders.

"Halt!" The boys collapsed at his feet. Stone helped the closest boy up to his feet, the fair-haired youngster who had the nerve to beg him for mercy. Stone smiled at the boy, who reminded him somehow of himself at that age. He rumpled the boy's hair. "Good work. You'll all make good soldiers. Squad dismissed!"

The young boy beamed under Stone's praise. Stone smiled over at him broadly, pleased that his approval meant so much to the boy. As the student cadets dispersed, two older boys approached Stone. They were in their late teens, and from their attitudes, it was clear that they considered themselves "peers" of their slightly older squad leader. A Japanese boy, Peter Tonzu, regarded Stone with admiration.

"That was a great display, Sir. You're sure to have the best squad this year."

The dark-eyed, curly-haired boy, Anton Benattar, born in Morocco, was more of a wise guy. "C'mon, Peter, if you kissed his butt any more..." Stone watched their bickering with some amusement, always happy to be fawned over. Peter took offense to being chastened, especially before his hero.

"Listen! Stone's always gotten anything he's set his sights on, and he always will. Which is more than I can say for you!"

Peter looked up at Stone, as if to ask, "Right?"

Stone smiled haughtily. "Yes, of course that's right."

Anton shook his head at Peter, indicating that Stone was peering over at Francini's office where Gabriella was just opening the door. Anton smirked. "Until now, maybe. But that"—he indicated Gabriella—"is one match you're going to have some pretty stiff competition to win."

Stone looked amused. "Oh really? And who would my competition be in this particular...match?"

"Eyes right," Anton hissed under his breath.

The trio turned to see a dark, rugged cadet crossing the quad. Stone roared loudly. "Fausto Monticelli? Please! He's hardly a man at all! And his pathetic squad consists of mewling underclassmen still learning how to lace their boots and not drool into their spaghetti."

All of their eyes followed Fausto as he proceeded across the campus. "His father is a NATO commander," Anton added, conspiratorially. Stone leered at Anton, annoyed now.

"Pardon me, Mr. Benattar—they don't give you the Squad Leader Commendation because of who your father is. If that were the case, I wouldn't even need to compete, would I?"

The three sets of eyes turned to watch Fausto's elegant form as it proceeded toward Francini's house. Now, Stone himself was starting to get rattled. *What was that cretin doing over there?*

Anton was still wincing from Stone's last comeback, but he persisted in making his point. "I wasn't talking about winning the *graduation* honors, Sir, as you yourself can now see." All eyes were on Fausto, sitting on a bench in the courtyard, waiting for something. Or someone. The door opened suddenly, and Gabriella emerged from her father's office. Stone and his cohorts silently watched her chatting and laughing with Fausto.

Peter and Anton watched as Stone's eyes narrowed; the sudden foulness of his mood seemed to draw its life out of the very air itself, and his two squad mates shuddered with the sudden chill. And it wasn't in their imagination. Suddenly, there was a distinct coldness in the air, and a chill breeze blew over the mountaintop campus. Leaves swirled around the general's deck as the chill moved in and shook Gabriella to her core.

Stone watched with satisfaction as she wrapped a shawl around her shoulders and nodded a quick good-bye to Fausto, now left standing alone in the courtyard, the cold winds whipping through his hair and light uniform jacket.

Stone beamed, stomping off across the campus. Peter and Anton both noticed that the sudden windy blasts had vanished as quickly as they came, and they exchanged looks of utter mystification.

# CHAPTER ELEVEN

My bounty is as boundless as the sea,
My love as deep;
The more I give to thee, the more I have,
For both are infinite.

—William Shakespeare, *Romeo and Juliet*


Pray that ye enter not into temptation.

—Luke 22:40

Music filled the airy quad as the cadets performed an outdoor classical musical concert for the benefit of friends, family and the local community.

Stone was in the midst of a virtuoso violin solo. It was Johann Sebastian Bach's *Violin Sonata No. 4 in C Minor*, one of Bach's most haunting and difficult pieces. Stone's fingers flew across the instrument as if magically. Nothing seemed difficult, or even challenging, for this young man. Was he merely a genius—or was something guiding him to greatness? The faint smile on Stone's face presented a clue—to anyone who wanted to see, that is.

In the audience, Gabriella sat next to her father and mother. She was moved to tears by the sonata and stared at Stone as if he were some kind of demigod, which, perhaps, was something of an understatement. Slowly, as he reached the crescendo of the piece, he raised his eyes to meet Gabriella's. The expression on his face was deeply penetrating. Gabriella flushed, feeling that familiar warmth in her heart.

His ability to undress Gabriella with his eyes didn't hamper his playing one jot. He completed the crescendo of the piece to a rousing applause, and Gabriella sank weakly back into her seat as if utterly fulfilled. There was no doubt in anyone's mind, neither Generale Francini's nor his wife's, nor Fausto's, nor Gabriella's, for that matter—that Stone had been playing just for her.

While the orchestra took its bows, the audience compelled Stone to come forward for a standing ovation. Stone emerged from the group, staring over haughtily at Fausto, and then seductively at Gabriella. As he bowed for the second time to the frenzied applause of the mostly local peasant audience, Stone's mouth drew up into a disarming smile. Gabriella simply beamed with pride.

Francini and his wife exchanged troubled looks. They had seen this intense passion between Stone and their daughter, but never in such a blatant exhibition as tonight. From the look on the faces of Gabriella's parents, there could be no doubt that they seriously wondered—and worried—what would come next. Or rather, *when* it would come.

Everyone in the audience had noticed the obvious flirtation—the rich American cadet and the general's daughter. That made for good dinner table gossip over a glass of wine and a loaf of homemade Italian bread. Gabriella wriggled in her seat uncomfortably as all eyes fell upon her. Sensing her discomfort, her father put an arm around Gabriella, leading her away from the bleachers. Rosa followed but two steps behind. There was sure to be a heated conversation behind closed doors that night at the Francini house.

# CHAPTER TWELVE

...Her candle goeth not out by night.

—Proverbs 31:18


This bud of love, by summer's ripening breath,
May prove a beauteous flower when next we meet.

—William Shakespeare, *Romeo and Juliet*

The Francini Academy was nothing if not secluded, and getting both in and out of there meant traversing a long, twisting road through dense mountain foliage. But this was not a hindrance, but rather a challenge, to any cadets with a free day. It was off to Rome for the cadets old enough, and lucky enough, to possess wheels of any type. For the unfortunate others, there was an anti-quated procession of buses and trains that winded their way—at an interminable pace—to "*la bella citta.*" And on this day, the over-crowded old buses were packed with liberated teenage cadets.

The school had adjourned on December 12 in honor of *La Festa de Santa Lucia,* patroness of the academy. There was to be an elabo-rate parade in honor of the martyred saint passing before the Spanish Steps in the heart of Rome, and the ancient stone steps were thick with camera-laden tourists as well as Lucia-loving Romans of all ages, all waiting anxiously.

Sitting at a quaint outdoor bistro, accompanied by two of her cousins, was Gabriella Francini. It was only under the "protection" of her older, married cousins that Gabriella had managed to temporarily escape the watchful eyes of her parents. Getting away from the academy made Gabriella feel somehow lighter. She was effervescent, freed of inhibition, here in Rome. Sitting at the bistro, free of her parents, Gabriella had a small glimpse of what it would be like to be a woman.

She was entranced by the trio of Neapolitan singers who had just finished a rousing rendition of *"Marechiare,"* as she then heard the unmistakable mandolin chords that announced the beginning of her favorite song. She felt goose bumps running up and down her arms as, accompanied by the guitar and mandolin, the singer started up once again in a voice both melodic and haunting.

*"Sul mare luccica, l'astro d'argenot; placida e' l'onda prosptero il vento; Venite all'agile barchetta mia; Santa Lucia! Santa Lucia!"*

The entire bistro crowd went wild after hearing the saint's theme song, and the three *cugini* had polished off a bottle of Chianti by themselves. They chattered away nonstop, only pausing briefly to hear a mandolin solo or a chorus from a favorite tune.

*"Venite all'agile barchetta mia; Santa Lucia! Santa Lucia!*

Gabriella was smiling broadly, yelling out, *"Brava,"* to the band, when she noticed a limo headed their way. In the back seat was Fausto Monticelli, in full uniform, along with four of his most bois-terous comrades.

Having also spotted Gabriella, Fausto instructed the driver to pull over immediately. The limo pulled to a full stop in front of their table—much to the dismay of the people in minis and Fiats behind them, who cursed and honked as only infuriated Italian drivers can.

Fausto called over to Gabriella, who at first coyly pretended not to notice him. "*Señorina. Piacere?* May I come and have a drink with you, once I've gotten rid of these..."

His friends were making fools of themselves in the limo, whistling and laughing at Fausto's valiant attempts at ardor. Monticelli was deeply embarrassed, but tried not to show it.

"Imbeciles." He flashed a deadly look at his friends that shut them right up. A little tipsy, the normally reticent Gabriella held up her wineglass invitingly. She yelled back at Fausto.

"*Si. Va bene.* If you can park that...thing."

Fausto's eyes gleamed. In a flurry of Italian, he instructed the driver to hurry up and park. The driver paled. A parking space?

"*Impossible!* Santa Lucia herself is coming down the stairs!"

Fausto pressed a handful of cash into the driver's hand. He reluctantly drove off, muttering a stream of expletives in Italian under his breath. This day had already cost Fausto a bundle—but it would be well worth it if it meant getting time alone with Gabriella Francini.

"*Si, signore...*"

Fausto smiled as the limo took off—at about two miles per hour, the traffic jammed for as far as the eye could see.

As the limo passed by, Gabriella's cousins immediately started interrogating her in rapid Italian.

"*Che bello!* He is so handsome! He must be very rich...Is he your *amore*? The one you were telling us about?"

Gabriella just laughed and chugged down another gulp of Chianti from a fresh bottle. "Maybe yes, maybe no," she teased. "Fill it up," she said to her cousin, holding out her empty wineglass.

Her cousins were seeing a new side of Gabriella, acting the gleeful ingénue for the first time in her life. They were getting a sudden glimpse of who the woman Gabriella would become.

Laughing and drinking as the procession solemnly began down the Spanish Steps, the women's eyes were temporarily diverted from their banter by the sight of a priest and his entourage, carrying a life-sized statue of Santa Lucia, clothed in a long, white dress, wearing a crown of holly berries in her long flaxen hair. Interspersed between the holly and the berries was a circle of brightly lit candles, heralding Santa Lucia as *Luce* itself—Light, bringing the flame of hope to famine-stricken people throughout the world. There were flowers, prayers, incense and the incessant chanting of rosaries. Gabriella's mood became somber. Not only was Lucia the patron saint of the Francini Academy, she was Gabriella's own personal role model.

She greatly admired Lucia's outspoken attitudes at a time when women were virtually bought and sold as little more than slaves or cattle. Since she so often felt like little more than a slave, a possession, herself, Gabriella was inspired by Santa Lucia's unwillingness to submit, her tenacity in "bucking the system" to reach her own ends and her bravery in traversing the world, alone, in her little boat to bring hope and liberation wherever it was most needed.

*As the statue of Santa Lucia passed her, Gabriella felt so inspired that she too wished to defy her parents—to tell them that she would never marry a man they had chosen for her; she would not marry at all, unless it suited her. If she, like Lucia, had been chosen to live alone and spread light throughout the world, she too would have gladly accepted the mission. At least, such was the strength of will she felt at that moment. Tears ran down her face in rivulets as she thought of what it must have been like for the young Lucia, a girl in her mere teens, adrift in the Adriatic alone, letting the winds guide her to wherever she was needed most.*

*Gabriella too often felt adrift like that—even though she had lived her whole life on top of a mountain. Stone made her feel adrift...out of control. Could she become Lucia—take up Lucia's work—spending her life in devotion to good deeds—and still be with Stone? Stone, who commanded her complete attention, captivated her completely. She couldn't imagine a life without Stone—his power over her was so vast—he intoxicated her; and yet, she was also intoxicated by the Light. Could those two obsessions ever be reconciled? Could she truly commit herself, heart and soul, to a man, to Stone—and still maintain a lifelong commitment toward serving the Light? What would her life bring?*

*Gabriella sat pensively, utterly absorbed in the dazzling image of Santa Lucia as she floated down the street. She could feel the purity, the strength of spirit, emanating from Lucia—even though it was merely a porcelain depiction of her.*

*She suddenly felt that Lucia's spirit was probably hovering very close by—radiating her message of charity and hope to all those who chose to embrace it. Gabriella felt it; she tapped right into Lucia's raw energy—and it filled her with a sense of oneness with everything around her. She knew right then that she had been touched by spirit, blessed by this most sacred of angels—and with that knowledge came a sense of responsibility, an overwhelming desire to continue the work Lucia had only begun here on earth.*

The cousins could only watch the dramatic change in Gabriella from moment to moment—the flirtatious bombshell one second, the devout daughter of Lucia the next. Their cousin was a beautiful, delicate creature—but decidedly complex, they thought. She continued to stare after the statue long after it had past them, and seemed utterly transformed.

$$\Omega^2$$

Fausto seethed as a line of stern-looking *carabinieri* stopped his limo, which had finally moved a grand total of one hundred feet. Incensed by the interruption, Fausto opened his window and started yelling at the police, who stayed uncharacteristically calm, merely pointing at the advancing procession. Fausto sank back into his seat, cursing the police.

It became instantly clear that the limo was going nowhere until the lengthy parade had passed through the area. Livid with frustration, Fausto looked back to where Gabriella was sitting, her head now respectfully cast down as the parade winded its way past the bistro. She was never more beautiful in his eyes than at that moment—when she was so completely out of his reach.

But just when Fausto thought that things couldn't get any worse, his eyes suddenly grew as wide as clamshells. He watched in horror as a tiny Vespa carefully wove its way around the cobblestone square, right through the bistro, stopping at Gabriella's table. Recognizing the young, sandy-haired cadet on the buzzing scooter, Fausto screamed out to his friends.

"*Morte de fame...che diavolo sta facendo?*"

The cadets in the back seat craned their necks backwards to see the source of Fausto's grievance. To them, this was a fabulous diversion. It was Stone Alexander, and he had succeeded where Fausto had failed—and was now nodding politely to Gabriella's matronly escorts! The laughter in the limo was loud, hard and most certainly at Fausto's expense.

Giovanni was the first one able to even get out a comment without cracking up. "Looks like the American had the same idea you did to celebrate Santa Lucia, eh, Fausto?"

Monticelli fumed silently as he saw giggling and laughing at the far distant bistro. He turned to Giovanni with a look that shut him up immediately. As amused as they were by this turn of events, Fausto was their "leader," and they feared his wrath. But even their fear couldn't stop another torrent of riotous laughter over Fausto's predicament, the boys rolling around the back seat of the limo while Fausto silently seethed.

# CHAPTER THIRTEEN

O, swear not by the moon, the inconstant moon,
That monthly changes in her circled orb,
Lest that thy love prove likewise variable.
—William Shakespeare, *Romeo and Juliet*


While ye have light, believe in the light,
that ye may be the children of light.
—John 12:36

The young man gliding by on the Vespa pretended—but not too hard—to be surprised to see Gabriella. He gave her that sublime smirk that always made her heart quiver and her body quake to the core.

"Señorina Francini—I see you have decided to grace the Steps with your beauty."

The cousins now had still more cause for giggling. Gabriella's second suitor within fifteen minutes—and both so "*belle fatte*," they whispered to each other. "*This* must be the *amore*." But Gabriella heard nothing. She was completely absorbed in Stone's gaze. Finally, she rose to the occasion, choking out a witty retort.

"Cadet Alexander. I see you have decided to risk your neck on that death trap."

Stone laughed, looking over at the procession and pointing to the diminutive saint in her equally diminutive boat.

"Certainly no riskier than your Lucia sailing the seven seas to help the poor. *I* have sought only to find you. A risky proposition, per-haps, but life without risk is rather boring, don't you think?" He nodded once again in the direction of Lucia being carried through the streets by a host of somberly clad priests. "I believe that she would agree."

Gabriella wasn't sure what color to flush, as if she had a choice. Stone had once again cornered her, captivated her. Finally, she stut-tered out, "Yes. She would have agreed. But to take a risk, a truly great risk, it must mean something. *Capisce?*"

Stone nodded at her, smiling. "Yes. But finding you meant a great deal, *capisce?*

The cousins noticed how discomfited Gabriella became at Stone's compliment. This one, surely, was the suitor she had spoken of.

Stone looked up the block to where Fausto's limo was being blocked by the *carabinieri*. He pointed over at Fausto's rented limo with a broad smile.

"See—much like your Lucia, I realized that a little ship was infi-nitely better equipped to get to hard-to-reach places. Which, in my case, would be anywhere alone with you."

Gabriella, flushing crimson, shared a laugh with him, partly at Fausto's expense. Her cousins prodded her to introduce Stone. She shook herself back into the real world.

"*Scuzi. Piacere*—Stone Alexander, I'd like you to meet my cousins, Maria and Paolina Francini."

The matronly Francini women stared at Stone hungrily, like starving dogs before a butcher shop window. They couldn't fail to notice the hold he had on Gabriella. Flustered by their own state of mild arousal, they merely nodded their heads at him and smiled coyly.

"Would you care to join us for *una tazza de Chianti,* Cadet Alexander?" Gabriella asked, trying to sound cool. But cool was anything but how she felt. Stone made her so...flustered.

"*Grazie,* Signorina. But I do not imbibe. I was, however, wondering if you'd like to come with me for a little spin?"

Gabriella was dumbstruck. Such a brash invitation—and right in front of her cousins!

"A...spin?"

Stone laughed almost warmly. "I'm sorry. I meant a little ride. It's such a lovely day. And, in honor of the saint and all...perhaps we can perform some heroic deeds on her behalf. Throw out some loaves of bread to the masses?"

His look reached down to the depths of Gabriella's soul. He fixed her with a look so intensely romantic that she felt a sense of urgency, that same burning, that always made her feel like Stone's captive. There was no fighting it. She couldn't fight it, and frankly, she had no desire to.

Gabriella choked out a little giggle as she struggled to catch her breath and maintain some sense of decorum. "All right, Cadet Alexander. Let me make my apologies. I think it is very good that my cousins speak only Italian."

Stone laughed. "I think that despite the language barrier, your cousins have clearly understood everything."

Gabriella laughed nervously. Of course, Stone was right. Her cousins may have had no idea what they were saying, but they could hardly fail to notice the vibration between them. Stone nodded politely at the cousins like a well-brought-up young cadet, then leered over at Gabriella with a mischievous grin. He extended his hand to her gallantly, but the look in his eyes was challenging.

"Are you afraid?"

She grabbed hold of his hand, and they felt an electric current between them that could have lit up the whole piazza. Her legs shaking like overcooked spaghetti, Gabriella tried to stand, desperate not to let Stone know how much he'd gotten to her.

"You forget. I come from a long line of army generals. We Francinis fear nothing."

"Well then, say *Auf Weiderzein* to your lovely *cugini.*"

Stone again nodded politely to the two women as Gabriella hopped onto the Vespa. The cousins protested, but Gabriella lied—telling them in a flurry of Italian that she'd be back in only a few minutes. The women reluctantly waved good-bye, stupefied by the sight of their modest young cousin bouncing off with her arms around the dazzling young cadet.

$$\Omega^2$$

Gabriella's arms were clenched around Stone's waist as if for all eternity as he high-tailed it as far from the Spanish Steps as he could. Bouncing along the back streets of Rome on the tiny Vespa at break-neck speed, Gabriella felt more free, more excited and more out of control than she had ever felt in her life. It was exhilarating, to say the least. Stone turned for a quick glance at the dark-haired maiden holding on to him for dear life.

He shouted over his shoulder, "So, you fear nothing?"

Gabriella shouted back, calling upon the bravado her lineage entitled her to. "That's right."

By way of an answer, Stone suddenly put the pedal to the metal—whisking them off into the mountains beyond. "I'll have to find something to frighten you, then. That'll be my challenge," Stone tossed out with a laugh.

Little did he guess that very close to the exterior, poor Gabriella was quaking with fear. Not fear of the rollicking ride. Not fear of heights, not fear of her parents' wrath or even of the young man controlling the machine. She was quaking with fear of herself.

$$\Omega^2$$

As Stone tore off across the square, Fausto and his friends sat there in their limo, deadly silent. All eyes were on Fausto. His face was as grim as murder itself, and none of the young men, not even Giovanni, dared to laugh at him now.

# CHAPTER FOURTEEN

And it shall be, that he that is taken with the
accursed thing shall be burnt with fire...

—Joshua 7:15


The midwife wonder'd, and the women cried
"O Jesu bless us, he is born with teeth!"
And so I was, which plainly signified
That I should snarl and bite and play the dog.
Then since the heavens have shap'd my body so,
Let hell make crook'd my mind to answer it.

—William Shakespeare, *Henry VI*

Stone stood before his squad, dressed and fully equipped for a paintball battle in the dense woods surrounding the academy. He paraded before his squad with the authority and demeanor of a general before a critical campaign.

"This is not just an exercise! This is the first step into your future! In battle, there are two kinds of soldiers: those who live, and those who die. To live, you must learn to kill. Killers win wars.

"Cadet Monticelli and his squad have been selected to defend the mountain against our attack. As you know, the victors will receive a regimental citation and will graduate with special honors. The vanquished will be required to complete one month's further training before they are allowed to graduate. It is imperative that we are the victors today! We are practiced. We are soldiers. We are killers. Do you understand me?"

The squad stood before Stone as if enchanted. His speech had profoundly inspired them all.

"I said, do you understand me?"

The young men were filled with raw energy and nerve. In unison, they screamed out, "Yes, sir!"

A satisfied smirk came over Stone's face. He lowered his voice. "Well then, take your positions!"

$$\Omega^2$$

Colored smoke drifted through the trees. Fausto and his squad were defending their flagged position against probing attacks from separate units of Stone's squad under Peter and Anton.

Vincenzo seemed quite agitated. He called over to his squad leader, "Fausto! They're up to something!"

Fausto was clearly taking this as seriously as if this was a real war, which for him it was—a war between himself and his rival, Stone Alexander. In his heart, he wished they were using real ammunition rather than paintballs.

"Yes, I know. That bastard's trying to smoke us out. Instruct everyone to be on guard!"

$$\Omega^2$$

From their position at the rear of the hill, Stone watched from behind cover, his attack strategy well planned. With a motion of his hand, Stone instructed his well-trained squad to charge Fausto's rear guard head-on.

SPLAT! Blue paint suddenly splattered against the face shields of

Fausto's camouflage-clad cadets. They recoiled, wiping the paint off their faces with their jerseys.

Two of Fausto's squad opened fire on Stone's men. Their yellow paintballs splattered into the air, missing Stone's men by a mile. Fausto fumed, expelling a string of expletives in Italian.

The leaders exchanged looks that would blister ordinary men. But these were not ordinary men. Fausto was the titled son of a diplomat. Stone, well, Stone was extraordinary for reasons all his own—having nothing whatever to do with his father's position of power over the media.

Stone curtly gave orders to his squad with a series of precise hand signals and a proud nod. Peter moved forward to Fausto's flag position. Fausto exercised his prerogative—cutting down Peter's team in a hail of yellow paint pellets. Concentrating all of his energy on Peter, Fausto completely missed Stone's other squad, led by Anton, coming up on their flank. Anton's men opened fire on Fausto's cadets.

Fausto saw the flanking attack and realized too late—"Pull back! Pull back!"

He heard a sound and spun around—Stone stood on their fortified position, Fausto's flag in his hand.

"You seem to have lost this...?"

Stone took off his paintball goggles and issued a look of disdain that only Captain Bligh could have one bettered. Stone's crack elicited most unsportsman-like howls from his team. Stone didn't chastise them, but instead basked in Fausto's humiliation.

Fausto's squad boiled under the skin and began to advance on Stone's team. Fausto too had lost it. He unthinkingly swung his paintball rifle to bear on Stone—THWAMP! The paintball hit Stone right in the forehead at close range and knocked him over backwards.

Anton and the others ran to their fallen leader. Peter got right into Fausto's face. "Hey! Fausto! The game was over! That's a violation!"

Vincenzo pushed the smaller Asian cadet aside. "Shut up, Tonzu! When's the last time your country even won a war? I mean, against something other than Godzilla?"

Fausto felt the heat rising on the field. A real battle could mean a possible dismissal. This was something he didn't dare risk so close to graduation. He tried his best to get things back on an even keel.

"Hey, Alexander, no hard feelings, heat of the battle, you know?"

Stone rose slowly to confront Fausto, wiping the yellow paint slowly off his forehead with Fausto's flag. Fausto vainly tried not to show how much this angered him. Fausto felt as if Stone was virtually burning a hole through his forehead. Peter pulled Stone aside and whispered in his ear.

80

"Don't fall into his trap! You can see what he's doing. He wants you to provoke him, Stone; that way you take all the heat. He'd love nothing more than for you to smack him in the mouth, and he'd go running off to Francini..."

Peter's comment immediately changed Stone's demeanor. Stone turned back to Fausto with an entirely different expression on his face.

"Absolutely. Heat of battle. No offense taken whatsoever." Smiling, Stone lightly tossed the paint-soaked flag at Fausto's feet.

Fausto restrained himself physically, but he couldn't resist taking Stone down a peg.

"Don't think you're the ultimate winner, Stone Alexander. This is only round one." He stared at Stone menacingly. "As we say here in *Italia, 'La Donna mobile.'* Young girls are very fickle."

The tension mounted once again. Everyone knew this was no longer about a mock war. It never had been. This was more like the Fall of Troy; it was about a woman.

Stone wryly lifted an eyebrow. "If what you imply were true, then surely Senorina Francini would have waited for you to park your ridiculous limousine yesterday and driven off with *you*. Has your father rented it for you on a long-term lease, Monticelli—hoping it will help you toward your lifelong goal of finding your manhood?"

Both sides roared at this comment. Secretly, even Fausto's own squad thought he was an awful show-off hiring a limousine to chauffeur himself around. Stone's crack won a point with both sides, as it was intended to, and the cadets all had a good laugh at Fausto's expense. Fausto clenched his paint-covered fists to keep himself from slugging Stone Alexander right in his irresistible jaw.

Fausto was so enraged that his brain literally froze, and he was unable to respond to Alexander's jibe. He just prayed that he could restrain himself from decking him. He uttered a quick "Hail Mary" under his breath before Stone hit again.

"But then again, Fausto, I don't know why you even trouble to concern yourself about the waxing and waning of a young girl's affection, when you have the accommodating Vincenzo here..." Stone pointed over at the stocky Sicilian boy, now inflamed beyond description at Stone's accusation.

Any homosexual innuendo among a group of principally teenaged boys was a sure-fire laugh-provoker. Stone won again, as both teams howled with laughter. But Vincenzo leaped at Stone—"I'll get you...!"

Fausto shook with anger, but still had the presence of mind to issue orders. "Get him off him! Now!"

It took four strong cadets to keep Vincenzo from getting to Stone. They continued to restrain him as he fought to get up, screaming in a virtually undistinguishable Sicilian dialect. Stone feigned amusement—or perhaps, he truly was amused. He smiled wryly at Fausto.

"Did I hit a nerve...?"

Fausto began to move in on Stone. His patience was gone. All thought of graduation honors were gone. All thoughts of Gabriella were gone. All he could see was red.

His team—suddenly remembering who their captain was—clustered around in support of Fausto. Stone's squad backed him up. It was a long, tense moment—a moment that could instantly become a conflagration.

Fausto and Stone stood no more than five feet from each other, both splattered in each other's paint. From the intensity of their reactions, you'd think they had been covered in each other's blood.

Fausto, having had ample time, had finally composed a whopper of a comeback. He set the stage, turning to his squad now for support. With one eye on Stone, he addressed Vincenzo, still frothing at the mouth.

"Vincenzo? I'm surprised at you! You gonna let a crack from a baby killer bother you? Stone only kills babies in the cradle! Isn't that right, *amazzate i bambini?*"

No one dared utter a word. A murmur ran throughout both squads. Stone's eyes narrowed, but he kept his composure. A long, tense moment followed. Peter again approached Stone, warning him not to go for the bait. Stone heard Peter, but he was already plotting a strategy.

Stone played out the moment for all it was worth. He wiped off his hands. Wiped the beads of sweat from his forehead, staring at the ground. Finally, after what seemed like an hour to both teams, he looked up at Fausto, smiling broadly.

"I think...I think what's needed here, under the circumstances, is a contest."

The silence finally broken, Fausto allowed himself a hearty laugh. "*Perfetto.* A battle in the old style, *mano a mano.* What did you have in mind, Signore Alexander, pistols at dawn? Or perhaps a sword fight for the fair lady's hand?"

Laughter amongst Fausto's cadets. *Touché.*

"Well, under the circumstances..." Stone looked over amiably at Vincenzo. "Perhaps it should be *sword swallowing...*"

Fausto grabbed Stone around the throat, his thumb pressed hard against his Adam's apple. Stone was choking. "There's not going to be any contest, because I'm going to tear you apart right now with my bare hands!"

Two of Fausto's men pulled him off of Stone, who took a moment to rub his reddened neck. The cadets tasted blood, and began hooting and cheering. "Fight! Fight!"

Fausto, finally having regained control, fixed his men with a stare. They immediately backed off. Knowing the kind of disciplinary action he could be up against, Fausto negotiated with Stone in a far less accusatory tone.

"All right, Alexander. A fair fight. What is it you propose?"

Stone too had regained his composure.

"Who said anything about a fight? Fighting is against the laws of the academy. I said a *contest*. No swords. No fists." They all stared at Stone, wondering what he meant.

"Tonight, Fausto, after lights out, a race."

Fausto burst out laughing. "A foot race? Are you kidding? I'll beat your lily-white American tail!"

Stone shook his head. "No, no. I meant nothing so pedestrian. I propose a race across the lake."

The entire crowd murmured in unison. The lake? In the chill fall water? At night? Anton and Peter both tried to get Stone's attention. Peter whispered to him, "Stone—Fausto has been the captain of the swimming team since third form!"

Stone hushed the boys with a look. He turned back to Fausto. "My men accurately point out that I give you unfair advantage here— you being captain of the swimming squad. But it is for that express reason that I make such a generous offer. I do so because, when I win, my success will taste that much sweeter!"

Stone bowed at Fausto in a highly exaggerated manner.

"But this is hardly the season. That water is like ice!" Fausto rejoined, clearly dismayed. Stone cocked his head, looking over at this far less cocky Fausto. He goaded him still further. "What's wrong, Fausto? You can get the limo to pick you up afterward so you don't catch the night chill, and your Vincenzo can wrap you up later in his arms. Or, do you need your *father* there to help you? He won't be, you know."

"Neither will yours, Stone Alexander," Fausto spat out. "Tonight it is."

Stone met Fausto's eyes. This was now a pact.

"Tonight."

Stone and Fausto finally broke apart and returned to their respective squads, with a great deal of attendant patting on the backs. Just as Fausto was almost out of earshot, Stone turned to fire one last blast: "Oh, and by the way, Fausto, I understand that fools, like witches, sink like stones."

Fausto froze for a moment and then turned away, the pumped-up cadets on both sides finally disappearing into the dusky fall evening.

# CHAPTER
# FIFTEEN

And from that torment I will free myself,
Or hew my way out with a bloody axe.
Why, I can smile, and murder while I smile,
And cry "Content," to that that grieves my heart,
And wet my cheeks with artificial tears,
And frame my face to all occasions.
I'll drown more sailors than the mermaid shall;
I'll slay more gazers than the basilisk;
I'll play the orator as well as Nestor,
Deceive more slily than Ulysses could,
And, like a Sinon, take another Troy.
I can add colours to the chameleon.
Change shapes like Proteus for advantages,
And set the murderous Machiavel to school.
—William Shakespeare, *Henry VI*


But when the night had thrown her pall,
Upon that spot, as upon all,
And the mystic wind went by
Murmuring in melody–
Ah, then I would awake
To the terror of the lake.
—Edgar Allan Poe, *The Lake*

The shore of the lake was bathed by moonlight, revealing at least three or four dozen assembled cadets, half friends of Fausto and half boosters of Stone, gathered on the bank to exchange wagers and watch the hotly anticipated race.

Fausto was the first of the contestants to show, the omnipresent Vincenzo at his side, as well as the rest of his squad. Vincenzo saw how nervous Fausto was, decked out quite appropriately in bright yellow scuba diving gear.

"He's not gonna show, Fausto. He's full of it down to his..."

Vincenzo never got to finish his sentence. Noise behind them drew their attention to the rustling in the forest.

While most of Stone's squad were already assembled on the lake shore, Stone now emerged from the woods in nothing but a pair of bathing trunks, a towel tossed casually over one shoulder, flanked by Anton and Peter. All conversation—and gambling—ceased when Stone appeared. He strode up to Fausto, looking up and down at his yellow scuba gear.

"I've heard of being yellow, Fausto, but this is really too much, honestly..." Stone taunted.

"You said nothing of dress, Cadet Alexander," Fausto rejoined through clenched teeth.

Stone laughed, rendering him the victor even before the race had begun.

"Well, yes, but these are Mediterranean waters, are they not—not the Arctic. The scuba gear seems a bit, well, overkill. But to each his own."

Stone tossed his towel at Anton and started stretching. Money changed hands quicker than at Las Vegas roulette tables.

The men locked eyes, Stone beamed broadly in his typically infuriating fashion. While the crowd held its collective breath in anticipation, Stone turned to Fausto tauntingly.

"See you in Florence." Stone dove into the river and started swimming with long, strong strokes. Vincenzo turned to the livid Fausto.

"Cheat! That man is a contemptible cheat!"

But Fausto had no time for long good-byes. He, too, dove right into the black lake, as the cadets now ran up and flanked the lake, chanting for their heroes.

$$\Omega^2$$

The two well-matched adversaries swam in long, proud strokes. Fausto quickly ate up the distance between himself and Stone. On the shore, Anton and Peter led their squad yelling out encouragement.

"Swim, Stone! Swim! Don't look back!"

But Stone did look back. He saw Fausto gaining on him. Though he started later, Fausto's long, muscular legs pushed him along faster, and soon, he pulled up even with Stone, and then, with a splash of wake in Alexander's face swam on—pulling ahead. The crowd was going insane with excitement.

All this commotion was far too much not to waken Generale Francini and all the schoolmasters. Rushing down to the lake in their bedclothes, Francini struggled to find a face he recognized in the dark. He pushed his flashlight up into Vincenzo's face. The boy stared at the general like a frightened rabbit.

"What's going on here?" Francini demanded.

Vincenzo choked out a reply as teachers, priests and even nearby villagers descended on the lake. "It's...it's that Alexander. That son of a b...*scuzi*, Generale Francini, he challenged Fausto to a swimming contest!"

Francini's eyes grew wide. Never in all his years—he thought to himself, *That's Daniel Alexander's son out there...one of my oldest friends—and the son of an important diplomat as well. If something happened to either of them...* Francini felt his whole world about to crash down around him.

"It was a matter of honor, sir," Vincenzo protested. "Fausto could not turn down his challenge without..."

Vincenzo was wasting his words. Francini was already at the lakeshore, along with all the others, frantically looking for any sign of the two men. Francini turned upon hearing a soft voice behind him. "Can you see them, Papa?"

Francini turned to see Gabriella, shivering in her thin bathrobe, tears running down her face.

"Can you see Stone? Oh, this is all my fault. My fault." Gabriella broke down completely. Her father put his arm around his darling daughter reassuringly.

"This has nothing to do with you, *figlia mia*," he lied. "This is just two young men seeing who can spit the farthest."

"I wish that were true," Gabriella cried, as she stared riveted at the still, black water for any sign of movement.

Every once in a while, someone shouted out, "I see them! There they are!" And with each new alert, the herd of onlookers would run along to that section of the lake, hoping to catch a glimpse of either of the participants, remaining absolutely silent in the hope of hearing their arms moving through the cold water or even a gasping breath.

# $\Omega^2$

On the shore, a cassock-garbed man watched quietly in the midst of the cadets. But this was not one of the parish priests. This was Stone's Guardian.

The Dark Angel disappeared from the crowd, moving behind a thick cluster of trees. As he dipped one foot into the lake, his body began to shimmer, as if becoming water itself, and then he dissolved entirely, slipping into the water like a flume of ink.

While the contestants were swimming just about neck and neck, each fighting for breath, the Guardian congealed into the form of a twenty-foot-long ink-black shark—his powerful tail propelling him forward. Francini and some of the others, including Gabriella, were amazed to see the fin of the demon shark, jet-black against the moonlit water. The cadets began screaming. Gabriella blacked out momentarily and had to be supported by her father. When she finally came to, she turned to him, her eyes betraying her love and concern for Stone.

"What was it, Father—what *was* it?"

Francini spoke only the truth, crossing himself without even thinking. "I have no idea, *figlia*. Pray to the Holy Mother."

Francini, Gabriella and the others stared mechanically at the massive finned creature illuminated by the bright moon. Following the creature's movements, the crowd finally caught their first glimpse of Stone and Fausto.

"There they are! There they are!" The group seemed to scream out *en masse*. The creature came up behind Stone. Gabriella screamed out in fear—but the creature glided past Stone to the next swimmer, much easier to spot in his yellow rubber suit—Fausto.

Fausto heard the commotion in the water and turned to see the horrific creature coming his way. Incredulous, yet terrified, he thrashed at the water, uselessly trying to build up enough momentum to distance himself from it.

Back on the shore, Vincenzo's eyes opened wide with fear. He screamed out to his comrades.

"*Madonna! Che diavolo sta facendo!* We have to do something!"

But all were so frozen with fear that they didn't even dare to open their mouths. Paralyzed, they could do nothing but wait—and let "nature," or whatever it was, take its course.

# $\Omega^2$

Under water, the demonic shark opened its mouth unnaturally wide and clamped down on Fausto's midsection. Those near enough to get a bird's-eye view witnessed a sight they would never forget—and indeed, would see over and over again in their worst nightmares. Those lucky enough not to see it, however, were unfortunate enough to hear Fausto's last pleas for assistance.

"Help me!!! *Piacere*...O God!!"

Stone too heard the screaming, though he had been so absorbed in his own strokes that he hadn't noticed the shark advancing on Fausto. Upon hearing Fausto's pleas, Stone, some twenty feet behind Fausto, stopped swimming—treading water and trying to make out what was happening in the dense mist ahead of him. When his eyes finally began to focus, he saw the creature toss the top half of Fausto's body some twenty feet into the air, which finally landed with a loud thud back into the water. Stone, along with the others, waited for the inevitable. With one quick motion, Fausto's upper half was abruptly yanked under the water. Suddenly, the water was still, without so much as a whirlpool indicating Fausto's final resting place. As stunned as everyone else, Stone continued to tread water, watching the scene before him as if in a trance, the piercing screams from the shore reaching him like voices in a prophetic dream.

# CHAPTER
# SIXTEEN

Swearest thou, ungracious boy?
Henceforth ne'er look on me.
Thou are violently carried away from grace,
There is a devil haunts thee...

—William Shakespeare, *Henry IV*


Give him all kindness;
I had rather have such men
My friends than enemies.

—William Shakespeare, *Julius Caesar*

Later that night, Generale Francini, his head bowed deep in thought, sat before his office fireplace, with a cognac snifter, filled to the brim, clutched in his shaking hands. Beside him, wrapped in one of Francini's own robes, sat Stone Alexander, lost in his own thoughts and mesmerized by the fire. The silence was deadly and was gently broken by Francini.

"Stone...this thing, this thing with Fausto—this is very, very serious."

Stone continued to stare into the fire. He was not grief stricken, but he certainly was somber. Francini tried again to get through to him.

"Stone?" Stone was startled out of his reverie.

"I said, Stone, that this thing, this horrible accident, is a very serious matter."

Stone was jarred by Francini's voice. He turned to Francini slowly. "Of course. Of course, Sir. What could be more serious than the loss of a man's life?"

Francini stared at the profile of the young man before him, looking so much like his old friend, yet so very different. "Yes. Stone. Despite my affection for your father and your outstanding record here, which no one can dispute—I'm afraid there must be an official inquest."

Stone virtually jumped out of his seat, trying to maintain some degree of decorum. "An inquest? For what reason, Sir? Surely you're not accusing *me* of any foul play...as if it would be the first time..."

*Stone moved away from the fire, stopping before the Bosch print that had so intoxicated him when he first arrived at the academy some fourteen years earlier. The images of the damned, in all their suffering, held the same lurid attraction for him now as they did back then, when he was a disgraced youth accused of fratricide; when he had been abandoned by his father only days after his mother's death. The shame, the pain, of those first days at the academy all came back to him in flashes: his father's abrupt departure; the taunts of the merciless young cadets; his running out into the rain and finding solace in the chapel.*

*Stone's consciousness was wracked with anger, shame and despair—the sense that no matter what he achieved, and he had achieved a great deal despite his virtually orphaned state, he would somehow always be the scapegoat. The images of the damned he had seen in the fire of his father's house so long ago, on that last night he had ever spent under his father's roof, flooded his mind now, combined with the hideous sounds of Fausto's final moments in the clutches of the mysterious beast.*

Francini was, as always, political. He rose and slowly went over to Stone. He placed an arm gently on the shoulder of the young man he had grown to love, to respect—and to fear.

"You must try to understand, Stone. This has nothing to do with me. You are like...you have become...like a son to me."

Stone turned to Francini, his eyes now flooded in tears.

"Frankly," he replied. "That is the kindest thing anyone has ever said to me." Stone choked back his tears. "I...I thank you for it, Sir. From the bottom of my heart."

Francini squeezed Stone's shoulder the same way he did to Daniel Alexander fourteen years before, the day he arrived with Stone. *How strange fate is,* he thought. *Could there be some curse upon the heads of the Alexander family?* He and Stone shared a moment in silence, neither knowing what to say. Finally, Francini spoke up, as kindly as he knew how.

"As I said, my son, none of this is up to me. If it were up to me, the matter would be deemed a terrible tragedy; the books would be closed, and we could all go on with our lives. But the school board, the Monticelli family, *they* will demand an inquest."

Francini paused briefly, lowering his voice. "It is especially unfortunate that it is widely known that you were the one who extended the challenge."

Stone turned to face Francini, his face burning with genuine emotion. He paced around the room like a wild animal, his usual composure gone.

"I challenged Fausto to this contest because I believed it would be sport, and nothing more. If I had wanted him dead I could have easily taken him out in a duel—or even with my bare fists! *Those* were the choices he first proposed to *me*! I knew I could beat him cold in fencing or in fisticuffs. I felt it would be unmanly of me to challenge him to a contest at which I would be the inevitable victor. That seemed unfair to me. Unheroic. It was *I* who suggested a race. A swim. A sport at which Fausto was widely known to excel and would therefore put him at an advantage—so that it would be considered an even greater conquest on my part when I beat him cold." Stone sighed in utter exasperation. "Well, cold he is..."

Francini hung on Stone's every word, longing to believe him, and seeing no rational reason not to. Stone continued ranting as he paced the room. "What happened was a tragic accident! What has that to do with me? How can I be accused of prearranging such horror?"

For the first time, Francini's face betrayed him. Stone saw that Francini could not meet his eyes. "Stone..."

But Stone wouldn't let him get in a word. Not until he'd convinced

Francini completely of his innocence.

"Everybody saw this...this...monster. Even I saw it. I saw it open its jaws and devour Fausto! It was hideous, yes—I will never forget it as long as I live—but what has it to do with *me*? It could have just as easily been me that the demon devoured..."

Francini couldn't help it; something inside of him told him that the shark had been meant for Fausto alone. He remained silent about his feelings, however, his eyes still downcast. This only made Stone more insistent, more defiant.

"You saw it yourself! You must have seen it!"

Francini chose each word very carefully. "I...I am not so sure anymore, Stone, of what I see, and what I do not." He shrugged his shoulders apologetically. "It is one of the privileges, shall we say, of growing older."

Francini's elusive manner did nothing but further incense Stone. He didn't understand Francini's reticence on an issue that could cost him not only his degree and his reputation—but also his very life. Out of control, Stone pounded on the wall furiously with his fists, like a helpless infant with no other way to express his rage.

After a long pause, Francini resumed again, speaking calmly, fearful of inflaming Stone even more.

"Stone, I know, it was well known, that there was...let's just say, a competition...something personal...between you and Fausto. That is another thing that would surely come up at the inquest."

Stone turned on his heels, staring at Francini through piercing blue eyes that almost seared a hole through Francini's skull with their intensity.

"That's right. There was. And I am not at all ashamed to discuss the reason for that 'competition,' as you chose to put it." Another pregnant pause. Francini didn't need or want to hear the explanation for their "competition." He already knew the reason quite well. Had known it for a long time.

"We need not go into that now, Stone...let's just say..."

Stone moved right before Francini. He wanted clarity between them, and he wanted it now. "Yes, we do need to go into it. *Now.* It's about time."

Francini was amazed at the frightening change in Stone's demeanor. What had happened to the tearful boy he had just called "son"? The boy who was just railing at the fates and banging his fists against the wall? He had suddenly assumed the tone of an equal, an army general. Francini tried to move away and change the subject—but Stone wouldn't let him budge. Francini desperately tried to diffuse the situation.

"Stone, it is true that you were nowhere near Fausto when whatever happened to him happened. We have many cadets who will confirm this, from Fausto's squad as well as your own. I can accuse you of...nothing."

Still assuming his haughty attitude, Stone coldly replied, "And nothing is what I am responsible for."

Finally, Stone allowed Francini to return to his seat by the fire, where he abruptly drained the entire snifter of brandy in one gulp. He sighed loudly. When he finally spoke, his voice trembled with emotion. "You have a great power in you, Stone. I have watched you over these many years."

Stone went over to him, nodding in appreciation of Francini's words, his face warming slightly. Francini thought he detected a slight quivering in Stone's voice. "That's more than my father has ever done."

Francini poured himself some more cognac, sipping slowly and feeling the warmth pervade his body. His lips turned up into an ironic smile. "Great leaders do not always have great fathers, Stone Alexander."

Stone cocked his head to one side, much calmer now. "You think that I am a great leader, Sir?"

"I think you have the potential to be, yes." Francini stared around the room at the portraits of the great generals, the famous leaders, whom he had long admired. "You share many of the traits, without a doubt, of the men whose faces line my walls. Julius Caesar. Winston Churchill. Your Teddy Roosevelt."

Stone beamed at the compliment. He arched an eyebrow. "Alexander the Great?"

Francini found himself laughing, a welcome distraction from the dreadful seriousness of the situation. "Yes. Alexander the Great." Francini steeled himself before delivering what, he knew, could be perceived as a bomb. "But...there is something about you, Stone...it's hard to put a finger on it. A kind of...detachment. Sometimes, you seem, almost...without human feelings."

Stone again felt himself back on precarious ground. He thought that he had won Francini over. But this time, he maintained his control. "To be humane could be perceived as weakness by an enemy, wouldn't you agree, Sir? Isn't that what you've taught us here—instructed me all these years?"

Stone smiled broadly at Francini, his most charming smile. It was so very out of place under these circumstances that Francini found himself shivering.

"I hope that I have not." Again, he drained an entire snifter of cognac in one gulp, hoping the alcohol would give him the strength to finish saying what he knew he must. "There is a big difference between being human and being humane. Sometimes you frighten me, Stone. When will you learn that there is more to life than war?"

Stone stared at Francini now, in deadly earnest. He knelt down beside Francini's armchair. "Generale Francini, with all due respect, Sir, I learned that there was far more to life than war the first moment I laid eyes on your daughter Gabriella, when I was but six years old."

Francini closed his eyes. He face grew pale as a ghost. This was a can of worms he had not wished to open that night, nor indeed any other night. He stared down into his empty snifter, searching for the right words.

"You know how I feel for you, Stone. I have bared my soul to you. But being suited to be a great leader, a man of eminence, does not necessarily make you well suited to be a loving, tender, husband and father. These are not the skills we have taught you here at the academy. But, whatever an old man has to say, it is up to Gabriella to chose her life partner, with her own heart."

Stone clenched his jaw, unsure how to proceed here—nervous about Francini's reaction. He lowered his voice, partly for effect, partly out of respect, and partly to cushion what would inevitably be a blow to the older man.

"In that case, Sir, I have every reason to believe that—since you already feel like a father to me, you shall feel even more warmly toward me when I become your son-in-law."

Unbeknownst to Stone, *nothing* could have cushioned that blow. Francini had lived in fear of this moment ever since the first time he saw Stone and Gabriella exchanging naked stares at each other, many years before. Still, the old military man fought to retain his composure. This was, as he well knew, a critical juncture. The last thing he wanted was to make an enemy of this powerful young man.

"Stone, I have known your father almost all my life. We are like brothers. Now, I have known you almost all of yours..."

Francini stopped himself abruptly. He was stalling for time, talking gibberish, and he knew it. Stone cut in.

"And you have just most kindly said that you felt like somewhat of a father to me, if I might paraphrase?"

Francini cleared his throat. He just couldn't win against this silver-tongued devil. "All right. Suppose you are cleared of any implications in Fausto's death? Suppose I give my daughter to you...what then, Stone? What can you give my Gabriella? Can you swear, honestly, on your dear mother's soul—that you could make her a good husband?

That you could truly make her happy?"

Poor Francini had tears in his eyes. Stone stood before him, and then got down on one knee like a suitor. He looked the general, now nothing more than an anxious father, right in the eyes.

"We belong together, Gabriella and I. We always have. We always will. There is nothing on earth that can stop it."

Stone's eyes seemed to burn right through Francini, and he could not continue to meet the boy's stare. He averted his eyes to the fireplace, which emitted far less ferocious flames. For a long moment, he considered what Stone had said.

Suddenly, in the wordless chamber, the young cadet's shadow grew larger and larger on the wall behind him—finally congealing into the form of the Guardian. Francini's eyes were frozen, eyes opened wide in mute terror, as the Guardian's eyes met his own. For that moment—however long it lasted—Francini saw into the depths of his own soul; he experienced all over again every sin he had ever committed throughout his life sequentially, almost as if he were on his deathbed. It was a harrowing experience. An unwelcome taste of hell.

Stone had no idea what was happening; the Guardian appeared only to Francini, but Stone couldn't help but see Francini transfixed before a vision of some sort. To Stone, the old man seemed to have aged ten years in the blink of an eye. As quickly as it appeared, the shadow of the Guardian disintegrated, leaving Francini a wobbly wreck of a man.

Stone placed a hand on his arm, shaking him ever so slightly, afraid that the old man might have suffered a stroke. "Generale...Signore Francini..."

Francini slowly became aware of Stone leaning over him, touching his hand with a tenderness he never would have thought him capable of.

"Sir, are you all right?" Stone asked, pouring Francini a glass of water and holding it up to his mouth.

Francini shook himself out of his trance and looked up at Stone. He nodded his head and allowed Stone to place the cup of water at his lips. The old man thought that possibly, the tragedy that night might have unhinged him completely.

"*Si, si,*" Francini muttered, choking down a few sips of the water.

Stone appeared relieved. He smiled at Francini with genuine concern and affection. Francini looked up at Stone, and words just poured out of his mouth—without his even thinking them.

"Yes, yes, you are right. Nothing on earth can separate you..."

Stone was elated. He grabbed Francini's hand and kissed it fervently.

"Then I have your permission? I mean, of course, your permission to ask...?"

Still in a profound state of shock, Francini found himself nodding in acquiescence. Stone threw his arms around Francini, whose entire body shivered involuntarily at his touch.

"Now, you will truly be my father, for all eternity!" Stone declared. Smiling broadly, all talk of trials and inquisitions had disappeared from his mind. Gabriella was now his alone. Stone bowed and took his leave of Francini.

As Stone walked out the door of the office, Francini seemed to see a dark shadow following him. Francini sat there alone in his armchair, staring at the family crucifix hanging above his desk. It was his most sacred family heirloom, passed on to him by his father, Generale Michele Francini, and to him by his father, Generale Vittorio Francini—his own namesake. He slowly made the sign of the cross. Now, for no reason that made any sense to him, he thought he saw blood pouring out of the places where the nails had been hammered into Jesus' body. Staring at the bloody crucifix in disbelief, the general heard himself muttering, "For all eternity..." Upon saying these words, Francini's body began to quake uncontrollably in what appeared to be an epileptic seizure.

# CHAPTER
# SEVENTEEN

Death, be not proud, though some have called thee
Mighty and dreadful, for thou are not so;
For those whom thou think'st thou dost overthrow,
Die not, poor Death, nor yet canst thou kill me.

—John Donne

At night the Roman Coliseum echoed with the ghostly sounds of the thousands of Christian men and women who were murdered here in face-to-face combat with wild beasts. The more sensitive could smell the blood splashing up on the faces of the wealthy patricians who had cheered on the bloodbaths. The roaring of the lions that mangled and devoured the early followers of Jesus could even be heard.

But the less sensitive, only attuned to what they could actually see and hear on the earthly plane, heard only the descendants of those wild cats—much smaller cats, mewing and chasing each other around the vast stone pillars that kept the ancient Coliseum erect.

Gabriella had come well prepared for the visit, with a huge jug of milk and a gigantic bag of cat food. She walked carefully toward a herd of wild cats, calling them over to her in a soft, melodious voice, pouring out bowls of food and milk. Within moments, hundreds of emaciated cats surrounded Gabriella, each fighting for a spot at the bowls.

"*Basta...basta...*There's enough for all of you," she reassured them, picking up a tiny kitten in her hands and petting it sensuously. Stone moved up slowly behind her, putting his arms around her waist.

"I envy that kitten."

Gabriella turned to him with a smile. "Isn't it adorable? I have to take at least one or two home. Mama won't mind..."

Stone laughed. "Who could mind anything you do, Gabriella? Or should I call you Santa Lucia?"

Gabriella giggled at the compliment. The couple stood back, surveying the whole of the ancient stadium. "It is beautiful here, no?"

*Stone clutched her even closer, the sounds of earthly suffering resounding in his ears.* Without letting on what he was experiencing, he whispered to her softly, "Terrifying. But magnificent."

They walked arm in arm through the empty Coliseum. Gabriella heard nothing, but Stone's perceptions became more and more acute. He heard the sound of the cheering mobs, the screams of the dying as they were shred to pieces—and it tormented him. Yet it also exhilarated him. But he would not let on to Gabriella.

"Stone, you never told me what happened."

Stone paused now, trying to shake off the ghosts of the past that called out for their salvation—as if to him alone. Stone replied somewhat defensively, "What happened with what? With Fausto? Are you so sorry to see him gone?"

Gabriella sighed, "You are jealous, Stone, and for no reason. Of course I am sad to see him gone. How could I feel otherwise? But you are foolish to suppose there was ever anything between us."

"On your side, perhaps, that is true. But he was in love with you. You knew that, didn't you?"

Gabriella lowered her eyes. "Yes, of course I did. But all the cadets are in love with me, are they not? I am the only woman within fifty miles of the academy!"

Stone eased up, realizing the truth of her statement, and further realizing a far more important fact: Gabriella was *his*. They strolled along arm in arm.

"But you misunderstood me, Stone. I was not speaking of Fausto. I was speaking of my father. You never told me what you said to him. I always thought he was against our being together."

This comment hit a discordant note. Stone stopped and looked at Gabriella, his tone angry and imperious. "What made you think that? Your father and my father are old friends! It is only natural that he'd give us his blessing, isn't it? Well, isn't it?"

Gabriella knew she had blundered. She tried to cover it up as best she could. "Well, it's just that, he never...well, my father..."

"Never had a good word to say about me?"

Gabriella protested, a little too vehemently. "Oh, no, Stone! He only says the best things about you—that you are a natural-born leader, a *great* leader."

Stone frowned. Gabriella confirmed what Stone had known all along, what Francini had so much as told him that night: that he didn't consider him "marriage material" for his daughter.

"But not a great *man*."

Gabriella tried to laugh it off. "Silly. What difference does it make? A leader? A man? Is not a leader a man? I don't understand you sometimes, Stone Alexander."

*Try as he might to block them out, the anguished screams blasted intermittently through Stone's consciousness—the cries of martyrs resounding over two thousand years. Stone struggled to stay in the moment.*

"Sometimes I don't understand myself."

They continued to walk along in silence, the cats following after them, fighting over the stray bits of food Gabriella tossed at them, while still nuzzling the kitten in her arms.

"Stone, you must understand. An Italian father is an Italian father. He always said he would give up his *bambina* to no man. To tell you the truth, I believed him! I thought I was destined to remain alone all my life. Like Santa Lucia, with no husband, no children, healing the sick and feeding the poor. This is why I ask you what you said to him, Stone. For no other reason."

102

A faint smile formed around the edges of Stone's mouth.

"What I said to him, my dearest, was merely the truth, about how I felt about you. That when I rule the world, I want you as my queen, forever at my side."

Gabriella turned to face him. Her face was filled with sweet devotion. "Is that all?"

The specters of the unhappy dead all faded away before Gabriella's innocence. Hers was a face only the greatest masters of the Renaissance could have painted. Her grace came from somewhere not on this earth. Stone was overcome with gratitude for the gift of this exquisite jewel staring up at him with unbridled love.

"No. That is not all. I told him that I had loved you since I first saw you, when I was but six years old. That when I see you, I see an angel, with a crown of stars around her head. An angel unworthy of even Botticelli's hand."

She smiled. He moved closer to her. The intensity mounted. Gabriella giggled, embarrassed by his compliments. "And he believed that? My father must be getting old."

Stone pulled her in so tight that she could barely breathe. But she didn't want to. All she wanted was to feel this way forever.

"I meant it."

He pulled her chin toward him, and they kissed with the savage passion of the lions that once called this place their lair.

"I have never loved anyone else in my life," Gabriella whispered. "You know I was just playing with you, like a cat with a mouse."

*Despite the exquisite perfection of the moment, Gabriella's comment triggered once again a vision of the scenes of "play" and "merriment" at the Coliseum that took place over two millennia before. He fought to block out the screams of the faithful filling his head.*

Gabriella noticed his distress, and a look of empathy crossed her face. She could only assume that her comment had caused Stone pain. She reached out and held her soft hand against his face. He pulled her into a close embrace.

"Let us never play with each other again, my darling. It is far too dangerous a game." They kissed against the bleak but beautiful backdrop, the souls of the wretched dead soaking up their passion like wine on the blood-drenched ground.

# CHAPTER
# EIGHTEEN

The web of our life is a mingled yarn,
Good and ill together;
Our virtues would be proud,
If our faults whipped them not;
And our crimes would despair
If they were not cherished
By our virtues.

—William Shakespeare, *All's Well That Ends Well*

The strident blast of a military brass band announced the formal beginning of graduation day at the Francini Academy. Rows of hundreds of white folding chairs had been set up before a martially festooned dais. Each chair was now filled with the posterior of the proud parent of a graduating senior.

In one of these seats sat a far older Daniel Alexander. His jaw was set, but inwardly, he was inordinately fearful of this day. He had come to Italy to offer congratulations to a son he had fathered in name only. Or rather, to a son he had cared for only fiscally, by writing overly generous checks every year to the Francini Academy—not only to defray the cost of his son's education, but also, he hoped, to absolve himself of his sins. If he could have admitted it to himself, which he could not—this was the day, the confrontation that he had most dreaded.

David Alexander sat beside his father, now almost sixteen years old, and the resemblance between the two was striking. The difference between them was just as striking.

Unlike the tight-lipped Daniel, impossible to read, David was an open book. From the look on his face, David was far more excited than apprehensive that afternoon. Quite obviously, David Alexander was a different animal than either his father or his older brother. Innocence and integrity surrounded him. *What will he be like,* he wondered, *this brother I have never met? Will we look alike? Be alike? Will my brother like me?* David was on tenterhooks to find out the answers to the questions that had so often preoccupied him throughout his sixteen years.

General Francini stood at the podium outfitted in his finest dress uniform, every one of his many metals polished until they gleamed. He took a moment to survey the crowd, and smiled down at his old friend. Francini hemmed and hawed, tested the mike..."*Uno, due, tre...*" The slightly nervous Francini couldn't delay the proceedings any longer. He began to speak, in a tentative voice at first, and finally, more self-assured, as befitted his position as head of the Francini Academy.

"We all know why we are here. To congratulate the special young men who have completed their intensive training here and who will now go on to do great things—in the careers of their choosing. It is appropriate, I feel, to say that any young man graduating from the Francini Academy will reap the rewards of all he has learned here: resolve without cruelty; tolerance without weakness. Our graduates will find many doors open to them as our doors close behind them. I welcome everyone who has traveled from all over the world to be here, and to start our festivities, we have prepared an extraordinary regimental presentation. And now, the honor of giving the special regimental presentation goes to Cadet Squad Leader Stone Alexander."

The excited audience cheered wildly. Daniel and his son exchanged stares. Was it surprise on Daniel's face that his virtually deserted son had fared so well? David almost jumped from his seat in excitement, cheering louder than anyone, as the man who was his brother came forward on the parade grounds, followed by his well-oiled machine of men.

David watched in awe as Stone barked orders and his squad of dress-uniformed cadets pushed the field artillery piece out, running through their paces with an elegant precision, executing a flawless display of an arms drill. It was a presentation worthy of West Point, and Daniel Alexander turned, somewhat surreptitiously, to his young son—trying to gauge his reaction.

"David?"

But David didn't hear him. His eyes, as well as everyone else's, were glued to the parade ground, and his eyes were fixed particularly on the face of his starched and handsome older brother. David tried to hide his feelings, but he could not. He was clearly a young man who always wore his heart on his sleeve. He felt tears welling up in his eyes that he hoped his stern father wouldn't see. But he did. The sight of those tears made Daniel Alexander feel his own inherent worthlessness—as both a human being and a father. But he refused to own those feelings. He turned abruptly back to the brightly colored pageant before him. He watched Stone command the field and realized, in a flash, that with no help from him, Stone had become a man.

# CHAPTER NINETEEN

But, O, strange men!
That can such sweet use make
Of what they hate...

—William Shakespeare, *Measure for Measure*

A local band started playing a variety of Italian favorites, beginning with the academy's theme song, "Santa Lucia." A robust man with a resounding tenor voice launched into the first verse of the popular tune as groups of proud parents and cadets milled around the field after the presentation of degrees. Stone stood at the center of a small group of parents, who were congratulating him on his triumphant exhibition. He gave them his boldest smile by way of thanks, along with a curt, gentlemanly nod of the head.

Daniel and David Alexander, wandering across the field to meet him, heard snippets of his conversation.

"No, actually, I've decided to forgo a military career. I've accepted an administrative post with the European Union."

The parents smiled at him, and he bowed formally to the group before turning and walking back to the main festivities. He could hardly believe what, or *whom*, he saw up ahead. Stone actually missed a step, trying to decide whether to advance or retreat. He quickly decided that advancing would be the "better part of valor." Stone adopted a confident, almost cocky air, crossing easily to where his father and a young man stood waiting for him. Stone haughtily saluted the elder Alexander as if meeting up suddenly with a foreign dignitary—which, in fact, was exactly what his father was to him.

"I don't believe I've had the pleasure?"

Daniel Alexander fumed beneath his plastic veneer. He extended his hand to Stone in a pathetic gesture of peace.

"Congratulations, son." After a brief moment, Stone chose to take it. "Thank you...*Father*, is it?"

Daniel was now certain that Stone was playing with him—and it infuriated him. He was determined not to let it show. "It is."

The mercurial Stone performed a changing act right before their eyes. The haughty cadet was suddenly effervescent and cheerful. "Well! This really must be an occasion." He looked over at the shy teenager standing next to Alexander. It hadn't dawned on him that this could be...

"Then this must be...David!"

The slim, sandy-haired boy beamed. He felt immediately drawn to Stone. Stone embraced him warmly, then stood back and took a good look at his brother.

*They looked at each other. It was everything the meeting of two long-lost brothers should be. Both were touched to the point of speechlessness. There was an instant bonding between them that seemed to go far beyond blood bonds.*

Stone was the first to speak, albeit tentatively. "Well, I must say, you've grown into a fine young man."

*The silence went on, as the long-separated brothers continued to size each other up. Each liked what he saw more and more by the moment. Each recognized in the other, almost immediately, not only a true brother in blood—but a soul mate, or a twin soul. Whatever term one wanted to apply to their connection, the bond between them seemed deeper than life itself. And instantly, each of them knew that they'd been seeking the other—as if seeking their other half—all their lives. And now, together, they were complete.*

Watching them together like this, and knowing that he'd been responsible for their lifelong separation, made Daniel Alexander want to slit his wrists on the spot. But Stone was simply bubbling over with delight. He shook his head, smiling at David. "I had no idea...you're the missing link, aren't you?"

There was no trace of the usual irony or bitterness in his voice. Not when addressing his brother. That day, his sardonic side was reserved for Daniel alone. David was elated. He had no idea what to expect from this mysterious older brother he'd heard of only in bits and pieces, and usually in hushed whispers. David spoke from the heart. "Maybe to you I am," David said. "But to me—it's you who are the missing link!"

Stone glowed from within. Yes. They had been waiting for each other for so long, and neither of them had ever known it—at least, not consciously. "I suppose, David, that our...father is preparing you to follow in his footsteps?"

There was an awkward silence. Stone sensed that he'd hit a sore spot, much to his delight. David lowered his head shyly.

"Well, actually, I'm not all that interested in the media."

Stone was completely blown away, although most pleasantly, by David's reply. Daniel Alexander, however, was not pleased. Stone looked over at David, still shirking, and then at his father. "Well then, I suppose neither one of us is much of a 'chip off the old block,' so to speak!"

To Stone's satisfaction, he noticed that his father had caught the implied insult. David couldn't reply without offending either his father or his newfound brother. He chose to just smile awkwardly at both of them. Alexander, Sr. cleared his throat, determined to intervene before any more "brotherly bonding" could occur. He turned to David somewhat abruptly.

"David, if you don't mind, give me a few moments alone with Stone." David felt dismissed. The last thing he wanted was to leave his brother's side, but he played it cool. "Sure. OK, Dad. Stone, I'll catch up with you later."

Stone smiled fondly at his not-so-little brother. "Yes. We have a lot of catching up to do."

Stone followed David with his eyes until he was out of sight, mystified by the hold this young man had over him.

# CHAPTER TWENTY

After this I looked, and, behold,
a door was opened in heaven.

—Revelation 4:1


Be thou faithful unto death,
and I will give thee a crown of life.

—Revelation 2:10

Having shyly moved off from his father and brother, David looked around, feeling desperately out of place and trying to figure out what to do with himself. His Italian was atrocious, he knew, and he was afraid of making a fool of himself. He finally gravitated toward the crowd clustered around the food tent.

$$\Omega^2$$

With David out of the way, the gloves came off. Stone went right for the jugular. He was determined not to let Daniel off the hook. The pair began to walk aimlessly side by side so neither had to look the other in the eye.

Instinctively, both men had the same walking pattern; they walked at precisely the same pace, with exactly the same interval between steps—almost as if they had spent a great deal of time together, which most certainly they had not. Stone tossed off his first sally.

"I am absolutely amazed that you could find your way back to the academy, Sir, after, how long has it been—fifteen years?"

Alexander felt his blood pressure rising, but said nothing, marching along at exactly Stone's pace.

"But I suppose they included a map and directions along with the invitations as a matter of course, for *foreign* parents."

Stone glanced over briefly to catch how hard his first blows had hit Daniel Alexander. He had never wished so hard to hurt someone, genuinely hurt someone, in his life. Not consciously, at least. Alexander tried not to show his anger, but Stone could feel his father's blood boiling just beneath the surface.

"I could never forget my way here. I lived here as a young man for many years, if you recall."

Stone laughed. "Oh yes, of course you did. I guess you knew the way here backwards and forwards, didn't you?"

They moved along a few more steps before Stone added, "But I suppose it was difficult for *your father* to find his way here—during, say, holidays and school vacations. You must've spent a lot of time alone."

As a media mogul of over twenty years duration, Daniel Alexander had learned to be the soul of tact and diplomacy. But this young man at barely twenty-two years of age instinctively knew just what buttons to push to set him off.

After a lengthy pause to regain his composure, Alexander decided to change the subject entirely. If he had been a negligent parent, he was unwilling to admit it, not to himself, and most certainly not to this young rapscallion.

"The European Union isn't the right place for you, Stone. You aren't cut out to be a bureaucrat." The elder Alexander paused. This was far harder than he thought it would be to get out. Yet, he tried his best to sound at least vaguely congenial. "There's a place for you, Stone, in my organization. You would have to work hard, just like everyone else, but with your confidence, you could easily work your way up in a year or two. Have you ever thought about coming back to the States?"

Stone stopped in his tracks, pausing for deliberate dramatic effect. "Coming *back* to the States? How can you come back to somewhere you have never lived except as a snot-nosed child?"

Alexander cringed, but Stone continued to vent. "America is your country, Sir, not mine. I follow Italian football—that's 'soccer' to you, not baseball. I eat a farinaceous diet—not Big Macs. I go to *La Scala* for a night on the town—not drive-in movies. In short—I belong to *this* world."

Stone's putting him to task for what he perceived to be his sins or failings as a father unnerved Daniel in a way he had hoped it wouldn't. If he had been a praying man, he would have prayed that this meeting wouldn't have bothered him like this. But he wasn't a praying man. Never had been. He was a pragmatist. Now he found himself shaky, unprepared for this attack.

He had somehow thought they would just reconcile. At the worst, he had figured that Stone would treat him cordially, as if he were an utter stranger—or perhaps as the anonymous "benefactor" who had "sponsored his education." But these hopes were clearly not founded in reality. At least not in Stone's reality.

Emotional confrontation was something new to Daniel Alexander. It was something he had managed to avoid his entire life. He found it had worked exceedingly well over the years as a defense mechanism against feeling pain. His life as a twenty-four-hour manipulator of the media had served its purpose very well until now; it had provided him a refuge against any possible human contact. But now, back at the academy, he was being called on the carpet—being asked, though covertly, to account for his actions by a man much younger than himself, a cunning and bitter man who also happened to be his son—and he didn't like it one bit. He would not accept the gauntlet Stone had thrown down. He was unwilling, or rather unable, to feel.

"America *is* your home, Stone, and I'm very sorry you feel the way you do. About coming home. About America. It's where you were born, and it's where you owe your loyalty." The empty platitudes resounded in Daniel's ears, and he sensed he was just digging a deeper hole for Stone to bury him in. "A man without a country is like..."

Daniel was spent. He'd really bungled it now, and he knew it. His quick mind immediately changed the subject once more, trying a new tack. "Stone, I, uh, have read your graduate treatise with some interest."

Stone feigned absolute amazement. His eyes opened wide with amusement. "*You* took the time to read *my* graduate treatise? A man with your rigorous schedule! I am absolutely amazed!"

All hopes of a *rapprochement* between them evaporated—the foolish dreams of an old man. Daniel keenly felt the contempt in which his son held him and everything he stood for. Every word that came from his mouth was pure venom, only lightly coated with sugar.

"How on earth did you even get it? I certainly didn't send it to you. I could have, of course, but I had no reason to believe you'd be interested."

Alexander felt trapped. To admit the truth would only open himself up to another torrent of abuse. He winced, as Stone waited impatiently for his answer. "The, uh, graduate committee sent it to me..."

The truth of the matter sank in. Stone jumped on the information, as Daniel knew he would. "Oh, of course. Along with the bill for my last tuition payment, I suppose. As if to prove to you that they had done something with me all these years; that you hadn't just thrown your money down a hole!"

*Touché.* Alexander tried to smooth things over once again. "They sent it to me along with your grades and your service reports to explain why you ranked number one in your class."

Stone was temporarily jolted—was that a compliment from his father? But then he realized that Alexander had merely been passing along information, not commending him on his performance. His anger escalated. He deserved at least that much from this man. He had graduated number one in his class! He was leader of the cadet corps! He deserved, at the very least, to be congratulated on his accomplishments. But Stone was determined not to show how much this hurt him. They continued over in the direction of the entertainment. Stone's response was courteous, though cool.

"So, you read my treatise. What did you think of it? I would be most interested in your opinion."

Alexander took a deep breath. He wished Stone hadn't asked him that. He found himself, for the first time that day—indeed, for as many years as he could remember—unable to contain his anger.

"You want the honest truth? I thought it was utter rubbish. A hodge-podge of socialism, communism, utopian idiocy..." Stone saw

116

that he had gotten his father into a highly agitated state. Now he could relax. He had achieved his goal.

He was the agile cat who had finally cornered the old mouse.

"Those are such old-fashioned words, Sir. Philosophies that were tried and abandoned, and for good reason. My treatise speaks of the ideas that are shaping the future of world politics. One day you'll wake up and discover what a dinosaur your beloved capitalism has become...*Father.*"

He delivered this last word with an irony that cut Alexander to the quick. A moment passed without either man speaking as they walked in tandem, each step in precise alignment.

"I know you think I'm wrong, but I'm not. You'll see. History will bear out the truth of my claims. There is nothing that can stop me."

*A chill ran down Alexander's spine. He flashed back to that night long ago when Stone had set fire to David's crib. Then, there was the long, silent trip up into the mountains. No, Daniel thought, nothing could stop him—even then.*

Before the conversation could get any further out of hand, Daniel gratefully saw General Francini approaching the quad from his house. Just as they were about to greet him, Stone dropped a bomb.

"Oh, yes. I forgot to mention that I am to be married."

Daniel turned involuntarily to face Stone, completely taken off guard. Stone continued, enjoying Daniel's discomfort. "Yes. That pretty much settles the issue of my returning, as you put it, 'home.' I doubt that my future wife would appreciate the crassness of the States. She has led, well, a very sheltered life. And I would like to keep it that way."

Daniel Alexander was literally down for the count. He actually stuttered. "Your...your...marriage, did you say?"

Cheerily, Stone continued. "You mean you hadn't heard? I thought everyone knew! Gabriella Francini and I are to be married. We are deeply in love. And the best part is, now Generale Francini will truly be my father—which is only fitting, as he has *functioned* as one these sixteen years."

Stone looked over at his father with a charming smile—completely inappropriate considering the dagger he had just thrust into his back. Alexander's face was ashen. Stone reveled in his father's mortification. He realized that he had finally delivered a mortal blow. Stone savored the delicious moment and the sickly sweet taste of revenge.

# CHAPTER
# TWENTY-ONE

If ever you prove false to one another,
Since I have taken such pains to
bring you together,
Let all pitiful goers-between be
called to the world's end
After my name...

—William Shakespeare, *Troilus and Cressida*

Under the billowy white tent, cadets, attended by elegantly dressed parents from all over the globe, hovered over the sumptuous buffet, arrayed with platters of shrimp, calamari, roast beef and a dessert table that challenged the waistline and defied the imagination. While the jabbering in foreign tongues, along with the jangling of utensils, created quite a din around the buffet, young David Alexander stopped a few feet from a small table set off to the side that was set up exclusively for nonalcoholic punch.

David stood before the table, dumbstruck by the sight before him—the most beautiful woman he had ever laid eyes on. It was Gabriella. The temptations of the food table suddenly paled before the young woman's glorious charms, and he just stood there, riveted, watching her as she was framed by the warm sun, her hair fairly glowing like a halo. Having completely lost his appetite, David stared at the vision of loveliness for a long moment before he could will his legs to walk over to the punch table.

Hypnotized, David's feet moved as if in slow motion toward her. Gabriella couldn't help but notice the effect she was having on this shy boy, and she smiled at him encouragingly. Her smile gave him the courage to walk up to the table and extend his empty hands, like a beggar looking for a handout. Gabriella filled the ladle and then looked down at his hands.

"You'll get all wet," she smiled at him. The youngster was most certainly appealing. Classically featured, young, vigorous—very much like Stone, but sweet and innocent in a way that Stone never was, and never could be. David was so entranced that he couldn't take his eyes off her, or even begin to take in what she was saying. He stood there foolishly, feeling like Lancelot when he first beheld Guinevere. David finally stumbled out, "Huh? I…"

Gabriella showed this pathetic, infatuated youth the same benevolence she had shown the kittens at the Coliseum.

*They were somehow alike in the way they looked at her. Needy. Like a motherless child. It was nothing like the way Stone looked at her—obsessively, compulsively, commanding her attention. With Stone, she was powerless. She could do nothing but give him whatever he wanted. Some things were just fated, she thought. She could tell in an instant that it would be different with this boy. With him, she would always be the one holding the reins.*

"You'll need a glass if you want something to drink," she whispered to David, who continued to stare at her as if Venus herself had suddenly jumped out of her clamshell. He thought to himself, *Am I acting like a total dork, or what?*

He hastily picked up a glass. She poured him some punch, smiling at him all the while with a combination of attraction and pity.

"Thanks," he muttered, almost under his breath. Just when he thought he had completely blown it, this goddess incarnate extended her soft hand to him.

"I'm Gabriella. Gabriella Francini."

David clutched his punch in one hand, squeezing her hand with the other so tightly that he spilled the punch all over himself. Gabriella laughed wildly at his discomfiture, handing him a stack of napkins. This boy was adorable. Finally, while still blotting the bright red punch on his clothes, he mumbled out, "Francini? Like Generale—?"

She laughed. This young boy grew more charming by the moment without even trying. He was definitely American, she had decided. "He's my father," she offered.

David laughed, delighted to have finally found some common ground between them. "That's great! My dad went to school here. He and your dad are really good friends!" David couldn't believe the synchronicity.

Gabriella smiled at him brightly. "That seems to indicate that we will also become good friends, does it not?"

David gushed, "Gee, I sure hope so! I mean, I guess you couldn't have known my father. It was a long time ago when he went here. But maybe you've heard about him. From your father, I mean. He works...I mean, we live in America."

David suddenly realized that he was still holding Senorina Francini's hand. He looked down to confirm it. Yes, he was clutching her hand in his as if for dear life. *Jeez,* he thought. *I am such a dork.* He was mortified. He laughed awkwardly, finally allowing her hand to drop to her side.

Gabriella tried to diffuse his embarrassment. "Now, would you care for some punch?"

David froze, then nodded. "Yeah. Oh, definitely I would."

While she poured out the punch, he continued to run on at the mouth. "This just...I mean, this is, like, such a coincidence! I mean, our fathers knowing each other, and me meeting you, and you being so...so..."

*Gabriella looked up at him with genuine sweetness, basking in his obvious admiration. But there was more to it than that, and somewhere deep inside, she knew it. She was as attracted to this young, goofy boy as he was to her.*

"Yes, it *is* interesting. So, what brings you all the way over from America? Are you looking over the school—are you thinking of coming here next year?"

David laughed nervously. "Oh, no. No way. This isn't for me. I'm not into the whole military thing at all, I mean, no offense. I want to do something that...helps people."

She laughed. "No offense taken. I think that helping people is a very fine ambition."

Once again, she had gently lifted him off the hook and placed him back down on the firm ground. *If she had been an American girl,* he thought, *she'd have made mincemeat out of me already.*

David started running off at the mouth, and Gabriella struggled to follow his line of thought. "I mean, it's so weird and all, because I hardly ever even see my dad, and I've never even met my brother before, and it's like, well, it's like...very, very—well, it's just so weird! And I'm all worried about, like, is he going to like me; what's he going to be like and all, and then, I meet him, and it's like, POW! He's, like, the greatest person I ever met! He's like...he's like..."

David couldn't even finish the sentence. But still he gushed on. "And I've missed out on that, all my life, not knowing him. But I'm going to make sure I make up for that. I plan on seeing as much of my brother as I can from now on!"

David suddenly turned beet red. He couldn't believe how much he'd just revealed to this girl! He felt even more like a complete idiot than before. He pretended to drink some of the punch, but found himself choking on it. Gabriella found all of this most amusing.

"I'm really sorry. I didn't mean to tell you the whole story of my life..."

"That's quite all right," Gabriella replied sincerely. "I enjoyed hearing the story of your life."

*Their eyes met briefly, and he knew she wasn't playing with him; she had really meant it. He was utterly and entirely smitten.*

In the distance, Generale Francini had finally joined Stone and his father. Francini shook hands with Stone and hugged Daniel fondly. David spotted them too, and excitedly pointed over to where they were standing.

"Look! There they are now!" David glowed with pride at the image of his tall, elegant father and his mythical older brother.

Gabriella looked over to see her father, Stone and another man talking. "That is my father, yes. Is that your father with him?"

"Yes," David replied proudly, "and my brother."

Gabriella looked at the boy. Then back at Stone. Now it was her turn to feel embarrassed. She suddenly paled.

*Of course. This boy was Stone's brother! What else could have explained her instant attraction to him? She laughed to relieve the wave of panic she felt sweeping over her.*

"Stone Alexander...is...your brother?"

David seemed surprised. "Yeah! Do you know him?"

Gabriella softly, almost reluctantly, delivered the news she knew full well would break this boy's heart.

"Yes. I know him very well. We are engaged to be married, Stone and I."

*Gabriella was right. David felt his heart, his hopes, sink to the ground. He fumbled for words. Any words.*

"Oh. Wow. Gee. That's, wow, I mean..."

Gabriella laughed again to relieve what was a decidedly awkward moment for both of them. David joined in the laughter, the absurdity of the situation hitting him like a brick in the face. There was nothing else to do but laugh.

"I suppose that we are destined to be more than just friends, then," Gabriella offered, trying to soothe his disappointment.

*Gabriella had dashed enough young men's hopes in her brief life to know when she had utterly destroyed one. This one, she knew, she had left bereft. She felt overwhelmingly guilty at flirting with him so shamelessly, only to destroy his dreams.*

She tried to start up another conversation, trying to deflect from the pall her "announcement" had cast over both of them. *But why,* she wondered, *am I so upset? I have only just met this boy.*

"So, it is David, is it not?

David nodded absentmindedly, still looking over to where Stone and the two fathers rapidly approached them.

"Stone has often spoken of you," she lied kindly.

David appeared to recover slightly. "Really? That's great!" he replied, somewhat heartened.

*Now he remembered. Stone. His newfound brother! It seemed like only moments before that he was enraptured by the opportunity to rekindle, or rather, to start up a relationship with him. And just as quickly, upon meeting this girl, he had forgotten him completely! What was wrong with him? Now, he looked over at Stone coming toward them, his heart pounding in his chest. Yes, it was Stone he had come here to meet. This "incident" at the punch table had been a mere diversion. Hadn't it?*

Gabriella tried to keep the conversation going, inadvertently opening a powder keg. "So," she laughed, "tell me, David—is it true that Stone tried to kill you when you were a little baby?"

*Suddenly, David snapped. His vision blurred. All before him was ablaze. The screams of the damned filled his ears. Before him, gaping wide, were the very pits of hell, and circling around it, just waiting for it to drop into its jaws, was a white crib containing a bawling infant.*

Gabriella could hardly miss David's transformation.

*Now, she knew that both brothers were alike in one way, at least. Both of them saw visions. Not necessarily the same visions, but visions nonetheless.*

Seeing the acute pain on his face, Gabriella tried speaking to him, trying to bring him out of it. "David...David?"

*But David didn't hear a word she said. He was perched, ever so precariously, before the terrifying vision of hell.*

Gabriella reached over and put a tender hand on David's arm, and he instantly returned to real time, smiling awkwardly, trying to shake off the disturbing vision.

"What did you say? Did Stone try to...Oh, no. No, no. That's just one of those tall tales passed down by a long line of nannies. I heard people mention it a couple of times over the years, but I never brought it up to my dad. But then, he was never around much to mention it to, even if I had wanted to."

*So,* Gabriella thought, *Stone's father had kept himself at arms' length from* both *of his sons.* Coming from her own experience with a doting, devoted father, she found this both perplexing and sad.

But before the conversation could go any further, they were jolted by Stone's imperious voice. Both of them tried to regain their composure.

"*Perdonne me*...but you're both wrong. In the future, the world will be won by a new method—one that makes your warfare, Generale, obsolete—and makes my father's manipulation of the media look as crude as a stone-tipped lance compared to a laser-guided cruise missile."

Stone walked over quietly behind David, and a hand suddenly appeared on David's shoulder.

"Stealing my bride away, David?" Both David and Gabriella were shaken. Despite their furious efforts to hide the instant intimacy that had sprung up between them, Stone had intuitively known what had transpired. *How did he know...how could he know?* they both wondered.

Despite the fact that Gabriella was engaged to be married to Stone, there was a great deal about him that she didn't know or understand. She knew that he saw visions, but she had no idea of the extent of his psychic powers.

*The moment he entered the tent, Stone saw the attraction between David and Gabriella. He sensed a purity that disturbed him greatly. The energy between Gabriella and him indicated the power of their mutual attraction, yes, but certainly not any purity of feeling.*

Why is the energy between her and David so different? *he wondered, wracked with jealousy. And even if he had not possessed this remarkable psychic power, his suspicions would have been immediately aroused by the look of profound discomfort on both their faces—looks that each of them had tried so desperately, and unsuccessfully, to hide.*

*But Stone was far more clever than either of them. He prided himself on the fact that no one, ever, had been able to read his thoughts—and they never would. He was able to smile at both of them as if nothing had happened, relieving their tension and guilt. However, he carefully filed this information away for future use.*

"You wouldn't be the first to try, believe me," Stone laughed.

*That is true,* Gabriella thought guiltily, suddenly recalling Fausto's hideous screams for help as the shark ripped him to shreds. *Over me?*

Stone moved over to Gabriella and draped a proprietary arm over her shoulder. He looked over to David, radiating with happiness. "This is truly my day. Not only do I graduate with highest honors, but I also get a bride, a father and a brother in the bargain. I must have done something right to deserve this bounty!"

Daniel Alexander and Generale Francini stood off from the group, sharing a moment alone as they stared over at their children. Alexander looked over at his old friend, lowering his guard only for this brief moment. "What have you made of my son, Vittorio?"

Francini merely shook his head dolefully. "You must believe me, Daniel. I don't think either one of us had a hand in making him."

The two men stood in silence, watching Stone holding court, hovering over Gabriella, with David standing mutely by. The men exchanged a look that clearly indicated that neither of them was pleased with what they saw. Finally, Daniel spoke up, a sense of defeat apparent in his voice. "I suppose we should join them." Francini nodded in agreement, and both men advanced slowly toward the tent, a funereal air surrounding them.

Daniel Alexander recovered his composure, an art he was well practiced at, and strode over to introduce himself to his future daughter-in-law. Congratulations and introductions made their way all around. And despite Stone's frantic attempts to lighten things up, the tension in the air remained as thick as blood.

# CHAPTER
# TWENTY-TWO

Thou should'st not have been old
Till thou had been wise...

—William Shakespeare, *King Lear*

The peaked, ice-capped mountains, the winding mountain road and the placid lake surrounding Francini Academy had remained the same—but much else had changed in twenty years. The faces, the clothes—all were different. But the voice speaking before a large crowd assembled before the stage hadn't changed—except in tone and resonance.

Stone Alexander, now forty-two years old, stood at a podium before a hundred or more elderly men and women, some squeezed into ancient military attire.

"This noble establishment has served as both father and mother to me, as well as to so many others, for many decades. And that is but one of the reasons why I'm so proud to be introducing the Class of 1946 and congratulating them on the occasion of their fiftieth reunion. This school has always prided itself on birthing many of the world's great leaders—generals on the battlefields, captains of industry—including my own dear father...Daniel Alexander."

Stone extended a hand toward the front row of the assembly, where sat Daniel Alexander, now in his early eighties, and David Alexander, now almost thirty-six. The crowd cheered as Stone pointed to his famous father.

The demeanor of the men seated together had changed drastically. David was now far more confident and had finally learned the necessity of adopting a poker face when he had to. Daniel appeared old and tired far beyond his years. He also seemed deeply troubled.

Stone continued his speech as the cheering subsided.

"We will call upon him later on to dedicate this lovely concert hall in the memory of another father, the father of my dear wife, Gabriella, Generale Vittorio Francini, a man whom many of us came to regard as a true father."

Stone fought to speak over the resounding applause. Many of the old-timers had tears in their eyes, recalling their own fond memories of the general.

"So, please take some time to enjoy the fine wine and music. Later, we will bring up my father to bore you all to tears."

The audience applauded wildly as Stone descended the stage and crossed to his brother and father. David was apprehensive, but disguised it well, smiling at his older brother and warmly extending his hand. Stone shook David's hand enthusiastically.

"Brother. It has been too long." Stone held on to David's hand for a long time.

*David stared at his brother, wondering, from the depth of his heart, why had it been so long since they had last met. The bond between them felt as strong as it did the first time they had shaken hands, when David was but a mealy-mouthed teen.*

*He looked Stone right in the eyes, trying to ascertain if his brother felt the same way. Stone had become a very polished statesman, but David felt the same passion in his handshake that he had felt when they first met, and that buoyed him. He sensed that beneath that slick veneer, Stone too had keenly felt the loss.*

"It's been way too long, brother," David said, in all sincerity. Stone smiled back, but David felt that he was not reaching the real Stone at all—but speaking only to his persona.

"Yes. I'm so glad we could all meet together like this again. Even if it took us twenty years to do it!"

"Well," David said, trying to get some real emotion out of his brother, "let's not wait another twenty years for the next Alexander family reunion." Stone nodded in the affirmative, and David felt he had seen something real, though only a mere glimpse of it, on Stone's face.

Daniel Alexander looked up from his seat at his elder son. He tried his best to be flattering, but the undercurrent of deep resentment between them was obvious to anyone who cared enough to observe. David, who had himself become quite a good student of human dynamics, noticed it immediately.

"Well, I've lived to see both of my sons become better speakers than I ever was."

Stone smiled down at his father. "Nothing...neither of *us*, surely, has ever prevented you from having your voice heard, Father." David turned to his father, seconding Stone.

"Yes, you may not speak a lot, Dad, but I think pretty much everyone in the world always knows what's on your mind! Everyone that counts, that is."

Even this attempt at a compliment failed to get a smile out of the elder Alexander. He appeared in a deeply contemplative mood. He spoke as if to himself. "Through others, perhaps. Yes, maybe I've made my voice heard through others."

David couldn't help but notice his father's strange mood. He misinterpreted it as performance anxiety.

"I hope you're not nervous about speaking tonight. It's just a group of old soldiers. I'm sure they'll be all be adequately lubricated before your speech, so you could go up there and recite 'Jabberwocky,' and they wouldn't even notice."

But Daniel remained preoccupied. "Thank you, David. Will you give me a few moments alone with your brother?"

*David was taken aback. He flashed back to twenty years before, when his father had said the exact same thing to him, and he had felt precisely the same way: dismissed. He wondered why it must always be this way with the three of them.*

David politely honored his father's request and, nodding to both Stone and his father, walked off out of their hearing range.

But now, David was no longer a schoolboy with no social graces and no idea what to do with himself. He headed toward the dance floor that had been erected on the quad for the special occasion. He had only one thing on his mind: finding Gabriella.

In an instant, he spotted her. She stood alone in a corner of the tent, as stunning as ever, absentmindedly holding a cocktail in her hand, her mind obviously somewhere far away. A string quartet warmed up as David slowly approached Gabriella from behind.

# $\Omega^2$

As David moved out of earshot, Alexander's tone became far more serious. He looked up at Stone. "Where can we be alone?" Stone instantly picked up on the urgency in his father's voice. *What is this about?* he wondered.

"Follow me," he rejoined cordially. Stone had the key to the Francini home, now housing the current president of the Francini Academy and his family. Stone lead his father up the narrow, stone steps into Francini's old office. As they reached the door, Stone noticed the older man fighting to catch his breath. Stone said nothing, but turned on the light, entered the musty old office and looked around.

"It looks the same as it did twenty years ago."

Daniel Alexander looked around the room as if in a dream. "It looks the same as it did fifty years ago when I was a cadet here."

Stone smiled. "You see. If you wait long enough in life, everything comes around full circle."

Alexander was a bit tipsy. He shook his head wistfully. "Good old Francini. I miss him. He was like a father to us."

Stone sat down behind Francini's desk, saying pointedly, "Yes, he was like a father to *all* of us."

Alexander didn't miss the slight, but he chose to ignore it. He had bigger fish to fry that night. "How is it you have access to this office, Stone? Isn't the current president...?"

"Gabriella and I have our own wing here. She insisted on leaving her old room and her father's office exactly as they were. So, we come here often on holiday...that is, Gabriella does."

# CHAPTER
# TWENTY-THREE

My bounty is as boundless as the sea,
My love as deep:
The more I give to thee
The more I have.
For both are infinite.

—William Shakespeare, *Romeo and Juliet*

W e have to stop meeting like this." Gabriella turned to see the familiar face of David. She beamed and pulled him in for a big hug.

"You're right. This is the second time in, how long has it been, David?"

"Twenty years," he replied softly. Gabriella nodded, her face saddened. But she kept the conversation light.

"Yes. People will surely begin to talk. How are you, David?"

*David stared into her eyes, surprised to find himself as intoxicated by her as he was that day so many years ago. Twenty years ago.*

"I'm good. So tell me, before I botch things up—how am I supposed to address you? What do you call the wife of the head of the European Union? Are you the First Lady? The Empress? High Priestess?"

Gabriella smiled warmly. "To you, David, I am always Gabriella."

*A tender moment passed between them. If Stone had been there, he would have surely noticed it. But despite this overwhelming feeling between them, they continued to exchange small talk.*

"Don't think I haven't been following your career, David. You haven't exactly been groveling in obscurity on your side of the pond all these years, have you, *Senator* Alexander?"

David laughed. "Not that it matters much, but I'm a congressman. But to you, I'll always be David."

Gabriella smiled, but David couldn't help but notice the deep, pervasive sadness in her eyes. "No, Gabriella, I haven't been groveling in obscurity all these years. But I have been suffering."

Gabriella showed immediate concern. "Suffering? What do you mean? What's going on, David?"

The stringed orchestra finally started up, and David took the opportunity to lead her out onto the makeshift dance floor. A haunting mandolin started playing the first strains of "The Neopolitan Boat Song"—more commonly known as "Santa Lucia." Gabriella sighed in delight upon hearing her favorite tune starting up. *"Sul mare luccica; l'astro d'argento placida e l'onda prospero il vento..."*

"I'll tell you..."

*He held out his hand and she automatically reached out for it. She paused for a moment, surprised at herself. With that touch, they both experienced a strong sensation coursing through their bodies, a sensation that was impossible for either of them to deny.*

"I'll tell you...while we dance."

Gabriella and David glided along the dance floor. He didn't say a word, savoring the moment, as the baritone's voice moved both of them almost out of their bodies with the haunting tune. *"O bella*

*Napoli, o suol beato, ove sorridere volle il Creto...* " Finally, Gabriella spoke up, uncomfortable with the depth of her own feelings.

"So, we are dancing now. Tell me."

David was no longer the timid sixteen-year-old boy who had spilled punch all over himself the first time they met. This David, though still undeniably sweet, was a poised, finessed man.

"All right, I'll tell you. You feel wonderful in my arms."

"Thank you," the startled Gabriella replied, marveling at the change in him. His power over her terrified her to the core of her being. Again, she tried to initiate a more innocent conversation. "You know that's not what I meant. Tell me, why are both Alexander brothers so unhappy?"

David pulled back ever so slightly and looked deep into her eyes. "*Stone* is unhappy?" Gabriella sighed, unable to meet his glance. "It can't be because we're both in love with the same woman. He *has* her."

*David looked at her and smiled warmly, and this time, she found she couldn't avert her eyes from his. She didn't want to. There was an intoxicating undercurrent of sensuality behind his words. She wondered if he meant what he had just said. Or was he just flirting with her? She tried to gauge the truth by looking deep into his eyes. To her surprise, his eyes told her that he had been in earnest.*

"You Alexanders are nothing if not direct," she responded cautiously, hoping to stop this intimacy before it went too far. "But I thought you were asking about Stone."

David sighed. "I was. I am. Tell me about Stone."

Gabriella struggled to find the right words. In the background, the singer struggled to sing out a verse of the song in English. "Hark how the sailors cry; joyously echo nigh; Santa Lucia! Santa Lucia!"

David saw how nervous and preoccupied she was and tried to lighten things up. "Is *that* what that song's about? I never had any idea!"

Gabriella could only laugh, which relieved the tension somewhat. "It is about Santa Lucia. That is all. You don't have to know Italian to know that."

David looked at her more seriously now, lowering his voice. "OK, so what's going on with Stone, Gabriella?"

"I...I don't really know what to say. Stone acts happy enough. You would think he is happy. But it's much more than that. It is like, well, he's...consumed." *Gabriella winced, feeling that on some level, her words were a betrayal. But, after all, this man was her husband's brother. He cared about him. There was nothing wrong in her sharing her concern with him.*

David's mind was elsewhere. He spoke as if only to himself.

"Funny. I would have thought..." David stopped himself from finishing the sentence, but Gabriella prodded him.

"What? What did you think?"

*David found that once again, he couldn't help himself. He had planned on acting like Errol Flynn—light, vivacious and nothing more. But Gabriella made him feel and act like a teenage fool. He found himself saying things he never would, indeed, never had, to another woman.*

"I would've thought that he...or any man...would have been happy just having you as his wife."

Gabriella blushed bright red. Her head fell down upon his chest. David picked up her head gently, touching her cheek. Tears suddenly filled her eyes.

David whisked Gabriella to the end of the dance floor and out into the star-filled night. He could not stop himself from saying what he felt.

"Tell me. Tell me, Gabriella? Why has Stone never come to see me? Why has he never let me see him—get close to him—in all these years? Tell me! Please!"

She looked up at him, eyes brimming over with tears.

"He knew," she whispered. "Stone knows everything. Everything you think; everything you feel. He knew..."

David picked up her meaning right away. "How I felt for you? That very first day? But we had just met!"

"That was enough. He was determined never to let us be alone again—even for a minute—even if it meant cutting you out of his life completely. Which is exactly what he did. You see, David, I am his most valuable possession."

This revelation, or rather, revelations, crushed David.

"I would never have believed it. I mean, I never would have believed my feelings were that transparent. But I was just a *kid*..."

Gabriella was apologetic. "I know, David, but..."

He held her gently around the shoulders and met her eyes. "But Stone was right. I would have done anything to steal you away from him. Anything. Even though I was just a kid, I would've found a way."

She looked up at him and, against her better judgment, softly replied, "And...you might have succeeded."

A look of steely intent came over David's face. She had seen that look before—Stone and Daniel had perfected it to a high art form. David was showing his Alexander blood at last.

"I still might."

David reached out and gently brushed away her tears with his fingertips.

135

# CHAPTER
# TWENTY-FOUR

It is a wise father that knows his own child.

—William Shakespeare, *Merchant of Venice*


It is a wise child that knows its father.

—Homer, *The Odyssey*

Sitting alone with his father in the general's office, Stone himself took in the familiar surroundings with some yearning.

"I haven't been here in a long time."

The elder Alexander sat across from Stone—sitting in the very chair in which Francini had interrogated him about Fausto's death. But Daniel had no way of knowing that. Stone took a perverse pleasure in the reversal.

Daniel, having finally caught his breath, focused in on his son's face. *Yes,* he thought, *he is my son.* He looked at Stone and saw himself as a vigorous, young man in the peak of health. He sighed audibly. Clearly, he was no longer at the peak of health—in fact, he wasn't even on the mountain.

Stone sensed that his father had something to say, and he remained quiet, just sitting there and waiting. Finally, after a prolonged pause, Daniel began.

"They say you begin to reappraise your life as your own mortality becomes more apparent to you. Well, I've been reappraising my life, and I don't like what I've found."

Daniel now stared away from Stone, out the window to the twinkling party lights. The festive music and joyous atmosphere outside provided an odd contrast to the old man's pathetic confession. Stone remained still, uncharacteristically letting someone else hold court.

"With all my success in business, in making myself filthy rich, I've come to see that I failed in accomplishing what should be the most important responsibility in a man's life: raising my two sons."

Stone countered now without much sincerity—frankly, without any sincerity at all. "Nonsense. I rather like what I've become. And I'm very grateful for all that you've done to bring that about."

Daniel knew a load of manure when it had been dumped in his lap. "Don't patronize me, Stone. I blame no one but myself for what you've become. And as for David, he could have had it all—all of Alexander Enterprises. But he let it be known long ago that he had no interest in that. His interest was in 'serving the people.' And somehow, Alexander Enterprises had no part in that. Alexander Enterprises was dirty. Corrupt. Unlike himself. Mr. Liberal. Mr. 'Incorruptible.' Of, by and for the people. Well, hurrah for that! The people can have him! And if I know people—which I dare say I do— they'll tear him to pieces at the first scent of blood, just like wounded wolves before a plump, juicy rabbit."

Alexander paused, tired from this prolonged confession. He looked over at Stone, who was cocking his head as one would upon encountering a sideshow oddity. Stone was just waiting. He knew what was coming next: his father's appraisal of his own career. Finally, Daniel regained the strength to continue.

"And what of my eldest son? Stone Alexander. A great leader, they say. Creator of the New World Order. What's it all about, Stone? What's it *really* all about?"

Stone raised an eyebrow as if ignorant of Daniel's meaning. Daniel was cool and guarded as always, but there was seething anger under that tight control.

"I've watched you, Stone. I've been watching you very carefully, following your every move, since you left the academy. I can't say I know what's behind your pushing all this 'One World' mumbo jumbo, but I can tell you right now that I don't like it. So, whatever the hell you're plotting, whatever you've got going on in that robotic brain of yours, you won't be able to do it using my resources anymore."

Stone actually did a double take.

*Daniel noticed it, and was glad to have finally witnessed it—a sign that, underneath that suave façade, Stone was indeed vulnerable. It looked as if Daniel might have just discovered his son's Achilles heel. This gave him the strength to continue on with some vigor.*

"The TV and cable stations, the wire services, the satellites, the websites—I'm donating all of it to the public. Every bit of it. I'm all but gone, Stone. Every day I spend here on earth is on borrowed time. All I can do now is try and keep you from destroying your own life—as well as the lives of countless others."

Possibly for the first time in his life, Stone was genuinely stunned. *How was it that he had not seen this coming?*

Realizing the importance of what was at stake here, Stone replied ever so quietly, leaning forward in his chair. "Excuse me, Sir, I don't quite understand...?"

Daniel frowned. "You don't get it? OK, let me spell it out for you in blood. I'm dying. I'll be dead in six months. Three, if I'm lucky. Just as you've been 'elected' as head of the 'New World Order,' whatever that means—I've 'elected' to give it all away! That means the networks, the print media, whatever is left of it—not that anybody can even read anymore—but all of it will be put into a public trust. In short, the Alexander family will no longer control any part of Alexander Enterprises. Have I made myself perfectly clear?"

The old man sank back into his chair, feeling as if the weight of the world had just been lifted from his shoulders. Stone replied in a virtual whisper, "Is this what you wanted to tell me?"

"That's right. And I'm going to tell *everyone* when I make my speech tonight."

Daniel watched Stone desperately trying to keep his cool, and it gave him deep satisfaction. His lips turned up into a sardonic smile.

"Don't worry, Stone. I'm not going leave this world and give you boys the satisfaction of saying that your rotten old man cut you off and left you without a penny."

Stone's ears perked up like a dog hearing its master's footsteps approaching.

"Well, actually, I'm not leaving either of you a penny. I've given David the estate in Virginia, right near his beloved White House, and you, since you love your adopted country so much, will be happy to know that you're getting the Roman villa. I trust that this bequest will make both of you very happy."

Daniel may have been a sick, spent, old man, but he was doggedly intent on venting his spleen, finally, to the son who had, to his mind, become a disgrace to the family name, an inveterate power monger. Stone watched in silence as Alexander struggled to his feet so as to more properly wield the axe.

"Everything else—the vast machine that I've built to shape public opinion all over the world—and used so unwisely for over half a century..."

Daniel paused to summon up enough physical stamina to deliver the fatal blow. His breathing was erratic, and it was obvious that every move he made caused him excruciating pain. Still, he drew himself up to his full height, looking every inch the patriarch he had been forty years before.

"To sum up, Stone—neither you nor your brother will have the opportunity to control and manipulate public opinion as I did. As I did without any sense of humanity or conscience. Now that I'm going to meet my Maker—whoever he, or perhaps *she*, to be more politically correct, may be—I've come to recognize the stupid farce that my whole life has been, and I have chosen not to pass on that stupidity to my sons. I trust that you will respect my decision, Stone, and perhaps, someday, might actually come to see the wisdom of what I've done. Wisdom is, perhaps, the only benefit old age has to offer."

Daniel sank back into his chair. Expressing his emotions, for the first time in his life, had thoroughly wasted him. He poured himself a glass of water from the pitcher on the table with a shaky hand and swallowed it down along with a handful of pain pills.

Stone slowly moved over to his father's chair and reached out and touched his shoulder affectionately.

*Again, Stone had a strong sense that he had played out this scene once before. Yes, it was most oddly like the night he had told old Francini that he was taking his daughter away from him.*

Daniel looked up at Stone, mystified. This seemed like the first time in his life that Stone had ever really touched him.

"Perhaps you shouldn't speak tonight, Father," Stone said in a singsong voice. "You're dreadfully tired. You're not yourself, and you've been drinking."

The elder Alexander saw right through this obvious ploy. *Had he actually allowed himself to think, even for a moment, that his son actually cared for him? What nonsense!* He shook Stone's hand off his shoulder and looked up with eyes of steel at this son who was never a son.

"I've never been more myself. I've been planning this for months, Stone, and tomorrow, it becomes reality. At least I'll be alive long enough to drink a toast as I watch my empire crumble. Which is more than most men in my position could say. My only regret is that I didn't have the horse sense to do it decades ago."

*Daniel saw Stone's mental machinery at work. He saw his son desperately trying to figure out how to turn this situation to his own advantage. This pleased him, and he turned the screws even tighter, a faint smile coming over his face.*

"I just thought that you should be the first to know."

Stone stood up and began to pace. *He was well aware that his thoughts, his weaknesses, were transparent to Daniel, and he needed time to plot his next move.* He paced slowly around the room, finally speaking.

"This, this revelation...your illness, is very saddening. Very saddening, Father, I must say; I thought you'd never die."

Daniel just sat back in his chair, enjoying Stone's discomfiture, not allowing himself to be fooled for a moment that there was any true feeling in anything he said. He rolled his eyes at Stone's professions of dismay.

"We all die," Daniel said firmly. "That's life."

Stone continued his pleas with vigor. "I can see you are in terrible pain, Father. I really must insist that you go back to your hotel and rest. Tomorrow, we can talk."

Daniel became angry now, his face reddening. "Listen, Stone. I've said my piece. There will be no tomorrows. I will be heard— tonight. And there is nothing that you can do about it!"

Silence filled the chamber. Stone continued to pace, stopping before his favorite Bosch print, still hanging exactly where it was on the day when his father first brought him to the academy.

*How well he remembered that day. Catching his first glimpse of Gabriella through the window. The limo door closing with a thud as Daniel abandoned him there in the mountains—a thud as final as the sound of the closing of his mother's casket. The shrieking of the boys, "Amazzate i bambini...Amazzate i bambini..." His rushing out into the frigid night, hot tears of hatred and rage melding together with the cold, steady, stream of rain. His being beckoned by an inner voice, and finding refuge in the church. It all came back to him now in a rush of unwelcome emotion.*

Stone slowly approached his father's chair once again. Daniel looked up at him. There was no longer any pretense of charm. No boyish smile to try and divert Daniel's attention from his true motives. There was nothing but naked malice in his eyes. Daniel's eyes lit up.

"That's better, son. I feel like I'm seeing the real you for the first time!"

"I will have what is rightfully mine!" Stone raved, all theatrics gone. "I'm not like you, Father. I have a vision. Your 'media empire,' as you choose to call it, isn't just some roadside tomato stand! It's a tool—an invaluable tool that in the right hands, *my* hands, can help bring my vision into reality. One world—*my* world."

Daniel Alexander seemed to crumple at these words. He had been having a good time with Stone, playing with him. But this had gone too far. He sighed audibly, all pretense gone from his voice and his visage. He looked the sickly, pathetic old man he truly was.

"You're even crazier than I thought, Stone. I should've believed Francini all those years ago when he said that neither one of us had a hand in making you. I hope he was right, or I'm going to have to pay the piper when I get to the other side!"

Stone just leered at his father, further infuriated by this alleged quote from Francini. But Alexander just sank down further into his armchair. He was too tired. Too sad. Too sick—sick in body. Sick in heart. Sick at the sight of this ambitious, immoral brute he had fathered. Virtually whispering now, Alexander looked over again at Stone.

"Tell me, Stone. Who's your role model? Mussolini? Hitler? No— I've got it. Of course. Why didn't I see it before? It's Alexander the Great!"

Alexander shook his head and chuckled. Stone was livid. If it hadn't been for all the noise outside, the echoes of his fury would have resounded throughout the entire mountainside. A frigid wind suddenly blew open the shutters with a crash. Even the air itself seemed to solidify, to congeal. Stone's features became terrifying, horrific, as he screamed at the old man.

"Who are you to judge me? You, who swept the world away from a six-year-old boy! You, who took his mother away, and then deserted him—left him here an orphan. Just like Quasimodo's mother—ridding herself of her monstrous offspring on the steps of Notre Dame, praying to be freed—not of her responsibility, but of her guilt and torment! Well, now, that boy, *your* Quasimodo, is going to reshape the entire world in his own image! I know what the future holds, Father, because *I* am the future!"

Alexander smiled up at Stone contemptuously. "Alexander the Great wasn't good enough, eh Stone? So now you want to be God, too?"

# CHAPTER
# TWENTY-FIVE

This is the monstrosity in love, lady;
That the will is infinite,
and the execution confined:
That the desire is boundless,
and the act a slave to limit.

—William Shakespeare, *Troilus and Cressida*


Perdition catch my soul
But I do love thee!
And when I love thee not
Chaos is come again.

—William Shakespeare, *Othello*

Outside, the party was in full swing. The old-timers worked up a sweat dancing the rigorous *Tarantella,* the swinging Italian lanterns casting shadows in crimson and green over the revelers.

Only two people on the quad were not participating in the dance.

David and Gabriella stood off to one side, the dense foliage hiding them from prying eyes. Common sense told Gabriella to leave, to run away, but her emotions silenced those voices.

Staring into her eyes, David had never seemed so serious, so intent on his purpose. "If you are unhappy, Gabriella, there's nothing keeping you with Stone. You have no children..."

Gabriella's head sank lower. Her voice trembled as she replied, "That was Stone's decision. Not mine."

"*His* decision? What, did he have you sterilized? If he really loved you, would he deny you the chance to have children?"

Tears welled up in Gabriella's eyes, while David's burned with love. Stone's eyes had burned into her many times, but never this way. With intensity, with desire, yes. But never with love.

"He doesn't love you. You've as much as admitted it! You're his favorite *possession*! How does that feel, Gabriella? How can you live like that, knowing that you're no longer a living, breathing woman, but an object?"

Gabriella wept sadly. "I don't know. I don't know. I stopped feeling long ago. All I know is...it's...my life."

David rubbed his fingertips across her wet cheeks, both of them aching with love for the other. He wanted this woman for his own, more than he had ever wanted anything in his life. Yes, even more than his precious official titles. He tried to instill her with the confidence she needed to make that giant leap—into his heart, into his life.

"You can't tell me you don't feel *now*. I know what you're feeling. The same thing I'm feeling. You can just walk out on him, Gabriella! There's nothing to stop you. Stone's 'brave new concepts' don't even acknowledge marriage as a legally binding contract! Take him at his word. Leave him...and come with me."

*Gabriella saw her life over the past twenty years in her mind's eye—the deadliness of it: Stone's coldness, his utter indifference to her and yet, his possessiveness. She wept on David's shoulder, whispering into his ears, "David...David..."*

David was sorely tempted, but he held himself back. The truth was, he felt that the fulfillment of a desire so heartfelt, so exquisite, so long yearned for, could have, under the circumstances, just as easily destroyed both of them as it might have brought them together forever. He could not, would not take that chance.

*He would never take her while she was still his brother's wife. Nor would he take advantage of her vulnerability. This would have to be her conscious decision. She would have to make the commitment to come away with him, to leave Stone for good. Then, they could give themselves to each other without guilt and with full commitment.*

"Gabriella," he whispered. "Please come back with me to Washington. Please leave Stone. Come with me..."

"No," she said weakly. "I cannot. It is fated. It is fated." He squeezed her hands in his own with all his power, his tears dropping down on her now upturned face. He spoke as if he were praying, praying for his only chance at earthly happiness.

"Fated? I don't believe in fate. We each make our own fate. If any two people were ever fated to be together, it's you and me, Gabriella."

Her mind was filled with doubts and self-recrimination.

"Gabriella, I want you to be the mother of my children. Gabriella...there is still time! We are still young..."

Gabriella buried her head against his sweat-drenched chest. *She imagined the world David could make for her. Children! Their children together.* She saw the bright promise in his tear-clouded blue eyes.

"You could have a wonderful new life, David..." Gabriella sobbed. "I would be happy...just to have...life."

Gabriella's comment filled David with despair, but also with resolve. "I've never loved a woman as I've loved you, Gabriella, all these years. You have to believe that. It has only been you."

Gabriella looked up at him, incredulous at this revelation.

"But all these years, David...all these years we've been apart? How can I believe that you've never loved another woman?"

David looked her right in the eyes. She could see that he was in earnest. "I'm no angel. I've made love to women. But I never found what I wanted, the qualities I wanted, in any of them. I tried, but I couldn't love...I never wanted any of them to be the mother of my children. And it wasn't for want of trying. Believe me, Gabriella, there is nothing I've tried harder to do than to erase you from my mind. There's nothing I wanted more than to forget I ever met you!"

Gabriella caved completely. She believed him. Trusted the truth of everything he had said. *This was a man who would belong to her alone—not the world. A man who already belonged to her. She loved him with every fiber of her being. And for that moment, however long it lasted, time ceased to exist. There was no one else in the world but the two of them.*

147

# CHAPTER
# TWENTY-SIX

When I was a child, I spake as a child,
I understood as a child:
but when I became a man,
I put away childish things.

—1 Corinthians 13:11

tone hissed like a serpent in his father's face. It seemed to the elderly man that Stone's voice had changed, deepened, seeming to echo throughout the chamber. Even his face appeared monstrous and distorted. Daniel felt as if he had been thrown into one of Edgar Allan Poe's eeriest tales—where any manner of *grotesquerie* was commonplace. Maybe the combination of all the pain pills—he had taken far more than usual tonight—along with the potent Italian wine had put him into this hallucinogenic state.

He blinked, trying unsuccessfully to focus on Stone's face. But blinking didn't help.

*Stone's face still seemed like nothing more than a mottled blur. His voice seemed as if it were coming from somewhere far outside of him.*

"You never really understood the power you had, Father. Using your networks to settle petty issues. To extort silly political favors. You can believe I won't be so foolish."

*Daniel Alexander felt hypnotized by the swirling images before him as they pulled him to his feet. Yet he still retained enough of his faculties to hear exactly what Stone was saying. To his mind, as rattled as it was, these seemed like the ravings of a madman.*

*Alexander's body felt as if it simply didn't exist anymore. The thought crossed his mind, suddenly, that perhaps he had actually crossed over. Was he in hell? Still, he heard his own voice, even though he knew, or thought he knew, that he hadn't opened his mouth.*

"Too bad I won't be around to see it. Alexanderland, that is."

"Yes," Stone lied, in a guttural cry. "It is too bad."

*As he spoke, Stone's very shadow seemed to drop off the wall, melting into his body. Time itself seemed to slow down. Daniel could only watch in mute fascination as Stone extended his hands. Within seconds, a furious sphere of black energy formed between Stone's hands. Stone spread his hands, and the energy of the Netherworld flew at his father with supernatural speed and power, blasting the old man back— and out the office window through the shattering glass.*

# CHAPTER TWENTY-SEVEN

Then everything includes itself in power,
Power into will; will into appetite,
And appetite, a universal wolf,
So doubly seconded with will and power,
Must make perforce an universal prey,
And last eat up himself.

—William Shakespeare, *Troilus and Cressida*


Nature mourned, for its parent had died.

—Edgar Allan Poe

Outside, the elderly cadets frequented the dessert table, taking a well-deserved rest after the challenging *Tarantella*. An intrepid few still remained on the dance floor, trying to remember the steps to the dances popular in their academy days.

Standing beneath the trees not far from the tents were Gabriella and David, trembling like Tristan and Isolde, hearts still beating as one. From the look of devotion on her face, David was sure that within moments, Gabriella would declare herself free from her bond with Stone and accept him wholeheartedly as her husband.

Suddenly, a loud crash, followed by a sonorous thud, was heard. Everyone beneath the tent was suddenly screaming—holding their hands up to their faces in horror.

David and Gabriella rushed toward the sound, following the mortified partygoers clustered *en masse* around the end of the tent, peering toward the old Francini house.

"What is it, David?" Gabriella murmured apprehensively. David led her through the crowd, clutching her hand tightly.

"Excuse me! Excuse me, please!" David cried, finally reaching the edge of the tent, where a group of elderly alumni and their wives stood weeping openly. David and Gabriella didn't have to waste much time figuring out why everyone was so upset.

There, on the patio, was Daniel Alexander—crumpled into a broken, lifeless heap. Gabriella closed her eyes at the grim spectacle. "Santa Lucia, pray for him," she whispered softly. David blanched. After a long moment, he turned to several of the old-timers, his voice strangely calm.

"What happened? Did anybody see it happen?"

One of the elderly men, still recovering from the wild dancing, rubbed the sweat from his face. "I saw it. I was just coming off the dance floor, and suddenly there was this loud noise—like glass breaking, which I guess it was, and then suddenly—it was like he was flying out the top story window. I never saw anything like it in my life. 'Cept, of course, in the movies."

His wife chimed in, "The poor thing. First he landed face down on that..." She pointed over to the stone staircase. "Then, his body sort of just toppled over. He was already dead by then, from hitting all that stone, so at least he was out of his suffering. The poor thing. I wonder who it was?" The old woman turned to David. "Do you have any idea who he is, or well, was?"

David's face was pallid. Gabriella clutched his arm to give him moral support. She understood; she too had lost her father.

David just stared uncomprehendingly at his father's body. "Yes," he replied in monotone, pulling out of Gabriella's grasp and rushing over to his father.

153

David was the first to reach the body. Daniel Alexander lay in a spreading pool of blood. The others stood far back, partly to keep a respectful distance, but also, because they were too sickened by the sight to want to get any closer. Only seconds after David had arrived at the scene, Stone darted out of the building, out of breath from running, instantly kneeling down next to his father and reaching for one of his lifeless hands, clutching it to his heart. David too got down on his knees. Both brothers just stared at the pathetic, broken body that used to house the soul of Daniel Alexander.

David turned to his brother, his voice cracking. "Do you have any idea what happened?"

Stone seemed beside himself with anguish. Tears streamed down his face. Gabriella remained among the crowd, the spectators now finally realizing the identity of the doomed man. They gossiped about the Alexander family until Gabriella could stand it no longer. She turned proudly to face the crowd.

"*Cose state guardando?* A man is dead! It would be better to hold your tongues and show some respect!"

She lifted her head high and broke free from the crowd, moving toward her husband and David. *Which one should she go to first? Whom should she comfort? Where did her loyalties lie?* Despite everything that had just transpired between David and her, Gabriella found herself silently walking toward Stone.

Stone turned from Daniel and looked over at David, his eyes bloodshot. "Yes. Yes, I know what happened. He...he was drunk, David, he wouldn't stop drinking. He was in a lot of pain. He...he told me he was dying, David!" He looked into his brother's eyes. "Did you know?"

David was stunned. "No, I didn't know. He didn't tell me."

Stone continued, his voice cracking. "Yes. It was the first I heard of it, too. I suppose he was trying to be brave. He told me he had terrible cancer; he was in excruciating pain—and that he wanted to kill himself, put an end to it now. That's why he invited us both here tonight. To say good-bye."

Stone began sobbing uncontrollably. He struggled to complete his piece. "At the very place we both grew up."

David slowly shook his head, feeling as if he were the subject of an old newsreel. *This couldn't really be happening, could it?* Stone's sobbing soon turned into full-blown hysteria. His eyes were wild with grief as he began to rant. "I tried to talk to him, David! To get him to come stay with me. Spend his last days in peace. But no. He was determined, David! Out of his mind. He ran for the window..." Stone threw himself into his brother's arms, crying like an infant for its

154

mother in the dark, lonely night. "I tried to stop him, David. I tried to stop him..."

Stone had broken down completely. The crowd looked on at this tragic performance, which rivaled anything Shakespeare ever penned in its authenticity and dramatic appeal.

Gabriella, reaching the scene of the accident, could only stare at the body—lying there on the patio where she had once gaily scampered as a girl. *That blood can never be washed away,* she thought, wondering if she could ever come back there again.

The sound of Stone's wailing brought her out of her trance. She knelt down beside the brothers, still huddled together as one—*just as she and David had been only moments before. The irony of this pierced her heart.* She reached out to touch her husband tenderly.

"Stone. Stone, I am here. I am here, Stone." But Stone was oblivious to her presence. His head was buried in David's chest.

"David, I tried to stop him...forgive me. Forgive me!"

*While Stone clung desperately to his brother, and Gabriella to Stone, David and Gabriella exchanged a look—a look that said a thousand words. One more minute, perhaps, and they would have been joined together forever. But now...now, things were different. Now it was Stone who commanded both of their attention. The moment was surreal; the three of them huddled together, hands and bodies intertwined. To Gabriella, it felt as if the three of them were somehow melded together in their grief into one united soul.*

David fought to regain control of his faculties. Finally, he found the strength to yank Stone off of him. He spoke to him in a calm, though shaky, voice. "Stone, you have to pull yourself together. We have to do something here. Fast."

His chest still heaving with emotion, Stone looked up at his baby brother. "What—what should we do, David?"

"Listen to me, Stone. We can't let on that he killed himself. It would destroy his empire. The stockholders would pick it to pieces. He would have hated that. If there's no will, and knowing the old..." His eyes darted over to his father's body. "He didn't make a will. I'd put money on it. We have to agree, Stone, right here and now, that it was an accident. If we don't, we could lose everything he spent his whole life building. It just wouldn't be right."

Gabriella, running her hand mechanically through Stone's hair, stared at David in amazement. *How could he find such tremendous inner strength? How could he think at all at such a time?*

Stone looked at David, trying to process what he said. David took a brief moment to survey the havoc surrounding them. *The crowd of onlookers. The bright, red blood gushing out of his father's head.*

155

*The sight of Gabriella running her hands through his brother's hair. Her husband's hair. Had he been wrong? Did she really love Stone? He was overwhelmed with grief and confusion.*

But, as a politician, he'd become adept at dealing with crises as they came up—and going to pieces later. He turned to face the crowd, calling out in a strong, firm tone, "Call for an ambulance!"

Gabriella echoed him in Italian. *"Chiamate un'anbulanza! Sbrigatevi!"*

David put a reassuring arm around his trembling brother and helped him to his feet. Gabriella helped to steady him.

"This is the only way, Stone. Trust me."

As his brother and his wife supported him, one on each side, Stone's eyes turned back once more to his father's body. He heaved a loud and wistful sigh. Still, Stone slowly seemed to be calming down under their soothing influence. He spoke quietly now, his eyes still fixed on the body.

"I...I...suppose you're right, David. So be it. I wish that I was as strong as you are." Stone made the sign of the cross. *"Requiescat in pace,* my father."

Gabriella stared at Stone in utter shock. From the look on her face, it was quite clear that, in all their years together, she had never *once* seen him cross himself. *David noticed her expression, and the thought crossed his mind, though only for a brief moment, that perhaps he was being duped. That perhaps both of them were being duped. He instantly dismissed the thought from his mind, ashamed of himself.*

David turned Stone to face the crowd, still helping to keep him on his feet. "Let's do this together, bro..."

Gabriella released her hold on Stone, as arm in arm, the Alexander brothers approached the crowd. David sucked in a deep breath before speaking.

"I'm afraid...there has been...a terrible accident. My...our father...is dead."

The crowd moaned in collective sorrow at the sight of the two grief-stricken brothers. Gabriella advanced toward them, still standing off to the side. David continued, "I'm terribly sorry that the evening had to end this way..." He passed a sideways glance at Gabriella, speaking ever so softly, "For everyone concerned."

Gabriella moved over to Stone and David as the crowd quietly dispersed. Stone appeared virtually catatonic, but at least, he was quiet now. She looked over at David and whispered softly, "David—I'm so sorry...about *everything."* She reached over to take his hand in hers and squeezed it gently. David looked down and saw that both of their hands were covered in blood. His father's blood. Suddenly, his body convulsed as he was thrust into a hideous vision.

*He saw himself on a battlefield—a scene of great devastation. Tanks and men were twisted together into a tableau of horror. He felt himself drawn to one body lying amidst the masses, a crow picking at its face. He watched the bird fly away. Staggered by the recognition, David realized he was looking at himself—or was it Stone?—lying there dead with one eye socket empty. He felt himself falling frantically into a black hole and clawing to get out...trying to get a foothold...He heard himself crying out for his brother, "Help me, help me!" But Stone refused to extend his hand.*

"David! David!" A familiar, caring voice pierced time and space, bringing David back up through the black hole and into the even more horrific present. David opened his eyes, taking in the scene around him, and felt the bile rising up in his throat. Unable to even look at Gabriella, David dropped Stone's arm, running out of the courtyard, getting as far away from the academy as he could—running out into the mountains beyond.

Gabriella, struggling to support Stone's weakened body by herself, called after him. "David!?" But he was gone. Gabriella sighed, shaking her head at this sad, tragic turn of events. She turned to look at her husband and was stunned by what she saw. There appeared to be a look of smug satisfaction on his face as he watched his brother disappear into the night. Seemingly oblivious to her presence, Stone muttered to himself, "Run, poor little orphan."

A broad smile started to come over his face—when suddenly, he remembered Gabriella. He looked over to see that she'd been watching him, very carefully, the whole time. The look on her face was absolutely incredulous. Stone immediately did a quick-change act, tears welling up in his eyes as he looked plaintively over at Gabriella. But he knew. He knew she had seen the look in his eyes. Stone berated himself. How could he have been so careless?

*Gabriella too started wondering. Wondering if she—if she and David had both been duped? What was that look on his face? What did that mean, "Run, little orphan"? Had Stone actually been taking pleasure in David's pain? Who was this stranger she was married to? Why was she still here and not running after David? Did she truly love Stone—could she ever love Stone again, after what she had just witnessed with her own eyes? Did she love David, and if so, why was she still here? Could it be that she really loved both brothers—despite Stone's many flaws?*

Gabriella looked over at Stone, now contrite. Trying his best to repair the damage, he reached over and grasped her hands in his own.

"You must be strong. Strong for me, Gabriella. I need you now, more than ever."

*He knew, Gabriella thought. He knew that she and David had been together. It was just as she thought. Stone knew everything. That was why he was so happy to see his brother run away like that—and call him a poor little orphan. That's why he was clutching at her now so desperately, trying to win her back again, make her feel needed. Stone had triumphed over them once again. He had once again succeeded in keeping them apart. Who knew for how long this time?*

Stone's head sank to his chest, and he whimpered like a child. Then, just as David had done, Stone looked down at his hands intertwined in Gabriella's. They were covered in blood. Bright, red blood.

The sight of his father's blood on his hands shook Stone profoundly. His eyes widened in fear as he tried to stifle a scream. Stone suddenly pulled away from Gabriella, fleeing across the courtyard and up the narrow stairs into Francini's office, slamming the door behind him. *Gabriella just stared after him, her mind whirling with conflict over everything that had happened that night. What she had felt. What she had seen. What she had heard, with her own ears, coming from her husband's mouth.*

In the distance, she heard the roaring of the ambulance and police cars navigating the twisting mountain road. The brightness of the flashing red lights caused her to wince. In a flash, she realized that both brothers had abandoned her. It was now up to her to deal with bidding her father-in-law farewell, forever, from the Francini Academy. It was for her to remain strong, for both of them, and give the official statement to the police. She steadied herself for that challenge. She put on a brave front, as she had watched the Alexander men do so often over so many years, and as she had witnessed her own father do so many times over the years—as the sirens resounded in her ears. She seemed completely under control, even haughty, as the *carabinieri* approached her. But inwardly, she was a mass of confusion. *What a night! Literally, it had gone from the sublime to the incomprehensible. What had it all truly been about? Right now, there was only one thing she was sure about: From now on, she was going to watch Stone like a hawk.*

The seeds of deep distrust had been planted.

# CHAPTER TWENTY-EIGHT

Go to, a bargain make:
Seal it; I'll be the witness.

—William Shakespeare, *Hamlet*

The air was frigid, but even the coldest of Mediterranean nights could hardly be considered bitter. It was about three o'clock in the morning when Stone quietly left Francini's office. He was in a highly agitated state, much like his first night at the academy. His breath was coming so fast that his chest felt as if it were bursting. He knew he must get out into the open and get some air.

*It wasn't grief, anxiety or even guilt that was causing this intensity of feeling. Something was calling to him. Someone was compelling him. Willing him to come to them. When the voices called, he would always respond. Always.*

*Stone walked across the courtyard in a light trance, looking out into the mist-covered countryside and the mountains beyond. He was breathing more easily now; he felt freer now, out in the brisk air. But still, the voices were beckoning, and he followed their command.*

*Suddenly, he felt something smack him hard across the back. He grimaced in pain. He swiftly wheeled around to confront his assailant. Was it David? No. It was only a heavy, wooden plank. He realized that this had been a sign. He was meant to stop here.*

*Stone planted his feet into the soft ground and waited. Waited for the next sign. Behind him was the ancient academy chapel, long since boarded up and on the list to be demolished and replaced by a new building.*

*Although the chapel had been closed to the student body for over twenty years, its cross was still firmly in place on the old roof—its shadow falling exactly where Stone was standing. Yes. This was the message he had been waiting for.*

*Stone walked deliberately toward the building. Heavy wooden planks, like the one that had just "assailed" him, had been hammered up across the entrance to the chapel. But this did not deter Stone from his mission. With superhuman strength, he tore down the boards with his bare hands, oblivious to the fact that he was virtually tearing up his hands in the process.*

*Stone was transfixed now and feeling no pain. He slowly opened the creaky door, moving into the remains of the chapel. He failed to choke on, or even notice, the revolting, unearthly stench pervading the place, or even the dense smoke filling the air.*

*Stone trod through the smoky chamber, his eyes fixed on the dim light flickering before the altar. He heard words being spoken in a language that seemed to resemble Latin—though he could not make out any of the words or see who was speaking them.*

*As he finally reached the altar, Stone faintly made out the image of a man. He had his back turned to Stone and was murmuring prayers and invocations that were indecipherable to him, even though he was* fluent in six languages. But strangely, he felt no fear. In fact, he was beginning to feel far more at ease, even lighter, than he had felt in years.

His eyes narrowed to focus in on the man standing at the altar. The density of the incense, the dimness of the light and the dust filling the air made it difficult to make out just who it was. Would it be someone he knew?

Slowly, he discerned that the man was attired in the black cassock of a monk, a hood shrouding his head. Stone saw before him on the altar an ancient book, a gold athame, a silver goblet and an old wooden crucifix. Stone thought he recognized it as the Francini family crucifix—the one that had blessed the general's office, his father's office and his father's father's office before him. Now, that crucifix had been defiled by Stone's transgression before it. How had it gotten there?

Stone fell to his knees as if hypnotized, crawling the last few feet to the altar on his knees. He put his head to the cold, wood-planked floor, covered by decades of debris. The fresh blood from his wounded hands fell in puddles around him. Finally, the man turned around and looked at Stone through penetrating eyes. Stone felt those eyes upon him, and he knew he must look up at them. Upon looking at the man, Stone felt some sense of recognition, but he couldn't place the face. He knew that there was a deep bond between them, but he neither knew who the man was nor why he felt so close to him.

Most people under the same circumstances probably would have asked, "Who are you?" But not Stone Alexander. To him, it was far less important to find who the man was than to discover what he wanted of him—and what he could offer in return. Stone simply said, "Why have you summoned me?"

The man smiled, replying softly, his words caressing Stone like a gentle ocean breeze. "Don't you recognize me, Master? Don't you know who I am?"

Stone stared up again into the man's eyes—as deep and blue and penetrating as his own. Something finally clicked. He flashed back to another night, long ago, when this same man had appeared before him, the night when, as a miserable and lonely six-year-old, he had sought refuge in the old chapel. He instantly calmed, feeling a sense of familiarity and peace flooding his body. It almost felt like returning to the womb.

"Yes," Stone responded, "I think I do."

The cassocked man descended the altar steps, as if floating on air. Now, Stone was sure. This was his Guardian.

162

"I have always been with you, Stone, whether you've been aware of my presence or not. I've been watching over you these years, since your earthly parents abandoned you."

Stone began to understand. The mixed-up jigsaw puzzle of his life began to come together.

"Yes."

"It is I, in the name of our lord, who have nurtured you, protected you and insured your rise to power on this earthly plane."

Stone continued to stare at the "man" before him, now floating several feet above the grimy floor. Finally, Stone asked, "What is your name?"

The unearthly creature smiled at Stone enigmatically. "My name is unimportant. I am but the minion of the Ancient One."

"Why have you summoned me?" Stone reiterated.

The Guardian surrounded Stone now, his cassock encircling him, the wind filling it up like a sail. But there was no wind.

"Because the time was right, Stone. I have been biding my time these many years, until you were ready."

Stone cocked his head. "Ready? Why am I ready now? And for what?"

The Guardian loomed before him now larger than life, taking on the appearance of an archangel, bathed in gold and white light.

"Because you have spilled the blood of your earthly father and proven yourself ready to assume your rightful place..."

Stone looked confused.

"...beside your true father. Do you understand me, Stone?"

Stone did not understand. He became suddenly disoriented. Distorted voices, vivid images, echoed throughout his consciousness—images of plague, war, death and destruction that seemed to span all of eternity. The Guardian picked up immediately on Stone's vision—and the trepidation it was causing.

"Don't be afraid, my son. You have done no wrong. By the murder of your earthly father, you have allied yourself with your true father, the Dark One, who seeks to regain the kingdom of heaven from the Most High, who unjustly cast him from glory into eternal darkness, and to sit rightfully on the throne of eternity. By joining the army of Lucifer, you will become his Thane, his earthly embodiment, and will bring about the destruction of the empire of Jesus Christ, the resurrection of our Dark Lord, Lucifer, and his final and complete conquest of the throne of heaven. Is this what you desire?"

The words came out of Stone's mouth automatically, without his even thinking them. He heard himself saying, "Yes. I do desire it."

"Do you then renounce Jesus Christ? Do you believe in our Dark Lord, he who was cast from the heavens to make way for the usurper?"

Stone replied in monotone, "I do believe."

The Guardian had floated back to the altar, gesturing over the old crucifix. Now, he took the cross and placed it face down before Stone on the plank floor of the chapel. Stone well remembered that crucifix, always hanging over the pious old general's desk. But that memory now felt like nothing more than a dream from another lifetime.

"With this act, we forever cast out Jesus Christ, defiler of the Dark Lord."

Stone needed no further instruction. He automatically rose to his feet, crushing the wooden crucifix to shreds with the heel of his shoe. The Guardian beamed. He stood over the desecrated crucifix and spat upon it. His spit was like venom, bubbling up on the cross as if it were boiling. Stone followed his lead. He too spat down on the splintered remains of the cross. To his surprise, his sputum was pitch black.

"Because of the fealty you have shown him, our great lord offers you a pact. Your commitment to him—in exchange for earthly sovereignty and the promise of a throne at the right hand of our father in the End Days to come."

The Guardian looked Stone in the eyes once more, to see if he was waffling. He was not. Pleased, the Guardian continued.

"Do you then hereby consecrate yourself to the Dark One, and by the spilled blood of your earthly father, acknowledge Lucifer as your father almighty?

Stone's face was transformed. "I do. The devil is now rooted in my heart."

The Guardian now removed a Eucharist from a gilt vial on the black satin-covered altar. He floated before Stone, proffering the "sacrament" to him.

"This host is the body of our Lord Lucifer. Take it, and become one with him."

Stone extended his tongue, and the Guardian placed the host upon it. The Eucharist immediately turned black as coal. Stone closed his mouth and chewed on the host, swallowing it instantly.

The Guardian now raised Stone to his feet, leading him toward the altar. As they ascended the steps, the blood from Stone's hands continued to fall on to the chapel floor, now morphing into a rippling, crimson mass. The Guardian reached for the silver chalice, lowering it to the floor and easily filling it with Stone's blood. He placed the chalice in the center of the altar. Then, the Guardian placed a black cassock and hood, just like his own, over Stone's head. He looked over to Stone as if to say, "This is the final challenge." He slowly proffered the chalice.

"Repeat my words. 'I drink this blood and, in so doing, grant Lucifer absolute power and dominion over me.'"

The Guardian's lips turned up into a smile as Stone repeated the words with firm intent. His voice was vibrant with emotion. "I drink this blood and, in so doing, grant Lucifer absolute power and dominion over me."

"Now, repeat these words. 'May this cup be full with the blood of my enemies...spilled in my true father's name.'"

Stone did not falter. He repeated the words with finality. The Guardian nodded in acquiescence. "Now, drink."

Stone picked up the chalice and brought it to his lips. He paused only for a brief moment before fully imbibing its contents. He looked over at the Guardian. The pact had been sealed in blood.

Within moments, Stone's body erupted in a series of cataclysmic convulsions. The Guardian once again enveloped Stone in his flowing robes, as if to protect him. A dark cloud hovered over Stone's body, finally melding into it. The convulsions subsided immediately thereafter, as they were meant to, and the Guardian smiled. His mission had been accomplished.

"You have done the right thing, my son. You have fulfilled your destiny."

Stone, having recovered from the enormous shock his body had just undergone, separated from the Guardian, trying to get his bearings. He looked over at the altar and saw the desecrated crucifix—Francini's crucifix—lying crushed into the befouled floor. In a flash, everything became crystallized in his mind. He suddenly understood his reason for being on the earth. The recognition filled him with an indescribable sense of strength and power. Stone looked over at the Guardian now with a newfound luster in his eyes. His voice was triumphant.

"I must thank my father for his blessings. I am become the Thane!"

The Guardian raised his hands to his charge proudly, the dark mass concluded. From out of nowhere, a deep voice resounded in the dark, smoky chamber. It belonged to no man.

"My name is Legion, for we are many."

As these words were spoken, Stone watched as the pieces of the crucifix burst into flames and disintegrated into ashes before his eyes.

# CHAPTER TWENTY-NINE

That misbegotten devil...
In spite of spite, alone upholds the day.

—William Shakespeare, *Henry V*

The banner-strewn hall was packed to the rafters with dignitaries representing every country in the world. A very tense media gathered before their respective computers and satellite uplinks. Sound engineers jockeyed for the best position to pick up the latest breaking news and send it off to every corner of the globe.

Chuck Farrell, a square-jawed man in his sixties whose face had obviously been stretched once too often by the plastic surgeon's knife, was one of the United States' top television anchormen. People regarded anything he said in that sonorous, well-trained voice as gospel all across the country.

While his diligent makeup men finished up with some last dabs of powder, Farrell's face was being framed and monitored by a team of technicians in the rear of the room—working to combine his face electronically on the television screen with a map of the world's continents, divided into ten zones. Graphics differentiated between the "committed zones" and the "uncommitted zones"—China, the United States and South America. Chuck received the cue in his earphone and began his preliminary announcement.

"During Stone Alexander's reign, he has, quite literally, changed the face of the world. Using his great wealth, he has all but ended the problems of world hunger and drought, brought about peace to the Middle East and laid the ground work for his utopian ideal, a new world government united under one flag…"

# CHAPTER THIRTY

Behold, I come quickly.

—Revelation 3:11

What shall I do?
And do my tears lament myself,
Or this poor city,
Held in gloom?

—Euripides, *The Phoenician Women*

A sleek limousine carried David Alexander through the final checkpoint at the White House. David had been watching the ceremony on a flat plasma screen monitor. He turned off the monitor as the limo pulled up under the White House portico. He jumped out of the car, escorted by two Secret Service men.

David entered the White House, formally greeted by a familiar staff of assistants, caretakers and bodyguards as he made his way toward the president's situation room. He stopped and knocked on the door. A Secret Service man answered. President Benson, seeing David, called him over.

"C'mon—he's just starting."

David walked in, nodding apprehensively at the president.

Richard Benson, in his late sixties, was a tall, hard-nosed Midwesterner. The room was filled with the presidential chiefs of staff as well as a score of Secret Service men. But there was a seat waiting for David—right next to the president.

David leaned over and whispered to him, "Got a call from Breckenridge."

Benson whispered back, "About us pulling our delegates from this circus?"

David nodded. "Yeah. Said he's afraid of sending the wrong message to the World Union."

"We're sending that nut job—excuse me, David—exactly the message I *want* to send! That we ain't coming to your little clambake, ain't that right, boys?" The Secret Service men snickered in unison.

"Sure is right. What kind of loony tune does this bozo think he's dealing with, anyway? Wait..." He turned to David. David grimaced, almost ashamed of his relation to the man they were all referring to. No, he was ashamed of his relation to this man. The eyes of both David and Benson were glued to the screen, listening to Chuck Farrell's commentary.

"Stone Alexander's rise to chairman of the European Union has been meteoric. National borders have been erased as the world has been divided into ten democratic zones, with each zone's secretary-general having one vote in the World Union Parliament. But with Alexander now ordained as sole chancellor that will..."

Benson looked over at his vice president, who watched the events unfold with a look of unfathomable sorrow. David muttered under his breath. "Zones. The United States Zone."

Benson saw the look on David's face. "I know why *I* didn't go to this dog and pony show: I had a point to make. But you could have gone, David. I wouldn't have held it against you. I don't think anyone in this room would have held it against you. After all, the man is your brother."

David's eyes narrowed, remaining fixed on the screen. "Stone has been no man's brother for many years."

Benson pulled back, not wanting to push an obviously very sensitive subject. Everyone in the room listened in silence to the unfolding news.

"The excitement mounts as we all await the inauguration of Stone Alexander as the first-ever chancellor of the United World Union, here on historic Mount Jerusalem. All nearly came to a crashing halt two weeks ago when Alexander was gunned down by a would-be assassin's bullet. Eyewitnesses report that Alexander was shot in the head, as our footage clearly shows."

On the screen, they all watched as Stone stood addressing a crowd and a sniper stepped forward, pointing a revolver right at Stone's head. Before he could even react, the bullet hit him right in the temple—blood splattering everywhere. Stone went down. A group of Stone's bodyguards succeeded in capturing the assailant, while others whisked Stone's inert body off in his private limo.

"And yet, despite what should have been, by all accounts, a fatal head wound, the world has witnessed a recovery nothing short of miraculous, as Alexander appears before us today for his inauguration without so much as a Band-Aid."

Benson and David exchanged looks, utterly mystified. The news anchor touched his earphone. "Dana?" A woman reporter appeared within the temple mount, where a stage had been erected for the proceedings.

"Yes, Chuck, let's go inside, where, I believe, the chancellor is about to make his acceptance speech...wait a minute; an entourage is entering the building. I believe they are escorting Alexander..."

Benson turned to David, his voice filled with sarcasm.

"Here comes Big Brother..."

David frowned. Cheers exploded from the crowd as the familiar, sandy-haired man entered the hall. Flanked by a herd of bodyguards, Stone entered the room, smiling triumphantly and looking as boyishly charming as when he was a young cadet. He waved to the riotous throng. The heads of the European Union each took their turns congratulating Stone.

President Benson slumped down in his chair dejectedly.

"Maybe I should have ordered some popcorn and soda for this extravaganza."

The Guardian, although unrecognized as such by the crowd, was standing at the podium. He placed a purple ceremonial stole around Stone's neck. Cheers rang out from the crowd as Stone moved toward the microphone to make his acceptance speech.

"You are all here to witness the dawn of a new, united world. One currency. One language. One goal: to strive every day to make the lives of all men better and better. I have always pledged that I would set my throne above the stars of God, and it has come to pass! I have done what no man has ever been able to do. I have become both king and god!"

There was unilateral cheering from the audience, who obviously idolized their new leader. But back at the White House, there was only silence. Finally, the president broke the ice.

"Is there anyone who'd care to break open an old bottle of brandy with me?"

Everyone clustered around the president as he uncorked an antique bottle of fine brandy—the year, 1900. He poured drinks all around and held his hand up in a wry toast.

"Well, here's to the new king and god. So much for our cherished 'separation of church and state.'" Everyone groaned by way of reply, including David.

Benson grumbled, "Well, you won't find *me* kissing the hand of this new 'messiah,' I'll tell you that." Benson walked around to his desk and stood behind it, staring out at the Rose Garden.

Rick Howard, an affable black man of forty and head of the Secret Service, chimed in. "The man acts like Hitler—with an overinflated ego."

Staring out at the peacefulness of the garden before him, the president contemplated, "Now that he's got almost everybody lined up on his side, he'll be looking for new ways to put pressure on us."

David nodded, still seated. "Yes. A logical first step would be an economic embargo. If he cuts us off from the world markets, we're in a lot of trouble."

The president turned around, addressing his chiefs of staff. "David's right. You better get on that right now. Where do the Chinese and Latins stand?"

David handed Benson a thick folder. "Still uncommitted. This is from our intelligence group. Satellite photos show a lot of activity at Russian nuclear weapons storage sites."

Benson narrowed his eyes as he scanned the folder. "Are they moving stuff around?"

David sighed. "CIA said somebody offered them a load of money for some nukes."

Benson lifted an eyebrow. "Any idea who that could be?" Everyone in the room smirked. Everyone but David, that is. "Well, let's keep an eye on them."

Benson turned back to David. "You sit down with those labor

union honchos yet? I don't want them believing the lies your brother is telling them about free trade. We need them, David."

David nodded perfunctorily. "Already done. They're drafting a resolution in support of our policies."

Benson grinned as he looked over at his vice president. "Well, then, looks like everything will be just hunky-dory."

David tried to lift Benson's spirits somewhat. "Listen, at least we're not alone. The South American Zone wasn't present at the ceremony either."

Benson raised his hand as he downed another brandy. "Well, here's to the South American Zone!" Benson shook his head, utterly baffled, yet displaying great strength of will.

"I have to tell you, son—your brother's already gone beyond the wildest dreams of both Julius Caesar and Genghis Khan—and now he expects us to grovel at his feet. Well, if he thinks I'm going to kiss the hem of his garment, he's got the wrong man!"

The phone rang. One of the White House aides picked it up. His face blanched. "Yes. Could you hold on one moment?"

The aide turned to the president with trepidation. "It's him!"

Benson looked over at David. "He doesn't waste much time. Guessed he noticed our...lack of participation?" David didn't react as Benson headed for the phone. "Well, let the games begin..."

Benson tapped on his videophone. Stone was standing with his back to the camera, looking out of a hotel suite in Jerusalem. In the background, they could make out a fleet of helicopters circling the Mount of Olives. Benson took a moment to gather his composure.

"Benson here. Congratulations, Chancellor."

Stone smiled, though his back was still to the videophone. "Thank you, Mister President. I'll be staying in the Middle East for another day, but I'd like to see you in Rome when I return on Wednesday."

Benson was clearly taken aback by Stone's abrupt request. He looked over to David, who was equally stunned. "I'm, uh—gratified that you want to see me, but I'm a busy man, Chancellor Alexander. I have a country to run here. The United States of America? Land of the free, home of the brave? You may have heard of it?"

From the looks on their faces, it was obvious that David and the others all respected the hard line that Benson was taking with Stone. But Stone was, as ever, insistent. "I'm afraid I can't take no for an answer, Mr. President."

Benson frowned, rolling his eyes. "And just what is *that* supposed to mean, Alexander?"

Stone replied casually, "I'm off to take care of one more thing here in Israel, and then I'll be on my way home. My people will meet your plane at Rome in thirty hours. Then we'll talk. You might bring my brother along with you. It's been years..."

The screen suddenly went black. Everyone in the room sucked in their breath, wondering how the president would deal with this "edict" from Stone. Benson remained quiet for a moment, then turned to David. "David, what's the position of the Sixth Fleet?"

"Off the coast of Italy, sir."

Benson smiled. "Mighty fine place for it, don't you think?" The president headed briskly for the door, tossing a comment at David over his shoulder. "Pack your bags, Mr. Vice President."

David's face fell. He just sat there, staring at the blank screen, feeling as if he had entered a black hole.

# CHAPTER
# THIRTY-ONE

He that hath an ear, let him hear.

—Revelation 2:7


I...have the keys of hell and of death.

—Revelation 1:18

A vast desert, formerly covered by only a few stray cacti, was now filled with a herd of school buses. The ruins of the legendary city of Megiddo, on the mountain overlooking the Valley of Jezreel, were currently hosting several school field trips as part of a historical study of the area to help "bring history to life" for the fifth grade classes of Jerusalem public schools. They were going to get a chance to take part in, or at least observe, an actual archeological excavation, funded by the University of Jerusalem, to unearth the ancient city of Megiddo.

On the northern most observation point overlooking the vastness of the valley were at least four or five dozen Israeli boys and girls, all vying to look through the one observation telescope on the point. As the boys and girls fidgeted, happy to have a day outside the school room, their dark-haired young teacher tried to gain their attention, hoping to give them some appreciation of their relatively new country's most complex and fascinating history. She tried to speak over the voices of the kids still blabbering in the background.

"The city of Megiddo was founded over six thousand years ago. Its strategic location, here, at the opening of the Eron Pass, made it vital to anyone who wanted to rule the Middle East. And that would be everyone—Romans, Canaanites and Israelites. Whoever controlled Megiddo in those days controlled Jerusalem. And whoever controlled Jerusalem controlled the rest of the world."

Back by the telescope, two boys, Jacob Levy, eleven, and his chief foe, Ilan, were scuffling. Ilan wore a WWF Cyber-Wrestling T-shirt; Jacob, a rabbi's son, wore a yarmulke, and their fighting seemed to consist of his classmate trying to yank it off his head. Jacob was getting steamed. "Look, Ilan—quit it!"

But the boy in the wrestling T-shirt goaded Jacob. "What? You think you're so special just 'cause your father's the rabbi? Big deal! My father says that rabbis don't even pay taxes! That they think everyone else should support them because they're 'men of God.'"

Jacob spat back, "My father may be a rabbi, but he's an Israeli citizen too, just like everybody else. You want to talk trash to me just because I wear a yarmulke, go ahead. It won't be the first time."

Ms. Herman couldn't help but notice how heated the debate was getting between the boys. "Stop it back there, you two! I'm trying to talk here, and all I can hear is you boys squabbling!" The boys settled down, Jacob moving away from Ilan. Ms. Herman picked up her lesson where she'd left off.

"OK, so, Megiddo reached the height of its glory during the reign of King Solomon. At that time, believe it or not—it was over twice the size Jerusalem was!"

The kids murmured among themselves. That was, indeed, an interesting thought. This old pile of stones was once a city more powerful than Jerusalem. They were so impressed with this information that many of them looked around with new interest at Megiddo, surveying the ruins, excited about the chance to get to see what was down in those ruins close up.

While Jacob was contemplating a fallen column some fifty feet before him, obviously the remains of an ancient temple, Ilan sneaked up behind him again, plucking the yarmulke from his head and tossing it, like a Frisbee, down into one of the excavation pits that had been roped off to prevent school children from falling into it. The whole group stared in awe at the depth of the hole and how the yarmulke never even seemed to reach the bottom.

Jacob was incensed. He clenched his fist, trying his best not to smack Ilan. "You son of a..." Ms. Herman hadn't missed a trick. She grabbed Ilan by the arm, whispering something in his ear that seemed to indicate a lengthy detention and a call home to his parents. The boy's bravado suddenly vanished, much to Jacob's satisfaction.

Feeling vindicated, Jacob joined the rest of his classmates, and Ms. Herman began to lead them into the heart of ancient Megiddo. "OK, now that there are no further interruptions, let's go get a closer look at the city's incredible underground water system. Please try to stick together now."

Ms. Herman led the group down from the observation point and onto a path set aside by the excavators as the one safe place that school children were allowed to enter. They were, however, handed safety helmets at the entrance to the excavation in case of any unexpected earthquakes or cave-ins.

But Jacob's mind was not on getting the tour of the excavation. As soon as the group was out of sight, he climbed over the railing, scurrying down the hillside into the heart of the deep excavation that had been well terraced off against intruders. He was terrified—and not for any reason one would suspect. He knew what would happen to him if he returned home that night without his yarmulke. He would be disgraced in his father's eyes. Jacob was determined not to let that happen.

The boy easily climbed over the six-foot high screen surrounding the excavation, and then jumped off—rolling down the steep hill into the heart of the excavation, hitting hard as he landed. He got up and brushed the dirt off his clothes, stopping for a moment to get his bearings and to adjust to the darkness. He looked around him, noticing how each specific excavation—some for artifacts, some for bone specimens and hair samples—had been numbered and set off with sandbag walls by the diligent team of archeologists.

With relief, he spotted his yarmulke, rather the worse for wear, in the depths of a square pit—the beginning of a relatively new excavation—and intrepidly jumped down to retrieve it. Dusting it off as well as he could, Jacob proudly placed it back on his head and began to climb out of the pit when, suddenly, he looked up to see a man standing over him. He had no idea who he was; he could only see his shoes.

The boy was mortified. *Busted!* he thought. *Man, am I going to get it!* But before Jacob could worry much longer, the man—Stone Alexander—suddenly knelt down before the pit, looking at him kindly with eyes that indicated no threat to him. Jacob breathed a deep sigh of relief, thinking that maybe this was no archeologist or policeman at all—but just someone who sneaked down here into the excavation, just as he did, to survey the "digs." Still, Jacob didn't move a muscle.

Suddenly, Stone spoke to him in the strangest voice he had ever heard. It was unearthly, somehow, and echoed throughout the deep chamber. "I have been here before," he said, almost kindly. Jacob slowly raised his head, climbing slowly out of the pit to see that the man had stood up and was pacing around the ruins.

The boy watched in wonder as the immaculately dressed man—he had never seen such fine clothes—stretched his hands out over the remnants of a stone wall, as if having an actual, sensory memory of the surface of the long-gone edifice. It was a strange feeling for Jacob—almost like seeing a ghost. Or a prophet. Stone continued in a lilting voice that absorbed Jacob completely.

"I was here when these walls stood tall. When this soil was red with blood. Oh, the flowers that bloomed afterwards, nourished by the blood of my enemies. When the Egyptians turned back the Canaanites—a thousand years before the Second Coming was even the seed of a plan in my rival's mind."

Stone became more contemplative now, looking up out of the excavation at the plain of Jezreel. He continued to speak, aware of the boy's presence, but really speaking aloud to himself. Jacob remained riveted, having no clue of what the man was talking about, but just understanding that this man was, in some way, very special. He was especially happy that it didn't look like he was going to turn him in!

Still, the man captivated him. He continued speaking, as he walked slowly along, touching the ancient walls. "Later, when the earth trembled beneath two thousand chariots, King Ahab rode against the Assyrians. But that was nothing. Nothing compared to the battle that is coming."

Stone turned to the startled boy. "Your teacher is right. Megiddo *is* the key. Even into the last century, when England drove the Turks from this land, armies have assembled here and marched into war, their drums beating. The good and the evil have been cut down like winter wheat. All meaningless."

Stone moved closer to the boy, his tone almost conspiratorial. "For five millennia we have tried to win the world with violence. But we were going about things all wrong."

Jacob appeared confused, but it didn't matter. Stone was talking to himself. He continued, "'And he gathered them together into a place called in the Hebrew tongue Armageddon.' Your rabbi father ever read you the Christian Bible, Jacob?"

Stone met the boy's eyes. Jacob was really scared now. How did this man know his name? Know about his father? The boy found the courage to speak from somewhere deep within. "Who...who are you?"

"I am one who is older than this very place," Stone smiled, but looking very melancholy. Something rumbled not too far off in the distance. Jacob's entire body shook in fear. Would he be forever buried in this excavation, never to see his parents again? But Stone's voice became excited, almost gleeful, and that reassured him. He felt that, at least, he was in no immediate danger.

"You hear that? It's coming. The horsemen are beginning to ride. The final battle is ready to begin. Run! Run home and tell them! Tell them all! And take a look at that New Testament. The Book of Revelation. It has quite a tale to tell."

Jacob scrambled up and out of the ruins as fast as he could, clutching the Bible Stone had thrust in his hands. *Who was this man?* he thought. *What was he saying that he should tell his father? Tell his father what?* His brain was nearly exploding as he finally reached the top of the excavation and saw his class ready to board the school bus in the distance. Spotting him, his relieved teacher waved at him frantically to hurry over. The boy tore off after the school bus as if it were home itself.

$$\Omega^2$$

Back inside the excavation, Stone laughed to himself, amused by the encounter with the young boy. "Tell them, boy. Not that they'll listen."

Then, he raised his hands to the heavens, and screamed out, in a thunderous, resounding voice, "How about You? Are You listening? Are You ready?"

There was nothing but silence by way of reply. But Stone waited, lips quivering, for the response he knew would come. Suddenly, in the distance, was the sound of explosive thunder. "Ah, yes! He has heard me." Stone smiled broadly, clucking in contentment.

# CHAPTER THIRTY-TWO

Ancient mother,
I hear you calling.
Ancient mother,
I hear your song.

—Traditional Chant

The Blessed Damozel leaned out
From the gold bar of heaven;
Her eyes were deeper than the depth
Of waters stilled at even;
She had three lilies in her hand,
And the stars in her hair were seven.

—Dante Gabriel Rossetti

A panel truck that had obviously seen better days creaked to a halt in the dusty village of Santa Maria Teresa, somewhere in Central America. But this crippled village only exemplified hundreds, no, thousands, of others just like it south of the Mexican border. Volunteers helped sweat-soaked soldiers begin to off-load much needed supplies for the desperate villagers. Gabriella, dressed in a simple khaki dress, emerged from the passenger side of the truck. She took her first look around the pestilence-ridden town. Moans of anguish and despair emanated from the hastily assembled huts peppering the village, huts that had been constructed by the villagers to nurse their sick and dying after their homes had been destroyed by the earthquake. Babies wailed away in the universal language of misery. Gabriella noticed grimly that the entire village had virtually been leveled, with several small haciendas still burning on the hillside above the village.

Seeing Gabriella standing there in the middle of the village square, her official Army escort moved before her like a battering ram—trying to stop her before she could step a foot into town. The terror-stricken sergeant pleaded with her, and it sounded like a well-practiced plea.

"Señora, *por favor*—do not go any further. Please get back in the truck."

Gabriella protested. "Sergeant Jimenez, you don't think I've come all the way down here just to drop off some food and run away, do you?"

Jimenez rolled his eyes. "I know you far better than that, Señora, but you don't understand. This is a plague area. Quarantine, *comprende?* Let the general's men help the people to unload the food, and then, let's get out of here!"

He now pulled a well-worn rabbit out of his hat, a rabbit that usually won over this particularly tough crowd of one.

"We have many more towns to visit before dark, as you know, Señora. Towns where they have great need of you..."

The sergeant tried once again to escort Gabriella back to the truck, but once again, she resisted. "*Lo siento,* Jimmy, but you've used that rabbit trick on me one too many times. You're not getting me out of here that easily!"

Jimmy sighed deeply. He knew that if the rabbit trick didn't work, they wouldn't be moving on any further that day—or probably that night, either. Who knows how long he'd be stuck in this plague-infested inferno because of this *loca Italiana,* as he had nicknamed her affectionately.

Gabriella saw the sergeant pouting. "Jimmy, I came here to see what's going on—and that's what I'm going to do. You should know better than to try and stop me." She turned on her heels, heading off into the heart of the desolate village.

"*Sí, sí*, Señora. I should know better by now!" Jimmy called out to her, jocularly.

Gabriella turned back to him once more, tossing back her own quip this time. "No one is asking *you* to jeopardize *your* health, Sergeant Jimenez. Why don't you just curl up in the back of the truck for a little siesta—like you always do?" She had mischief in her eyes as she spoke, and Jimenez could only chuckle as he watched her dust.

Yes, he knew there was no point in trying to talk Gabriella out of anything once she set her mind on it. He was just her official escort, along for the ride. He climbed obediently into the back seat, curling up into a fetal position and closing his eyes. He smiled to himself at the spirit of this singular woman.

"*Que loca Italiana...*"

# $\Omega^2$

Gabriella was smiling, too. *Poor Jimmy,* she thought. She really kept him on the go. But somebody had to get to these out-of-the-way places; someone had to be there to minister to the sick, the wounded and the hungry. And usually, it seemed, that person was Gabriella. Whether it was Africa, Asia or Central America, Gabriella was a one-woman army of love, bringing with her an abundant supply of hope, joy and faith—and almost as importantly, food, water and medical supplies.

As she moved into the shambles of the town, Gabriella noticed several people up ahead, hovering over someone on the side of the road in obvious distress. This would be only the beginning, she knew. One person on the roadside would be nothing compared to what she'd find in the makeshift hospitals and lean-tos. She had visited many such villages, and each one had its own story to tell. Each person had his or her own story to tell. She wondered what the stories of these people would be, here in Santa Maria Teresa.

*Gabriella sighed, full of deep regrets. What earthly use was it to her to have a castle in Rome, when she was so painfully aware that people were starving all over the world? People were sleeping like dogs by the side of the road, while she dwelled in a mountaintop castle overlooking Rome. What a ludicrous life! To live in such opulence, with people everywhere going hungry! If the decision had been hers to make, Castle Alexander would be sold, and the proceeds would go to buying herself a well-outfitted schooner, which* she would stock with food, medical supplies and a full medical staff so she could sail off around the world. Just like Santa Lucia. And all this could be paid for by the simple sale of her home. She would do it in an instant, if it meant saving the life of even one child. The only thing she'd really miss was her garden.

Up ahead, General Juan Garcia watched as an exhausted, elderly, brown-skinned nun carried a bucket of clean water to an old woman, who was obviously dying, propped up on a bench against a wall. General Garcia was in town not only to survey the damage, but to make sure the food and supplies were distributed among the people—and not carried off by a roving horde of *banditos*.

Gabriella moved up alongside the general and the nun, just watching the scene unfold. The placid nun sat beside the old woman, starting to moisten her filthy face and bathe her arms with a damp rag, when suddenly, she felt faint and collapsed by the side of the road.

"*Madre Mia*...give me strength," she whispered.

Someone reached over and took the cloth from her hand. The nun looked up in surprise as General Garcia sat down on the bench, cradling the old woman's head in his lap, dipping the cloth in the bucket of spring water and wringing it out. Gently, he began laying cool compresses on the women's face. Parched and dry from fever, she just moaned at the relief of the cool water on her brow. The haggard nun looked over at Garcia, touched beyond words. The old woman opened her eyes, looking up at the serious but kindly man who was now tending her. She struggled to focus her eyes, noticing all the gold braids, medals and doodads on his Army uniform. Her eyes opened wide. "*Gracias...General?*"

Garcia smiled down at the old woman, tears welling up in his eyes. "*Permítame, madre mia*," he replied, as if asking to kiss the hand of the fairest woman in the land. His humble response only made the general seem even more beautiful in the nun's eyes.

Gabriella came up upon the unlikely trio, which struck her as a heart-rending variation on Michelangelo's "Pieta." She saw the nun sitting on the ground at the general's feet, while he sat on the bench above her, cradling the head of the old woman in his strong arms. The symbolism of it affected her greatly.

Seeing the nun's weakened condition, Gabriella knelt down before her, offering her some bread and wine. Taking the food in her shaking hands, the nun struggled to choke down a few bites. Gabriella admonished her gently, "You have not eaten for days, *Madre*. I can see that. How can you stay strong if you don't eat?"

The nun replied almost apologetically. "There is just so much to do, Señora."

Gabriella paused for a few moments, letting the woman eat in peace. "*Madre,*" she said, as delicately as possible, "how many people have you lost in your village?"

The nun fought back tears, which wasn't too hard because she didn't even have the energy to cry. "I don't know, Señora. Two hundred, maybe more. Tomorrow—it will be twice as many. We have an infirmary; it is outside, but there is no doctor and no beds, except for straw. Tomorrow...I do not want to think about tomorrow, Señora."

Gabriella put her arms around the gentle, caring woman. "I will help you. I have brought food and medicine that can help your people."

The sister looked over at the strong, courageous woman before her, not knowing what to think—except that she had been sent by the Holy Mother herself. Gabriella sat by as the nun slowly managed to swallow down a few bites of the bread. Gabriella held the jug for her so she could get a revitalizing drink of the good red wine. Revived in both body and spirit, the nun looked up at Gabriella with gratitude.

The two women talked as the general soothed the old woman to her eternal rest with a Spanish lullaby. Gabriella sensed that this was probably the first time the nun had actually been off her feet for days. She took off the woman's well-worn shoes, but she had trouble removing her stockings. It had been so long since she had bathed that her stockings had actually stuck to her feet. Gabriella finally succeeded in getting them off and began to rub the nun's feet. She moaned, in a combination of pleasure and agony.

"How do you do it, Sister?" Gabriella asked, awed by the woman's fortitude and devotion.

"Do what?" the nun asked, luxuriating in the sensation of Gabriella's hands massaging her sore and blistered feet.

"How do you...look at all this every day and still believe?"

The nun now seemed suffused with inner light. "It is because of 'all this,' as you say, that I do believe. It is when we experience the deepest of human suffering that our faith is challenged. Many cannot face that challenge and will turn away. But faith is always there, *mi hija*—but if we don't open ourselves up to it, we cannot receive it."

Gabriella looked over at the old nun with profound respect. "It is wise women like yourself that help show others the way. It has been that way since the beginning of time."

The nun nodded humbly. "I only do what I must, Señora."

"Call me *hija*—please, *Madre,*" said Gabriella to indicate her respect. The old woman nodded at her, smiling.

"*Hija* it will be then, my daughter." Gabriella now trained her eyes on the dying woman. *If it weren't for this extraordinary general,* she thought, *this poor soul wouldn't even have had a place to rest her head as she lay dying.*

*This is not how it is meant to be. This is not how one should die. Out in the middle of the dirty street, with no husband, no children, no grandchildren; no one to meet her eyes and bid her farewell. No one she loved to whisper "Vaya con Dios" in her ear. Who knows? Maybe none of her family had even survived the earthquake. Maybe her sons and daughters, and even her grandchildren, were now lying on the ground of the makeshift hospital, expiring of the plague. At least then they would all be together again.*

Gabriella found herself whispering a soft prayer—one of the few prayers she ever said on her own behalf: *"Blessed Mother, when it is my time to come and sit by your side, please, don't let me cross over alone. Please let there be someone I love holding my hand when you call me to you. For then, I will not be afraid, and shall most willingly make that journey. This is all I ask for myself. Not my will, but thy will be done. Amen."*

When Gabriella opened her eyes, she took in the strange triumvirate they made—united only for this one, anomalous moment, frozen in time: the nun, the First Lady and the Army general, all come together to minister over an anonymous dying woman. The general noticed Gabriella's eyes upon him. He looked over at her kindly. "You must be the famous Señora Alexander. I must thank you for all the supplies you have brought here today. My men will make sure it is distributed fairly among the people. My name is Juan. Juan Garcia, at your service."

Gabriella nodded politely at the humble man in the uniform that proclaimed him one of his nation's highest-ranking officials. She respected that Garcia had introduced himself, under these circumstances, as just "Juan." He was, after all, just a man now, not an Army general, keeping the death watch over an old grandmother. It was curiously just as she had done with the nun—asking her to call her merely "sister." They all noticed that the old woman's breath was becoming more and more faint.

"You have come here at a very sad time," Garcia offered, in hushed tones, not wanting to disturb the old woman.

Gabriella just smiled over at him compassionately. "If things were good," Gabriella said simply, "there would be no need for me here." They shared a look. Yes, they were needed. Desperately needed. And that was why they were both here. Garcia nodded his head in appreciation, recognizing a kindred spirit.

He watched as Gabriella looked out upon the remnants of the old village. She became very upset. "I don't know why this is happening.

I pray and pray, but still...there is nothing but devastation."

Garcia continued to run the cool, wet rag over the old woman's fevered brow, smiling philosophically. "What is it you are wishing for, my sister? A miracle? You want the earthquakes to stop? The famine? The plague? Just like that?"

"Yes," Gabriella said sincerely. "I just want them to stop. I pray that they will stop." She looked up at Juan. "Don't you believe in miracles, Juan?"

Garcia smiled over at the beautiful woman rubbing the nun's feet. "Of course, my sister, I believe in miracles."

"Well," the nun said gently, "I think that such a miracle will require a great deal of prayer. More, perhaps, than just yours alone, *hija*."

Gabriella nodded, realizing how silly, how childish, her impatience must seem to this wise woman, who had learned the lessons of temperance and was satisfied to have her prayers answered in their own time. She had a lot to learn from this stoical healer of bodies and souls.

While they were talking, the old woman leaned her head back and died. The nun struggled to put on her shoes, limping over to close the dead woman's eyes while looking at Garcia with great admiration. "We will continue to pray. But right now, we must take comfort in the little miracles that come our way. Like right now—a general risking his life to wash the face of a dying woman. That, to my mind, is a nothing less than a miracle!"

The nun made the sign of the cross over the dead woman, whispering under her breath as they all dropped their heads for a moment of silent prayer. "I will go find some people strong enough to carry her." She looked over at Gabriella. "We will have to burn her body right away."

The nun looked away now, a profound sadness on her lined face, toward the end of town, which had obviously become a crematorium. She tried not to sound as distressed as she clearly was. "We had to burn all the bodies. To keep the disease from spreading." She now looked at Gabriella, concern in her gray eyes. "You are not meant for burning. Please..."

Garcia still sat there, cradling the dead woman's head in his arms. He spoke to Gabriella pointedly. "I think Sister Antonia wants you to go, *mi hija,* for your own safety—but she doesn't want to offend you by saying so."

Gabriella smiled over at Garcia. "Thank you, *mi hijo*." She turned back to the wise woman now, smiling courageously. "Just show me the way, *Madre.*"

Smiling in recognition of Gabriella's resolve, Sister Antonia motioned for Gabriella to follow her. She turned to Garcia. "Well, I suppose there are to be two miracles today in Santa Maria Teresa!"

Gabriella picked up her heavy bag of medical supplies and took off after the rugged old woman. General Garcia could only smile in awe as the raven-tressed Italian woman trying single-handedly to save the world disappeared around the corner.

"She might just do it at that..." he mused.

# CHAPTER
# THIRTY-THREE

There are some defeats more
triumphant than victories.

—Montaigne

ir Force One winged its way over the Atlantic. The lights were turned down low, and most of the Secret Service men were sound asleep. President Benson was playing poker with Rick Howard on a small table near David, who sat at his laptop computer, utterly absorbed. Before him were images of Stone Alexander's "meteoric rise to power," with stock footage of him shaking the hands of the foreign dignitaries who had now united under his banner. *David just stared at the image of his brother. Was there anything there of the man who was Stone Alexander?*

Benson turned away from his card game. "Hey, you! What are you up to?"

David sighed, coming out of his reverie. "Just trying to figure out what makes him tick."

Benson let out a belly laugh. "I can tell you that in a second. Power. Power is the ultimate aphrodisiac, and your brother obviously takes mega doses of it before bedtime. That's not what I need, David. What I need is something that will give me an edge. Something tangible I can use when I face off with your brother."

David shook his head, obviously deeply conflicted about something. He slowly opened his attaché case and tossed a report on to the president's table, upsetting his hand.

"Whoa, boy—that was the beginning of a straight flush..."

But David's dead seriousness intrigued him. "You may want to have a look at this," David said in a virtual whisper.

Benson pushed the cards off the table and began leafing through the report. "Barnsdahl Group Insurance Actuarial Study? What the hell is this? Can't you just cut to the verb, boy?"

David joined the president and Rick at the table. "I can. But I don't know that I want to." He paused, and then continued, "All right. Basically, the report says that there are over two hundred people, whose names are listed in that report, who at one time or another opposed my brother, either in political or business dealings, over the last three decades."

Benson stared at David. "Let me guess how this ends. They're all dead."

David nodded.

"All of unnatural causes?"

David shook his head. "No. That's the weird part. *None* of them did. They all suffered organic trauma. Heart attacks. Cancer. Strokes..."

Benson was baffled. "OK? And...?"

"I had the numbers crunched. The odds of all these people dying of organic trauma in this particular time frame were over two million to one."

Benson pounded on the table. "What the hell are you saying, David? That your lunatic brother is giving people cancer and heart disease—in absentia? How do you expect me to make any kind of logical sense out of that, David?"

David averted his eyes. From the quavering in his voice, it was obvious he was speaking what he felt to be the truth. "I don't have a clue. All I can say, Sir, is, in light of these figures, I would advise you to avoid any close, personal contact with my brother."

Benson rose to his feet, blustering at David. "How in hell am I supposed to do that? We're traveling three thousand miles just to meet the joker! If I want to show him we mean business, I have to do it face to face, man to man. What am I supposed to do, talk to him through a Krypton screen? I never heard such nonsense."

Rick and David exchanged looks. The head of the Secret Service spoke up. "I think the vice president has a good point, Sir. As head of your security force, I would be derelict in my duties if I even let you get near the man!"

Benson stormed off in a huff. He turned back to them again, frustrated and angry. "You know, when you two get to be president, you can do what you want. But for now, I have to play cards *my* way." Fuming, he brushed the remaining cards off the table, strewing them all over the floor of plane. David and Rick watched the president storm off to his bunk.

Rick called out to him before he reached his cubicle. His voice was firm, yet kind. "I repeat, Mr. President. I will do everything I see fit to protect you. Whatever it takes."

Benson stopped in his tracks for a moment, then just shook his head and ambled off to his bed.

# $\Omega^2$

David and Rick sat alone. Fear was etched on both their faces. The deck of playing cards lay strewn across the floor of the plane almost prophetically. There was an awkward moment of silence.

Rick spoke out quietly. "Do you believe in omens, David?"

"I don't know," David replied in all honesty. Rick looked over at the playing cards that Benson had strewn on the floor. Something caught his eye. He reached over and picked up one of the cards. His face dropped.

"Look at that. The Jack of Spades was covering the King of Hearts—and it was upside down." Rick kept hold of the card, just staring at it. "The nastiest dude in the deck, the Jack of Spades."

David smiled wryly. "So, the Jack of Spades is the worst card in the playing deck; is that what you're telling me?"

"You bet I am," Rick replied. "All race issues aside, this Black Jack, the Jack of Spades, is like a harbinger of doom! Didn't you ever hear anyone say, 'Don't blackjack me, man'? That card's a hex! And to see it covering the King of Hearts like that—that's too much for me, man." Rick was trembling.

David laughed. "Here you are getting all superstitious on me!"

"Superstition or no superstition, all I can tell you is that I don't feel good about this. It makes me feel real creepy."

David stared over at the King of Hearts lying forlornly on the floor. His impression was of a courageous man, a kind and gentle leader. Then he looked over at the card that Rick still held in his hands. The Jack of Spades. A shiver ran down his spine. There was something about the image on that card that connoted pure evil—although he couldn't for his life figure out how or why it did. It was all rather unnerving.

Rick stared down at the maleficent card in his hand, deep in thought. "I don't like it. I gotta be everywhere at once tomorrow. We gotta save that stubborn..."

David shook his head. "It's not that he's stubborn, Rick. It's just that he doesn't really believe that true evil exists. He has no conception of it."

Rick nodded, understanding exactly what David meant. "I got a feeling we're gonna come up against it real soon." Rick continued to stare at the card in his hand. David noticed that his hand was shaking.

*The Jack of Spades had covered the King of Hearts. Why did that strike both of them as so unnerving? As an evil portent? They were both being ridiculous. Weren't they?*

# CHAPTER
# THIRTY-FOUR

I have fought a good fight,
I have finished my course,
I have kept the faith.

—2 Timothy 4:7

President Benson's limousine glided through the dense traffic of downtown Rome, especially vicious today because of the dignitaries in town for the speech that was taking place before the Circus Maximus. Flanking every inch of the stage was an intrepid bodyguard. A familiar voice could be heard against the ubiquitous background noise of everyday Rome.

"One currency. One language. One goal: to strive every day to improve the quality of life for all mankind."

Stone looked over the huge crowd. The people gathered closest to the stage were already devotees. Their faces were smeared with tears, their eyes wide with admiration and outright devotion. But toward the back of the crowd, Stone noticed a formidable cluster of dissenters laughing among themselves, obviously holding Stone in contempt.

Stone zeroed in on the cocky young man who was clearly the leader of the group and sent a subliminal message to the young man to meet his eyes. Within moments, the man looked up and met Stone's eyes. A shiver ran through his body. How had Stone honed in on *him* in this crowd of thousands? Had Stone been reading his very thoughts? If so, he was doomed. His friends noticed the instant change in their leader's demeanor. Stone continued his monologue—staring at the young man and his friends all the while.

"I know what some of you are thinking. That I am nothing more than a modern-day Caesar! That I seek only self-aggrandizement, to control you..."

Stone's gaze seemed to burn a hole in the young man's forehead. "So, to those of you who believe that, I pledge that you are wrong! These are nothing more than thoughts born out of fear of the unknown—the same kind of fears that caused Julius Caesar to be bludgeoned to death by his closest friend and allies. But I am no Caesar! You have no need to fear me. I am no conquering hero. I am your father, your brother, your friend. I ask to work beside you, not above you. I ask you not to follow me, but merely to accompany me on this journey to a better world."

The crowd exploded in cheers. Dozens tried to mount the stage, hoping to get to touch Stone—even his trouser leg—but they were tossed aside like dirty laundry by the bodyguards flanking the stage. The applause and cheering continued undiminished. "Stone! Stone! Stone! Stone!" Stone met the young man's eyes one more time. Something in his smile told the man to just give up; he was powerless to stop him.

The young man and his friends stood quietly in the background, startled by what was happening around them. People were leaping up on the stage to touch Stone's vestments—as if he were Jesus

Christ! But the young man knew that Stone was far from the Second Coming. He also knew that there was nothing he or his friends could do to stop this overwhelming tide. While the crowd threw themselves before their new messiah, the young man turned away and motioned for his cohorts to follow him through the dense mob. He knew there was no point in their sticking around.

$$\Omega^2$$

The press leaped in unison toward the stage, shooting rapid-fire questions at Stone in a head-splitting cacophony of languages. But he moved quickly away from the podium, deftly sidestepping them and heading backstage, flanked by bodyguards, to the makeshift "Green Room," where he saw that President Benson, David and the Secret Service entourage were waiting for him.

As the crowd roared and cheered for their new leader, Benson turned to David and Rick with a smirk. "He gives a good speech. I'll give that to him."

A chill ran down David's spine. He steeled for the shock of seeing his brother again—for the first time in so many years he couldn't even count them—and this time, there could be no doubt that they were on opposite sides. To say he felt awkward would be the grossest of understatements. He was enraged, distraught—fearful even—and a lot of other things as well, but he had no time to catalog them as Stone suddenly emerged from the stage door and saw him.

Though naturally David and Stone immediately locked eyes, it was Benson who spoke first. "Chancellor."

Stone moved toward the group—moving more effortlessly than a teenager, hardly seeming a man who had been gunned down and thought fatally wounded only two weeks earlier.

"Mr. President. Brother David." Stone moved in to hug David, but Rick quickly moved between them. Stone bristled, but then extended his hand warmly to Benson. Once again, Rick intervened. Stone pretended not to notice. Stone stared over at his brother and nodded as if proud of his worldly accomplishments.

"Mr. Vice President."

David nodded, barely polite. "Stone." Stone immediately picked up on his negative mood. He smiled at his younger brother, then over at Benson.

"It's been a long time since I've seen this one. You keep him very busy in your employ, President Benson."

Benson cut right in. "Look—before you start getting all teary-eyed and reminiscing about the old days, and before we all start blowing

199

smoke up each other's hindquarters, let's get down to brass tacks. OK, Alexander?"

Stone's eyes widened. He nodded, impressed by the president's directness. "Well said. There will be ample time for reminiscing after negotiating."

Stone cordially extended his hand to a corner of the room where an impromptu sitting area had been arranged. Rick immediately followed them—but Benson stopped him with a glance. Rick didn't know what to do. He couldn't disobey an official order, but he couldn't lose his chief client, either. He looked over at David for guidance. David just shook his head. Benson had taken the matter into his own hands. He had taken the ball, along with the responsibility for his own safety—and now he had to run with it. David and Rick just sat close by, ready for anything.

## $\Omega^2$

Stone and Benson sat opposite each other on high-backed chairs. Stone politely waited for Benson to begin, pouring himself out a glass of sparkling water. Benson cleared his throat, then started right in. "Look, Alexander. I know you've got this whole mess of Third World countries and socialist paradises lined up like sitting ducks. And I'd be a moron to think that you brought me here for any other reason but to convince me to join you."

Stone nodded, listening attentively as Benson took a brief, but significant pause. Benson just shook his head back and forth, slowly. "It ain't gonna happen."

Stone nodded thoughtfully, politely, as if actually considering what Benson had said. Then he laughed. "You know, Benson, I admire you. I truly do. You're the last of a dying breed. You remind me of my own father, rest his soul."

Benson fired back caustically. "I knew your father quite well. I'm not sure whether to take that as a compliment or an insult."

Stone roared with laughter. "You *are* one of a rare, dying breed, Mr. Benson—the honest man!"

But Benson didn't laugh. He met Stone's gaze head on. "Back to business, Mr. Chancellor...?"

Stone emerged from this interlude wearing a quite different face. Benson actually did a double take. *Was this even the same man he was just talking to?*

"Back to business it is. But unfortunately for your side, the Yank side, this conversation is moot. The decision is simply no longer yours to make."

200

Benson yanked his sleeves up now, ready to get down and dirty. "And what exactly do you mean by that?"

"You see," Stone continued, "the United Nations and the European Union have very nicely folded themselves into my organization. Even your own representatives to the UN have voted for the accord."

Stone smiled cordially at Benson, like a very polite Old West sheriff telling his prisoner that, with great apologies, he'd be hanged by the neck until dead the next morning. But to Stone's surprise, Benson had a trump card up his sleeve. Benson smiled right back at him.

"With my regrets, Mr. Chancellor, I'm afraid I had to withdraw those inept ambassadors from service. Some of them, between you and me, weren't really qualified for office. Well, we all make mistakes."

Stone was obviously taken aback by this new strategy of Benson's, but tried his best not to show it. He raised his eyebrows and nodded his head, trying to make this look like it really was a conversation— which it was not. It was no more than a monologue. Still, Stone continued to work on Benson, though he now considered that he was wasting his time. He would take this charade only so far and no further. But at least he would put on a good show—for his brother's sake. He raised his voice, sure that David and his companion would be listening.

"Sir—you don't want to be the only boat paddling against the tide of progress. The North American Zone must..."

Benson rose to his feet, as imperious as an Army general—which, indeed, he had once been. Benson became somehow taller than life, his voice loud and imperious.

"North American *Zone*? Listen, Svengali—I don't care what *you* want to call it. But as long as *I'm* living and breathing, your so-called 'North American Zone' will remain the United States of America! It's a good name, I like it, and I plan to keep on using it." Benson eyes shot out fiery beams at Stone, who truly admired the man's bravery. He let Benson "vent" and "say his piece," and then he rose to his feet, smiling warmly at the president.

"Well, it certainly looks like I've brought you a great distance for no reason, doesn't it, Sir?"

Benson lowered his voice so that only Stone could hear him. "I flew three thousand miles just to say my piece—face to face. Man to man. And I'll do it again if I have to. I sure hope I won't have to."

Stone led Benson back into the Green Room, where David, Rick and a handful of bodyguards and agents from both sides were eyeing each other cautiously. Stone thought for a moment, hearing the implied threat behind Benson's words. He then smiled graciously at Benson, extending his hand. Rick and David jumped to their feet, running toward the president. Benson stopped them with a wave of the hand. He had everything under control. He had Stone exactly where he wanted him.

"I truly appreciate your honesty, President Benson. It's very refreshing. Shall we agree, at the very least, to be friendly adversaries?"

Benson guffawed and nodded in approval as he extended his hand. "Sure. I'll shake to being 'friendly adversaries.' You bet."

Rick jumped between Benson and Stone, but he got there too late. Something was wrong. As Stone clutched Benson's hand, David and Rick saw something tangible pass from Stone into the U.S. leader. They watched in horror as a ball-like shape raced into Benson's hand, went under his skin and into his pores—his entire arm turning as black as the Jack of Spades.

The Guardian, in the form of an antibody, moved silently up Benson's arm, into the subcutaneous fat layer and finally into his blood stream—aiming straight for his heart. Blood raced into the atrium as the black form swelled—filling his heart. Rick and David could only stand by helplessly as Benson fell to his knees, clutching his chest in agony.

Stone looked over at his brother with great concern. *It seemed to David he had seen that look on Stone's face before; yes, it was the same look he wore on the night their father died.*

"David! Help me!" The plaintive voice came through as completely hollow this time. David and Rick bent over their fallen leader. David leaned right over his face. No trace of breath. He turned toward Stone accusatorily. "What happened? What did you do to him?"

Stone put on a ludicrous display of histrionics.

"I don't know...we had just agreed to disagree, be friendly adversaries, and suddenly, he began grabbing at his chest, gasping for air..."

Rick turned Benson over and felt for any trace of a heartbeat, any trace of life. David just watched the show, muttering, as if to himself, "He's stone dead."

Rick was already on his shoulder microphone calling for the limousine. The other CIA agents in the room drew their weapons as a matter of course. The limo pulled up, and David, Rick and the other agents shuttled the president's limp form into the car.

As the limo tore out of the square, David stared back at Stone watching the removal of his opponent's body with a smug, self-satisfied look that he would never forget.

$$\Omega^2$$

In the car, David stared over at the limp form of the president, while Rick screamed commands into the video monitor. Rigor mortis was already setting in the president's lifeless body.

"Stone dead," he muttered, just loud enough for Rick to hear him.

# CHAPTER
# THIRTY-FIVE

Beloved, I wish above all things that thou mayest prosper and be in health, even as thy soul prospereth.

—3 John 2

The sky was turning from blue to pink as the sun prepared to set over Rome. David stood on the parapets of Stone's castle and watched the golden light recede. A familiar voice kissed his heart.

"*Buona notte.*"

He turned around to see Gabriella standing before him.

"Hello, David." They each took a moment to get used to the way they looked—ten years older than the last time they saw each other.

"Gabriella." David embraced her, then took a step back. "What have you been up to? I haven't seen you in any of the coverage of Stone's public appearances. Don't you travel with him?"

Gabriella replied almost mechanically. She was still beautiful, but something about her had changed. It didn't escape David's notice. "No. I am busy with my own work. And when I am finished, I come right home. Stone is happier when I am here."

David tried to smile. "His most precious possession?"

Gabriella began to walk around the garden, puttering with her plants as she walked by out of habit. "I rarely leave these walls, unless it's to do my work. I do what I can for the poor and helpless, and Stone does not interfere. He appreciates that I have a higher calling. But Stone is afraid of his enemies, of what they might do to me to get to him."

David smiled awkwardly. "Stone still has enemies? I thought they were all dead."

His meaning was not lost on Gabriella. She spoke caringly. "How is your president?"

David winced. "Dead."

"He was a good man?"

"The very best."

"Then I'm terribly sorry."

"That's the problem. I always seem to lose the people I care about."

This comment made Gabriella extremely uncomfortable as she moved over to a reflecting pond. She stared into the depths of it, catching her reflection and David's standing behind her. She spoke with the wisdom she had accumulated on her life's path, learned from working with women all over the world like Sister Antonia. "You cannot lose something you never possessed."

David moved up beside her, saddened by the drastic change in her. "Gabriella, why do you stay here, really?"

Deep inside, he was hoping to recapture some of the magic that had brought them together the night of his father's death. Hoping that with just one spark, it might once more turn into a raging

205

inferno, but Gabriella had changed. She had become far more distant, not only from him—from everything. She almost seemed like a creature not of this world as she moved away from him again, tending to her rose bushes and camellias. She smiled wistfully. "You should know, David. I could not leave and live."

David finally caught up with her and stopped her. He tried in vain to get her to meet his eyes—but she would not. There was a long ebb in their conversation as David just walked alongside of her as she tended to her flowers. Finally, he pointed over to the familiar building in the distance.

"You see that?" he said.

She looked over in the distance, confused. "The Coliseum?"

"Bread and Circuses. Emperors, dictators, from Nero to Commodus gave the people what they wanted so they wouldn't complain while their freedom was slowly being ripped out from under them. That's what Stone is doing, Gabriella. You know that, don't you?"

Gabriella continued to stare at the Coliseum through glazed eyes. She remembered when she, Stone and the tiny kitten took a jolting ride up the mountain on the back of his Vespa. That seemed like a lifetime ago.

She spoke as if she were under heavy sedation. Or, the thought passed through David's mind, she might have been systematically brainwashed. "Every leader throughout history has done that. Do you think your brother is worse than all the others?"

"Yes. Yes, I do," David said, in hushed tones.

Gabriella froze. He took her by the shoulders, the way he did the last time he saw her—the night of his father's death—when he hoped her would win her away for good.

"Gabriella, please. Come away with me."

Gabriella smiled faintly, trying desperately to stifle any hint of emotion. "Why, David?"

"You want a list? Well, for one, because you don't love Stone. But even more important, because he's sick...he's deluded."

For the first time, Gabriella looked up shyly and met his eyes. He saw that she had not been sedated or brainwashed; she had just become well practiced in holding in her feelings. David felt that old rumbling in his heart once again as she teased him pitilessly.

"More deluded than a man who waits for a woman he's seen twice in thirty years?"

*Touché*. David tried to get back on surer footing, playing the pompous fool. "Where did you get the idea that I was waiting for you? I'm the vice president of the United States..."

He sadly recollected the incidents of that day. "I mean, I guess, now, I'm the president of the United States, and I've been, well, kind of busy. I don't have a lot of time for...you can jump in here anytime and stop me, you know."

Gabriella smiled warmly at him for the first time. She even suppressed a girlish giggle, still very becoming even at her age. In fact, it was even more becoming now than when she was a teenager. "I was having too much fun watching you squirm. For a moment there, I imagined you the awkward teenager I met so many years ago. The boy who spilled the punch all over himself."

David shook his head. This woman would either be the death of him one day or bring him back to life. He knew not, and didn't much care, which it would be. She was both his angel and his temptress. "You make me *feel* like a teenager, Gabriella," David admitted.

They had finally succeeded in getting back on firm footing with each other. "Hah! An old woman like me? My only purpose now is to nurse the sick and dying, like the *strega* of old *Italia.*"

He touched her softly on the shoulder. She now remembered how much she had loved his touch. She sighed with a long-forgotten joy. "Do you still love him, Gabriella? Did you ever really love him?"

She looked up at him sadly. "David—I am *supposed* to be with him. Remember, long ago, I told you that?"

David stepped closer, almost taking her in his arms, when they sensed another presence nearby. They looked over to see Stone standing imperiously on the deck staring at them.

"*Still* trying to steal my bride away from me, little brother?"

Stone smiled falsely. David looked like the deer caught in the proverbial headlights. He looked over at Stone, almost accusingly. "Your timing, as usual, is impeccable, Stone."

Stone smiled, "I try to do everything impeccably." David turned back to Gabriella sadly, forcing a smile.

"I'll see you later. But I hope not too much later..."

Gabriella smiled back, ever so faintly. "If it is meant to be, we shall, David. You must believe that."

David just stared at her. He wondered if that had been a coded message, meant for his ears alone—or was that actually how she viewed life? Whatever it was, David couldn't think about it now. He shook himself free of all thoughts of Gabriella and proceeded across the deck toward Stone.

Scenes from the movie

MEGIDDO

A shadow demon pounces from the rafters, anxious to greet his new master.

The Guardian's blood congeals into an upside-down cross on Stone's head during the blasphemous baptism of the Antichrist.

David and Gabriella sneak a dance at the reunion.

Stone Alexander's "Black Mass" empowers his next step toward world domination.

Stone bids farewell to the American president with a "lethal" handshake.

One of God's furious "bowls of wrath" hurtles down upon the Coliseum.

The leaders of the seven loyal zones grovel at Stone's feet.

Gabriella risks her life in plague-quarantined Mexico to help the dying and diseased.

*Photos by Justin M. Lubin*

Stone calls down fire from the sky.

David and Rick brief the leaders of the loyal Sixth Fleet aboard the aircraft carrier.

*Photos by Justin M. Lubin*

David turns to God
for help.

Stone stands atop
Megiddo, confident
of victory.

*Photos by Justin M. Lubin*

The Latin forces sweep in from the east.

Stone's forces launch a counterattack.

*Photos by Justin M. Lubin*

The Beast has David right where he wants him.

American soldiers attempt to hold back Stone's relentless forces.

*Photos by Justin M. Lubin*

# CHAPTER
# THIRTY-SIX

Treachery, though at first very cautious,
in the end betrays itself.

—Livy


Do not presume too much upon my love;
I may do that I shall be sorry for.

—William Shakespeare, *Julius Caesar*

Stone sat before a bank of television monitors in his downstairs office. David walked around the room uncomfortably, wondering how much Stone had seen—or heard—of his encounter with Gabriella. Stone was the first to break the ice.

"I don't know whether to say 'I'm sorry' or 'congratulations,' David. I suppose both would be appropriate, under the circumstances. Benson seemed a fine..."

A strong, firm voice interrupted Stone's finessed opening.

"You did it."

Stone swiveled around in his chair to face David, laughing.

"*I* did it? I did what, David—killed Benson? Really, David, your imagination is quite vivid. What do you think—that I reached into his chest—in front of you and your entire Secret Service—and gave your president a massive coronary?"

Stone was making David feel like a flustered child, and he resented it. "Yes...no...look, Stone, I know what you did. I just don't know how you did it." David paused, then looked over at Stone, dead serious. "It seems that everyone who opposes you ends up dead."

David forced Stone to meet his eyes. *Yes, there it was again. That bond. That unspeakable, unfathomable bond between them. Both of them felt it, but neither of them spoke of it.*

"I will not accept that responsibility. But neither will I deny that I have benefited from my enemies' misfortunes."

David leaped on him, metaphorically speaking. "*Misfortunes?* Either you're the luckiest man on earth or..." David stopped. He really didn't know where to go, what piece to move. Stone easily took over, filling the space in the conversation with a warm, convivial remonstration.

"My brother. A decade since I have seen you, and *this* is what you want to talk about?" Stone's eyes smiled at him, and David did, indeed, feel guilt. He was confused. Stone was the master of confusing issues, confusing people.

"I'm...I'm sorry, Stone. But I think it's understandable that I'm pretty shaken by the day's events." He found his mouth turning up into a sad smile in spite of himself. "But you're right, Stone; it has been a long time."

*The brothers now locked eyes for a long moment, each sizing the other up, much like the day they first met at the Francini Academy. All those feelings swelled up in both men. Feelings that had nothing whatever to do with their meeting that day, but was "unfinished business" strictly between the two of them.*

*David couldn't help but notice that Stone, despite his recent near tragedy, looked exactly the same as the last time they met. Even younger, perhaps. Now, David thought, it was* he *who appeared the older of the two.*

"So, what's your secret, Stone? You have some secret fountain you've been drinking from?"

Stone looked puzzled. "Why is that, David?"

"Why...you look so young!"

Stone laughed out loud. "No. No fountain of youth, David. It is my work that keeps me young."

David frowned. "I wish I could say the same."

Stone cocked his head to one side, leaning forward toward David. "You could—if you were on the right side."

There was a long, pregnant pause. Then Stone whispered, almost seductively. "Why have you stayed away, David?"

David was taken aback by the question—jolted, in fact. "Boy, Stone. That's a good one! Well, I had...good reason, plenty of good reasons—to think you didn't want me around. Besides, it seemed like we were following different roads..."

Stone laughed out loud. "But 'all roads lead to Rome.' These same roads have now brought us back together, and with a most fortuitous timing."

David sighed, recalling the tragic incidents of the day. "I'd hardly call the president's death 'fortuitous.'"

Stone raised an eyebrow. "No? It certainly is for *you*, Mr. *President*. Now, we can truly be like brothers, for the first time. We can work together."

David stood up, holding up his hands. "Whoa, now, Stone. Wait a minute. My views on this subject are the same as Benson's. I have no interest or intention of joining your 'New World Order.' And the U.S. is not the only holdout, as you well know."

Stone paused strategically, as if thinking something through, when in actuality this was all part of a carefully conceived plan.

"Well, as I see it, David, with the North American Zone in, the Latins and the Chinese would quickly follow. They'd have no choice."

David shook his head vehemently. "Of course they'd have a choice! My joining with you would have nothing to do with their decision."

Stone held up a finger. "No. The North American Zone is the key, and they know it. They wouldn't dare hold out once you gave your endorsement."

David exhaled emphatically. "No. I will not join. America will not be party to whatever it is you're doing." He stared at Stone accusingly. "I'm not saying I understand what you're trying to do, Stone, but I know in my heart that it isn't right."

Stone pulled out all the punches. "*Right?* You've seen the polls! You know that the American public supports the One World. If you resist me, you're going to have trouble with your own people. They want to share in the great New World I am creating. Why wouldn't they?"

"Well, brother, I'll just have to let the chips fall where they may. I'm sorry, but there is no place for me in your...scheme."

Stone's face fell. He hadn't anticipated such active resistance. He tried another approach, lowering his voice now, adopting a wounded and nostalgic attitude.

"I am truly hurt, David. I have always been so happy to help you achieve your dreams. First a congressman, then a senator, a vice president—and now, well, you're 'The Man.'"

David only grew more indignant. "What do you mean, *help* me, Stone? How have you ever helped me?"

Stone was deliberately vague on this point. "Well, let's just say that...I just saw where you wanted to go, and I helped you to get there. It's fairly simple, David."

David became furious at Stone's implication. "Look, Stone—every office I've obtained has been through my own hard work and the people's choice...I'm an elected official..."

Stone laughed aloud. "You really are so naïve, David. As if elections had anything to do with power..."

David began shouting. "What are you getting at, Stone—that you got me my jobs? You're trying to tell me that my long-lost brother—who hasn't even seen fit to contact me over the past ten years—has helped me get where I am today?"

A look of profound pain came over Stone's face. "You may not have seen me, David, but I have seen you. Many times. And I've wanted nothing but the best for you. I would hate..." His voice trailed off.

David got in his face. "You would hate what?"

"Well...I would hate to see anything happen to you, that's all."

David sucked in a deep breath. "Is that a threat, Stone?

"You are my brother, David. My own flesh and blood. I would never harm you."

David became overwhelmed with long-repressed rage. "Really? Is that why you tried to burn me to death in my crib?"

Stone's eyes opened wide. "Really? You remember that?"

David moved in even closer. "No, I don't remember it, Stone. But I know it. I *feel* it. I've *seen* it..."

Stone completed the sentence for him. "In your visions, David?"

David was completely knocked out by this. *How did he know?*

221

Stone remained calm. "David, don't you think that if I had wanted you dead, you would have died in that crib?" David was speechless. "I want you alive. I want you by my side. I need you."

David was horrified. It *was* true! All those "apocryphal stories," the chattering of the nannies when they thought he was long asleep. The visions of burning, falling into the abyss...Stone's voice thankfully interrupted what could have easily become another of David's horrible visions. Seeing himself in the crib—the doors of hell gaping wide before his innocent soul.

"There are many in your own Congress who see things my way. If you try to rise against them, you'll fail, and I won't be there to help you anymore. How could I be, when it would then be entirely against my own best interests? Think about that, David."

But David was unwavering. "Stone, you don't stand a chance in hell of getting what you want!"

Once again Stone laughed out loud. But this laugh did nothing to ease the tension between them; it only increased it. "Oh, trust me, little brother. I always have a chance in hell, David."

The brothers seemed to have reached an impasse. Stone had to hand it to his brother. He was a true Alexander—he would not fold. Stone admired him for this. He crossed over to the wall of video monitors, sighing deeply. "Really, David, I didn't want things to go like this. Especially when it's been so long since we've seen each other. But honestly, you give me no alternative."

David's ears perked up immediately at this, like a dog picking up a high-pitched noise in the distance. He was on alert, ready for anything. Stone picked up the remote video controller, waving David over to him. Cradling the controller in his hands as if it were some kind of secret weapon, Stone looked over at David, almost apologetically.

"This is, as you'll see, a rather rhetorical question, David. Of course, you remember the night our father died?"

David was riveted by Stone's performance, wondering what the next act would be. He replied mechanically, no trace of emotion on his face. "Yes, I remember."

"Well," Stone rejoined, "I wonder what all those senators and congressmen and all those 'little folks down on the farm' might think if they saw this..."

Stone pressed a button, and suddenly, the wall of monitors came alive with image and sound. At first, David had no idea what he was seeing. But he concentrated and thought he could make out the inside of the old Francini house. Stunned—he saw his father on the screen. He looked just as he did the last time David had seen him alive—old and tired. This must have been filmed just before his death. David involuntarily shuddered as he thought, *What is this about?* But before he could wonder for too long, the video continued to unfold, telling a story, and David could do nothing but watch—eyes riveted to the screen.

The video image showed David arguing with his father, calling him "a tyrannical brute"; he saw himself struggling with the old man, and finally, pushing him off the balcony of Francini's office. Stone froze the video image on the elder Alexander, arms flailing, halfway over the balustrade, sheer terror in his eyes. It was hideous beyond description.

David could do nothing but shut his eyes. This was awful, hideous—the contorted image of his father's face as he confronted death. David was outraged and bewildered. Stone sat back down in his seat, calmly sipping an iced tea. David slowly opened his eyes, hoping this was just another vision, or perhaps a nightmare. But it was not. There was his father's face on the screen, frozen in fear of the unknown. David was both bewildered and hurt. He clenched his fists in fury. Stone, however, remained unruffled. In a lighthearted voice, he tossed off, "I rather think he looked more like you than like me, David. You can see it best in this close-up. What do you think?"

David didn't know what to do. He was filled with grief and rage, rendering him momentarily speechless. He looked over and saw Stone sitting there, cool as a cucumber, just waiting for his reaction. Finally, David had the strength to turn and face him. His first words were jumbled, incomprehensible.

"I just...I can't...I can't even think! What is it you want from me, Stone? You want to know what I think? What do I think? I think you're a heartless, soulless..."

David stopped himself in midstream. Seeing the cool expression on Stone's face only infuriated David more, and he paced around the room, fuming. Trying to come up with something to say. Something effective. Something "to the point." Finally, he turned back to Stone, seething with anger. "Stone, that never happened, and you know it!"

Stone was all sympathy. "Of course not, David! I know that. You know that. But let's just boil things down here. The fundamental point is, no one else knows it. How long do you think your moral constituency would follow a man whom they believed had murdered his own father? Even if you and I both know that you did not."

David sputtered, "But it's a fake—just a computer-generated sick joke!"

Stone commiserated, talking as if to a small child crying over a spilled ice cream cone. "But people won't know that, David. This was over a decade ago. People believe whatever they see on television. Father himself always said that. You yourself know that."

223

David stopped pacing. He finally comprehended what Stone was saying. He grasped the magnitude of his plan. At last he knew what he was up against: Join in with Stone, or have his reputation and career blown to bits. He mustered up all his confidence and confronted his brother face to face. His voice was quavering with emotion. "You would do this...you would use this against me? You, who just said you would do nothing to harm me not more than ten minutes ago?"

Stone looked over at David apologetically. "I will not harm you—physically. But I would do this, David, if you fail to see things my way, and, I should add, so that things will be crystal clear between us, I'd do far more besides."

David picked up a chair and hurled it at the video screen, smashing it to bits. His face was white with fury. Stone spoke to him condescendingly, each word driving a stake through David's heart. "David, this has nothing to do with you and me. It's more like that old film—what is it, *Casablanca*—where they say, 'This is bigger than the two of us.' It was a rather beautiful moment, if I recall. Well, it's rather corny, but in this case, it is nevertheless true. I do love you. You are my true brother, born of our same poor mother. But this *is* bigger than the two of us! You have no idea of the magnitude of my dream, my destiny!

"I have helped you, David, watched after you these many years, whether you want to believe it or not. I have always prayed that someday you would join your power with my own, and that united together, our power would be exponentially multiplied."

Calmer now, David walked over to Stone and stared at him for a long time—as if for the first time. The furrowless brow. The still boyish grin—unmarred by the inevitable wrinkles of middle age. David shook his head. "What happened to you, Stone? You've become like the picture of Dorian Gray. You're not even human anymore. I wonder if you ever were, or whether I just wanted so much to believe that you were that I thought it was true."

Their eyes met. Suddenly, something clicked. David heard himself saying the words he never thought he'd never even let himself think, never mind say aloud.

"You did it, Stone. You killed him. You killed Father..."

Stone merely opened his eyes as wide as he could, strangely, to David's mind, nonplussed by this accusation. "I despised him, true. But I never laid a hand on the man."

But now David was pressing for the truth. He had to know. "You never laid a hand on Benson, either, except to shake his hand, and now he's lying in the morgue! You killed him, Stone; you murdered our father! And now you're trying to make me the scapegoat!"

David's tirade finally succeeded in getting a rise out of Stone. *He felt long-suppressed emotions, human emotions, bubbling up inside of him—feelings that he had thought he had ridden himself of many years ago. He felt both pain and rage rising perilously close to the surface and hated David for causing it to happen.*

Stone exploded, his face beet red with fury. "You mean media mogul Daniel Alexander? *That* man my father? He was never a father to me. He was no kind of father to either one of us. He was merely the sperm donor. *My* father, my *true* father, is much more powerful. Invincible, in fact. He believes in loving and protecting his favorite son, as good fathers are meant to do!"

David fired back. "That father you fail to acknowledge must have been very psychic, Stone. He must have known exactly what sort of man he had fathered when he named you. *Stone!* How entirely fitting the name he gave you! Because that's what you are! Hard as a rock. Incapable of feeling..."

"Yes, and like a stone, I have existed for millennia, outliving generations of mortals. When all were dying around me, I lived—a stone is indestructible."

"A rock that feels no pain? An island that never cries?" David whispered.

Stone went right for David's Achilles heel. "Is that why you persist in trying to steal Gabriella away from me? Because you are so much *better* than I am, David? So much more in touch with your feelings...your 'animal instincts,' shall we say?"

*Touché.* David saw the bait, but didn't go for it, much to Stone's consternation. "No, Stone. It's not that I'm better than you are. It's just that I'm human."

Stone smiled, forging on in his attempt to enrage David. "For someone who is so inhuman, so incapable of feeling, it's odd that I should feel so sorry for you because you are 'carrying the torch,' as it were, for something that is merely mine alone."

David was losing control. He knew he had to get away from there—out of Stone's clutches—as soon as possible. He pulled his portable phone out of his pocket and pressed in a code. Then he turned back to Stone, anger in his eyes. "By 'something,' Stone—do you perhaps mean Gabriella? That's all she is to you, Stone—a *thing*. And yet, you keep her under virtual house arrest! It seems you can't be happy unless everything on God's green earth is yours alone. And the sad part, Stone—the irony is that you won't be happy even if you get it! How can you ever know true happiness if you are incapable of feeling it?"

Stone smirked, haughty now. "*When* I get it. And you're wrong about that, David. Not only will I be happy, but I will also be amply rewarded. And I will have Gabriella at my side as my queen."

David spoke into his portable. "Get me back to Air Force One!"

Stone saw his last chance with David slipping away. He appeared greatly agitated. This was not the way he planned it. This was not how this was supposed to work out. He moved in front of David—sounding more genuine now than he had before. There was something in his tone that indicated that he might be speaking sincerely, perhaps for the first time in his life.

"David, please. Make a bargain with me. Join with me. I will...I will let you have Gabriella. Then, we shall both finally have what we have always wanted. You shall have her—and I shall have my brother."

David could only stare at Stone with a combination of fascination and pity.

"It would be a great trade-off for each of us. You throw in your lot with me, and you get Gabriella. I get my brother, my equal, my twin soul—but I lose my wife. My queen. We both stand to gain much and to lose much by this deal. And yet, David, I offer it to you. I believe that it is a pact that Gabriella would agree to gladly."

David couldn't believe what he was hearing. Surely this was another one of Stone's sarcastic jokes. He looked over at his face and saw that he was deadly serious. "Stone, I...that's an incredible proposition. Really incredible. I'm so flattered."

It was such an incredible proposition that David surprised himself by actually thinking it over. Would it be worth throwing in with Stone in order to get Gabriella? And he'd get his brother back to boot. It was a tempting offer. A decidedly tempting bargain. But after clearing his mind for a moment, he realized how ludicrous the proposal was. He tried to let his brother down as gently as he could.

"I've got to hand it to you, Stone; you sweetened the pot so much that you actually had me thinking about your crazy scheme. But I realize that you meant your offer in good faith, and I want you to know I appreciate it. I truly do. I think you were willing to make quite a concession to have me join with you, giving up Gabriella. I think that was a noble, generous offer. But, unfortunately, I could only accept Gabriella into my life if she chose to come to me—because she wanted to, not because she'd been instructed to. Otherwise, there would be no joy in it. How would I know she wouldn't be pining away after you, lying there in my arms?"

Stone demurred. "I doubt that sincerely."

"And as for you always wanting me, wanting a brother—you have to remember that this is all news to me, Stone. You've never given me any indication that you wanted a relationship with me, of any kind, in the last twenty years..."

Stone interrupted, anxious to be heard, to be accepted. "But I did, David. I always did. From the first moment we met."

David looked at Stone's face now, plagued with doubt and self-recrimination. The man was the absolute master of disguises, he had decided.

"I wish I could say that I was happy to hear that, Stone, but right now, it just plants the dagger even deeper into my heart. I too wanted nothing more than a brother all my life. It wasn't easy growing up alone, with nothing but a nanny and schoolmasters to talk to. I needed a brother. My brother. *You.* But you turned your back on me, Stone! And now, it's too late."

Stone was actually speechless. His face fell, and he suddenly appeared his true age—perhaps for the first and last time in his life. Rick and several other Secret Service agents appeared at the door. Without looking back, David strode out of the room. Stone watched them go, and then drained his drink. In one motion, he crushed the glass, blood gushing out of his hand. He seemed impervious to the pain. Stone watched as the door shut behind David and his troop. He had never felt more alone in his life.

"Good-bye, little brother."

# CHAPTER
# THIRTY-SEVEN

I...will fight against them
with the sword of my mouth.

—Revelation 2:16

avid's motorcade moved through the sluggish traffic on Rome's *Via Del Corso*. On a street filled with minis and Vespas, it was like trying to maneuver a whale through a school of restless sharks. David sat across from Rick, on a video conference with his now vice president, Charles Breckenridge. "We're heading for the airfield now. I want a full Cabinet meeting as soon as we touch down."

Breckenridge saw naked defiance in David's eyes. "David, please. Don't buck your brother. It's a battle you can't win. It just isn't worth it."

David yelled back, clearly in charge. "You're the vice president of the United States now, Charlie! If you don't think the country is worth fighting for, you'd better resign. Over and out!"

David clicked off the video screen with a loud sigh. Suddenly the limousine stopped short. David's body was propelled forward—almost smashing into the glass separating him and Rick from the driver.

"What the hell—?"

The panic-stricken driver spoke into the microphone. "It's Jeeps, Mr. President, blocking the road!"

Rick and David looked through the side window. Two Italian Army Jeeps had indeed set up a roadblock. Soldiers with machine guns slung across their chests signaled the limousine to come to a halt. The Secret Service men in the back seat instantly produced MP-5K submachine guns from under their jackets and extended the stocks. Rick cautioned them, "Steady, now. We don't want to start an international incident unless we have to."

David looked over to Rick for their next move. "I say we stop and see what they want."

Before they got a chance to ask, the soldiers opened fire on the limo. Armor-piercing nine-millimeter shells tattooed a line of spider-web cracks across the limo's bulletproof windshield.

David remained calm. "OK...now we know what they want." He leaned over and shouted into the microphone, "Get us the hell out of here!"

The driver stomped on the gas pedal, and the limousine rocketed forward—scattering the soldiers and battering the two light Jeeps aside. The soldiers regained their momentum, jumped into their Jeeps and tore off after the limo. But the traffic was at a virtual standstill. The frantic limousine driver veered up onto the sidewalk and cut across a crowded square—pedestrians leaped out of the way as the two-ton rocket smashed through a magazine kiosk.

As Army vehicles bounced across the cobblestone square, the soldiers fired their weapons at the fleeing limo, their bullets cutting down innocent bystanders.

One of the Jeeps raced ahead of the other and pulled alongside the limo. David's eyes grew wide with fear as he saw the gun muzzle pointing right at him. SLAM! The limo driver cut the wheel to the right and battered the Jeep out of the way. The Jeep careened out of control and plowed into a fountain—tossing the soldiers into the air.

David retained his cool. Rick shouted to the driver, "Get the hell out of here! There's too many people...!"

Rick turned to David. "David, keep your head down!" Bullets continued to ricochet off the limo's well-reinforced body. The driver squinted through the cracked windshield, searching for a way out.

In the one remaining Jeep, the soldier on the passenger side attached a rifle grenade to the muzzle brake on his AR-70 rifle. The limousine sliced sideways as the driver threw the wheel to the left. Wheels skidded—leaving a trail of smoke as the driver accelerated toward a narrow side street.

David, Rick and the others were slammed forward once again as the limousine hit the end of the too narrow street and stopped dead; the impact was so severe that it blasted the windows out of the vehicle.

David instinctively scrambled out his door and started to run up the narrow street. Rick climbed out and rushed after him. "David! David! Get back in the car! David!"

One of the soldiers fired his rifle grenade—WHOOSH! The limousine exploded—shattering store windows for blocks. David was thrown to the street as the car behind him erupted into a fireball. David got right back on his feet, running for his life.

The soldiers saw their target running away, but they couldn't follow around the flaming wreck of the limo. They jumped back into the Jeep as it whirled around, tearing out of the square.

David jogged down the street, taking an inventory of his arms and legs. Still there. He ran his hand through his hair—no blood. He saw lights and heard music and people up ahead. Breathing heavily, he ran into the *Campus Martius*. The square in front of the Roman Pantheon was filled with tourists and nighttime revelers eating and drinking at outdoor cafés. David ducked into the dense crowd.

*SCREECH*—!

He turned at the sound of brakes squealing and people screaming. The Jeep had pulled up onto the road behind him.

David angled for the sidewalk and a row of Vespas parked in front of the *Trattoria Cinzia*. The sidewalk was filled with terrified pedestrians. David leaped over the row of Vespas, looking for a way out.

The Jeep plowed into the row of scooters, knocking them down like bowling pins. David was just one step ahead of them. David leaped onto the back of a parked Mercedes sedan and rolled over its hood, then back to his feet, running alone down the middle of the street.

The persistent Jeep flung the last Vespa aside, but the driver couldn't turn the Jeep quickly enough to avoid hitting the parked Mercedes. David didn't stop to look back, waiting any moment for bullets to rip his body to shreds, when suddenly a Fiat slid to a stop no more than two feet in front of him. The driver jumped out of the car and began a tirade in Italian. *"Che stupido! Che cosa stai facendo? Madonna mia..."*

David ignored the raging Italian. He turned to look behind him. No Jeep! He uttered a sigh of relief, stopping to catch his breath. Suddenly, a hand grabbed hold of his shoulder. David whirled around to see Rick, agitated and exhausted. He looked at David sternly.

"OK, here's the deal. I protect you. You stay with me so that I can protect you; got it?" David managed a smile as Rick put an affectionate arm around his shoulder. "That was a very nasty scene. You could've gotten yourself blown to shreds! Mr. President, David, please, don't ever run away from me again. For a minute there, I thought I was going to lose *two* presidents in one day! I couldn't even have gotten a job shoveling it in Louisiana! Can't you show a hard-working man a little mercy?"

David managed a weak smile at another of Rick's always priceless comedic gems; they always seemed to come at exactly the right time, too—just when he really needed to laugh or to lose his mind completely. He didn't know what he'd do without Rick. He was just about the only stabilizing force in his life, and he supposed that Rick felt pretty much the same way. The deal was implicit: They took care of each other.

David and Rick finally shared a good laugh over the incredulity of the whole situation. The uncomprehending Fiat driver finally got back in his car, still cursing under his breath as the two men went off arm in arm.

*"Americanos..."*

Rick pulled the new president around the corner, and the two men disappeared like gypsies into the foggy Roman night.

# CHAPTER
# THIRTY-EIGHT

Take therefore no thought for the morrow; for the morrow shall take thought for the things of itself. Sufficient unto the day is the evil thereof.

—Matthew 6:34

No one was allowed to enter Stone Alexander's "meditation room," or, as he sometimes called it, "his inner sanctum." No one, not even Gabriella—especially not Gabriella—ever. There was much there to want to keep hidden. A huge, crackling fireplace on one wall faced a huge fresco of the crucifixion of Jesus Christ. Stone paced before the painting, hurling vile epithets at the colorful depiction of his immortal enemy.

"Two thousand years of power. Can You feel it coming to an end? First, You cast down my immortal father into the pits of Sheol. Then, when it looked like they had all but forgotten Your very existence, You sent down Your mortal son to try to win them back with love. And You saw how well that worked! They *murdered* Him! Haven't You learned that mortals are filled with hate? That they understand nothing but hate? They will abandon Your Son, just as You abandoned my father."

Stone moved over to an altar covered with a black cloth and satanic relics. A gold chalice. An athame. Picking up the well-sharpened athame, he carefully opened a vein on his left forearm, his blood dripping out onto the floor. He dipped a wand into the blood and flicked the blood so that it splattered the face of the crucified Jesus.

"Taste that? Does it taste good? I've had to swallow my pride for two thousand years! Well, now it's going to be Your turn!"

A knock at the door stopped him in mid-rant. Stone became enraged. "What is it? I told you never to bother me here!"

A chastened voice came through the thick door. "I'm very sorry, Chancellor. I thought you'd want to know that the American president made it to his plane."

Stone paused, looking over at the painting. "Thank you."

He heard the footsteps rushing back down the hall. Stone stood riveted before the fireplace, blotting the blood on his arm with a black silk handkerchief. "In the scheme of things, my earthly brother is but a minor inconvenience."

Stone stared into the myriad shadows cast by the flickering fire. The shadows drew in upon themselves and slowly congealed into the form of the Guardian. Stone stared into the Guardian's powerful blue eyes. "It is time."

The Guardian beamed back at him in adulation.

# $\Omega^2$

Stone climbed to the top of his castle, looking out over the twinkling lights of Rome. He smiled, raised his hands to the heavens and shouted. "Well? Are You ready?" There was nothing but silence. Stone waited, lips quivering. "Bring it on, I say!"

In the distance, Stone heard thunder. A cautious smile formed around the edges of his mouth. Within moments, fire began to rain down from the sky. Now, the smile erupted into a bold, satisfied smirk. He nodded prophetically. "My will be done," he said, still addressing his heavenly adversary.

# CHAPTER
# THIRTY-NINE

A sound of battle is in the land,
and of great destruction.

—Jeremiah 50:22

n a French schoolyard, a husky fourth-grade schoolboy kicked a soccer ball over to his friends. The ball scooted across the playground, and three boys scrambled for it—knocking the smallest of the boys down. The fourth grader, Etienne, ran over to the smaller boy crying on the ground.

"Are you all right?" Etienne said. The little boy sat there on the ground as the other boys ran off with the ball. Etienne noticed that the boy had scraped his knee. He bent down and looked at it. "*C'est dommage*," Etienne said kindly. "I guess that was my fault, Paul."

Paul looked up at the older boy, embarrassed that he was crying. "I don't want them to see me crying. They won't let me play anymore!"

"Don't worry," Etienne reassured him. They'll have to answer to me if they try that!" Paul managed a weak smile, staring in terror at the blood running down his leg.

Etienne dug into his pockets and extracted some of the objects you'd expect to find in a ten-year-old's pockets—some loose change, trading cards, a few crumbs from this morning's hastily consumed croissant and finally, a dirty, crumpled tissue.

Etienne shook the crumbs out of the tissue and blotted the blood on the younger boy's knee. "Now, you have to apply pressure to it. That will make the bleeding stop."

"Are you sure?" Paul said, obviously scared.

Etienne pressed on the wound with his dirty tissue, which instantly soaked up the excess blood. "Voilà," Etienne said, remembering how scared he used to get when he got a bloody nose or a scraped knee when he was only in the first grade. It had always seemed like a terrible tragedy—like nothing would ever stop the blood. But his father had shown him this trick, and it always worked. He tried to be brave so that the little boy wouldn't feel so lonely and scared.

"Do you want me to walk you home?" Etienne asked.

"I don't know if I can walk," Paul replied, still choking back his tears.

"*D'accords*," Etienne said. "It'll feel much better once you start to walk on it. Trust me."

Etienne held out his hand to the younger boy, still sitting on the pavement. He nervously held out his hand, letting the bigger boy help him to his feet. "See?" Etienne said. "That doesn't hurt so much now, does it?"

It did hurt, but Paul was determined to be brave. "*Oui. C'est ne pas trop mal.*"

Suddenly, the boys heard a loud, rumbling sound echoing off the buildings. The boys playing soccer stopped their game, looking up to see a squadron of Apache helicopters roaring overhead, heading toward the Eiffel Tower.

"*Quest-ce-que c'est?*" Etienne yelled out to one of his friends, as

239

the boys picked up their soccer ball and huddled together in the middle of the schoolyard.

The boys shrugged their shoulders, almost in unison. "*Je ne sais pas,*" one of them said, his eyes glued to the skies where the copters were just passing overhead.

Etienne looked over at Paul, still clutching his wounded knee. Wordlessly, he took the boy's hand. Before any of them knew what was happening, hailstones began to fall—hailstones the size of soccer balls. The boys were stunned, rooted to the ground.

Paul yelled out, "*Je ne sais rien de qui ce passe!*"

Etienne grabbed Paul's hand, running out of the schoolyard. All the others followed Etienne's lead, scrambling for cover. "*Foutons le camp!*" Etienne screamed, as he pulled Paul past the chunks of ice smashing into parked cars—crushing their roofs and blasting out their windows. The soccer squad hastily dispersed. Etienne looked around for a place to hide, finally deciding on an old school bus parked right outside the school gates.

"*Vite! Vite!*" Etienne yelled, rolling Paul's slight body under the bus and following quickly after him. The boys lay there in silence, listening to the sound of the enormous ice mallets pounding down on the bus, shaking it like a roller coaster. They clung to each other in terror.

$$\Omega^2$$

In the heart of gay Paris, the ice spheres pummeled the city to its knees. The area surrounding the Eiffel Tower was filled with tour buses, and now, thousands of tourists visiting the city's main attraction scrambled for cover—screaming in a cacophony of foreign languages. The tour guides yelled into their microphones, "Everyone back on the buses! Please! Take cover inside the buses!" But the tourists weren't listening. They were hysterical, running around screaming, as the icy cannon balls smashed at them furiously.

But it was not only people who were in peril. The Eiffel Tower itself was battered by the barrage from the heavens. Many of the tourists had foolishly clustered beneath the Tower, believing it indestructible, and there was screaming as its steel girders buckled with a loud groan. The tourists bellowed, trying in vain to escape from beneath the steel mausoleum. But it was as useless as trying to escape from Pompeii after the volcano.

Tottering on its axis, the Tower finally collapsed onto the street below, amidst the unearthly sound of groaning steel. Thousands lay wounded and dying beneath the tonnage, moaning and crying out for aid. But not a soul dared go to their rescue.

# CHAPTER FORTY

O Lord, what shall I say, when Israel turneth their backs before their enemies!

—Joshua 7:8

Moving down from a Jerusalem skyline dominated by the Dome of the Rock, a young schoolboy ran through the ancient, narrow streets. It was Jacob Levy, the same boy to whom Stone had given a New Testament at the excavation site at Megiddo. The shopkeepers waved and called out to him as he passed. The young boy passed the Wailing Wall, weaving by a squad of Israeli soldiers carrying M-16s. He stopped at the wall for a moment to pray. As he stood there, a shadow passed over his face. He looked at the sky, and his eyes grew wide with shock. The sun's edges were turning black and beginning to flake away like crumbs falling off burnt toast. Terrified, the young boy ran on, huffing and puffing in fear.

$$\Omega^2$$

Inside the Knesset the conference table was packed with Israel's primary decision-makers: the prime minister, politicians and military leaders, as well as the chief rabbi. Rabbi Aaron Levy was engaged in a heated argument with a top Israeli Army general. "We do not need Americans. We have the Almighty! *He* is our protector."

The prime minister frowned, seeing that things were getting nowhere. Diplomatically, he suggested, "Gentlemen, perhaps we should take a short recess?"

The men and women nodded in agreement and dispersed. Only the chief rabbi, clad in a dark blue robe and prayer shawl, remained in the room, collecting his papers. The young boy came dashing into the room, bumping into a steward and sending a tray of water flying. But he didn't care. He ran up to the rabbi, pulling on his robe. "Father! The sun! It's crumbling! Look!"

The boy pulled open the curtains, revealing the darkening sun. His father stepped back in horror. Jacob pulled off his backpack and nervously fished out a book. At first, he held it behind his back, then finally got up the nerve to hold it before him. His father's eyes opened wide with anger when he saw it was a copy of the New Testament.

"What are you doing with that, Jacob?"

"In the Gentile New Testament, Father, Jesus-Yeshua says that before His return the sun would be blackened and..."

His father's eyes filled with fury. Ashen-faced, he grabbed the Bible and threw it across the room.

"Jacob! You disgrace me with blasphemies! *Cheelool hashem!*"

But the boy was insistent, still pulling on his father's robe in an attempt to get him to listen. "Father, please—listen to me! Remember the man I told you I met at Megiddo? It was he who told me to read the New Testament. The Book of Revelation..."

"And *I* have told you, the old ways are the best ways. The Old Testament is the *only* Bible. The only true word of God. You are but a boy. Leave the work of God to the men of God."

But Jacob persisted. "But Father, the man said..."

Rabbi Levy was furious now. "The man said? *What* man? What man was this, trying to lead you away from the teachings of your father and your father's fathers? Was this the prophet Elijah himself—with a special message only for you? Or was it some demon incarnate, trying to turn you from the ways of the true God?"

Despite his bravado, and having just reduced his son to tears, the rabbi turned once more to the window, standing transfixed before the warning in the sky.

$$\Omega^2$$

Jerusalem and Paris were not the only places where strange events were occurring at a lightning pace. Apocalyptic warnings were ravishing all the wonders of the modern world.

The Taj Mahal was experiencing a hailstorm just like its Parisian counterpart—the Eiffel Tower. While thousands of tourists and native Indians alike visited the elegant palace, walking amidst its peaceful gardens, they were jolted as the savage ice mallets began to rain from the skies.

Thousands fled for cover, but there was no cover to be found. Many hundreds were inside the building, oblivious to what was going on outside, when the magnificent edifice began to quake. People ran to the windows, witnessing the unearthly ice storm turning tourists into bloodied heaps on the sacred ground. Everyone panicked—rushing for the stairs—trying to get out. Trying to get *somewhere.*

But going outside was not the answer. As a crowd fled the quaking building, huge chunks of the parapets fell into the courtyard, crushing countless visitors beneath them. The air was filled with the screams of the dying, trapped beneath the tonnage of what used to be one of the most magnificent palaces the modern world had ever created. Now, it was no more than a jigsaw puzzle for future archeologists to reconstruct.

Only a hairsbreadth from what used to be the Taj Mahal, a group of Indian teenaged boys, many of them cut and bruised from the hailstorm, approached the crest of a hill overlooking a herd of sacred cattle grazing in what had been lush grass, but now covered with a blanket of fine crushed ice. Armed with a plethora of weapons—axes, hammers, scythes—the boys formed a mob, a mob that wanted revenge. Revenge for what the blitz had done to their homes, to their families—many wounded or dead. They wanted blood for blood.

The young man in charge uttered the battle cry. Yelling out in one united primal scream, the boys rushed the placid animals with their weapons, mangling and mutilating them—until every last one of the sacred cattle had been bludgeoned to death. It was an eerie reenactment of some ancient Dionysiac rite, where the followers of Bacchus, the god of nature, were imbued with preternatural strength and tore their god to pieces in a ritualistic sacrifice.

Their blood lust sated, the boys sank down exhausted on the icy grass, breathing hard, seemingly frozen in place, the blood of the cattle passing over them until the whole field glimmered with fresh blood. As the warm blood began melting the ice, the boys began, one by one, to come to their senses—realizing the enormity of the sacrilege they had just committed.

As the world was literally collapsing around them, people were losing their grip on reality. The things they had held sacred were gone. The world seemed to be going mad.

# CHAPTER
# FORTY-ONE

She stretcheth out her hand to the poor; yea,
she reacheth forth her hands to the needy.

—Proverbs 31:20

Seven heavily guarded limousines were parked outside the main gates to Stone Alexander's Roman castle. Seven world leaders, the chairmen of the World Union zones, sat around a huge, semicircular table, presided over by Chancellor Alexander. Armed soldiers lined the walls and the windows. The leader of the Northern European Zone was hysterical.

"They're rioting in the streets of London. Paris. Dublin. They think it's the bloody end of the world!"

Stone raised an eyebrow. "I am absolutely astonished! Are the people so quick to forget how much we have done for them?"

The leader of the African Zone spoke now, ever so cautiously. "My people are not ungrateful, Sir, but when a hailstorm destroys a third of our continent's vegetation, there is bound to be some...resistance among the people."

The leader of the Arab sector threw in his two cents. "There are many factions growing, Chancellor, dissident factions. We must construct a unilateral policy to deal with them..."

Stone raised his hands as the representatives grew quiet. "You seven. You loyal seven. Without you, there'd be no chance of uniting the world into one seamless unit. Cease your worrying. There are plans underway even as we speak to bring your populations back in line."

There was a murmuring among all the delegates.

"But we don't have enough troops," the head of the Russian sector protested.

Stone shook his head. "You misunderstand me. Force will not be necessary! Your troops will make their presence known, yes, but only to comfort the populace, not to control them."

"But what about the renegade zones? What will we do about them?" the Russian leader blustered. "The Chinese have two hundred million soldiers on our border..."

Stone rose to his feet. The meeting was at its conclusion. Stone nodded for the armed guards to open the door and escort the disgruntled delegates to their limos. Stone addressed them all *en masse*.

"Everyone—you have trusted me before, and I must ask you to trust me again. Especially during this most trying of times. The final solution *is* underway. All will be settled at Megiddo. On that, you have my word."

The assembled leaders stopped in their tracks, exchanging looks. Megiddo? What, or where, on earth was *Megiddo?* To them, it was no less baffling than if he'd said, "It will all be settled at Morgan Creek." They had absolutely no frame of reference from which to understand that comment. They realized that they'd better find out what, and where, Megiddo was—and fast!

Stone stood at the door, shaking each representative's hand as he left. When they had all gone, Stone was startled to see Gabriella standing alone, framing the doorway. She seemed aghast. Stone tried to make light of things. "Hello, my dear."

But Gabriella had no intention of letting this go. The great strength of that long line of Francini generals instilled her with inner strength and resolve. "What did you mean by that, Stone?"

Stone took Gabriella's arm and tried to lead her out of earshot of the guards, but she pulled out of his reach. Stone was clearly startled. "Gabriella?"

"'The final solution is under way.' What does that mean, Stone? What were you plotting in there?"

"Gabriella, darling, it's nothing for you to worry about. You must understand. These are powerful leaders, from cultures very different from our own. They all have different value systems—so, if I am to lead them, I must tell them what they want to hear. Your father taught me that a long time ago."

But Gabriella was not taken in. "Is that what you're doing now, Stone? Telling *me* what you think I want to hear? Millions of people are dying, in every one of your 'zones'—and I don't see you lifting a finger to do anything about it! You don't even seem to care!"

"But that's your job, darling," Stone joked. Stone tried to pull Gabriella in for a hug, but she resisted. "Darling, you must understand. These people are but pebbles in the pond."

Gabriella stared at him in horror. "The...pond? What pond is this?"

Stone replied matter-of-factly. "My pond. They are necessary casualties, my dear. Unfortunate, but necessary. For the good of all mankind, of course." Gabriella backed away from him, seeing Stone as he truly was for perhaps the first time in her life.

"I...I don't understand this. David warned me. He said that anyone who got in your way ended up dead. I didn't want to believe him. But he was right!"

Stone put a reassuring arm around his wife. She felt a chill rush through her body, as if a corpse had reached out for her.

"My brother, Gabriella, is looking for answers to the tragedies and disappointments in his own life. He's chosen to demonize me to absolve himself of any guilt or wrongdoing. You must not believe anything he says against me." He looked her in the eyes, trying to make her feel guilty. "And we both know that my brother has, shall we say, 'ulterior motives' to try and turn you against me."

Gabriella remained stiff in his arms, the stench of death filling her nostrils. Stone continued to try and lull her into complacency. "Just answer me one question, my dearest. If I didn't care about the people, about the future of the world, why would I have spent my entire fortune creating systems to feed the poor? To purify the water all over the globe so people wouldn't die of thirst or of dysentery? Encouraging you to go out and feed the homeless and blanket the blanketless? Why would I even encourage such activities if I were so bad?"

Stone saw that Gabriella remained unmoved. "Will you deny I've done these things?"

Grudgingly, Gabriella nodded. "Yes, you have done *these* things. It is the *other* things that you have also done—and are now doing—that I question." Stone shook his head, trying not to display his anger. He spoke through clenched teeth.

"Thanks to my dear brother. He arrives here for one afternoon, and suddenly, a lifetime of trust between us is in doubt."

"Don't blame David, Stone. There is nothing sudden about this. I have had my doubts for a long time."

He ignored her words and caressed her face. Again, a chill coursed through her body. *Why had she never felt it before? Or had she just failed to acknowledge it?*

"If I am such a villain, my darling, why have you stayed with me all these years? Why didn't you run off with David when he begged you to ten years ago? Or when he asked you again yesterday?"

Gabriella sighed. It was useless to deny anything, impossible to hide anything from Stone. "*Could* I have left yesterday, Stone, even if I wanted to...and remained alive?"

Stone feigned the utmost dismay. "Gabriella! What a terrible thing to say. I have always been completely devoted to you..."

"I am not denying that," Gabriella replied.

"If you truly love David, or if you love David more than me, I would simply have to understand. It's not all relations between men and women that are lucky enough to survive so many years, particularly, so many happy years. At least, they've been happy years for *me*."

Stone's "confession" had the desired effect. Gabriella felt terribly guilty. She lied through her teeth. "I don't love David, Stone." Stone read the lie on her face instantly. She was a terrible liar.

"I am glad of that," he replied. "But I want you to know that I told him yesterday that if you wanted to leave me, the choice was yours. The door was open. Only a fool tries to bind people to himself. It is only the Almighty to whom we are each inextricably bound—forever."

250

Gabriella was shaken by this information, but didn't buy it. Not anymore. "You would have given me up, Stone? Your 'most precious possession'?"

Stone looked up at the heavens. "Darling, my most precious possession is my relationship with my father. You see, Gabriella, I understand human frailty, perhaps even better than you do—even with all your Santa Lucia ministering to the masses. And I do believe, by way of a compliment, that you've done old Lucia one better!"

Gabriella was confused, conflicted, guilt-stricken and buoyed by the overwhelming compliment, but still paralyzed by doubts. "I only do what I can do. All I meant was, Stone, I don't understand you..."

Stone smiled generously. "It has always been said that the greatest men would be misunderstood in their own time—and I suppose this is the case with me. Another little axiom I picked up from Generale Francini..."

Gabriella moved in closer to Stone, softening her tone. "Stone, I am truly sorry if you feel misunderstood. I try—I have always tried, to understand you. It is your methods that I don't understand. Perhaps that is my failing. One day you are compassion itself, feeding the poor and helpless, and that person—that method, I understand. But now, I'm seeing old women dying in the streets, as part of some 'master plan.' That 'method,' as you call it, is something I cannot understand, though I try to. But as much as I try, I can make no sense of it."

"You simply must trust me, Gabriella. It is a cruel world, my dearest. If I am to move it toward a lasting peace, which no man has ever even attempted, well then, as your father always said, 'sometimes the means must suit the ends,' as unpleasant as they may be. Believe me, I'm not relishing this upheaval any more than you do."

The constant mentioning of her father jolted Gabriella back to reality. *Why was she buying this total nonsense? How long would she continue to let this man con her? Her eyes burned with the fire of truth. For perhaps the first time in her life, she demanded a reckoning.*

Her voice was stronger than Stone had ever heard it before. "I wonder what my father would say, Stone, if he heard you twisting his old sayings to your own advantage? I can't help but feel that he is turning over in his grave right now."

Stone appeared wounded, but Gabriella, for once in her life, would not let him off the hook. "Stone, I am not an Army general; I am but a woman who seeks to help those in need. I will not deny that I have not the benefit of your vast experience. But that does not make my opinion worth less than anyone else's. And *this* is my opinion, Stone: What good is it to gain the whole world if you lose your soul in the bargain?"

Stone whirled her around to face him, laughing, his face lit up like the Christmas tree at Rockefeller Center. She couldn't imagine why her comment, spoken in the deepest sincerity, would strike him as the world's funniest joke. She certainly had not meant it as one. His transformation did not reassure her; it took her aback. "Gabriella, you must believe this above all things. I swear to you that *that* is *never* going to happen!"

Gabriella remained unconvinced. Stone turned back into the empty chamber, still chuckling to himself over his private joke. Gabriella followed him. "Stone—I have not finished. I have not even begun..."

Stone spoke to her like a parent to a petulant three-year-old. "We can go over all this again tonight, my dear, but right now I have to get back to work. You have my word that I am trying my best to set all things right."

He opened the door to his boardroom to let her out. Just as he was closing the door, she whispered to him. "Stone?"

He stopped and raised an eyebrow.

"Who *are* you?"

Her question made him stop momentarily. But he caught himself and smiled back at her winningly, looking strikingly—no, *exactly* like the cadet she had so willingly embraced in the Coliseum some thirty years before. But they both knew that those warm, loving embraces had stopped many years ago. Decades ago. Now, it was unusual for them to even be in this close proximity to each other. Perhaps that was why, she thought, she had never noticed the iciness, the deadly chill, which accompanied his touch.

"Why, who do you think I am, silly? The man you married!"

Stone shut the door to the boardroom, leaving a sorrowful Gabriella in the hallway. "Yes," she said aloud, "the man I married."

Gabriella walked slowly to the French doors leading outside to her garden. As she looked around her, she felt the blossoming flowers to be her only friends—and the only living, breathing things at Castle Alexander.

Her mind began to wander. She wondered what her life would have been like if she had taken David up on his proposition to go away with him so many years ago. She imagined them waking up together, laughing and playing with their children before a handsomely decorated Christmas tree; then she saw them taking their family hiking through the mountains. She laughed to herself, not even knowing if they were any mountains anywhere near Washington, D.C.!

252

As she stared at the brightly blooming flowers, she suddenly understood that she had been meant to be a mother, and it was a hole, an emptiness in her life, that had plagued her for years. The camellias. The fig trees. The stunning long-stemmed roses in varying shades of yellow and pale orange. They all proved it. Look how they grew! Everything she touched seemed to blossom under her soft, nurturing touch. Children. She sighed aloud.

Still holding on to that lovely vision of herself and David beneath the Christmas tree, Gabriella continued to indulge her fantasy. She saw the children she should have had, before it was too late. It was quite a group. There were two boys, one a sandy-haired twelve-year-old opening an ornately wrapped present. Another was younger, also a boy, sitting on a brand-new fire engine. He was squealing with joy. Then, at her feet, were two little girls—one, about five years old, with dark ringlets and black eyes—the spitting image of herself at that age. The age she had been when she first saw Stone. Finally, there was an infant girl, cuddled in David's arms, who also had her dark hair, but the penetrating blue eyes that belonged to all the Alexander men.

They would have blossomed and grown just like her garden, becoming healthy and strong men and women. She saw David as a doting father, nuzzling the infant girl in his arms while instructing the boys which presents they were to open next.

Gabriella felt calm and peaceful, knowing that somewhere, on some plane of existence, this reality must have occurred—or was it just *meant* to have occurred in this lifetime?

This thought evoked a profound sense of regret—of genuine loss—causing the whole lovely vision to disappear. Gabriella dissolved into a fit of tears. She had no sandy-haired young sons. She had no beautiful daughter who was her double. She had no one, except herself. Of one thing, she was absolutely sure: She did *not* have Stone. She wondered if she ever did.

# CHAPTER
# FORTY-TWO

O Israel: thou canst not stand before thine enemies,
until ye take away the accursed thing from you.

—Joshua 7:13


It's a hard rain's...gonna fall...

—Bob Dylan

F ar from Castle Alexander, across the Atlantic Ocean, was the
heart of the one earthly stronghold of democracy still hanging
on by a mere thread. Pennsylvania Avenue, in the center of
Washington, D.C., was clogged with thousands of protesters, each
carrying banners or placards, their insistent chanting and banter filling
the air with turbulence mirroring the weather. The sky above them
was filled with angry, swirling clouds, threatening to open up and
pelt them with hard rain at any moment.

The persistent rumblings of the protesters echoed their way into
the Oval Office. David stood before a window, watching the demon-
stration, seemingly transfixed. Rick called over to him quietly. "Mr.
President, please don't stand in front of that window. You're like a
sitting duck."

David realized his foolishness and reluctantly returned to his clut-
tered mahogany desk. "That's one angry mob out there, boyo."

"You bet they are," Rick rejoined. "They'd eat you or any of us
alive if we so much as showed our heads."

David raised his eyes to the heavens. "Would someone kindly tell
me why I wanted this job? I could have been a bricklayer, a car-
penter..."

Rick replied in monotone, always with an ironic twist. "Because
then you'd be out there with them, yelling at some other poor fool
sitting at your desk. Besides, Jesus went the carpentry route, and look
where it got Him."

Rick looked over at the vice president, wrestling with a miasma of
computer printouts. Rick nodded his head in Breckenridge's direction.
He leaned toward David, whispering, "I wish he'd go take a walk out
there. They'd probably wrench his fool head right off his neck."

David laughed, relieving the tension ever so slightly. They had long
suspected that Breckenridge was less than trustworthy; they knew he
had designs on the Oval Office.

"I can't believe you're complaining about your job," Rick continued. "The pay's not bad—and you got that great benefit package
that goes along with it. You get to see the world, go to swanky cocktail parties, have babes up to your ears..."

*David felt himself falling into one of his trances. But unlike his hor-
rific, apocalyptic visions, this one was sweeter than honey. He saw
himself holding Gabriella in his arms, cuddling in front of a blazing
hearth, with a long line of Christmas stockings hanging over the fireplace. He even made out the names on the stockings. David. Gabriella.
Daniel. Lucia. Emily. It was a big family. Suddenly, a herd of children
bounded down the steps, stopping in front of the twelve-foot
Christmas tree and trembling in awe at the munificence of Santa Claus.*

*The boys were carbon copies of David, and a little girl looking just like Gabriella came over and squeezed both of them tightly around the necks. Then the children ran in unison toward the tree, ripping up paper and strewing it all around the room. David bent over to kiss Gabriella softly. They looked up and met each other's eyes. There were no secrets between them, only love.*

An insistent voice interrupted David's sweet reverie. "Mr. President, have you seen what's going on?"

David was startled out of his vision. He was surprised to open his eyes and find himself in the Oval Office, with Charlie Breckenridge staring down at him accusingly.

"Mr. President...?"

David shook himself, but frankly, this was one dream from which he never wanted to emerge. It had been so sweet. It was what might have been, if it hadn't been for Stone. Stone. The very name sent David plummeting back to earth.

"I haven't been living in a cave, Charlie."

Breckenridge pointed to the television monitor. "I wasn't implying you were, Sir. But *this* is something you have to see..."

David, Rick and Charlie clustered before the monitor. On the screen, balls of fire fell from the skies, crashing down on moving buses, setting them on fire like dry straw. Fields all over the world lay parched, the earth cracking open as if creatures from the underworld were fighting to make their way to the surface. A volcano came to life, ripping its way up through the ancient pyramid at Giza, spewing rock, lava and black soot into the air. In New York Harbor, meteors rained down in the distance as volcanic geysers erupted in the water, spewing fire and debris. Another volcano erupted within the heart of New York City—right under Rockefeller Center. The building slowly began to wobble, and huge chunks of rock crushed the fleeing crowds who had the misfortune to be shopping on Fifth Avenue that day. On Ellis Island, a geyser erupted, hurtling the entire Statue of Liberty into the air. The most glorious monuments of civilization had been razed—remaining now only in photographs and news footage such as the one they were watching.

David stared contemplatively at the footage. His mind wandered to the Seven Wonders of the Ancient World, all gone forever. He spoke quietly, as if speaking a eulogy to the world as they knew it.

"The Hanging Gardens of Babylon. The Temple of Artemis. The Colossus of Rhodes. And now, the Eiffel Tower and Statue of Liberty. All gone with the wind."

Oblivious to David's mood, Breckenridge turned up the volume. "Yeah—if you want to call this 'wind!'"

A reporter was interviewing a Spanish priest at a makeshift hospital set up under an enormous tent. The buildings around him had been leveled as far as the eye could see. The priest seemed to know the secret that David had fought with himself desperately to deny.

"Fire rains from the skies and destroys everything around us. The earth opens up beneath our feet. Our seas and rivers are turning to blood. What used to be Barcelona is nothing now...we are a lost city. All men and women of God understand the signs. We have known for a long time that there is only one explanation for what is happening..."

Suddenly, a discordant musical chord was struck. The scenes of destruction were suddenly replaced by a heavy-metal dude wailing on a dual-necked Stratocaster. "It's Guitar-mageddon! The guitar sale to end 'em all! Get down to Guitar World for Fender, Yamahas, digital Sonys..."

Rick looked over at David knowingly. "I think we can thank our beloved chancellor for that interruption. I'm surprised he hasn't found a way to stop all television coverage completely..."

David scowled. "If it were in his interests, you can bet he would have done it already. This is better. This way, it's more like a soap opera. He keeps everyone tuning in, just waiting for more..."

Rick nodded. "You gotta hand it to him. The man has a brain."

"Yeah," David replied bitterly. "If only he had a heart and soul to go along with it."

The chanting and screaming from the street seemed to grow louder and more insistent. It was driving Rick out of his mind. He pointed outside to the protesters. "These idiots! They think this could have all been avoided if we had joined the One World. They think this is some kind of personal vendetta between you and your brother. I mean, where are their minds?"

David pounded on the wall, plaster shattering onto the floor of the executive office. "What in hell is the connection between fireballs raining from the skies—streets opening up and devouring carloads of people—the sun breaking down into little pieces and setting Jerusalem on fire—and my less-than-ideal relationship with my brother? It's just ridiculous! How am I somehow responsible for all this? What are these people thinking?"

"That's just the point—they aren't thinking at all!"

David shook his head in utter consternation. He passed by the window again, standing off to the side this time, staring out at the vicious crowd. Mothers with children hoisted onto their backs were screaming out, "End the hunger!" Boy Scouts on bicycles rode in unison, carrying a banner that said, "World Union or Die." The mob was united behind one common goal: to convince the president to enter the World Union. Not for political reasons—many of the protesters were former "die-hard" Americans who only weeks before would have fought to maintain American independence at all costs. But given the recent reign of terror all over the world, they were ready not only to join, but also to pledge allegiance to the flag of the World Union. David could only shake his head in frustration.

"Do they really think that our joining the One World is going to stop all this? Do they think I like what's going on out there? Don't they think I'd stop it if I could? If it were that easy, I'd put in a call to Stone right now."

Rick poured himself a drink. "Maybe that's what you should say to them. Make an official statement—televise a State of the Union address. Maybe a little logic wouldn't hurt."

David shook his head adamantly. "Did you take a good look at those faces out there? These people are way beyond logic, and no State of the Union address is going to help that. I probably couldn't even get it on the air if I wanted to."

Rick nodded. David was probably right about that. David continued, "Stone's magnificent manipulation of the worldwide media has made it seem like our holding out is causing the world to fall apart!"

Rick downed his brandy in one gulp. He turned to David. "That brings up a very interesting point, David. Something we haven't really talked about." David looked over at his best friend and protector. "I mean, if your brother isn't bringing the world to its knees, *who—or what—is?*"

David was pulled up short. Rick continued on, treading cautiously. "I mean, what was that priest saying—before he got cut off, that is— that the holy men know what's going on, that they've 'recognized the signs' for a long time? What do you think that means, David?"

David brushed him off. "The so-called 'holy men' always want you to believe they know what's going on. That's been the principle way every religion has managed to keep their people in line. They know what's going on and you don't—so you'd better give them money! They're no better than Stone. You start listening to the priests and the gurus, and the next thing you know, they'll be starting up their own world union."

Rick backed down, not wanting to inflame David any further. But nothing could keep his keen mind from mulling it over.

Charlie Breckenridge left his seat behind the television monitor and sat down in the fine leather chair before David's desk. "David, whatever is causing the catastrophes has nothing to do with the political situation at hand. Right now, the people of this country want to join the World Union. You're right; your brother is a master at manipulating the media. Let's face it—you're not. You're...an honest man. If we don't join..."

David leaned forward in his chair, not believing what he was hearing from his second in command. "What are you saying, Charlie? That I'm going to have a mutiny on my hands? Are the people going to set me adrift on a lifeboat, with three days supply of food and water—like Fletcher Christian did to Captain Bligh in *Mutiny on the Bounty*?"

He looked over at Rick. "I must have seen that movie fifty times—the Clark Gable and Charles Laughton one, not the one with Marlon Brando. What I love about it is, that even though Captain Bligh is a foul-mouthed, murdering bastard, Fletcher Christian is still a good enough guy to give him a chance to make it home safely. Revenge is never his motivation; all he wants is freedom for himself and his crew. There's something archetypically beautiful about that, don't you think?"

Rick smiled. He understood David's parable. But Breckenridge did not. He paused for a moment after David's thoughtful soliloquy. "That wouldn't have been exactly the analogy I would have chosen, David, but I think I see what you're getting at. But to use your own analogy—at this point, I don't even think they'd give you a lifeboat!"

David fell back into his chair. "Well, that's honest, at least." Then he just exploded, smashing his fist hard into the wooden desk. "Then what the hell am I even doing here? I might as well just shoot myself in the forehead before some wacko takes me out on the street!"

Breckenridge faltered slightly. "I'm sorry, David—but it would be unfair for me to misrepresent the truth of the situation as I see it."

David calmed himself down and stared at his vice president. "So, that's the people's choice from your point of view. No lifeboat for me. But what about you, Charlie? What do you think?"

Breckenridge stumbled over his words. "Well, I, it's not up to me, sir. I mean, I'm not the president..."

David sighed. "Not yet, anyway."

David didn't fail to notice that Charlie could not meet his eyes. Instead, he jumped out of his seat as if it were burning a hole in his backside and darted over to the DVD player. "I have to show you this, David. I didn't think it was relevant at first—just some lunatic complicating things even more—but this guy seems to be gaining momentum, taking away the thunder even from your brother!"

David looked over at Rick with an impish grin, delighted by what seemed like an opportunity for a most welcome distraction. "This I have to see."

Charlie nervously tapped on the DVD player. "I can't figure out what this guy's game is, but I pulled this off the wire service to give you an idea..." The image came across the screen. The camera moved in on a middle-aged man, garbed only in a simple black cassock, making a public appearance before an assemblage of the United Arab Emirates. A swarthy young reporter spoke over the news footage.

"A frightened and confused populace, seeking desperately for answers, have embraced this self-proclaimed 'prophet of the New World.' When asked his name, this extraordinary man will only call himself 'the emissary of the one true godhead.' This nameless prophet has been traveling all over the globe and is said to have performed countless miracles at many of the locations decimated by natural disasters."

As the reporter spoke, the screen was filled with images of the cassocked man, passing his hands quickly over the wounded and dying—and healing them instantly. Hordes of people gathered around him as dying men and women rose virtually from the dead—right before their eyes! They knelt before the Guardian and proclaimed him the new messiah.

David and Rick just stared at the screen in utter amazement. This was indeed a diversion. Rick was the first to comment. "You know, Charlie's right about this guy. He's good. Maybe he'll take away some of your brother's action. I mean, even Stone can't do that stuff."

David just stared at the image on the screen. "I wouldn't be too sure." David appeared deep in thought, his eyes glued to the footage of the Guardian performing "miracles." He turned to Rick and Charlie, completely deadpan.

"Say, if this guy can raise the dead, maybe he can do something about the Statue of Liberty?"

Rick just roared. Charlie interrupted, annoyed by this superficial turn in the conversation. "Only one thing's for sure. This guy's making his presence felt all over the world!"

David's brow furrowed. "Well, who is he, Charlie?"

Breckenridge just shook his head. "I've checked all our sources. No one has a clue. NCIC, CIA, Interpol—nobody has anything on the guy. It's like he just came out of nowhere!"

"'The Man from Nowhere.' That's a catchy title," David rejoined.

"Just listen to this part, here—" Breckenridge interrupted. The three men turned back to the screen. This time, a young African woman in a dashiki and turban was speaking into a microphone. "Sanctioned by no known religious or political organization, this nameless 'emissary of the true godhead' has vowed to lead the world out of this dark time. Here in Africa, where fires have destroyed almost half of the continent's food supplies, over a million have begun a pilgrimage to Nairobi, where this self-appointed prophet is next scheduled to appear."

The screen now showed aerial footage that looked like an enormous snake winding its way across the desert. But it was no snake; it was nearly a million people—entire villages, mothers carrying their young on their backs, elderly men and women leaning on their children for support—all heading for the same destination: Nairobi.

The three men watched the footage on the screen while the wails of the protesters outside threatened to deafen them. After watching all this, David felt unable to move. He spoke quietly, as if to himself, "Maybe *I* should go to Nairobi. Maybe, if I asked him nice enough, this 'emissary of the true godhead' would take this cup away from me..."

Rick looked over at his tormented best friend with great empathy and compassion. He wouldn't have his job for anything in the world.

# CHAPTER FORTY-THREE

Up, sanctify the people, and say,
Sanctify yourselves against to morrow:
for thus saith the Lord God of Israel,
There is an accursed thing in the
midst of thee, O Israel: thou canst not
stand before thine enemies,
until ye take away the accursed
thing from among you.

—Joshua 7:13

A small stage had been erected right in the middle of a deadly, dry African plain. The empty stage was surrounded by a sea of African faces. The air was filled with cheers and chants to bring on the prophet—the emissary of the true godhead. It was without a doubt the largest gathering of people that had ever assembled in one place on earth.

Backstage the Guardian stood with Stone Alexander. Stone listened to the united voice of the people and smiled triumphantly, turning to the Guardian.

"The first angel sounded: And hail and fire followed, mingled with blood, and they were thrown to the earth."

The Guardian smiled back at Stone as he knelt down before him. "Yes, my lord. The first trumpet has sounded." Stone peeked through the curtain at the swarm of helpless souls—all ready to be plucked. Stone turned back to the Guardian, who had now returned to his feet, adjusting his robe before going on stage.

Stone and the Guardian seemed to speak in their own "shorthand."

"*They've come for the answers,*" Stone said.

"*Give them the answers, my son. More will follow.*"

Stone nodded in agreement, as the Guardian slowly moved out onto the stage. As he passed the proscenium arch, the assembled masses jumped to their feet and cheered.

"Welcome...welcome to all of you. I know how long and hard it was for you to make your way here today. But you had no choice, my brothers and sisters. You received the call from the one true god of this world."

The people bowed and prayed, amazed that they could understand every word the Guardian said without an interpreter—and he was speaking in English! This in itself seemed proof of his divinity. The Guardian continued, "Yes, we are all brothers and sisters. We breathe the same sweet air. Toil beneath the heat of the same sun. Taste the same rain upon our lips. But—the world we share is changing! You look around you and see a storm of fire that sweeps across your fields. Destroys your crops. Kills your animals. You see a sky black as sackcloth in the full light of day. You see a pestilence that rips through your families till they are but skin and bones."

The masses nodded in agreement. Yes, yes—every word he spoke was true. The False Prophet began to pace across the stage. "You see the world we share threatening to tear itself apart at the seams! And so you have come here today for answers; you have come here for my help!"

The crowd rose to their feet in unison, their arms outstretched toward him. The Guardian stopped abruptly and glared at them. "I am afraid I cannot help you."

A hushed cry went through the crowd. There were the beginnings of unrest. Suddenly, the Guardian tore into them—lambasting them like a fire-and-brimstone preacher. *"I cannot help you because you have brought this punishment down upon your own heads!"*

The audience was utterly confused by this attack.

"You had been given peace. Nourishment. Shelter. Clean water to drink and to make your crops flourish. You were taken to the mountaintop and shown a better world. You were given all these gifts by a powerful and almighty benefactor. But what have you done with these gifts? Have you shown your allegiance to the new lord who has granted you this bounty? No! You have not knelt before him. You have not offered him your faith. You have merely taken his gifts. This is not enough! *This* is why he has caused the earth to crumble at your feet!"

Some of the crowd started to rebel. The Guardian became still more intimidating. "You reject him, and you reject the light of your god! Your *one* god! And so he turns your land to darkness!"

Just as the rebellion was starting to escalate, the skies around the entire area began to darken. The image of the Guardian began to grow—a holographic manifestation over a hundred feet high. Screaming, the crowd began to run away from the stage, falling over each other and causing pandemonium. But the Guardian's voice, now booming, stopped them in their tracks. They turned back, mesmerized by the spectacle before them.

"You cannot run from me! I am the emissary of your one true god! The only one who can bring back the light and offer you eternal salvation! Will you remain in darkness?"

Cries rang out from the terrified crowd as the sky continued to darken. Only the Guardian, glowing against the darkness, could be seen.

"Will you remain in darkness for all your days?" Lightning bolts pierced the sky, and the crowd unanimously sank to their knees.

"The time has come to unite behind he who is the true resurrection and the life and to free the world from the infidels who would keep us from our glorious New Age. If you would bring about an end to this plague—an end to this famine—you must pledge your troth to your true lord and master..." The Guardian paused only a moment for dramatic effect.

"Stone Alexander!"

The African people were dumbfounded but silent as Stone now emerged from the wings, striding to center stage. The Guardian, still huge and glowing, stood behind him. His voice boomed out in the darkness. "Bow and swear your allegiance to the son of your one true god!"

Most of the crowd immediately fell to their knees in adulation. But many of them resisted, struggling to escape from the throng. Lightning bolts slammed into the back of their legs—knocking them off their feet. Not a soul missed this. No one else dared try to escape. United, they sank to their knees and prayed. Stone's ice blue eyes looked out upon the glorious ocean of souls. This was the moment he had been waiting for, plotting and planning to bring to fruition for many years. And now, the moment had come.

"I am the son of the one true god. You cannot fight me. Place your heads on the ground and pledge your allegiance to me. Pray to me!"

With their heads pressed into the parched earth, there was a mumbling of prayers in a cacophony of African languages. Stone was jubilant; the intoxication of power sent a current of pleasure down his spine.

"I shall take away all your troubles as I did before, my children, in exchange for your fealty. Soon, the earth will again turn green. Herds of animals will again blanket your plains. All will be as it was—only better. Because your lord will be with you, and you with him, for all eternity! Rise, my children, rise!"

The crowd jumped to their feet, cheering and applauding.

Stone beamed, raising his hands toward his heavenly rival.

His face turned away from the microphone, he whispered, "Soon all that You have taken from my father will be mine, and I shall once again sit at the right hand of my father on his heavenly throne!"

# CHAPTER
# FORTY-FOUR

He will be a master of deception,
defeating many by catching them off guard.
Without warning he will destroy them.
He will even take on the Prince of princes in battle,
but he will be broken, though not by human power.

—Daniel 8:25, NLT

Night fell on Tokyo harbor. An old fisherman sat resting and smoking a hand-rolled cigarette aboard his tiny junk, just as he had done every night for the past fifty years. Lanterns glowed around him as he settled down for a peaceful smoke.

Suddenly, he heard the sound of loud rock music intruding on his solitude. Annoyed, he looked over the side of his boat to see a small skiff approaching, staffed by two very drunk Japanese teens— one wearing a Dodgers baseball jersey; the other sporting a *Wasabi* T-shirt, the name of a Japanese rock band, hair dyed bright yellow; both of them swilling beer as their boom box blasted. Infuriated, the old fisherman yelled over to the boys in the skiff.

"Hey! Turn off that noise or beat it! I am trying to rest!" The old man turned away, figuring that his warning would scare them off. But the boy in the Dodgers' shirt yelled back at him.

"Hard day trimming *bonzais*, old man?" His pal, stoned out of his mind, started laughing uncontrollably. "Nah, too many tokes at the opium den, right, Grandpa?" Both boys shared in the joke at the old man's expense. The old man simply shrugged and sat back down to finish his smoke, figuring that eventually, the boys would tire of bothering him and just go away.

Drawing in a deep puff of tobacco, the old man stared up at the sky, the stars twinkling brightly over the glistening water. He would ignore these ignoramuses. They had obviously been reared with absolutely no respect for their elders. *Ah,* he thought to himself, *how times have changed.* Heaving a deep sigh, the fisherman continued his solitary meditation, trying his best to tune out the noise.

Suddenly, a giant mountain of fire ripped down out of the sky, hitting the ocean far off at the horizon. The fisherman jumped to his feet in amazement, leaning over his junk to address the boys. "Did you see that? Did you see? A mountain fell from the sky!"

The yellow-haired teen opened his eyes wide. "Oh, mountain fall from sky. Must be Godzilla. Run for hills!" Both boys cackled with laughter so hard that they almost fell out of their boat. Suddenly, the water beneath them began to boil. The old man just stared at the water in the moonlight. *Was it actually changing color, or was he losing his mind?* Both boats rocked violently back and forth. They all watched in horror as dead, rotting fish bubbled to the surface.

"Sick, man!" One of the boys stuck his hand into the water, pulling it out immediately, screaming in terror. His hand was covered in blood. The rickety old junk rocked violently, finally tossing the old fisherman into the boiling bloodbath. He struggled desperately, holding out a hand to the boys. "C'mon, c'mon—let's get the hell out of here!" the utterly stupefied, yellow-haired punk yelled. The other boy, equally frenzied, started up the motor and tore out of there as if his life depended on it—which it most surely did.

The old man called to them repeatedly, imploring, "Help me! Please!"

Without so much as looking back, the hysterical teens sped off into the night, leaving the old fisherman to perish in the ocean that had both housed and fed him his entire life. Now, it had become his grave.

# CHAPTER
# FORTY-FIVE

Behold, I will make them of the synagogue of Satan.
—Revelation 3:9


Men would be angels; angels would be gods.
—Alexander Pope

The voices of what sounded like millions of people were chanting in unison: "Stone! Stone! Stone! Stone!" Stone and the Guardian waited backstage, surrounded by their "flock"—armed bodyguards who had been instructed to keep their distance from both men, but to protect their lives at all costs. Stone was both enthralled and invigorated by the sound of the throng calling out his name. He turned to the Guardian, fully satisfied for the first time in his life.

"It *is* sweet. Sweeter than I ever thought possible. Everything is just as you said it would be."

The Guardian nodded his head, his mouth turning up ever so slightly around the edges. The two remained quiet, basking in the adulation of the unseen crowd. "Stone! Stone! Stone!"

Stone turned to the Guardian smugly. "I suppose it's easier than yelling out, 'Alexander! Alexander!'"

The Guardian did not smile now, instead looking over at Stone with flashing eyes. "Perhaps—but 'lord' would be better still."

The smile dropped instantly from Stone's lips as he remembered what he was there for. He stared ahead with steely determination. "Soon, *all* will call me lord *and* god."

The roar of the crowd only increased in intensity. The leader of the Latin American Zone had been allowed backstage by the bodyguards. He timidly approached Stone and the Guardian, bowing profusely. "My lords, welcome. They are all...clamoring...for you?"

Stone smiled at him sweetly. "Yes. Isn't it lovely?"

The man tried to convey his message as politely as possible. "If it could be, that you could begin at any time soon, everyone would be so honored, my lords...." The man knelt before Stone. Stone gestured for him to rise, nodding in acquiescence.

"Yes."

The man backed away from them without ever turning around, afraid of offending them and being struck dead by a thunderbolt. He had heard about what happened in Africa. Everyone had heard about what happened in Africa. The official was escorted out on to the stage. The voices of the multitude quieted down as they listened to the message from their leader, conveying that Stone would be appearing momentarily. When he finished, the crowd erupted in wild applause. The cries of "Stone! Stone!" became deafening and frantic.

Stone readied himself to go onstage, rolling his neck around to relieve some tightness there. The Guardian stood right beside him. "*The second angel has sounded,*" he whispered.

Stone closed his eyes, a beatific smile coming over his face. He spoke as if in a light trance.

*"Then the second angel sounded: and something like a great mountain burning with fire was thrown into the sea, and a third of the sea became blood. A third of the creatures in the sea died, and a third of the ships were destroyed."*

He opened his eyes, but continued speaking in a monotone.

*"And a third of the trees became burned and all green grass..."*

Stone paused, looking over at the Guardian. "There are five more trumpets and seven bowls of wrath left to come."

"There are only three heads of state still opposing you."

Stone's smile disappeared. He was clearly thinking of David. He spat out, "Still, after all that has happened, he continues to resist me!"

"He is strong, your brother. I wish he was on our side," the Guardian remarked, his words scalding Stone. His eyes peered off as if into another world. A dark world.

"He'll weaken. He'll join me. You must have faith. Didn't you teach me that?"

The Guardian bowed before Stone. "No one had to teach you anything, my lord. I merely awakened you to your calling."

Stone smiled. Yes. He nodded respectfully toward his minion. "Now go on," he teased, pointing toward the stage. "Dazzle them with your pyrotechnics! Get them all ready for me!"

The hooded Guardian silently moved out before the assembled Latin audience. They bellowed in excitement, falling to their knees, swearing their undying devotion. Backstage, Stone spoke quietly to himself, his eyes tightly shut.

"I have absolute faith...I am..."

# CHAPTER FORTY-SIX

And David said to Solomon, his son,
Be strong and of good courage,
and do it; fear not, nor be dismayed:
for the Lord God, even my God,
will be with thee; he will not fail thee
nor forsake thee, until thou hast
finished all the work for the service
of the house of the Lord.

—1 Chronicles 28:20

A group of people who had obviously seen better days stood amidst the burnt-out rubble that used to be Pittsburgh, Pennsylvania, all fighting to enter one of the few stores still remaining intact. In the background, there was a mass of tents with campfires burning; groups of people huddled around the campfires trying desperately to keep warm.

The people who had filled the "Techno-Wizard" megastore to its 1,300-person capacity had come to watch Vice President Breckenridge's press conference blasted over two dozen screens in the television department. There was a time in the nation's history that people didn't even tune in for presidential addresses, much less speeches by the vice president. But these times were so hopeless, so bizarre, that people followed everything that was going on around them—on the home front as well as around the globe. They were hoping for some glimmer of light. Some indication, however slight, that things were going to change for the better.

When Breckenridge's face appeared, the unruly mob in the back of the store started shouting out, "What'd he say? What'd he say?"

"Shut up! It's just starting!" The people closer to the screens admonished. Charles Breckenridge's smarmy countenance suddenly filled every television screen in the store. No one even dared to breathe. Breckenridge cleared his throat for what seemed like a lifetime to these people, and then began.

"I would like, at this time, to offer my prayers and my hope to the American people for all that they have suffered over the past few weeks. This has been a very trying time for everyone all over the world, and it is only by sticking together, working together, sharing our resources with one another, that we can get through this period of trial.

"Unfortunately, I have an announcement to make that will only cast your hearts down even further; although in the long run, this discovery should bring about the end to the misery we have all endured!"

There was a murmuring of approval among the crowd. Any hint, any indication of a potential change in their run of luck, was exactly what they wanted to hear. Breckenridge continued, addressing the American public with great sadness in his voice.

"I am very sorry to say that, after an in-depth investigation by the State Department, we have discovered that our president, David Alexander, whom we have trusted as our leader, is not the man we thought he was."

A ripple of horror made its way all the way through the crowd, like an electric current.

"I am very sorry to say that David Alexander has risen to his position by a series of false promises and immoral acts...including the murder of his own father!"

There was a muttering among the crowd after the announcement. But people remained somewhat calm—they had certainly heard bad things about their presidents before. This was not exactly newsworthy from their perspective. And it wasn't going to put food in their mouths either. But all that changed when the footage that Stone had so carefully created appeared onscreen: David hurling his father over the balcony to his death. Indeed, a picture was worth a thousand words. Having witnessed the act of bloodshed with their own eyes, the crowd went wild. Fistfights broke out. Men pulled the televisions down off their shelves, hurling them into the store, crushing and killing many of the onlookers.

It was a full-scale riot: the betrayed, starving and freezing Americans letting out their suppressed rage and frustration. And all that anger was directed at one man alone: David Alexander.

# CHAPTER
# FORTY-SEVEN

The enemy said, I will pursue,
I will overtake, I will divide the spoil;
my lust shall be satisfied upon them;
I will draw my sword,
my hand shall destroy them.

—Exodus 15:9

Abastion of liberalism and democratic thought for many decades, the University of California at Berkeley had managed to survive, though in name only. Really, the only thing that had actually survived was most of the faculty and student body. The university itself had all but succumbed to a devastating series of earthquakes, which had been felt all the way from Sacramento to the Mexican border.

Though the Student Union, once the rallying place for rebellious students and leaders throughout the country, had been leveled and the library burned to the ground, both students and faculty remained at the institution, continuing to live and work out of over a hundred double-wide trailers—precariously perched on the rubble of what used to be the university. The faculty, ever philosophical, chose to describe their "new teaching facilities" as much closer to the Socratic method—no buildings at all, just eager students before a wise and willing teacher. Many of the teachers preferred to have their classes *al fresco*, rather than inside the tin houses.

In one of these trailers, a group of cow-eyed students packed the smoky room, quietly watching a small television screen. They were tuned in to the same thing everyone all over the country was watching: the vice president's speech. The students were virtually speechless as Breckenridge spoke over the scene of David's "atrocity," now playing over and over again in slow motion, as if to verify its authenticity.

"This was a man who has held our trust. All of our trust, including my own. A man we rallied around because we believed in his integrity. But we have all been deceived. David Alexander, our president, is guilty not only of patricide, but also of selling out and destroying his own nation!"

Passing around a bowl of hashish, one of the students called outside to a group of students passing by. "Dudes! Check this out!" More students piled into the already crowded trailer like so many sardines, fighting to see the screen as Breckenridge continued his assault.

"Now, in our nation's darkest hour, the true nature of our leader is revealed. David Alexander is a man who would do anything...say anything...not only to rise to power, but to maintain it."

The students were dumbstruck. Finally, a contemplative girl in the middle of the trailer said, as if to herself, "Imagine him doing that. Stone Alexander's own brother!" She said Stone Alexander's name as if she were talking about some great mythical hero, like Odysseus or Hercules! The other kids grunted and nodded, obviously agreeing with her sentiment.

A boy majoring in psychology sat right up by the screen, eyes still riveted to the television. "I'll bet he did it out of jealousy. You know, his older brother being this big humanitarian and all—and who was he? He was trying to get back at his brother for being the 'favorite son.'" Again, a murmur of approval ran through the trailer.

An elderly professor stood at the trailer door, unbeknownst to any of them. He addressed the group. "Very astute observations. Sibling rivalry is a very potent force for evil, and has been, since the beginning of time. By gaining the presidency, David Alexander put himself in a position to actually compete with his brother—defy his brother—even if it meant betraying the people he had sworn to defend and protect. Well, now, at least, it seems inevitable that the United States will finally join the One World. And that's something we can all be happy about. You can be sure that our president, such as he is, will pay for his crimes." The kids nodded in agreement.

The professor continued to hold court in the Socratic style. "Now, if this were a Greek tragedy—how do you think it would end?" he asked, as if giving the group a pop quiz.

"That's easy," a girl with thick, braided hair replied. "He'd stab himself to death, before anyone else got the chance!" Cheers of approval rang out throughout the makeshift classroom. The professor smiled philosophically and walked back out into the rubble that used to be the university campus.

*Yes,* he thought to himself. *The girl is absolutely right.*

$$\Omega^2$$

At Nate's Truck Stop, on a dark stretch of the New Jersey Turnpike, a group of truckers watched the broadcast as they chowed down on their vittles. A sign behind them on the wall advertised Nate's prices: Hamburger, $15; Cheeseburger, $20. Even Nate himself stopped wiping the counter to listen to this astonishing speech.

"Even now he will tell us we have plenty of oil. He will tell us we have plenty of food. He will tell us everything but the truth...that we should have reached out and taken the hand of Stone Alexander when he first created the One World Union. *Why* has our president repeatedly declined this offer, while so many of his people were hungry and homeless? Is sibling rivalry so powerful a force that it allows a man to betray an entire nation, rather than to swallow his overbearing pride and succumb to his brother's plan, which would, in effect, ease all the suffering we have endured?"

Nate simply shook his head as he turned to the truckers at the counter. "You just don't know who the hell to trust anymore, do you?"

But unlike the students, these men didn't reply. They really didn't

283

care. They had learned from experience that nothing they could do or say would affect the quality of their lives, so why bother even thinking about it. Never even looking up at the screen, they just continued to devour their greasy burgers in silence. Breckenridge's accusations provided nothing but background noise. And then, it was back into their trucks for another seemingly endless cross-country drive. Only Nate, the owner of the dive, stopped long enough to actually listen to Breckenridge. He could only shake his head, his hand automatically washing off the counter in circular motions. "You just don't know what to believe in anymore..."

# CHAPTER
# FORTY-EIGHT

Whenever God erects a house of prayer,
The devil always builds a chapel there.

—Daniel Defoe

D avid and Rick watched the television monitor in dead silence as their limo negotiated the dense traffic of Washington, D.C. Rick looked over at his friend, sharing in his humiliation and disgust. "That son of a..." David didn't say a word, his angry eyes glued to the screen.

"If we are to survive this dark time, we must remove David Alexander from office before his personal vendetta against his brother destroys us all..."

David didn't utter a word because he was in a deep state of shock. *This couldn't really be happening.* Not that he ever trusted Breckenridge, but he never thought he'd stoop this low. Under his breath, he whispered, "Traitor." He gently punched off the television.

Rick tried his best to reassure him. "He's just a rat jumping ship."

Looking out absentmindedly into the dark night, David muttered, "He's always been a rat. I knew it. I just couldn't get rid of him. Legally, that is."

"We should've taken him out anyway," Rick replied. "Any way we could. This is my fault, David."

David turned to his friend, shaking his head. "Don't do this, Rick. Don't blame yourself. If you want to blame anyone, you can blame me. I'm supposed to be the guy in charge."

"Yeah," Rick demurred, "but I'm supposed to be the guy watching the backside of the guy in charge."

David smiled in spite of himself. "You're a lot more than that, and you know it. Without you..." David let the words hang awkwardly in the air. "Well, let's just say I don't know what I'd do without you."

Rick clasped David's hand. "Let's hope you never have to."

"Look," David said. "We tried to save Benson. We told him not to get too near Stone. But I let it happen..."

Rick nodded thoughtfully. "Well, I guess, all we can do is give it our best shot. And after that...it's out of our hands."

"Yeah," David steamed. "It's in *Stone's* hands."

"Oh, yeah. We used to think that guys like Bruce Lee had 'deadly hands!' Your brother's given a whole new meaning to the term." Then Rick grew far more serious. "I don't know what the man's doing, but I do know one thing; it's evil. There's evil in those hands. Evil in his heart."

David paused a moment. "I never told this to a living soul, Rick. I was ashamed. And I wasn't really sure until..." Rick looked over at him quizzically, wondering what on earth he was going to reveal. "Jeez, I'm really beating around the bush. Listen to me. Rick—it was *Stone* who murdered our father."

Rick's mouth just dropped. Finally, he looked up, as if suddenly struck by lightening.

David laughed a bitter laugh. "Yeah, you see—that's the *real* joke! He murders our father and then concocts this hoax to convince people that *I* did exactly what *he* did ten years ago: push our father over that balcony. He sets me up, destroys me and uses the details of his own crime to do it. It's really too much!"

Rick struggled to process this new information. "So, Stone is behind this whole thing with Breckenridge?"

David sighed. "Of course! What, did you think Charlie came up with it all by his lonesome? He hasn't got the brains."

Rick just nodded, over and over. Both men shared a long moment of silence, trying to take in the momentousness of all that had just transpired in the last ten minutes.

*David's mind was reeling. Breckenridge had threatened not only his presidency, but also his reputation—which was far more important to him. That people would think of him as a murderer—worse still, a "father killer"—cut him to the quick. His first impulse was to find the nearest hole in the ground, jump in and quickly shovel the earth back over himself. Then it would all be over: the agony of his betrayal by Stone; the hole in his heart caused by his futile, lifelong love of Gabriella; the strain of trying to be a good man, and a good president, under such appalling circumstances—and with such frighteningly poor odds. It would all be over. David turned his head ever so slightly toward Rick, failing to meet his eyes.*

"If you're truly my friend, Rick, maybe you'd do me the honor of putting a bullet in my head right now."

Rick grabbed his friend around the shoulders, recognizing the depth of his desperation.

"Don't talk like that, man! You can't! This isn't about you. You can't make it about you! This is about this *country*. This is about the whole damned world!" Rick smashed his fist against the bulletproof window. "What am I talking about? This is about the whole world being damned! You throw in the towel now, my brother, and—well, it's all over. You're the only chance this world has—and you know it. You've always known it!

"Everything happens for a reason! Because there's nobody else, David, who has what you have! Nobody has your drive, your integrity. Sooner or later, the Chinese will fold, and the next thing you know—but of course you won't know if you check out—there'll be nothing but the One World. And you and I both know what that means—the end of the world as we know it! Brought to you with the compliments of your host—Captain Bligh Alexander."

He smacked David hard on the back. "Hey man, wake up! I thought you wanted to be Fletcher Christian. The good man, fighting

288

the good fight. Putting the despot out of business and leading his loyal followers to the promised land. Or until the end, if need be."

David smiled despite himself at Rick's analogy. "You mean, this isn't the end? You could've fooled me."

Rick clutched David's hand and squeezed hard. "No! Not by a long shot it's not. No sir!"

David slowly began to lift his head, soaking up the encouragement from Rick's warm hand and his words. "You know, I'm not feeling all that much like Fletcher Christian right now."

Rick clutched David's hand so hard that it hurt. "Look! That scum bucket Charlie can make it look like this is all some bad blood between you and your brother. And I won't deny that a lot of people are going to believe him. But *I* don't believe him—and neither do you. It's you I believe in. The bad blood is inside your big brother. He infects everyone he touches. But the trick is, David, if you don't let him get to you—he can't destroy you."

David thought about that. After a few moments, he said, as if to himself, "He can't get to me—unless I let him..."

Yes. It actually made sense. David was suddenly flooded with a renewed sense of purpose and resolve. Of course he wasn't going check out. Give up? That just wasn't his style. Maybe Rick was right. Maybe he was the only one who could bring Stone down. Maybe that was why he was here. Maybe that's why he had to suffer so much personal humiliation—so that he could muster up the energy, the anger, not only to do battle with Stone—but also to defeat him. Just as these thoughts crossed his mind, an angelic voice spoke deep within him, reassuring him that yes, this was indeed the truth. He didn't recognize the voice, but it was definitely not of this world. The voice continued to reassure David that this was the right path. That this was his destiny.

David shivered from the impact of the angelic messenger. He knew it had spoken the truth.

Suddenly, David's entire body language changed. Instead of slumping down in his seat, defeated, David sat up straight and alert. He looked over to Rick and smiled in gratitude. "What would I do without you, man?"

Rick smiled back. "Hey, you're the captain. I'm just here to guard your backside and keep you on a steady course."

David's temporary elation turned to anger as he thought about Breckenridge's betrayal. "Charlie may only be a little cog in Stone's plan to get to me, but he's still a stinking rat."

Rick nodded. "You know what they say. Rats and roaches will always survive."

David sneered. "Not this one. Not if I get near him."

Rick laughed, seeing that David had regained his confidence. "That's the spirit."

The men were jolted back to harsh reality by the sound of the car phone. Rick picked it up. "Yeah?" He paused a moment, then put the phone on pause. He turned to David with one eyebrow tweaked. "The rat."

David shook his head. What perfect timing. He pressed the button for the speakerphone, so that Rick could hear the conversation. "Hello, Mr. President. Or should I call you, 'Chairman of the North American Zone?'"

David's confident tone took Breckenridge aback. He had anticipated a blast of belligerence. Breckenridge paced nervously, his cell phone clutched in his hand. In the background stood the battlements of Castle Alexander. "David, please. Let's put politics aside and just talk like two men who love their country. OK?"

David and Rick exchanged mystified glances, as if to say, "Is this guy for real?" But David remained cool. "OK."

David heard what struck him as true remorse in the voice of this Judas and was surprisingly touched by it. "David, I only did what I thought was best for the people. There seemed to be no other way..."

Rick shook his head at Breckenridge's attempts at justifying his unpardonable treachery. David replied cautiously, "Uh-huh."

Breckenridge was becoming increasingly frustrated. Why didn't David just yell at him and get it over with? He had it coming. He desperately *wanted* to be berated, called on the carpet, for what he had done. Perhaps it would help ease his guilt. But David wouldn't give him that. He said nothing, gave him nothing—just waited for him to make the next move. What was he waiting for? Did he want him to beg for his apology? *Yes*, Charlie thought. *Of course that's what he wanted.* But Charlie couldn't do it. Couldn't handle the depth of his own treachery. Instead, he turned back to business.

"Listen, David, based on the North American Zone charter, there are already enough votes to remove you from office. All I did was make it easier on the people."

David managed to maintain a calm veneer. "I agree completely. You did the right thing. That's what you want me to say, isn't it, Charlie?"

There was silence on the other end of the line. David reiterated, "Well, isn't it?"

Charlie just paced across the vast patio of Castle Alexander, feeling lower than he ever had in his life. David finally spoke up. "I guess you've said all you have to say. You did what you had to do, and it was extremely clever. You offered me up as the sacrificial lamb, turned the nation against me so they don't have to feel any remorse over kicking me out of office. It's sheer genius, Charlie. A brilliant strategy. I wonder how you came up with it all by yourself?"

Breckenridge heard the sarcasm in David's voice. He knew right then that David was on to him.

"So, what kind of deal did my brother offer you, anyway?"

Breckenridge stood looking out over the twinkling lights of Rome, his limbs shaking uncontrollably. *Why,* he thought, *did I think I could keep my alliance with Stone a secret from David? Why have I been fool enough to think I could convince David that I had done this alone—for the good of the country?* David didn't need to beat Charlie up; Charlie was doing an excellent job of it himself.

$$\Omega^2$$

Back in Washington, D.C., the limo had just turned on to Pennsylvania Avenue, the White House in the far distance. Still on the phone, Breckenridge, now a mass of guilt and fear, began yelling at David.

"David—you just don't get it! He's too strong! You can't fight him anymore! No one can!"

Tears were streaming down his face, and David heard the guilt and terror in his voice. Surprisingly, it didn't make him feel any better. In fact, he began to feel sorry for Charlie, wondering just what machinations Stone had employed to make him take such drastic actions. Had he been standing over Charlie during the broadcast, with Charlie knowing full well that if he didn't say exactly what Stone had wanted him to say—and had probably even scripted for him—Stone would shake his hand, and then, bye-bye Charlie?

David couldn't think of anything more to say. Poor Charlie. He no longer had any desire to make him feel worse than he already did. Charlie's voice came back over the line, whispering now. He confirmed David's suspicions. "I had no choice, David. You have to believe me. Please, please—be careful!" The connection suddenly went dead.

David turned to Rick sadly. "Looks like we don't have to do anything to the rat. Seems to me he's dead already."

$$\Omega^2$$

Breckenridge stood there holding the dead phone in his hand, trying to figure out what went wrong with the connection. He kept on trying to talk into the phone. "David? David—can you hear me? David!"

Charlie felt a strong presence behind him. Petrified, he turned to see Stone standing before him, smiling almost jauntily. Breckenridge offered up a knee-jerk smile to Stone, the best that he could muster. He struggled to meet Stone's eyes, trying to get out the words he knew he must say: "My lord..."

As the words finally came out of his mouth, his entire body shook involuntarily. Stone didn't miss it. "It is done. Your brother has fled the country, and as acting president I have ordered all of our troops in Europe and the Middle East to Megiddo."

Stone strode elegantly across the patio, talking to Charlie quite casually. "I am indebted to you, Mr. Breckenridge, for the service you have rendered me. I shall not forget it." Stone's penetrating eyes virtually burned a hole into Breckenridge's forehead. Stone now stared at the shame-faced vice president. He leaned over to him, as if telling him a secret. "But, there is something I feel I must share with you..."

Charlie now knew exactly how prisoners on death row felt when they heard the final turning of the key to their cell—knowing that sound foretold their imminent execution. Charlie felt Stone's breath upon his face. "Do you know what it is that I detest above all else?"

Breckenridge knew this was a rhetorical question, but even if it had been a question requiring a response, there was no way he could have uttered even a word. He was waiting for the inevitable turn of the key in the lock, the sound of his own death knell.

"Keep in mind, Mr. Breckenridge, that I was raised in a military academy. Among many of the things I learned there was the importance of team spirit. In my days as a squadron leader, I taught my men that the most degraded person on earth was a soldier with the capacity to sell out his own general."

Breckenridge remained mute. Stone strolled casually toward the castle door, and then turned back to Charlie, as if adding an afterthought. "The wisest thing one could do, once such a capacity for treachery was discovered, was to annihilate the traitor—before he had the chance to strike again." Stone paused for a moment, then said, "Sweet dreams, Mr. President..."

Stone shut the door behind him. Though there was no raspy sound of a key turning in a rusty old lock—Charlie Breckenridge knew that he had just heard his own death knell.

# CHAPTER
# FORTY-NINE

I am no believer in fate.
Men's' actions, in so far as their
relations with one another,
are largely under their own control.
But there are times when
malicious powers seem to order
our human affairs for their own amusement.

—Fletcher Christian in Nordhoff and Hall,
*Mutiny on the Bounty*

Yes, heaven is thine:
But this is a world
Of sweets and sours.

—Edgar Allan Poe, *Israfel*

As the limo neared the White House, David and Rick were surprised to see a crowd surrounding the presidential mansion. As the limo pulled up even closer, the men were baffled by the sight of the White House gates chained shut, completely blocked off by armed Federal marshals. David looked over at Rick. The implications of the chained gates, the marshals, were fairly obvious. They were not to keep the mob out; they were to keep them from getting in.

Rick instantly took control. "They ain't taking you!" he cried out to David. He leaned over to the driver, shouting out orders. "Get this thing turned around—now—and floor it!"

The limo squealed into a 180-degree turn and roared back up Pennsylvania Avenue. The commander shouted out to his troops, "Open fire! Stop that car!"

The marshals obeyed their commander, guns aimed at the president's fleeing limousine. Unlike Rick, David was beside himself. "What the hell are you doing, Rick? I...I can't just run away! I'm still the president!"

Rick stared at his friend through feverish eyes. "This is my job—my call, Mr. President!"

David was jolted from his seat by a hairpin turn. "But I don't want to run away."

Rick looked over at David intently, the limo virtually flying through the darkened streets at 140 miles per hour. "You stay here, and they're gonna shoot you down! They've already peppered this car full of bullet holes, and every one of those bullets was meant to take you out! I'm in charge of protecting your life, and I'm getting you the hell out of here—or die trying!!"

"But I can't run away," David protested. "It'd look like an admission of guilt!"

Rick turned to him. "David, remember the old adage: 'He who lives and runs away lives to fight another day.'"

David heard the logic in Rick's plan, but was still rankled by the idea of fleeing. Above all else, he did not want to be considered a coward. "But—where can we go? It's not like Stone wouldn't have anticipated this. He probably has people everywhere..."

Rick tried to act nonchalant, with the wailing of police sirens assaulting their ears, fear breathing down their necks. "I'm the best at what I do, David. Isn't that why I have this job?" David smiled faintly. Rick continued, "I've had a chopper on permanent alert at Langley for over two months now—just in case you ever needed to make a 'politically expedient' departure. It'll fly us out to a Navy bird that'll hook us up with the Sixth Fleet in the Mediterranean."

David was stunned by Rick's elaborate, well-thought-out plan. What a guy! But still, he was wracked with fear. Fear of being thought a coward.

"I...I can't do that, Rick! You want me to leave the country, with all these accusations being thrown at me? You know what they'll say? They'll say I fled the country in disgrace! I won't do it! It would be just plain chicken!"

Rick looked him right in the eyes. "Steady, David. There's no cowardice here. This is simple war strategy. The truth is, as far as they're concerned, you're not the president anymore. If you want to get the country back, if you want them to even get to hear your side of the story, your first job is staying alive! And *my* job is *keeping* you alive!"

David still wavered. "But if I just go to the press, deny the accusations..."

Rick reached over and shook David forcefully as the limo roared through the damp Washington night. "You're not hearing me! The time for talk is over, man! This isn't some reelection campaign mud slinging. You want to prove to everyone that turncoat was lying?"

David nodded.

"Well, how the hell do you expect to do that if you're dead? Is that how you want the history books to read, that you were thrown out of office for murdering your old man?"

David gritted his teeth. "I certainly do not."

"Then you listen to me. I'm telling you, my brother, this is all-out war! And sometimes, the best short-term strategy is retreat!"

David sighed in resignation as the limo raced to arrive at Langley before the herd of marshals caught up with them. Rick finally saw the flight control tower that told them that they had reached home base. "Yes!" Rick screamed out. He leaned over and yelled to the limo driver. "Get us over to hangar 12—and move it, buddy; move it!"

The limo tore through the base toward the hangar. Just as Rick had said, a helicopter was ready and waiting for them outside the hangar, propellers whirling. The limo came to an abrupt halt before the chopper. Rick leaned over to the limo driver once again. "Get this baby back out onto the highway and lead those suckers on a wild goose chase. You got me?"

The limo driver responded immediately. "Yes, sir!"

Rick grabbed his reluctant charge and pushed him into the helicopter, manned by a uniformed fighter pilot. "Take off! Now—let's go!" Rick commanded. The limo spun around at top speed, taking a back road to throw off the marshals. The helicopter was in the air within seconds, roaring up high into the dense night clouds. Rick breathed a profound sigh of relief. Then, when they were obviously in the clear, he started chuckling, proud of how well his plan had worked. He had done it. He had actually pulled it off!

David, however, just stared absentmindedly out the helicopter window—steeling himself for the long and hazardous journey that he knew, in his heart, he was only just beginning.

# CHAPTER FIFTY

Open thy mouth, judge righteously,
and plead the cause of the poor and needy.

—Proverbs 31:9

Lo! Death has reared himself a throne...

—Edgar Allan Poe, *A Dream*

The "War Room" at Castle Alexander was lined wall to wall with video monitors and maps of the world. The Guardian sat quietly in a corner of the room, while Stone was in the midst of a video conference with the Chinese premier. Stone was at his most ebullient. He had the confidence of a man who knew he held the world in the palm of his hand.

"I'm afraid the American president has been forced to leave office in disgrace. The people have seen the error of their ways and have voted to join the Union. I pray that you too have chosen to join us, without any force becoming necessary—which would, of course, be a tragedy for everyone, but for your people in particular."

Stone paused slightly for dramatic emphasis. "Will I see you there, Premier Chen, when we gather in the Middle East?"

The Chinese premier was far from ebullient. He couldn't believe that Stone could speak of such life-and-death matters as if he were inviting him to a tea party. He glared at Stone belligerently, keeping his reply terse. "Neither I nor the Chinese people will ever bow before you."

Stone continued his charade, hoping to warm up the Chinese potentate. "Premier Chen, I know what the famine has cost you. Tens of millions of lives have been needlessly lost..."

The rugged-faced Chen interrupted him. "China can lose half a billion and still remain strong."

Chen's face remained impassive, as inscrutable as Stone's own. Stone lifted an eyebrow. This last comment had tickled his perverse funny bone. "You would sacrifice so many?"

The premier smiled at Stone for the first time, daggers in his eyes. "Wouldn't *you*, Chancellor?"

The screen suddenly went dead. Stone turned away from the monitor, a smile of admiration on his lips. He looked over at the Guardian. "Wonderful. The man has a brutality that almost rivals my own."

The Guardian rose from his seat, something obviously troubling him. "The armies of the other nine loyal heads are beginning to amass on the plain of Megiddo. If all ten heads are not with you..."

Stone glared at the Guardian. "O ye of little faith! The Chinese shall be there. They shall all be there!"

The Guardian felt relieved, trusting that all would be as Stone said. It always had been, and it always would be. The Guardian got down on his knees, genuflecting before his master. "I am terribly sorry, my lord, for my weakness."

But Stone wasn't listening. The Guardian watched as Stone moved over to the windows, throwing them wide open. Stone sucked in a deep breath, drawing his own shadow off the floor and into his body.

His face took on the appearance of an ancient Chinese Mandarin.

When his eyes finally snapped back open, they seemed reptilian. Stone opened his mouth wide and expelled a swarm of millions of plague-ridden flies, which poured out of the open windows over Rome. The hideous black mass circled Stone's castle before heading east. Far East, that is.

Stone, weakened by the power of the expulsion, staggered back from the window. The Guardian came up behind him, rubbing his back like a bench coach seeking to resuscitate his top heavyweight after sixteen brutal rounds in the ring.

Stone, still recovering, was surprised to hear a voice from the suddenly opened door. Stone reeled around to see Gabriella. She stared at his face, his eyes still reptilian. In that instant, she realized that her worst fears had been true. A look of abject horror came over her face. Before anyone had a chance to speak, two armed guards came up behind her.

"I'm sorry, Chancellor, for the intrusion. The First Lady insisted she had vital information concerning the Chinese..."

Stone, still weakened, dismissed the soldiers with a flick of the hand. Gabriella too had vanished from sight, and Stone was far too debilitated to follow her. The Guardian put a hand on Stone's shoulder, his voice soft yet firm. "It's about time she knew. "

Stone nodded stoically, knowing exactly what he meant. "Yes. It is about time."

$$\Omega^2$$

Gabriella ran down the hallway, headed for the stairs, spiraling down them at a dizzying pace. All was a blur before her. She finally stumbled, falling to the tiled floor on the landing. More terrified than injured, Gabriella got to her feet, hobbling through the long entry hall. She kept looking back over her shoulder, knowing full well that she would be followed.

Gabriella struggled with the enormous bolts and finally managed to throw open the heavy front door. With the fresh air finally hitting her face, she felt momentarily revived. That is, until she noticed Stone, framed by the Roman night, standing only a few feet before her, encircling her like a dark cloud. Gabriella was paralyzed with fear. Caught. Like a rabbit in a steel-jaw trap.

"I am truly sorry you had to see that, my dear," Stone said, moving closer to her. She shuddered with apprehension. "I am sorrier still that you saw fit to violate my strictest orders never to enter my private chambers." He smiled at her, transformed once again into the sandy-haired, silver-tongued charmer she had known since childhood. It was utterly bewildering. "Even the closest of couples must have their secrets, Gabriella."

Gabriella had no idea what to say. She was revolted by him. Everything David had said—everything she had most feared—had proven to be most tragically true. "I am sorry," she managed to whisper.

Stone moved in closer and put a reassuring arm around her. This time, she couldn't deny that it was indeed the frigid arm of death itself. "My darling. I have loved you all my life, taken care of you..." Stone gestured around at the magnificence of their surroundings, "...in a style befitting a queen. I have always said I intended you to be my queen. Now, that dream has become a reality."

Gabriella stared at him with trepidation, but Stone continued. "Gabriella," he asked, a trace of genuine emotion in his voice. "Do you still love me—as you did so long ago?"

Gabriella was no fool. She knew what she had seen. The hideous image was forever etched in her mind. She could hardly face Stone— or whoever this was impersonating Stone. "Yes...yes, Stone. Of course I do."

Stone knew she was lying, and it wounded him deeply. He now sank to his knees before her. "Gabriella, look what I am doing. I am on my knees before you, offering to make you my queen, asking you to rule forever by my side. Will you cast me away? Destroy my dreams?"

Gabriella looked down on him with a curious mixture of pity and revulsion. Stone also picked up on this immediately. His eyes grew wide with anxiety. He reached up and took her hands in his own. "Gabriella. You must not look at me that way. It pains me more than you can imagine. I, who now rule both heaven and earth, should not have to sink to his knees before anyone—except my immortal father..."

Gabriella slowly found the strength to meet his eyes. "And just who is your immortal father, Stone?"

Stone feigned surprise. "Why, the one true god, of course! What makes you ask such a question?"

Gabriella shook her head. "Will you put your hand on the Holy Bible and swear that to me? That Jesus Christ is your Lord and Savior?"

Stone put on a fair display of indignation. He dropped her hands and rose to his feet. "You humiliate me, Gabriella, with such nonsensical requests!"

"I don't think there is anything nonsensical about it," Gabriella whispered, realizing that she was perched precariously before the jaws of a shark. But her vast store of inner strength made her press the issue. "If you accept Jesus Christ as your Lord, then how can you claim to rule both heaven and earth? That you virtually rule the earth, there is no denying—but is it not Jesus Christ who sits at the right hand of the Father, the most High God?"

Stone was actually flustered. He felt pain for the first time since his painful break with David. Of all the souls on earth, Gabriella was one of the select few who could still make him feel like a man. He realized at that moment that the jig was up. The words of the Guardian resounded in his ears: "It is time she knew."

*Yes,* Stone thought. *It is the only course available. If I truly want Gabriella to reign beside me, to be my queen, throughout all eternity, I must convince her of my sincerity, of the righteousness of my plan. If she does not accept me for who I truly am—I will have no queen.*

He moved closer to her, knowing full well that by his confession he might lose her forever. Stone was about to be more honest and open with her than he had ever been—in all their years together. The risk was almost more than he could bear to take. Still, he saw no other way. He was not a vampire. He couldn't just bite her neck and make her do his bidding. He could kill with a mere shake of the hand, he could decimate nations, but he could not make a woman love him against her will. He placed his hand softly against her cheek.

"My dear, my dearest; I must ask you now to take a tremendous leap of faith. I am asking you to believe in me and understand why I cannot honor your request."

Gabriella fortified herself against what was to come. She already knew enough. She didn't want to hear any more.

"Listen to me, Gabriella. I cannot place my hand on your Bible. It would just burst into flames. I am about to tell you something that will go against everything you have ever been taught, everything you have ever believed in. Now, I am asking you to believe in me."

Stone sucked in a deep breath. He spoke calmly, though his voice quavered with emotion. "Gabriella, you must trust me when I tell you that Jesus Christ was nothing more than an ingrate. A false prophet. It was He who has caused all the wars, the famine, that have plagued mankind for more than two thousand years! It is I who was born to sit beside my immortal father, Lucifer, the brightest of all angels—and you were born to sit beside me for all eternity as my queen. Do you understand this? Can you accept this?"

Stone said these words as if he were merely asking a woman for her hand in marriage, whereas, in truth, he was asking her to relinquish everything she had ever believed in, as well as jeopardizing her immortal soul. It struck her as ironic that this was probably the first time Stone had ever been honest with her. Ironic, and tragic. She had the temerity to stare Stone down, as no mortal man had ever dared to do. No man, that is, except his brother.

"No, Stone. I cannot accept this. And I never will."

Stone became enraged. He slapped her so hard that she fell to the ground, her mouth bleeding profusely. She began to cry, but Stone was oblivious now, flailing his arms over the parapets. "You would deny me your allegiance, I, who have been your husband and lord for over thirty years? I, who have spared nothing to protect you from the cruelty of this world?"

Gabriella watched in mute terror as Stone turned his eyes to the heavens and railed at his immortal foe. "It is You once again who stand in my way! It is You who took away my mother, and now you have stolen away my life's partner! From this moment on, I swear by my lord to double my efforts to cast You down from my rightful throne!"

He turned back to Gabriella, seething with the fury of rejection. "With or without you as my queen, I shall reign beside my father!"

# CHAPTER
# FIFTY-ONE

Sion lies waste, and thy Jerusalem,
O Lord, is fall'n to utter desolation;
Against thy prophets and holy men
The sin hath wrought a fateful combination;
Profaned thy name, thy worship overthrown,
And made thee, Living Lord, a God unknown.

—Fulke Greville, *Caelica*

D awn was breaking over the Gobi Desert in a swirling sorbet of colors. The majesty that was daybreak was calm and serene. A persistent, hissing sound interrupted the beauty of the scene, as the swarm of venomous flies came suddenly into view, careening over the Gobi Desert into Asia.

In Tiananmen Square, some twenty thousand people bustled about, opening storefronts, hawking rice cakes and trinkets, trying to start their day. Suddenly the sky grew dark. A group of Chinese vendors looked up as the swarm of flies virtually blotted out the sun. People ran out from their kiosks, fish markets and vegetable stands— all pointing up at the disappearing sun in terror.

Then came the sound of the huge, buzzing horde. Thousands congregated in the square, watching, waiting, as the flies congealed, forming a giant Chinese dragon. The mystified crowd muttered to themselves as the dragon loomed ominously over Beijing. The populace fell to their knees as the dragon began to speak to them in Mandarin.

"The kings of the East will assemble their armies on the plains of Megiddo..."

The dragon's eyes flared with anger and defiance.

"Thirty days...or all is lost."

The flies dissolved from their formation, nose-diving into Tiananmen Square. People fell over each other; hundreds were trampled to death trying to escape the deadly bite of the flies that furiously attacked them.

From his vantage point within the Parliament building, the premier watched in anguish as the plague descended upon his people. His cabinet aide stood beside him, babbling hysterically. "We are powerless! You can see for yourself the powers this man commands. There is nothing we can do but succumb, before he kills each and every one of us!"

The premier ran through his extremely limited options. "There is only one thing we can do."

He glanced out the window again at the sight of his blood-soaked people. Thousands were fleeing; thousands more blanketed the square, dead and dying, covered from head to toe with the disease-ridden flies. The sight nauseated him. He turned away from the window, staring up at his sacred shrine. He lit a fragrant stick of incense and a candle as an offering to the Buddha and meditated silently.

Finally, he turned back to his panicked aide. "Buddha will always be in our hearts—but we must give this man what he wants."

The aide breathed a sigh of relief. "Shall I get Chancellor

Alexander on the phone?" he asked anxiously. Premier Chen settled down in his armchair, lighting up a pipe. He nodded most reluctantly, sensing the downfall of the world he had known, the world of his fathers and his father's fathers. He stared around the room at the photographs and oil paintings of the great premiers of China who had gone before him, and felt utterly helpless. The nervous aide's voice interrupted his musings. "I have Chancellor Alexander for you, Premier Chen..."

Chen rose from his chair in resignation.

# CHAPTER FIFTY-TWO

I stand amid the roar
Of a surf-tormented shore,
And I hold within my hand
Grains of the golden sand—
O God! Cannot I grasp them with a tighter grasp?

—Edgar Allan Poe, *Spirits of the Dead*


"In God's name, Mr. Christian! What is it you do?
Do you realize that this means the ruin of
everything? Give up this madness!"
"It is too late," Christian replied coldly.
"I have been in hell…and I mean to
stand it no longer."

—Nordhoff and Hall, *Mutiny on the Bounty*

The Mediterranean Sea hosted only one lonely visitor tonight: a massive American aircraft carrier steaming into position off the coast of Italy. On the flight deck, a squad of Apache AH-64 assault helicopters idled on the deck. The roar of their propellers was deafening against the still, blue waters.

Inside the massive craft's map room, David, flanked by both an American Army general and Navy admiral, went over the floor plans to Castle Alexander. The general turned to him. "But this is so sketchy, sir...isn't there any other way we can obtain this information?"

David shook his head. "Not without alerting the chancellor's armies. This is it, I'm afraid, as best as I can remember. I wasn't exactly a frequent visitor to Castle Alexander."

The general frowned. "Then that's what we'll have to go with."

Rick entered the room, dressed entirely in a black commando suit. From the look on his face, David could tell there was bad news. "Premier Chen has caved in. China is sending troops to join your brother, and Breckenridge has committed our troops in the Gulf."

The military men groaned in despair. David, on the other hand, seemed filled with inner strength. "It looks like it's all up to us now, doesn't it?"

The naval commander sighed in consternation. "But we're only one ship—what can we do?"

David swept them all off their feet with his enthusiasm. "We can *win*—that's what we can do! We're now officially freedom fighters! Renegade warriors! We win this one, and our country—and the rest of the world—is free again. We lose, and well..." He looked over at Rick, and then at the officers, his face becoming grim. "We *can't* lose this one."

Everyone in the room was buoyed by David's infectious spirit. They all saluted David by way of support, returning to the main deck. David stood alone with Rick. "I guess I always knew it would come down to this. Brother against brother. Cain against Abel."

Rick nodded, impressed by David's courage and resolve. "Congratulations. You've become Fletcher Christian at last, David."

David thought about that for a moment. "Well, I don't officially become Fletcher Christian until I overthrow Captain Bligh."

Rick rolled his eyes. "All right then, how about, you're well on you're way to becoming Fletcher Christian. Better?"

"Better," David agreed.

Within the aircraft carrier, the soldiers fortified themselves for what looked to be the most significant battle of their lives. The Army commandos all smeared black greasepaint on their faces. One of the helicopter pilots zipped up his flight suit, grabbing a photo of his wife and two little girls and stuffing it into his pocket. The soldiers on deck were preparing for a full-scale attack, the clumping of boots running across the armor-plated flight deck as they readied themselves for war.

A slow but steady rain pelted the deck as the Army general issued his commands, and the first unit of Rangers boarded the idling choppers. A grim David Alexander, having assumed his prerogative as commander in chief of the Armed Forces, even if, at this point, his "armed forces" consisted solely of this one aircraft carrier, also wore a black commando suit. He stood watching the troops systematically board the Apaches. He saluted them as they prepared to take off, and the men saluted him back. David spoke to the entire group of assembled soldiers, both Army and Navy.

"I want you to know that I am a loyal American, as I can see by your strength and courage that you all are. But what is critical to understand is this: We're not just fighting to save our country. This has grown far bigger than that. Everything we do from here on in is for the good of the entire world!"

David now brandished the flag of the One World. Holding up a butane lighter, he set the flag on fire. The soldiers watched in silence as the thick flames licked up the silk. When the flames finally reached his hand, David tossed the burning symbol out into the night. Caught on a breeze, the crimson flag danced in the air, finally disappearing as the flames consumed it. The troops cheered as the choppers took off into the rainy night. David held his hand to his head in an official military salute. The battle was underway.

Rick turned to David. "Might doesn't make right, does it, Mr. Christian?"

David stared off at the choppers ascending into the gray Mediterranean sky. "Nope. It never did."

# CHAPTER
# FIFTY-THREE

Yet a little while is the light with you.
Walk while ye have the light.

—John 12:35


With the fruit of her hands she planteth a vineyard.

—Proverbs 31:16

The Apaches were like sure-footed Indian braves, surveying their enemy's turf, sweeping in low—only these braves had the benefit of being able to climb over cities, over treetops, and creep in between buildings. There was only one disadvantage that their Apache brethren of yore never had to deal with: They made a lot more noise.

A squad of silent Army Rangers followed the Apaches in a transport helicopter. David and Rick sat among the Rangers, their faces chiseled and determined. Determined, that is, not to think of the fight that lay ahead.

Coming up on Rome airspace, the pilot reported that there was no resistance in sight. The Rangers breathed a sigh of relief. Rick did a quick check on David. He had to shake his head. It was remarkable how his friend had instantly assumed the persona of the commander in chief of the Army and Navy. A man with no military training whatsoever. And yet, there was no doubt in his mind: The man was a natural-born leader.

David's exterior may have seemed implacable, but inside, his mind was whirling, filled with all the incongruities of the situation.

*How ironic this all was. How funny, since he had always been a pacifist at heart, valuing peace above all else. It was his brother who had grown up idolizing and pantomiming the world's greatest generals; his own idols had been the peacemakers. But now here he was, of his own free will, in full military gear, commanding the combined forces of the United States and going up against that very same brother. The same brother who had tried to murder him in his crib; who had killed their father in cold blood; who had contrived to destroy his name and reputation. And now, he was somehow supposed to compete with this maniacal, military genius, who now fancied himself not only a god, which would have been arrogant enough, but the one and only god. Boy, life sure had a way of turning things topsy-turvy.*

On a more philosophical level, David had put those personal matters aside. The murder of a father, the betrayal of a brother, fell to the sidelines when seen against the big picture. What did such picayune circumstances matter in the greater scheme of things? All that really mattered at this point was to give the world a chance at existing—a last chance of remaining free: free of Stone Alexander. Whatever David would do would be his very best—and however inferior or inadequate that might be, he forgave himself. Deep inside he knew that, even if he failed, at least he had been on the right side.

Rick interrupted this interior monologue. "David…"

David roused himself and turned to Rick. Rick could see that he was a million miles away. "I guess this would be a bad time to discuss the legality of assassinating a sovereign leader?"

David's mouth turned up into an almost sickly smile. "I suppose that would depend on what legal system we were using." Rick tossed him a sardonic glance. David continued, "As I see it, there are no laws anymore. We just have to make 'em up as we go along."

Rick raised an eyebrow. "We still have our consciences. That ought to do us just fine for now."

David nodded in agreement. "It'll have to."

David stared over at the blank faces of the men sitting across from him. They were all deep in thought. He wondered about their lives; what they'd left behind to come on this mission. Of all these men, he probably had the least to lose of any of them. No parents; no wife; no children to mourn him if something should happen to him. For once, David was glad to be so free of any attachments. He was truly a man with nothing, or no one, to lose.

David contacted the pilot on the intercom. "Time to target?"

The answer came in loud and clear over the loud speaker. "Three minutes, thirty seconds, sir." The soldiers all noticeably stiffened.

David turned to his best friend and now comrade in arms. "Looks like this is it, bud." Rick drew in a deep breath. David surveyed all the brave warriors now under his command. "Up!"

The soldiers stood at attention, weapons bristling in their nylon harnesses. Wind whipped around them as the massive side doors were slid open. One by one, the team of commandos climbed on to the chopper skids, dropping their rappelling lines into the dark night. Their destination: the castle perched high on the mountain, silhouetted by the lights of Rome.

Two dozen Airborne Rangers silently glided down into the battlements of Castle Alexander on black nylon ropes. Stone's security forces found themselves caught by surprise by this aerial attack. The Rangers landed, their silenced MP5SD3 submachine guns making quick work of the castle guards. A triumphant voice came in over David's intercom.

"Entering the main building. Third floor." David and Rick waited in anticipation, like Victorian children in line at the local bookstore waiting for the next installment of Dickens's *Great Expectations*.

Silent as death itself, the intrepid Rangers made their way into Castle Alexander, moving past countless rooms filled with medieval weaponry and arcane artifacts. The squad leader stopped to shine his flashlight on the map taped to his left forearm. He spoke quietly to his men. "Up ahead. End of the hall. Break left and right. Now!" The men broke into two lines and moved down the corridor, destroying each room with a "flash/bang" grenade.

Outside the fortress, the Apache helicopter set itself down, and the second wave, led by David and Rick, leaped out and headed for the Castle. As they moved swiftly toward the building, David heard the voice of the lead Ranger on his intercom. "Heading for Alexander's office." David, Rick and the rest of the back-up unit finally caught up with the commando squad. David pushed toward the front of the action, but Rick grabbed his arm, admonishing him to bide his time.

The lead Ranger kicked in the door and tossed in a grenade. BAMPH! A flash of light and smoke—then the commandos burst in, emptying their weapons and riddling the room with bullets. All were silent for a moment, waiting for the debris to settle. Xenon flashlights cut through the smoke.

David and Rick carefully entered Stone's War Room. They looked around for a body. Preferably, Stone's body. But the room was empty. Rick grit his teeth. "Son of a...!"

David tossed him an ironic glance. "You didn't think it was going to be *that* easy, did you?" Rick smirked as David led the troops to still another door. The men advanced, threw a grenade and blasted through the heavy door to Stone's private sanctuary, his inner sanctum.

The men were speechless, staring at the altar, all the trappings, of Stone's demonic religion. One of the soldiers trained his light on the wall to reveal a gruesome sight. It was a man, nailed to the life-sized fresco of Jesus Christ. Dried blood encrusted the nails going through his hands and feet. All that was missing to complete the picture was the crown of thorns. Rick was the first to speak. "Jesus..."

David shined his flashlight on the man's face. Breckenridge. David shuddered, going weak in the knees, but finally regaining the strength to mumble out a response. "Nope. Judas."

A report was coming in over Rick's earpiece. "What? Who the hell does he think he is—Elvis?" Rick turned to David in a huff. "It appears that Mr. Alexander has left the building."

A rumbling broke out throughout the ranks. David thought carefully for a moment. "He knew. That's why he just left a token guard force here. And a little token for our appreciation..." He motioned up at Breckenridge's frozen corpse desecrating the crucifix. David continued to think aloud. "Where the hell could he...?"

Before he had a chance to muse too long, a report came in on Rick's earpiece. His eyes instantly lit up. He turned to David. "They say they've found someone locked in the sub-basement. A woman!"

David paused only for a moment. "Gabriella?" David rushed out of the room, forgetting to give the order for the troops to follow him.

Rick immediately took charge. "Well, what're you all waiting for? Cover the president!"

The commandos all headed off after David *en masse*. The squadron, with David again in the lead, patrolled the lower levels of Castle Alexander, descending into what looked like the lowest levels of hell depicted in Dante's *Inferno.*

The soldiers carefully entered a narrow, stone corridor that dated back to the days of the early Christian martyrs, the walls lined with tiny cells where the Christians were kept before being taken to the Coliseum.

David moved solemnly to the end of the corridor where a group of soldiers had liberated a woman. She was lying on her back, and a medic was administering a shot of adrenaline into her veins to revive her. She came to, choking, and the paramedic tried to get her to drink some water from his canteen.

David walked over to the woman with trepidation, his heart pounding. He looked down to see Gabriella, the beauty of her spirit still shining bright though she was emaciated and weak. David knelt down next to her and took her hand tenderly. It took a few moments for her to focus her eyes and see who was kneeling beside her. "David?"

David smiled, trying, as always, to make light of the circumstances. "It's good to see you again, Gabriella. That's twice now in the same decade."

Gabriella managed a weak smile. "People will talk."

As he looked down at her, a woman in her fifties, hair streaked with gray, bones poking through her clothes, he felt such enormous love that it staggered him. In an instant, he realized that this was the only woman he had ever really loved. And this might be his last chance—not only to have her for his own—but also to save her life.

He bellowed at the paramedics. "Help her to her feet! Get her back on that chopper and out of here!" As more ground troops poured out of a second and third U.S. helicopter, David, flanked by a wall of armed men, walked Gabriella slowly up the stairs and out of the castle. For her sake, David tried to keep his emotions under tight control.

"Why did he do it, Gabriella? What happened?"

Gabriella smiled faintly, clearly in pain. He led her outside and deposited her on a bench until the paramedics arrived with a stretcher. When she had gotten her breath back, he asked the same question again.

"What happened, Gabriella? You found him out?"

Gabriella nodded, shamefaced. "Yes. I found him out. I did the unpardonable. I spied on him. And of course, he caught me. He begged me to stay with him, knowing what I knew after what I had seen with my own eyes. But I couldn't. I refused."

David's feelings went beyond fury. Still, he held himself in check, wary of both her physical and mental condition. "So he locked you up ...his own wife...like..."

Gabriella finished the sentence for him. "Like all the other Christian martyrs left there to starve to death? Or be thrown to the lions? Yes. That's exactly what he did." She smiled weakly. "Sometimes, I could hear their voices. Feel their pain. It helped me to understand. To feel less alone. Under the circumstances, I think it was very appropriate that he locked me up down there, don't you?"

David ran his hand through her matted hair. Though exhausted, she fought to speak. "All these years, living here, and I didn't even know they were there. The catacombs. I had no idea there was anything below the basement. But Stone knew. That's why he bought this place. He could still smell their blood on his hands."

Gabriella became faint. David lay her back against him on the bench. "Are you all right?" he asked.

Gabriella shook her head as she reached for his hand. He couldn't believe how cold and bony her hand felt in his. It had always been so warm, so comforting. But this time it felt like touching a corpse.

*A wave of panic overwhelmed him. For the first time it actually hit him—he might lose her!*

"I'm not all right, David. None of us are all right. None of us can be all right. Not until Stone is dead."

David knelt before her, feeling more love and pity than he ever knew himself capable of. "I'm more worried about you, right now, Gabriella..."

She stared at him with an otherworldly gaze, imploringly. "I am gone, David. Please do not worry about me. I am already in a better place. But you must understand, David, that you're fighting Stone for the wrong reason." He just looked at her, puzzled. "You still think this is about the One World?"

David's eyes grew wide. "Well, isn't it?"

Gabriella sadly shook her head. "No. It's not about the One World. And it's not personal..."

David did a double take. "Look, Gabriella, there's plenty for me to get personal about with Stone. Look what he's done to you! And now I know now that he killed our father."

He expected Gabriella to be surprised at this, but nothing could surprise her anymore. In the same quiet tone of voice, she asked, "How did you feel about that when you found out?"

David struggled to find the right words. "I've struggled for years over how I felt about it."

"You didn't think it was bad?" she questioned.

"I thought it was bad, sure. But it didn't really hurt me. I really never knew my father. Neither of us did. The only time I ever saw him was the occasional Christmas, where he basically ignored me and I just wanted to run back to boarding school. So, when I first saw him lying on the ground there, dead, my first feeling was relief. I've been trying to be a good public servant all these years—maybe partly to make up for the guilt I felt—that I still feel—over the lack of sorrow I felt when I saw him lying there dead."

A crow cawed from the trees above them as David held Gabriella close to his body, trying to envelop her in his warmth. But her body remained chilled. But weak as she was, she desperately wanted to make her point. "David—do you really want to do what's best for your people? For *all* people?"

"Well, of course. Yes," he replied.

"Do you remember any of your Bible?"

David was taken aback. "The Bible? Frankly, I never really had any use for it. It wasn't exactly part of Father's agenda."

Gabriella sought out his eyes. "I heard Stone talking about the 'bowls of wrath'...."

David wrinkled up his face, vaguely comprehending. "The wrath of God?"

Gabriella nodded. "My father gave me his Bible on the day I married your brother. He wanted me to read it, to get closer to God. You know me, *testadure*. I felt I was close enough to God already, so I never did. It wasn't until Stone had me locked up that I started reading it. I had to read the whole thing to understand what he was doing—but I found what I was looking for at the end, in the Book of Revelation." She looked at him pointedly. "Hear me, David. It says, 'The Beast suffers a mortal head wound, recovers and takes over the world from Jerusalem.' Does this make any sense to you, David? Does it help you to understand what is happening?"

David was slowly picking up her meaning. "You don't mean that Stone thinks he is—?" She swiftly interrupted.

"Not *thinks*. He *is*."

David felt that Gabriella was suffering from delusions. It was quite understandable, considering everything she'd been through. He'd see she got the best care, a long rest back in Washington. He replied softly, not wanting to offend her. "What are you telling me, Gabriella? That Stone is the devil? The Antichrist?"

Gabriella heard the disbelief in his voice. She looked at him, pleading with her eyes. "I know you think I'm a crazy woman, David. But there is far more to the world than what you choose to understand. Even I didn't understand it, and I was living under the same roof with him! I was blinded to the truth because I wanted to be. But as sick as I am, David, I see things more clearly now than ever before. All you have to do is look around you, David. The disasters that have been plaguing the world have not been from natural causes. They are the bowls of the wrath of God! When they are released, it is the countdown to the end of the world!"

David felt as if he'd entered the Twilight Zone. Still unwilling to believe, he at least made an attempt to follow her line of thought.

"This is why he is having the armies assemble at Megiddo, don't you see? This is where the final battle between good and evil is prophesied to occur. Do you understand, David? Can you believe me?"

David mumbled, as if to himself. "Armageddon."

Gabriella nodded. "Yes. Yes! Now you see! I am convinced of it. And *you* must be convinced of it too, or all is lost. If you have ever loved me, you must believe me in this above all else!"

David was baffled. All this biblical talk left him cold.

"Don't you see, David? You're the only one who can defeat Stone. He knows that. That's why he fears you."

Her last comment hit home. Gabriella had not been the first person to say that he was the only one who could take Stone down. Perhaps there was something to what she said. David just shook his head in confusion, watching as the commandos prepared to board their choppers. "I don't know what to say, Gabriella. I've...I've never even set foot in a church. You're asking me to take a fantastic leap here..."

She squeezed his hand. "Yes. That's exactly right. A leap of faith. It is only by taking that leap that you have any chance of defeating Stone, for he is Stone no longer. He is the Beast."

David saw how agitated Gabriella had become, and he tried to placate her, motioning for the paramedics to hurry up with the stretcher. "All right. We'll talk about it. Let's get you to the ship, get you some food, and we can go over it all again later."

Gabriella was crestfallen. "There is no later, David. You don't understand. You won't understand..." Gabriella closed her eyes. The stretcher finally arrived, and David rose to his feet, extending his hands to help Gabriella.

She started to rise, when suddenly, the carrion crow in the tree above them silently took wing, flying away from them and then turning back—transforming itself into a black arrow. The arrow quickly flew across the lawn toward Gabriella. The three-foot arrow entered her chest—lifting her off her feet, slamming her back against a tree and pinning her there.

"Gabriella!" David desperately grabbed the end of the shaft and yanked it out of her body without so much as a trace of blood. The arrow dissolved into mist in his hands. David screamed out in agony. Gabriella's body slumped to the ground. David cradled her in his arms, tears filling his eyes. "Gabriella! Please don't die. Please don't die..."

Gabriella had only a few breaths left, and they were for David alone. "David...you...must believe..."

Rick rushed over in time to see David holding Gabriella's crumpled body in his arms. David looked up at Rick through moist eyes. "Where did that arrow come from? There's not a sentry alive on this mountaintop!"

Rick could only shake his head. In his anguish, David automatically fell into a deep, trancelike state.

In his vision, he saw bodies writhing in the darkest pits of hell, in tiny chambers like the ones in Stone's sub-basement. The catacombs. A demon with fiery eyes arose from beneath the sea and breathed plagues of locusts onto hordes of fleeing people. In the midst of all of this he saw an empty desert plain. Only one word echoed through his mind as the vision played itself out. Megiddo. Megiddo...

"David, David, are you all right?" It had been several minutes since David fell into the trance. He came out of it slowly, seeing paramedics hovering over him, an oxygen mask over his face, a man pounding on his chest. When he finally opened his eyes, he saw Rick bent over him, terror in his eyes. "Oh, man. You scared the hell out of us. Your heart just stopped, man. For three minutes! Are you OK?"

David nodded, a stunning realization finally hitting him. He turned to Rick, a new light in his eyes. An inner light. "Rick, I've been so wrong. I've just seen it. I've been on the right mission, but for the wrong reason."

Rick looked over at him with pity, assuming that grief had afflicted his friend's mind. They both watched in silence as the paramedics covered Gabriella's body and carried it off to one of the choppers. "You'll be OK, man. I'm so sorry..."

To everyone's surprise, David suddenly jumped to his feet, completely invigorated. The man who had been technically dead only five minutes before had become a living dynamo.

"There's no time for this now. We've got a war to fight!" The small crowd of soldiers around him cheered. Their commander had returned. Rick followed David toward the waiting chopper, shaking his head at his friend's sudden transformation.

# CHAPTER
# FIFTY-FOUR

My son, forget not my law;
but let thine heart keep my commandments.

—Proverbs 3:1


We are never deceived; we deceive ourselves.

—Goethe

In Jerusalem, the faithful of the Moslem, Christian and Hebrew faiths assembled before the most significant icons of their respective religions—the Dome of the Rock; the Wailing Wall; the Church of the Holy Sepulchre—all clustered in the heart of old Jerusalem. Rather than infighting, as had been their habit for millennia, the faithful of all three religions prayed and wailed in unison, each according to their custom, begging God for help during these tumultuous times. All bickering, all animosity, of Jews toward Moslems, of Christians toward Jews, was gone now. They were joined together now by the power of their faith and their fear of an unknown evil. For the first time, they all prayed together as one.

$$\Omega^2$$

On King George Street, right across from the luxurious Plaza Hotel in Jerusalem, stood the most important symbol of the Jewish faith: the majestic synagogue *Beit Knesset Hagadol*. This foremost Israeli synagogue was the domain of Chief Rabbi Aaron Levy, as was only fitting, since he was the foremost among all the rabbis.

Alone in the *shul*, Rabbi Levy had just opened the *Aron Hakodesh*, the sacred closet that housed the *Torahs*, or holy books of the Jewish faith. He combed through pages of the *Torah*, seeking out a specific passage. Hanging on the ceiling over him was the *Ner Tamid,* or Eternal Light. The rabbi looked up at the *Ner Tamid*, praying aloud for any glimpse of light that God cared to send his way. He could certainly use it now.

Rabbi Levy was startled by the sound of footsteps running into the *shul*, and turned to see his son, Jacob. Jacob hesitated, always slightly afraid of his father, but finally approached him. The rabbi carried the *Torah* a few steps from the *Aron Hakodesh* to a high table beside the *bimah*, placing it down to practice reading the passage aloud before the empty synagogue.

"Father?"

Aaron turned and slowly approached his son. "Jacob, I have something to tell you. The Chinese have joined the World Union. Do you know what that means, my son?" Jacob stared at him blankly, prepared for anything. "It means that Jerusalem will fall this night."

Jacob dared to confront his father once more. "It has all happened just as I told you, Father..."

The rabbi now noticed his son clutching a New Testament Bible. He tore it out of his hands, infuriated. *"Cheelool Hashem!* Where did you get that book? I told you never to pick it up again. This is a blasphemy! Son, do not again dare to tell me the things of God!"

For the first time, Jacob got a good look at his father's face. It was covered in leprous sores. Jacob gasped, pointing to the Bible his father now had clutched in his hands. "Father, please! Let me read this to you..."

The rabbi relented, allowing the boy to take back the Bible. Nervously, Jacob fumbled through the pages. Now it was *he* who was looking for a special passage in a holy book. A holy book that was different from his father's—yet each of them represented the Sacred Word of their respective faiths.

"Just listen, Father, please. This is what it says. 'I saw another...coming up out of the earth... and he performs great signs—he even makes fire come down from heaven.'"

His father moved away from him. Jacob grabbed on to his prayer shawl, forcing him to listen. "He gave breath to the image of the Beast, that the image should both speak and cause as many as would not worship him be killed..."

The rabbi remained unmoved. "What does all this mean, Jacob?"

"Please, Father, if you would just read the book you would understand—then you could make the others understand. They'll listen to you! They always listen to you! We can't just give up! We can't give the Beast what he wants!"

"Beast or no beast, it is too late, my son. Jerusalem will fall. You must get down on your knees and pray, Jacob, that we may survive this plague. And if not—God will always have a place for the righteous at His side."

Jacob just would not accept his father's fatalistic attitude. He grabbed at his father's scabrous hand. "God would not want *this* to happen! Look at what the Beast has already done to *you!*"

The rabbi moved out of his son's grasp, resuming his prayer position. "You must prepare, my son. It would be best." Jacob saw that there was no use. He lay the Bible quietly open on the table next to his father.

"Good-bye, then, Father. I love you."

The proud rabbi would not turn to watch his son leave the synagogue, even though he knew it might be the last time he would lay eyes on him in this life. After Jacob was gone, though, his eyes slowly focused on the book his son had left on the table. Hands shaking, feeling that he was doing a blasphemous act just laying his hands on the New Testament, Rabbi Levy finally picked up the book, forcing himself to read where his son had left it open. After a few minutes of avidly devouring the pages at lightning speed, his eyes widened in terror.

*His son had been right all along.* He sank to his knees on the cold floor of the synagogue, wailing inconsolably.

# CHAPTER
# FIFTY-FIVE

Strength and honour are her clothing;
and she shall rejoice in time to come.

—Proverbs 31:25


Thine are we, David, and on thy side,
thou son of Jesse: peace, peace,
be unto thee, and peace be to thine helpers;
for God helpeth thee.

—1 Chronicles 12:18

Surrounded by Airborne Rangers, David, in a black suit, knelt down in the last pew of St. Lucia's Cathedral in Rome. David sat alone at a mass being performed over a closed casket. He listened as the priest read scriptures, his voice dreamlike and airy, floating in and out of David's consciousness.

*"I saw a new heaven and a new earth and heard a loud voice saying, 'Behold, I will wipe away every tear from their eyes. There shall be no more death or sorrow or crying or pain.'"*

David's head fell into his hands. He began to pray, for perhaps the first time in his life. "Please, Lord...I don't understand. I want to help...help me." He clenched his eyes tightly shut. "Not my will, but thy will be done."

Again, the comforting voice of the priest entered his consciousness.

*"I saw heaven open and behold, a white horse. And He who sat on him was called Faithful and True. In righteousness He judges and makes war and on His thigh is written: King of kings and Lord of lords."*

David looked up now, entranced by the words the priest spoke. The priest's eyes met his own. He now spoke directly to David, with a special message for him alone.

*"And I saw the Beast, the kings of the earth, and their armies, gathered together to make war against Him who sat on the horse..."*

David nodded at the priest, understanding, blinking through his tears.

*"But the Lord will consume the Lawless One with the breath of His mouth and the brightness of His return."*

The priest stared right at David, and David drew strength from his words. He was so absorbed that he didn't even notice Rick moving through the church and sitting down beside him. David finally sensed the warmth of the body beside him. He turned to see Rick, looking very upset. David whispered to him, "What is it?"

"Word came in from the Knesset. Those tough Israelis have suddenly decided to dig in. They're not going to let Stone's troops march into Jerusalem. Chinese and U.S. militia are rolling into the Middle East right now. What do you want to do?"

David looked over at Gabriella's white coffin. The priest was waving incense all around her as he prayed. His eyes met David's one last time. David jumped to his feet and headed for the exit.

"C'mon!" Rick finally caught up with him at the door of the cathedral. "Hey, Boss—where are we going?"

David smiled bitterly. "To do battle with the Beast."

Rick smiled, opening the door to the waiting limo. David yelled into the intercom at the driver. "Get me Premier Chen on the phone. Pronto!"

# $\Omega^2$

Inside the great cathedral, alone with Gabriella and his God, the priest concluded the mass.

*"I am the Alpha and the Omega, the Beginning and the End..."*

# CHAPTER FIFTY-SIX

Alexander, Caesar, Charlemagne
and I myself have founded empires—
but upon what do these creations of
our genius depend? Upon force.
Jesus alone founded His empire upon love,
and to this very day, millions would die for Him.

—Napoleon Bonaparte


He will give the devil his due.

—William Shakepeare, *Henry IV*

Rumbling toward Megiddo were at least two hundred million Asian soldiers, complete with tanks and supply vehicles. The troops of the world were assembling at Megiddo. One man had summoned them all: Stone Alexander.

The faces of the men and women comprising the world's united armies were varied: Africans, Indians, Russians, men, women, teenagers—all nervous, excited and scared. They fondled their assault rifles, grenade launchers and other weapons expectantly, still unaware of exactly what enemy they were being summoned to face.

A European platoon drilled in the fading sun; they were clean and pale, just off the plane. Huey battle helicopters roared right over their heads. A fully functioning military base camp had been erected amidst the ruins.

Standing on the mountaintop overlooking the plain of Megiddo was Stone Alexander. He took in the spectacle that he had wrought— the nine assembled armies, the light from countless camp tents, the dust clouds churned up by a thousand tanks—with great satisfaction. He turned to the cassocked man never far from his side, moving to a bank of microphones set up on the edge of the cliff. "I'd like to address the troops."

Obediently, the Guardian moved up behind his master, conjuring up an enormous holographic image of Stone that could be seen throughout the entire Valley of Jezreel.

Stone's voice boomed out across the valley. "My troops. You have taken the first step on the journey to the new world! We cannot be defeated because we are on the side of righteousness!"

Stone's chest seemed to expand with pride as a rousing cheer erupted from the combined forces, echoing throughout the vast valley. He turned and entered his command tent, continuing to watch the action on a bank of monitors. A speaker buzzed, and an alarmed voice came through with the latest intelligence.

"Lord Alexander, we've received word that the Chinese have arrived on the Eastern front!"

"Welcome them!" Stone smiled to himself. The tenth of the heads. He could almost taste the victory. Only one key person still remained to be conquered. And that, as Stone knew, would be the most difficult conquest of all. Speaking to himself aloud, Stone said bitterly, "It is easier to move an entire army than to gain the allegiance of one man."

# CHAPTER
# FIFTY-SEVEN

Ring in the valiant man and free,
The larger heart, the kindlier hand;
Ring out the darkness of the land,
Ring in the Christ that is to be.

—Alfred Lord Tennyson, *In Memoriam*


He shall come down like rain upon the mown grass.

—Psalm 72:6

The mountain bearing the ruins of Megiddo was silhouetted against the dust-filled sky. Figures moved in the tree line of the Jezreel Forest. A group of commandos, headed by David and Rick, moved to the edge of the cover.

Among them was General Juan Garcia, the Latin American officer who had cradled the dying old woman in his arms in the village of Santa Maria Teresa. He was here now on a mission of a far grander scale. Representing the Latin American forces, Garcia was there to offer his army's support to David and whatever American troops would still follow him. The general moved up to where David and Rick were standing.

"I am General Juan Garcia. On behalf of the Latin American forces, I would like to pledge our allegiance to you, President Alexander."

Rick beamed at Garcia. This was certainly an unexpected boon! "Glad to have you aboard, Garcia. We can sure use you."

Garcia smiled at David, intuitively sensing that he could trust this man whom he had known for exactly one minute. "How many of the North American troops are still loyal to you?"

David looked at Rick, who responded quickly, "The United States Army knows who their commander in chief really is. Almost all the troops on the field will strike with us when the time comes. We'll give you all we've got, and we've got a lot to give." David took the swarthy Latin general's hand warmly. "Welcome to the team."

"OK, so let me in on what you've got so far," Garcia said, anxious to get started.

Rick turned back to Garcia. "Well, this might seem crazy, but see what you think. Maybe the best approach here is the most direct. Our greatest question right now is how 'a few good men' are going to take out the united One World armies, right?"

They all nodded solemnly. Rick continued, "Well, we wouldn't need to worry about how many troops are with us—if we can take out Chancellor Alexander."

Garcia nodded slowly, taking in the idea. "Cut off the serpent's head."

Rick nodded. "Exactly. Do you think that's insane? I mean, from a military perspective?"

Garcia smiled. "Let me hear more."

Rick pointed at the map, "The chancellor's base camp is here, above the plain, and he has his Elite Guard with him. If we make a strike—do you think you can cover us?"

Garcia carefully appraised the situation. "Two hundred yards of clear killing field."

"Maybe we should try to take out the whole camp with a missile strike?" Rick suggested. Garcia shook his head. He noticed that David had been curiously silent during these negotiations.

"Surveillance photos show that he has enough missile defense systems to knock down anything we could throw at him." Garcia displayed a map of the immediate area on a portable monitor. "And with no cover for two hundred yards—we couldn't get men anywhere near that mountain. Which is exactly how our beloved chancellor planned it."

Rick frowned. "So what do you think is our best bet, General?"

Before Garcia had a chance to reply, David turned to Rick and Garcia with quiet resolve. "Listen, General, Rick, please don't take any offense here, but none of this is really necessary. I already have a plan."

Rick did a double take. *David* had a plan? *What* plan? Both Rick and Garcia turned on their heels to face David.

"Sir?" Garcia said apprehensively.

"I'm going up there," David stated firmly.

Rick couldn't believe what he was hearing. "You're going *where?*"

"You heard me. I said, I'm going up there."

General Garcia looked at David as if he'd just signed his own death warrant. Rick pushed David into the brush, out of Garcia and the other officials' hearing range. He got right into David's face. "OK, you're going up there with whom?"

"I'm going up to my brother's headquarters on that plateau. *Alone.*"

Rick was startled, but spoke cautiously. "Uh...you've arranged a meeting with the chancellor, Mr. President?"

David smiled awkwardly. "Somebody else arranged it. All I'm doing is keeping the appointment."

David walked out of the brush and back toward the military men. He addressed them all. "OK. Garcia's your top man now. You guys just hang tight and wait for the signal. Good luck."

Juan Garcia stood there, utterly dumbfounded, as his new commander in chief took off alone into the woods—leaving *him* in charge! Rick waited no more than a few seconds before taking off after David—finally catching up with him at the foot of the mountain. He grabbed him by the arm.

"What on God's green earth do you think you're doing? If you think I'm letting you go up there without at least a squadron of elites, you're off your rocker!"

David just kept on walking. Rick shouted after him. "I'm calling for backup right now! Don't think for one minute that I'm going to let you march up there and get yourself killed! You're playing right into his hands! You're giving him just what he wants, David."

David stopped only momentarily to comfort his old friend. "That's exactly what I want to do. Listen, please don't try to change my mind or have me followed, Rick. This is something I have to do myself. It's something I should have done a long time ago. I love you, brother."

Rick didn't know what to do. He had never heard David sound more sure of himself, nor more sincere. He looked at David with grudging admiration. "I...I don't know what to say, man. I just..."

David interrupted him, squeezing Rick's hand. "Just pray for me, OK?"

David took off once again, leaving Rick standing there alone in the desert. Rick sucked in a deep breath, whispering to himself, "God, he's on Your watch now."

# CHAPTER
# FIFTY-EIGHT

Methinks I am a prophet new inspir'd,
And thus expiring do foretell of him...

—William Shakespeare, *Richard II*


For at that time day by day there came
to David to help him,
until it was a great host,
like the host of God.

—1 Chronicles 12:22

Night had fallen on Megiddo. David was crouched beneath a tree with wide, protective cover. In the distance, far down the mountain, David could still make out the thunderous cheering of the armies, bolstering themselves for what they had every reason to believe would be the greatest battle of all time.

David looked down at his hands, clasping a Beretta nine-millimeter automatic pistol far too tightly. He pulled back the slide and took a magazine from his belt, but he stopped short of inserting it in the gun. His hands began to tremble. His mind started working overtime in the dark Israeli night.

*"What the hell am I doing? I didn't come all the way up here to fight, did I? There are millions of soldiers down there—what am I going to do with this little peashooter?"*

*David flashed back to the night, so very long ago, when his nanny had told him the story of David and Goliath. He had never forgotten that story or her prophecy: "Someday, my boy, if you keep tight hold of your faith...you might find your own Goliath to fight." An ironic smile formed around his lips. Stella had been right after all.*

*David tossed the gun as far down the mountain as he could. It hardly caused a ripple in the sand as it landed. David stood there raging, one soul alone in the wilderness.*

*"What am I doing? Trying to get back at Stone for what he did to Gabriella? Keeping us apart all those years. Murdering her—if that's what he did. But how could he do it? How does a crow turn into an arrow and an arrow into dust...unless...?"* His mind wandered. He heard Gabriella's last words over and over in his head like a mantra: *"You must have faith..."* Then, he remembered the words of the Roman priest presiding over her funeral. He had touched something deep inside of him, something he had never felt before.

*It wasn't love—he had known love all right, and the one he had loved most was now dead, lying stiff in a coffin in Rome. And it wasn't patriotism either. He'd known that, too. He'd always been a reformer. Always wanted to make a difference, to change the world. Must be something in the Alexander bloodline, he mused. And that overriding desire to serve his country. He'd always had that. He was no phony, like most politicians, and he had to fight hard to stay uncorrupted.*

*Sure, he had craved earthly power and position—he wouldn't deny he had coveted, even sought after, these things. He enjoyed the parades through the Midwest in limos, the American flag flying free on the fenders of the car as it zipped through the cheering crowds. But there were crowds cheering here and now, too, and what was it all for? What was it all about? Was it about power? Was it about*

341

freedom? Was it really so necessary for America to stay free—when the rest of the world had already succumbed to the One World? What could he do? What was he trying to do?

David sat back down on the sandy slope, still greatly agitated. He looked up into the night and stared at the starry configurations he had known so well as a Boy Scout. That he had pointed out and described in detail to his own troop when he had become an Eagle Scout. "That's Scorpio over there...you can make out the tail if you just follow the stars...and look, that's Mercury, the brightest star in the heavens..."

David smiled to himself at that memory. He had sought to serve even then. But now, everything he had ever thought he wanted was gone. The fame; the magazine covers; the titles—"Senator Alexander," "Mr. President"—were all useless to him now. As useless as his puny Beretta against a nuclear missile.

So then—who, or what, was he serving by this mission? Was he to believe Gabriella—that his own brother was truly the Antichrist? A living, breathing demonic entity? That was a big load to swallow, especially for a man who had cut Sunday school to hike in the woods and dream. He had never so much as picked up a Bible. But he had read a great deal in college—great novels, the classic Greek tragedies. Stories of the great overreachers—who desired to control not only their own destinies, but also the destinies of everyone they could conquer.

What had happened to these men? To Oedipus Rex? To Dr. Faustus? To all the great tragic heroes, both fictional and historical? They all ended up stripped of their earthly belongings and came crashing down to exactly where David himself now sat—alone with their consciences on a mountaintop in exile. Or dead.

Of course, Stone had grown up with a different set of heroes. David's heroes were all mythical or pseudo-historical figures like Fletcher Christian—real-life men and women never seemed to measure up to his picture of true heroism and leadership. Stone's heroes were men who had covered the earth with other people's blood—for their own ends. Men like Alexander the Great. He smirked. Alexander the Great, all right.

Both brothers had, each in their own way, succeeded in achieving earthly greatness. Even his own father had been a real life Citizen Kane. Though he had never held political office, he was as powerful in his own way as if he had been the president. All the Alexander men had sought power, and what had happened to them? Daniel Alexander, murdered by his own son. Stone Alexander, delirious with a lust for power and taking out the frustrations of his own life

342

on the rest of the world. At least, David thought to himself, his own ambitions had been more modest.

When he had fought for his position in the Senate, for the vice presidency, it had always been for the people. Hadn't it? He thought again. No, in all honestly, he had to admit that he had coveted power as well. He might as well be honest with himself. He had nothing to lose at this juncture. He, Stone and their father had all been cut from the same cloth.

As for God, or affiliating with any organized religion, it had simply never held an attraction for him. He had always seemed to be able to get what he wanted by visualizing it—and just making it happen. There was always a strong inner voice directing him—but that voice had been silent for a long time. Until, he remembered, when the angelic voice had spoken to him in a dark moment, reinforcing that he was on the right path. He had forgotten that.

Still, he had no faith. Nothing to believe in. No God. No country. Not even faith in himself. And yet, something had brought him here. Compelled him to go out alone into the mountains, preparing him to take on this "brother" who had never really been a brother...

It was clear that something, or Someone, greater than himself had brought him to this point. Had it been Gabriella? Was he doing it for her? David stopped and thought for a long time. Time was, after all, all that he had right now. He flashed back to the moments before Gabriella died, when he had clutched her shriveled hand in his. He had felt as much love for her then as he had when he was a pimply six-teen-year-old boy—but it was a far deeper kind of love. He had been there when she died. He had witnessed the crow turning into an arrow. He had felt the arrow turn to dust in his hand, just as Gabriella herself must now turn to dust. Just as all men and women must.

He'd seen broadcasts of the calamities all over the world; he'd wit-nessed the destruction of the world's great cities by no seen hand. Whose hand was this? The hand of God? The hand of his brother, now become the devil incarnate? Could all that had happened be explained as just one unrelenting freak of nature? Or—could this really be Armageddon? As much as he loved Gabriella, this was a big one for David to swallow.

Armageddon? That was just a fairy tale, wasn't it? A story, just as Mutiny on the Bounty was a story, and Fletcher Christian and Captain Bligh fictional heroes and villains. It must be. But if it wasn't, he mused, what the hell was he doing there, scaling the mountain, when the chances were he'd be coming back down the mountain in a body bag? He wasn't some religious zealot. Why would he be chosen, of all people, to fight Stone, if Stone were indeed the Antichrist?

David's mind was about to explode from all these possibilities. Or rather, from all these impossibilities. He had always tried to be a moral man. Was he meant to kill his own brother—as his brother had killed their father—an eye for an eye? He knew it said that somewhere in the Bible. The Old Testament, he thought. Frightened and confused, he screamed out into the star-filled sky.

"What is this all about? Do I have to kill my own brother—so that the world can live again?"

His statement echoed through the empty caverns in the mountains. His words came back to him a hundred times over. David suddenly became deadly still as he waited. He took a few deep breaths and tried to clear his mind.

"God, why me? I'm just a man. I know I really don't want to die up here, but if I don't destroy Stone, I am dead—along with the rest of the world.

"God, I ask for Your guidance and protection. Forgive me for doing it my own way and not following Your plan. I need Your strength; I don't have the strength to stand on my own. I'm in Your hands now."

Suddenly, he was flooded with a sensation of bliss. Everything around him seemed to glow. David heard a voice deep within the core of his being. He knew that it was the voice of God Himself. He was telling him yes, and showing it to him by allowing him to experience a state of euphoria. David luxuriated in the exquisite lightness he felt. In those few moments, or hours, he had no sense of time; David understood that he was on the only true path. Gabriella had been right.

He had the courage of his convictions. He had both right and might. What had been missing from his life all along had been faith. From everything he had ever tried to accomplish in his life, he had learned that he must have complete faith in his intentions, in his actions, or he would surely fail. But that had been a different kind of faith. That was faith in himself. Faith in his abilities.

Now, he joyfully embraced a higher form of faith—one that entered his heart and filled him with a joy he had never known. He now realized that faith was what had kept Gabriella alive in those catacombs. It was faith that had kept her spirit so vital while her body was ravaged by hunger and deprivation.

Yes, faith in God, and faith in Jesus Christ, the true Son of the Most High God.

David was filled with a rapture he simply could not fathom. But he didn't want to, or need to. It was a state of mind, a sense of peace that surpassed human understanding. He felt blanketed with conviction, love and faith.

These were not his usual "visions"—graphic images of destruction that tore through his mind like a pickaxe. No, this was more like a glimpse of heaven. An understanding that his power was still intact, even stripped as he was of his titles, his wealth, his loved ones and even his weaponry.

The voice continued to speak deep inside his head. This time it was saying, "So the world may live again." David had finally been blessed with the answer. He understood that armed with faith in God, he was more powerful than he had ever been before. Those who had loved him and had gone over to the other side seemed to surround him. He felt their presence, though he could not see them.

His mother, Emily, who had died in childbirth, covered him with her love in a way she never did, never could, on an earthly plane. And he knew that Gabriella was with him now, and he felt closer to her now than he ever did before. David had truly been touched by God's grace.

Now, he finally knew the truth. He was not doing this for power. He was not seeking revenge. He was not doing this for self-aggrandizement. He was doing it because he must. Because he had been chosen.

Gabriella had said that David was the only one who could take Stone down. He now saw that she had been right. The ultimate battle would be brother against brother. Right against might. This was the challenge his entire lifetime had prepared him for. This was the final challenge—and he must pick up the gauntlet.

Alone no longer, armed with his newfound faith and resolve, David fought his way up the mountain, eventually being engulfed by the formless shadows of the night.

Let the battle begin.

# CHAPTER
# FIFTY-NINE

He that leadeth into captivity
shall go into captivity: he that killeth
with the sword must be killed with the sword.

—Revelation 13:10

Stone, accompanied by several other high-ranking officials and well protected by international artillery, sat in the command tent. As always, the Guardian hovered near Stone. While David battled the jagged cliffs on the way to meet his destiny, Stone sat comfortably in a plush chair, speaking with the Israeli prime minister on the videophone.

"I have tried everything in the book to get you to see things my way, Mr. Prime Minister, but you have yet to make the right decision. I'm afraid that if you don't give up this senseless resistance to your inevitable defeat, I shall have no choice but to reduce Jerusalem to a pile of rubble. I have done it before, and I will do it again."

The prime minister's face was twisted with anger and hate. "As long as there is the love of God in the hearts of men, Jerusalem shall remain free! Do what you will."

Stone sighed. "That is a very noble sentiment, Mr. Prime Minister, but it won't keep your people alive. Are you willing to have the blood of your people on your hands? Every last man, woman and child?"

The prime minister almost gagged at Stone's vivid description. "If you order this attack, their blood will be on your hands, not mine!"

Stone exchanged a look with the Guardian. He then looked back over at the monitor, smiling. "Well, then, I'll be seeing you...dead!" Stone clicked off the monitor. He turned to his assembled generals and zone leaders, all terrified by Stone's prediction. But not one dared to question him. "Ladies and gentlemen, if you don't mind, I'd like some time alone."

One by one the generals and zone leaders dispersed, their hearts filled with foreboding. Stone was alone, with only the Guardian hovering in the distance.

Stone extracted a crucifix from a black box in his desk. He stared belligerently at the image of the crucified Christ for a long moment. Finally, he spat on the cross, the spit congealing into a thick, black, tarlike substance.

"Tomorrow, all signs of You will have disappeared from the face of the earth." He looked down at what used to be the crucifix and saw that the metal had melted in his hands. Stone shook the molten mass off onto the ground. With one quick flick of a bootheel, he covered it over with dirt.

# CHAPTER SIXTY

And ye shall know the truth,
and the truth shall make you free.

—John 8:32

The mountain bearing the ruins of Megiddo was silhouetted against the moonlit sky as David emerged from what seemed like the bowels of the earth. It was actually an ancient aqueduct, cut out of the living rock a hundred feet below the desert surface. Once it had carried water to the city of King Solomon. Now, it carried David toward his fate.

He emerged from the darkness, breath coming hard. He stopped, crouching down behind a pile of fifty-five-gallon oil drums. He heard the crunch of a footfall behind him. He crab-walked his way around the drums, trying to avoid the faceless sentinel. Still, the figure moved stealthily on, coming up to the spot David had just left. The figure knelt down.

David leaped out of the shadows and tackled the sentinel, and the two went rolling off in a scrambling ball of arms and legs—stopping with David astride, his arm raised to punch his assailant in the face. He looked down at the man's face, faintly illuminated by the flares in the distance.

"Rick? What the hell are you doing here? What about my orders?"

"I quit! I don't work for you or anybody else anymore. Now what are you going to do—let me come along, or kill me?"

David shook his head. "Come on." He pulled Rick to his feet, and they forged onward together toward the edge of Stone's encampment, hiding in the shadows of an olive tree.

Rick appraised the situation. "I don't like it. This was too easy."

David replied cautiously. "Don't be so optimistic. We're not in there yet."

Without a moment's warning, they were suddenly surrounded by seven of Stone's guards. Rick started to lift his M-16. David stopped him. "There's too many of them. Put it down."

Rick tossed down his gun as he and David raised their hands over their heads. The armed guards led them to the door of the command tent. The head officer spoke to the tent guards, who quickly delivered the message to Stone. David and Rick heard Stone say, almost cheerily, "By all means, show our visitors in."

David and Rick were pushed inside the tent. Stone's energy was so strong that it compelled David to look at him the moment they got inside. David was immediately struck by the fact that Stone seemed younger and more virile than he had ever seen him. Stone rose from his chair and moved to greet David.

"My brother has come to visit. What a pleasant surprise." Stone looked over at Rick condescendingly. "And you brought your little dog, too..."

Rick's eyes narrowed in anger. Stone smoothly pulled a pistol from the holster of the guard next to him, leveled it at Rick and fired two quick shots into his chest. The impact of the two slugs threw Rick to the ground. David knelt down beside him. "Rick! Rick—hold on, man. You'll be all right."

Rick spasmed in pain, grabbing on to David's hand, managing to squeeze out a few last words. "I...let you down."

David stared at his friend, clutching his hand. "Never. Not once."

Rick's eyes flickered for one moment before glazing over. "You were right all along. You had to do this...alone." With those words, Rick was gone. His hand fell out of David's grasp onto the hard ground. Stone smiled over at David maliciously.

"Everyone you love seems to die, little brother. Why do you think that is? Your mother, your father, your beloved Gabriella...and now this."

Before Stone could finish, David flew into a rage and leaped for Stone's throat. The guards clubbed him down with their rifle butts and pummeled him into unconsciousness. Stone looked down at his brother's broken body quite casually.

"It looks my brother's impromptu visit has been rather attenuated. How unfortunate. Have him put into the pit." Without a word, four guards pulled David along the ground and through the tent door. Another four covered Rick's bloodied body and dragged him out of the tent. With a whisk of the hand, Stone dismissed all the sentries. "That will be all for now. "

With the tent now cleared of unnecessary personnel, Stone turned triumphantly to the Guardian. "I knew he'd come."

The Guardian nodded, his expression bland. "Of course. He had no other choice."

"That's right. He had no other choice." Stone rose to his feet and lifted his head to the heavens. "I can feel it now, feel it all within my grasp. By this time tomorrow, all the wrongs of the world shall be set right and the imposter cast down from his throne."

He stared at the Guardian with affection. "How can I ever thank you? When I was a small boy scorned by my father, heckled by the world—you comforted me. It was you who showed me the true way. My true path. I pray that you will continue to watch over me and guide me throughout eternity, my dearest friend, my prophet."

The Guardian's face suddenly went cold. His icy blue eyes pierced Stone's heart. "Make no mistake about it, my lord," he said tersely, "I have merely been the facilitator. When you sit at the right hand of the most high, I shall sit at his left hand. I shall have my reward, and you shall have yours."

352

Stone was completely taken aback by this abrupt change in the Guardian's attitude, but pretended not to care. "Yes. Of course. Please leave me now."

The Guardian covered his head with his hood and disappeared into a puff of smoke, leaving Stone alone with his thoughts. His celebratory mood had passed; now, he felt himself as alone as he ever did as a young boy at Francini Academy.

# CHAPTER
# SIXTY-ONE

I know thy works,
and thy labour,
and thy patience,
and how thou canst not bear
them which are evil.

—Revelation 2:2

General Juan Garcia, flanked by the assembled American and Latin American troops, stood over an aide connected to a radio setup. The aide removed his headphones and turned to the general. "Well?"

"I'm afraid there's no word, sir."

Garcia gritted his teeth. "Then they are captured. Or dead. There's nothing more we can do. Everyone get some sleep. Like the president said, all we can do now is hold up and wait for the morning."

The men dispersed. General Garcia was left there alone, in the middle of a foreign land, thinking that if David *were* dead, it was now up to him to lead the renegade armies against Stone. Would the North Americans really follow him? The responsibility unnerved him to the quick. He looked over at his two armies, trying to get some sleep. He wondered if any of them would ever be able to sleep again.

# CHAPTER
# SIXTY-TWO

I have no brother;
I am like no brother;
And this word "love,"
Which graybeards call divine,
Be resident in men like one another,
And not in me: I am myself alone.

—William Shakespeare, *Henry VI*


No man ever became very wicked all at once.

—Juvenal

Badly battered and bruised, David lay in a crudely dug hole in the ground, covered by thick iron bars. Two guards appeared at the edge of the hole and looked down. David peered up at them, squinting through the blood congealing over his left eye.

The guards opened the grill, hands reaching down for David. He let himself be lifted out of the hole and found himself being pushed once more toward Stone's command tent. The guards threw him face first into the tent, onto the hard ground. Stone looked up, or rather, looked down, on David. "Sleep well, brother?"

David slowly brushed the dirt off and painfully rose to his feet. Every muscle in his body hurt.

"Isn't it a beautiful morning? The sun is up, the birds are singing, and all is right in the world." Stone turned to David with a venomous grin. "*My* world."

David grimaced. He wanted to wring Stone's neck right then and just get it over with, but knew he'd be stopped within seconds.

"Have a seat, David. Let me get you some breakfast. You must be famished."

David sat down, sensing the Guardian's malicious energy, his eyes piercing him like razor-sharp darts from across the room. He looked at Stone, motioning over at the Guardian. "You take this guy everywhere you go, like a pet chimp?"

Stone smiled. He saw that David planned on trying to unnerve him, as he did at their last meeting at Castle Alexander, and he was determined not to let it happen again. He had lost control that night. There was nothing he hated more than losing control. "Well, he's more like a good luck charm, I'd say."

David pivoted around in his chair to face Stone. He looked over at the Guardian, then back at Stone skeptically. "It seems to me that Gabriella was far more of a 'lucky charm' to you than this guy."

David was a power hitter. Stone pretended not to flinch. He was going to give it back to him, tit for tat. "Ah, so that's what's brought you here, baby brother. After all is said and done, it's really about *love,* isn't it?"

David raised an eyebrow. His body may have been weakened, but his mind was as keen as ever.

"Ah, yes, Gabriella. I must say that watching the two of you all these years, seeing how difficult it was for you both...how noble you were...never giving in to temptation...it was exquisite, really, watching you both suffer that way. Dwelling in a kind of perpetual living martyrdom."

Stone noticed David's wincing. "Did I touch a nerve?"

"It was a mistake from the beginning, Stone." David drew in several painful breaths. "She should have been with me, and you know it. I would have made her happy."

Stone shook his head. "You're wrong, little brother. Your life might have been fulfilled, but you never would have fulfilled your destiny. *Our* destiny."

Stone motioned for the Guardian to leave them alone.

David now trained his eyes on his brother. "Stone, I know who you are."

Stone smiled. "Well, good! It certainly took you long enough to figure it out. Took a woman to convince you, didn't it?"

David shook his head with conviction. "No. It may have taken a woman, a very special woman, to show me the truth, but *she* didn't have to convince me."

"Well, then, please tell me—I'm really interested. Who did convince you?"

David paused. "Oh. I don't know. I guess you could call it a 'lucky charm' of sorts. An angel told me."

Stone narrowed his eyes. "Hardly surprising." Stone moved over to the bank of monitors, suddenly jubilant, like a young boy showing off a new toy train. "We are but two pawns in a heavenly game, you and I! We can help the game along, but the winner has already been decided. Predestined, as it were."

David raised an eyebrow. "Oh, has it?"

Stone laughed. "It most assuredly has. I'll let you in on a secret. If you hadn't already guessed—I win!"

David frowned. "I don't believe in predestination, Stone. I believe that every man makes his own destiny."

Stone winked at him. "You keep that thought, David."

This new, giddy Stone unnerved David even more than the arrogant one. His brother had more faces than a child could make out of Mr. Potato Head. Now, Stone was standing before the video monitor, his face lit up like Winchester Cathedral on Christmas Eve.

"Oh, David—you must come see this!" David joined Stone before the monitors. They watched the Italian and Russian troops rolling onto the plain of Megiddo—their tanks jockeying for position.

Stone gloated. "The Chinese will soon follow."

David nodded. "I've got to hand it to you, Stone. I didn't think the Chinese would ever give in."

Stone leaned into his brother as if sharing a secret. "I gave them no options. So now, all is in readiness..."

David looked over at his peacock of a brother, prancing about as if he owned the world. David ripped into him. "Readiness? For what, Stone? Armageddon? A battle against *God?*"

360

Stone giggled. "Well, of course, silly!"

"Do you really think He's going to come—what with His busy schedule and all?"

Stone seemed amazed by this question. "Oh, He's coming, all right. Haven't you seen and heard the heralds?"

David sat down before the monitor bank calmly. "OK, so, how exactly is this all going to go down, Stone? Are the assembled armies of the world going to fight a host of angels? Is God going to show up loaded down with heavenly cruise missiles, flanked by His squad of archangel snipers?"

Stone moved over to his brother, placing a frigid hand on his shoulder, chuckling gently. "Of course not. How ridiculous." Stone motioned to him, almost kindly. "Come, little brother..."

Stone pulled David out of the tent and waved an outstretched hand over the armies assembled in the Valley of Jezreel. The two Alexanders overlooked the vast tableau of the largest full-scale military offensive in the history of the world. The scope of the operation stunned both of them. The valley was filled with nine different armies, with the tenth on its way. Millions of troops swarmed about like ants beneath them. A steady stream of vehicles winded into the valley from all directions—thousands of tanks, artillery and makeshift airstrips with jets of every type and description. Hundreds of helicopters hovered over the scene, constantly delivering more troops and supplies. The burning of Atlanta in *Gone With the Wind* was a back-street brawl compared to this spectacle. It was an awesome, breathtaking sight. Stone gloried in it, reveled in it. David was aghast.

"Do you understand now? Do you see? There will be no combat with my heavenly rival. The battle is already won. All bow to me. It is the art of fighting without fighting." Stone couldn't help but notice the confusion on David's face.

"You still don't get it, do you? The battle was for the *souls of man*. These *bodies* assembled here—they are not my armies—they are my *trophies!* Proof that every soul on the earth—excepting, unfortunately, you, has pronounced me the victor. And as you know, David, to the victor belong the spoils. And the spoils are rich. I get to rule not only the earth, but heaven as well. Not a bad haul, I'd say."

Stone looked up at the heavens and shouted, "You know, don't You? You see! Your greatest creation—the fragile, fleshly ones that You made room for at Your table—shoving Your loyal angels aside. And now, they all follow *me!* They have abandoned You! I have won!"

Taking a moment to compose himself, Stone returned his gaze to

David. But his voice still quavered with emotion. "My fallen angels will rise again and take their rightful place of glory."

David was horrified. If he had still maintained even a shred of doubt, Stone's tirade would have convinced him that he most certainly was whom he claimed to be. "Those 'fragile, fleshly ones' you speak of are men, Stone."

"It is of no consequence to me what happens to them. They are but pawns in my game. And as you can see, I play the game very well." Stone lowered his voice for effect. "I even know that there are some wolves among my sheep."

David froze, though remaining poker faced. "What are you talking about, Stone?"

"You didn't come to the Plain of Megiddo alone, David. I know there are a handful who are still loyal to you who might try to spoil my plans. I'm afraid I can't let that happen." He flicked on his radio transmitter. "Attack the Latin and North American armies!"

"What?! You're attacking your own men, Stone! Those armies are loyal to you, not me!"

"Well, yes. But there are dissenters among them—and it would be impossible to weed out those few who have remained loyal to you. I'd rather just destroy all of them than take any chances."

"You deranged animal..."

"*You* are the animal, David. Now, just relax and watch your fellow humans bleed like the animals they are."

# CHAPTER
# SIXTY-THREE

For the great day of his wrath is come;
and who shall be able to stand?

—Revelation 6:17


Resist the devil, and he will flee from you.

—James 4:7

It was Palm Sunday on the field of Megiddo, the day that commemorated Jesus' arrival in Jerusalem. Neither the day nor its significance was lost on either the One World armies or General Garcia's rebel forces.

Stone's command to attack made its way throughout the field like a current of electricity. Without a moment's warning, the One World armies suddenly opened fire on the Latin American and North American troops.

Garcia, stunned by the surprise attack, shouted into his field radio, "What is going on out there?"

"They've ordered an attack, General—not only against us, but against their own armies!"

Garcia stared ahead pensively, knowing that the time had come for action. Garcia shouted into his field radio, "This is it, men! Stand by and prepare for further orders."

The War to End All Wars had been mounted. The United Armies of the One World swarmed onto the battlefield with state of the art Heckler and Koch G33 5.5mm caseless ammo rifles, each division taking their orders from Russian Commander in Chief Jan Bratslavsky.

Before the Latin American troops even knew what hit them, three One World platoons had cut off a full quarter of Garcia's army, their guns shattering the unearthly silence of the rolling hills. The techno-tanks moved forward like beasts of prey, their aim accurate and deadly. Nothing could have prepared the renegade soldiers for this attack. Realizing in a panic that Stone had turned on them, the United States troops joined together with the rebels in an attempt to save their lives.

Looking over at the miasma of armies, their tanks proudly sporting the crimson flag of the One World, Garcia could only mutter one word over and over to himself, "Armaggedon…"

Despite his own worst fears, Garcia kept his troops on the move, rallying them by his seeming confidence. "First line, advance. Do not open fire until I command! Everyone else, dig in and stay down! Dig in, thick and high!"

The rebel first line battery swung into position, training their rifle barrels on the attacking armada and the swarm of soldiers flanking them. The remainder of the troops dug "thick and high," as Garcia had commanded, creating deep trenches into which they climbed, crouched and ready for action. They peered up apprehensively over their gun barrels—waiting for the inevitable.

As soon as the One World Armies were within firing range, Garcia bravely ordered the attack. "Commence firing! Open fire!"

The smoke from tank and small arms fire hung over the landscape like a thick, sprawling ghost, the rolling hills echoing with the staccato rattle of artillery and the occasional piercing commands of General Bratslavsky. Within minutes, the battleground smelled like an *abattoir*, but far worse was the sound of the screaming and dying echoing throughout the valley, filling the soldiers with despair.

A young Hispanic rebel on the front lines was giving it everything he had, his youthful enthusiasm and courage an inspiration to all those who fought around him. They all knew him as a nephew of General Garcia, a good-hearted kid, hoping to impress his uncle with his valor that day.

Young Garcia feverishly exchanged fire with a crimson-clad One World soldier, fighting fiercely for his own survival. Several soldiers zeroed in on him, opening fire. Bullets trailed the rebel Garcia, barely missing him.

Garcia's young nephew spotted an enemy machine gun nest about fifty yards ahead, and he saw his chance to make a difference. He pulled a grenade out of his pouch as he dashed toward it, outrunning the trail of bullets like a tailback sprinting for the end zone in overtime.

No more than a hairsbreadth from the gun nest, Garcia was suddenly racked by a half dozen slugs. All the bullets neatly hit him in the midsection. Clutching his bullet-riddled torso, trying to hold in his internal organs with his left hand, young Garcia stumbled the final few steps toward the machine gun nest. He fell over the sandbags into the surprised laps of three One World gunners. Young Garcia's head fell forward, and his butchered intestines filled the nest with the fresh profusion of carnage. Before they could even react, the grenade in Garcia's hand exploded, blowing them all to kingdom come.

Garcia bowed his head in a moment of prayer as he witnessed the incredible sacrifice made by his sister's son. He wondered how he could ever look his sister in the eye after what he had just witnessed. But there was no time for grieving now. Garcia saw the top of a sleek tank appear over the rise. Then another. General Garcia and his top men stood at their command base, stunned as they watched tank after tank appear over the dusky horizon, along with hordes of heavily armed soldiers.

The One World tanks, in addition to wave after wave of infantrymen looking for targets, opened fire. Dense columns of smoke rose from exploding vehicles, shells bursting in the air after being touched by flame.

The rebels seemed to move in slow motion as bullets whizzed by them at a lightning pace. A platoon of rebels, who had just witnessed their young comrade's self-sacrifice, carefully wound their way between the enemy tanks, looking for an opening. But there was so much flesh, smoke and debris in the air that it was hard to see more than two feet ahead. Still, they moved on toward the unknown.

It was a living nightmare. Massive explosions from artillery shells and mines tore the valley apart. Thousands of machine guns poured out a red sandstorm of bullets. A river of automatic weapon fire rained down on their heads, the bodies of the faithful torn to shreds at the feet of their comrades in arms. They were knee-deep in gore, their feet moving slowly through warm puddles of their companions' blood.

Hungry and operating on barely any rest, the Latin and North American soldiers were in a giddy, surreal state, slipping in and out of nightmare-plagued dreams as they advanced toward the killing field. Some of them just fell by the wayside. Some halted for a few moments' rest before attempting to rise again, while others collapsed and never again regained consciousness, their dead eyes helplessly focused on the stalwart, unbroken line of the One World's defense, lumbering toward them in the distance.

But though they were exhausted and half-starved, the renegades were buoyed by their faith. They had passed the point of fearing their opposition, and their faith gave them the fortitude to continue their advance against the overwhelming tide.

Unlike the rebels, the One World soldiers were well nourished and well rested. Their beloved chancellor had seen to that. Because of the strength of their sheer numbers, their attitude was aggressive, confident of their inevitable victory.

In the rebel base camp, Commander in Chief Juan Garcia's face was worn and haggard. His sense of foreboding only increased as he witnessed seemingly endless hordes of One World reinforcements snaking toward the killing field.

The rebels struggled to avoid falling into the craters caused by the explosions blasting all around them. They desperately tried not to think about those who had just died, whose very lifeblood they were now wading in knee-deep—but of those who might still have a chance to live.

The rebel's front line was rocked by mortar fire taking out their field hospital. The tents, containing not only the standard store of bandages, splints and morphine needed to tend the wounded, but also four medics, were blown to bits.

The scene was eerie, horrific beyond description, as grotesque, bloodied body limbs flew through the air, oddly reminiscent of the Bosch print that had hung so many light years-ago in the office of Generale Vittorio Francini. Stone Alexander had been obsessed with

Bosch's savage imagery—which may have foretold his vision of the battle that would decide who would rule forever—both in heaven and on earth.

After this first methodical attack, the orderly line of the One World suddenly broke—going berserk. Hollow-eyed rebels sprang to their feet with empty rifles—their ammunition supplies rapidly dwindling—and the entire battleground erupted into a hideous bloodbath. The One World zealots battered the rebels, engaged in vicious hand-to-hand combat. Men and women struck each other over the heads with rifle butts, flogged each other with their gun-stocks, even flailed at one another with their feet.

There was the sound of demonic triumph, as the One World soldiers knew, unequivocally, that they had gained the upper hand. There was no doubt in anyone's mind about who was spilling more blood on the field of Megiddo.

A simple country lad, clad in the crimson uniform of the One World, yelled in unholy triumph as he clubbed a Latin woman with his rifle, then whirled around savagely to dispatch still another victim, a Native American lad of no more than nineteen years.

Grabbing at each other's throats with dirt-sodden fingers, cal-loused, sweaty hands and singularly sharp fingernails, the One World troops rolled onto the ground like wild beasts, biting at their oppo-nents' throats, ears and noses with their bared teeth. Guns lay momentarily forgotten, strewn on the bloodied grass, as the soldiers pounded each other *mano a mano*.

Many of the rebels found themselves surrounded by a wall of bodies, a wall so dense, so revolting, that the living soldiers felt asphyxiated and trapped by the sheer volume of corpses surrounding them—the corpses of those who had recently been their comrades in arms, many of whom had become friends over the campfire, many of whom had been actual family.

Scores of infantrymen just sank to their knees, utterly overcome with despair, praying over the body of a dead son, a dead husband, a dead friend—now nothing more than one bloodied building block in the wall of bodies enveloping them.

Their grief was contagious. The mood of the entire renegade army became somber, the soldiers seeming almost catatonic. And yet the One World continued their advance, threatening to annihilate still more of their loved ones. To annihilate them all.

$$\Omega^2$$

Garcia watched in horror as the One World soldiers, seemingly possessed by blood lust, held his troops in a final death grip. It had become obvious that they were hungry for far more than just the taste of victory: They wanted to taste the very blood of their enemy.

The One World armies were savage beyond anything Garcia had ever witnessed, or even ever read about, and he had read and seen a great deal. He never thought he would see a day where he would witness a besotted enemy biting the very noses off his men, like intoxicated beasts, not even bothering to wipe the fresh blood from their mouths. To Garcia's mind, these soldiers were no longer men at all. They had become the henchmen of the devil.

Garcia knew that the strength of his troops was no match for the One World. With his troops outnumbered by at least ten to one, the enemy armies just kept advancing. Garcia grimly watched his troops being battered within an inch of their lives. Despite his orders urging them to hold their ground, their efforts became more and more fragmented and disjointed. None of them had ever been up against an army like this before. How could they? The One World forces had the strength and power of pure evil.

$$\Omega^2$$

From their mountaintop vantage point, David watched proudly as his rebels desperately tried to hold their own against the One World forces. Stone seemed merely amused by the spectacle before him.

"They do have spunk, your ragtag rebels," Stone said sarcastically.

"That's because they're fighting for what they believe in," David replied softly.

But Stone seemed nonplussed. "That hardly seems to matter, little brother. It is written that he who holds Jerusalem at the end of days will rule the world. *I* am that man." Stone turned to the closest radio operator.

"Send the bombers!"

# CHAPTER
# SIXTY-FOUR

And I heard a voice from heaven as the voice of many waters, and as the voice of a great thunder…

—Revelation 14:2

In the field below, only General Garcia had discerned the ominous rumbling over the sound of the pitched battle. Garcia looked up suspiciously at the sky over Megiddo. Suddenly, two bombers appeared overhead—bombers he had never seen the likes of in thirty years of professional army service. Except maybe in CIA diagrams marked "confidential." The bombers streaked overhead, their vapor trails leaving white streams against the sky. Garcia screamed over his intercom, "They're headed for Jerusalem!"

The bellies of the high-tech stealth bombers bore their deadly payload—nuclear bombs the size of Mako sharks, their sleek carbon-fiber bodies nestled in launching position, reflecting the softly blinking amber lights that designated their readiness status: Code Two—prepared to fire.

# CHAPTER
# SIXTY-FIVE

And it shall come to pass in the last days,
saith God, I will pour out my Spirit upon all flesh:
and your sons and your daughters shall prophesy,
and your young men shall see visions,
and your old men shall dream dreams.

—Acts 2:17

David stared over at Stone in horror. "You're bombing Jerusalem!?"

"Why, yes, of course," Stone replied matter-of-factly. "They have denied me access to their city."

"Do you have any idea how many people will be killed by a strike like that?" David screamed out, enraged.

"Well, approximately, yes," Stone answered coldly.

"Don't you have even a shred of human feeling left in you?" David asked, his voice trembling.

Stone shrugged. "No."

David seethed. "But you used to be a man, Stone. Weren't you? Weren't you a man when you embraced Gabriella? When you did everything in your power to keep her from coming to me? Wasn't that a man's passion—a man's jealousy?"

Stone waffled briefly, but pushed the thoughts away. "Never. I have never been a man. You were, and so was our father. Your kind shall be washed away like so much refuse."

David went for the jugular. "And those weren't human tears you cried over our mother, were they, at her funeral?"

Stone looked over at David, genuinely shocked.

"I saw it on an old news broadcast—you pulling away from Father at the cemetery, tears streaming down your face...screaming, 'Mother! Mother!' It was the day's top news. All the papers were writing about 'the poor little orphan.' But I guess that was some other boy. Probably another boy, too, who was so distraught over his mother's death that he set fire to his brother's crib to punish him for taking his mother away from him!"

*Touché.* Stone turned on David now, his eyes blazing with fire. "It was Daniel Alexander who killed my mother! It was he who made her bear another child when the doctors told her..."

Stone stopped short, his face red with emotion. He tried to compose himself. But David continued striking the nerve. He had finally stumbled on Stone's Achilles heel.

"Ah, I didn't know that. After you were born, Emily was told never to have another child?"

Stone spoke quietly now, his voice cracking. "There is much that you don't know, David. But I will tell you, if it makes you feel any better. Perhaps then you might understand that it was not you I meant to destroy in that crib—it was our father! To punish *him* by taking away his newborn son! Just as he had taken away my mother!"

David turned away for a moment, trying to process all that had been said. Then he looked back at Stone, this time with tremendous empathy for his sorrow. "I am truly sorry, Stone, for the bad hand that misfortune dealt you. But try to remember what it was like for me. At least you had our mother for six years. Six years is a long time, Stone. I never knew the woman at all, except in the womb."

David remembered his vision the night before, of his mother's comforting presence around him, and it flooded him once again with warmth and compassion. This man, this monster, was also her son.

"But I do feel her around me, Stone. At least, now I do!"

Stone was as close to tears as a man turned devil incarnate could be. David felt his pain and his essential loneliness. It was the pathos of a Frankenstein, destined to be alone throughout eternity.

"I pity you, Stone. I truly pity you from the bottom of my heart. I want you to know how sorry I am. About our mother, I mean. This is the first time I truly understood how you felt. That you thought I had actually taken her away from you. If she hadn't gotten pregnant with me, she might still be alive; I would never have been born; and you would have become an entirely different person. A happier person, most likely, not the personification of Lucifer."

Stone looked off into the mountains beyond, far from the troops, remembering that little boy who ran screaming and crying from his mother's funeral so many light-years ago.

"I wonder..."

David continued. "It seems pretty clear to me that life would have been a whole lot better for you if I had never born, Stone. So now I understand that that's one of the main reasons you're so...eager to see me go. Not that it would bring anyone back. Not Mother. Not Gabriella..."

Stone turned to David, begging for forgiveness with his eyes. Tears were streaming down his face. This was one side of his brother that David had never expected to see.

"David. Don't make me do this. They have all knelt and obeyed me as God! You must do the same, or I'll have no choice but to kill you! Just as I had no choice but to kill Gabriella. She knew far too much and believed far too little. She would not make the journey with me. She preferred to die a martyr's death. It suited her. It was not meant as a punishment—but as a reward. It was her choice. I didn't want to lose her, but once she saw who I really was, she hated the sight of me. I couldn't bear it!"

David felt Stone's ghastly ambivalence over Gabriella. Stone knew he had shown far too much and tried to lighten things up. "But it worked out well for me. It was a trap. A lure to get you here. I knew your 'fine sense of morality' would make you come up here and 'call me out' for what you perceived as my 'brutality.' It's all so, 'wild, wild West,' isn't it?"

David went right for the quick. "Didn't it bother you at all, Stone—murdering Gabriella?"

Stone sucked in a long, chill breath, though he kept his voice firmly under control. "Are you asking me if I feel remorse over her death—a woman we have both cherished, idolized? Well, as you might imagine, my dear brother, the man who used to be Stone Alexander would have felt remorse, yes, would have hated destroying the thing he loved—but, 'the devil made me do it,' as they say."

Stone emitted a boisterous laugh, but it was far from convincing—to either one of them. "You see, David, I cannot allow myself to have regrets. Any shadow or hint of remorse can do nothing but weaken my cause. My being a man—that is, my having *been* a man—is something that I must constantly cast down in myself. Feelings of love, of pity, of remorse—they only confuse me, distract my attention from my goal. All my concentration must now be at the task at hand: gaining back my rightful place in heaven. All else is naught; all else falls away before that."

Stone moved in closer to David, his voice trembling with emotion. "What I have just said does not alter the fact that Stone the man loved Gabriella with all his heart. *He* felt tremendous jealousy over her deep-seated desire to be with you rather than with him. "

David remained silent as Stone began to rant. David knew that he was truly seeing the real Stone, for perhaps the first, and probably the last, time.

"I wanted desperately to believe that Gabriella could never fix her eyes on another man as she did on you—my own brother. I tried to fix it so she'd never lay her eyes on you again. I came close to accomplishing that, I think. But that was a simpler time. At that point in my life, Gabriella was all I wanted and all I needed. I found out later on that there were far more important things in heaven and earth than the earthly love between two—or in this case, *three,* mortal souls."

Stone remained quiet for a long moment, though his hands shook noticeably. "And when I knew that she must die, of course Stone suffered—but then, many, yourself included, would argue that Stone had been dead a long, long time. She herself believed that to be so."

David saw Stone clench his fists, his back still turned from him. "That is the only way I have been able to endure the pain. I will admit to having been a man. Each time I cried. Each time I lost someone's love—to another human being—I have been a man." Stone was clearly at war with himself, and David did nothing but watch the show.

"But that person is no more! I had to kill him years ago to become who I am to become. Who I *am* become. Don't you see, David?"

David nodded. He knew *exactly* who Stone had become. Stone attempted to shake off his melancholy with a show of bravado. "I am no longer Stone Alexander, so all his puny mortal problems mean nothing to me! All are dispensable: wives, fathers, mothers and even brothers if they get in my way!"

Stone sighed and looked over at David, his voice softening once again. "You have wanted the truth, and I have given it to you. I have never held you responsible for my mother's death. The fault fell with Father. But when you fell in love with Gabriella, David—how was I to forgive that?"

David shrugged his shoulders. "And exactly how was I supposed to prevent that from happening? I saw exactly the same things in her that you did! I looked at her, and I loved her. That was all there was to it. It was hardly a premeditated crime. I was sixteen years old!" He smiled wanly at Stone. "I guess you could say that the Alexander brothers, for all their dissimilarities, have identical tastes in women."

Stone's face began to contort. "Yes. It does appear so." Stone started to shake uncontrollably with long-repressed rage. David fought to keep his senses about him.

"And it was I who was left behind! As always. Trying to reconcile having lost the two women I had loved in my life—*to you!*"

David felt Stone's pain acutely. He winced in sympathy as he watched his brother's physical and emotional upheaval. "But I give you credit, David. At least you never 'went all the way,' as it were—with Gabriella. You both remained pure as gold. Honorable...till the bitter end."

David demurred. "That's fiction, and you know it, Stone. I'm no saint. I never pretended to be one. And neither was Gabriella, though she came pretty close. We were just flesh-and-blood human beings! C'mon, Stone, if we're being brutally honest here, let's get it right: We longed for each other. All of our lives. And that longing will remain just that—a longing. Forever. I hope that gives you some satisfaction."

Stone looked far off at the twinkling lights of Jerusalem. "It should. But strangely, it doesn't. All I feel is pity. For you. For me. For Gabriella. Poor, poor, trapped mortals, with no hope in sight for their deliverance. Like me as a little boy, yearning for my mother's return and discovering that no matter how hard I prayed, she just wasn't coming back. I prayed and prayed. I even prayed to Jesus Christ!" He looked up at David, tears of rage streaming down his face and blurring his vision.

"That's when they came to me. That's when I learned who my true father was, and forever turned my back on that kind of prayer."

David held back, fighting to understand the complicated creature that was his brother. Softly, he whispered to Stone. "But she never came back to me, either."

Stone turned to him. Their eyes met, and finally, there was a real soul connection.

"I never had either of them. Ever. Only in my dreams. At least you knew Mother; she held you, nursed you, bathed you—you carry those memories with you forever. With your power, if you wanted to, you could find her love for you is still there—that it never died! That nothing ever really dies."

Stone lowered his eyes, taking in every word David said. David continued, though it was most painful for him. "And as for Gabriella, well, I don't want to get too explicit but...you...you enjoyed intimacies with her that I only ever dreamed of. You had her, body and soul. You shared time together. Just watching her move among the flowers was more than I..."

The vividness of David's description sent both men into a melancholy reverie. Suddenly, it seemed to both of them that she was actually there with them, her memory was so evocative. The sense of her was so keen that they thought they could smell her sensuous jasmine oil in the air. The brothers shared a look. An agonized Stone was the first to verbalize what was clearly palpable to both of them.

"Do you feel it, David? Do you feel her here?"

David looked over at his brother, replying grimly. "Of course I feel her. It's like she's right here with us." Stone seemed carried away by the reverie. David punctured it, letting all the air out of Stone's balloon. "Or maybe it's just the vestiges of your mortal conscience trying to get through to you, Stone, before it's too late."

Shaking, Stone could not even summon up a response.

# CHAPTER
# SIXTY-SIX

If my people, which are called by my name,
shall humble themselves, and pray,
and seek my face,
and turn from their wicked ways;
then will I hear from heaven...

—2 Chronicles 7:14

Dawn was breaking on Jerusalem when the news came down from the men who monitored the long-range radar station. Two planes, two single planes were headed for the heart of Israel. They knew what that meant. And they also knew that their missile defense screen would be unable to stop them.

Outside the Knesset, Jacob waited impatiently for his father. The rabbi was surprised to see him there. He put a proprietary arm around him and led him across the street. "Jacob! What are you doing here! I thought I gave strict instructions to your mother for everyone to go immediately to the synagogue."

Jacob sensed the urgency in his father's voice. "She did, Father. But I wanted to meet you."

The rabbi just shook his head. "That's the way I've taught you to respect your elders—by disobeying their orders?"

Jacob lowered his head. "I'm sorry, Father."

The rabbi grabbed the boy by his shirt lapels, urging him along.

"Why do we all have to go to the synagogue, Father? What's happening?"

The rabbi sighed deeply, pushing the boy along. "We have refused to let them into Jerusalem, so they have sent their bombs to destroy us. There is no time to talk of this now! We must run, Jacob! They will be here in fifteen minutes!"

Jacob tried in vain to keep his father's swift pace, grabbing at his long cloak. Finally, Rabbi Levy swept his son up into his arms, rushing off in the direction of the synagogue. Rabbi Levy shouted at his son. "I cannot believe you disobeyed me like this, Jacob! You persist in going against my orders, my express wishes—but this time, it could have cost you your life!"

Jacob looked up at his father's usually stern face. It was filled with what looked to him like fear—an emotion he had never seen his father betray, not even for an instant. It shook the boy to the core. "I'm...I'm sorry, Father. I just wanted to be with you."

At those words, Rabbi Levy began to sob, clinging tightly to his only son, tears of anguish running down his face. "My son...my son." Not slowing down for even a moment, the rabbi looked up to the heavens, his eyes streaming with tears. "My Lord God, I ask nothing for myself. I ask nothing for the holy city. But if it pleases you, O my Lord—spare the life of my son!"

Cradling Jacob like an infant in his arms, the rabbi ran as swiftly as he ever had in his life. He had to—because now he was running for his life. For *both* their lives. Jacob looked up into his father's face—so worn, so troubled, and he felt that he had never loved him so much as he did in that moment.

"Will you forgive me, Father?" Jacob asked innocently.

Rabbi Levy looked down at the tender face in his arms for a brief moment, the synagogue now within his sight. He spoke to Jacob with tenderness, for perhaps the first time in his life. "It is not me, but the Almighty, that we must *both* ask for forgiveness now, my child!"

# CHAPTER
# SIXTY-SEVEN

To him that overcometh will
I grant to sit with me in my throne,
even as I also overcame,
and am set down with my Father in his throne.

—Revelation 3:21

General Garcia urged his troops on. They continued to act as one force—lambasting the One World with everything they had, taking out squad after squad of One World soldiers. Even though the odds were against them, for the first time, Garcia thought that they might actually be able to pull off a miracle.

As if in answer to his prayers, General Garcia received a message in his earpiece. He turned to his top men. "The Chinese are here!"

Two hundred million Asian soldiers, equipped with tanks and supply vehicles snaking off as far as the eye could see, moved into the very the heart of Megiddo. Jockeying for position, the Chinese tanks formed an enormous circle around the One World base camp. An eager Russian field officer dispatched by General Bratslavsky trotted to the top of a hill to wave the Chinese into the camp.

Boom! A high-explosive shell from a Chinese tank took out the top of the ridge and the Russian officer along with it. Bratslavsky was stunned. The Chinese turrets were pointed right at the One World base camp!

He bellowed, "The Chinese! Those sons of a...they have betrayed us!"

But before he could ruminate on that thought, Premier Chen shouted into his field radio, "Fire! Fire! Fire!" Shells exploded. Flaming oil burned the ground. Cannon fire burst through the air, and Bratslavsky and his entire squadron were blown to pieces.

"I've never seen anything so beautiful in my life!" Garcia said, tears in his eyes. "I thought they'd never get here!"

Without their general, the One World soldiers were rudderless, on the defensive, running for cover to keep from getting blasted to bits by the Chinese. Blood showered down on the One World, taken entirely by surprise by the Asians' defection.

General Garcia, now safely ensconced beside Premier Chen in his tank, stood in midfield, shouting out to his revitalized troops, "If it wears the colors of the World Union—it bleeds!"

Indeed, everything bled. The field of Megiddo was packed with the bodies of the One World soldiers, bloodied, with mangled limbs—most of them already dead, the rest but a prayer away. The anguished screams of the barely living pierced through the gunfire and explosions, as if the valley itself were crying out for mercy. The Asian troops were proving as deadly as the flies that Stone Alexander had let loose on Tiananmen Square.

# CHAPTER
# SIXTY-EIGHT

How art thou fallen from heaven,
O Lucifer, son of the morning!

—Isaiah 14:12

At the sound of the first explosion, David and Stone stood together overlooking the field of Megiddo. They watched in stunned silence as the Chinese attacked the One World. From another vantage point, always keeping an eye on Stone, stood the cassocked Guardian.

Stone shouted over to the generals darting haplessly in and out of the command tent. "What the hell is going on?"

One of the dazed generals shouted back. "It's...it's the Chinese, my lord! They've turned on us! They're attacking our troops!"

Stone became irate. He looked down at the massacre going on in the valley below. He glanced for guidance over to the Guardian, but he merely shrouded his face with his black hood. Stone barked out loud. "But that is impossible! I had the premier's word only hours ago..."

David couldn't help but smile wryly as Stone raged at the sudden change in the tides. Stone, of course, noticed this, and turned to David accusatorily. "You knew!"

David shrugged his shoulders. "Well, brother, *c'est la guerre*..."

Stone turned on him like a junkyard dog as the cloaked Guardian slowly advanced toward Stone. "You knew they were going to do this! You planned this with the Chinese!" He screamed at David.

David demurred. "I may not have gone to military school, brother..."

"*I am no man's brother!*" Stone screamed at him, in a voice far deeper and more resounding than he had ever heard it before. David tried to remain rooted—wondering where that thunderous roar came from. But he didn't have to wonder for long. David could only stand by, thunderstruck, as Stone metamorphosed before his eyes.

There was the hideous sound of flesh ripping itself apart, as Stone's skin was virtually rent from his body and, within what seemed like seconds, replaced entirely by scaly hide. It almost seemed as if he had turned himself inside out. With a little assistance from the Guardian, the creature now swelled to well over twelve feet tall. Once it was fully formed, there could be no doubt as to who he was. This was the Dragon.

Let a person call him whatever he will—Lucifer. Satan. Or, more simply, the devil. But no matter what one may choose to call him, there was no doubt that this was the face of evil incarnate. The reptilian creature reared up over David. But for some reason, David felt no fear. He had gone far past the point where fear could reach him. He bravely raised his eyes to meet the creature.

"So, at last we meet face to face, alter-ego of my brother."

The two stood apart, like the lawman and the bad guy, each wondering who would be first on the draw.

While David was appraising the embodiment of his brother's dark side, the panicked generals and One World zone leaders huddled together within the command tent, witnessing Stone's transformation. They saw that they had been most abominably betrayed.

They joined together, trying to decide on an immediate course of action. They found it. Within moments, they were all rushing about, shouting orders to their respective teams, until in a matter of minutes, a group of expert technicians, working inside the command tent, had turned on every video and audio monitor to its fullest capacity—*sending the image and interplay between David and the monster into the video and audio transmitters at every station throughout the field of war.*

When the image of the Dragon first appeared on the screen, a hush came over the battlefield. The fighting stopped instantly. Soldiers on both sides, formerly in deadly opposition, crowded around the transmitters, weapons dropped at their sides, watching the American president being attacked by a monster of biblical proportions. The war had come to a screeching halt.

# CHAPTER
# SIXTY-NINE

Is death the last sleep?
No, it is the final awakening.
—Sir Walter Scott


Servant of God, well done!

Well has thou fought the better fight.
—John Milton, *Paradise Lost*

Outside, the creature who once was Stone slouched toward David with a nightmarish slowness. He began to speak, his voice deep and resounding, as befit his enormity. The very earth reverberated with each word he uttered. "Aren't you afraid, little brother?"

David remained resolute. "Not at all."

The Dragon growled with barely repressed fury.

"What did you think I was going to do, Stone? Did you think I was just going to run away? Did you think I was going to fight you? I can't fight you; I didn't bring my slingshot! But I'm not going to make this any easier on you, either. I'm not going anywhere." David dug his feet into the ground. "Call it passive resistance, if you'd like—but I'm not budging, Stone." Unarmed, without even a slingshot, this David could only use his wits against the hound of hell.

The monster was only further infuriated by David's intractability. "Believe me, I have walked through history under better names than Stone Alexander!"

The ten armies assembled in the valley below stared in disbelief at the savage titan on the mountaintop, his image magnified like a hologram upon the pillar of fire behind him. There was a deadly silence as millions of soldiers watched the final death match play out. They were all so absorbed that none of them noticed the rumbling that came from neither tanks nor bombs.

"Your brother was a mere vessel I chose, nurtured from spawning to do my handiwork—the perfect puppet to perform in my final drama."

David spoke to the monster confidentially. "You're right about that. You couldn't have picked a weaker, more infantile specimen than my brother. But I guess you knew that. I guess you targeted him the minute he tried to set fire to my crib!"

The Dragon burned. David felt the heat—but it didn't stop him. "You must have figured, 'This kid'll be a cinch to win over to my side. He's already halfway there!' And you were right. He was an out-and-out chicken, and a coward besides! You had such a hold on him that you got him to murder his own father. Even his own wife! And he loved her! He was such a wimp that he'd hook up with anybody—if they'd let him call them, 'Daddy.' And you're one pretty big daddy! Stone was just a poor, lonely sucker looking for a father, and I guess you more than fit the bill."

That was it. The Dragon turned to the mocking David. "Enough!" With one swipe of a clawed hand, he slit David's throat. David dropped to his knees. There was an immediate outcry from the field below, from those watching the scene on the monitors. David looked up at the savage titan, blood coursing from his neck.

"OK, you got me. But do you have any idea what's happening around you? I hope you combed your scales today, brother, because you're being broadcast in all your true colors—all over the killing field! It's over, Stone! They know who you really are. How many of them do you think will follow you now, now that they've seen you in all your glory? You should have taken some time to read The Book. I'll let you in on a little secret—God wins!"

The titan stepped back and looked down at the field of Megiddo. He saw that all fighting had stopped and that the soldiers stood riveted *en masse* before the video screens. And they were staring at him! He turned back to David, bellowing with rage. "This is all your doing!"

David, one hand clutched over his bleeding jugular vein, continued to goad the monster. He had nothing to lose. "Hey, Stone! Remember how you said that people would believe anything they saw on television? You know, I think you're right. Now, they're seeing you like they never saw you before—stripped of all your camouflage and charm."

The Dragon reared back its head and spewed venom onto the earth, but it was obvious that its power source was slowly beginning to subside. Fear of defeat was defeat itself, and the Dragon was beginning to have doubts. David sensed his weakness and continued to bait him.

"If it was all those souls you were after, I think it's pretty safe to say you've lost this time around. Maybe next time you should look for a stronger 'vessel.'"

This blow hit hard. David knew that the monster was growing desperate. David was surprised that suddenly the terrible pain from the neck wound was all but gone. In fact, even though he knew he was dying, he had never felt so good in his life, so at peace.

But there could be no peace for Stone Alexander. For Stone, the man beneath the mask, his state of mind could only be described as tormented. Inhabiting the body of the Dragon was the shell of a man with fear at the core of his very existence. The man who had allied himself with the damned in the grandiose hope of winning heaven was wavering. A shudder of sheer terror ran down his back. He roared once again, but it was no longer clear whether his aim was to terrorize or that he himself was terrified.

But it was clear to David. He understood that the Dragon was toppling—must topple—because at his core was but the soul of a mortal man.

# CHAPTER
# SEVENTY

And I looked, and behold a pale horse: and his name
hat sat on him was Death, and Hell followed with him.

—Revelation 6:8

The desert shall rejoice, and blossom as the rose.

—Isaiah 35:1

Although the war had come to a virtual halt, no one had bothered to tell this to the pilots headed for Jerusalem. They had been dispatched by Chancellor Alexander himself, and unless they heard otherwise, they would complete their deadly mission. The bomber pilots had been well instructed. Their mission: total and complete destruction. Their target: Jerusalem.

Inside the synagogue *Beit Knesset Hagadol* in Jerusalem, a mass of terrified Jews circled Rabbi Levy, shrieking as the sound of the approaching bombers filled the air. The rabbi pulled away from them, standing on the *bimah*. He addressed his fearful congregation. "Stop it! Stop it! All of you! You cannot fight the will of God. His will be done, and that is all. All we can do is pray for deliverance. His will be done!"

Jacob knelt beside his father, hand in hand, praying as fervently as ever he had in his brief stay on earth. Just as the bombers were preparing to drop their deadly poison over Jerusalem and the rest of the world—there suddenly came a jolt. A jolt so massive that it caused the entire world to halt. Speechless, the Jews sprung as one to their feet as a series of blinding flashes of light erupted, reflected through the stained glassed windows of churches, temples and mosques all over Jerusalem.

Out of simple huts, gardens and treetops, hundreds, thousands of beacons seemed to be lighting the way—like runway approach lights. What was it they were lighting the way for?

Suddenly, a massive white light, one sole power source, ripped out over the sky like a tsunami, illuminating all the ground beneath it like floodlights against a black sky. The ferocity of the light split the Mount of Olives and vaporized the stealth bombers as their bomb bay doors began to whine open.

Water blasted out from the earth hundreds of feet into the air. Shafts of light burst up from under the ground like crystal icicles. Healing water gushed down over Jerusalem, through the ancient city, flooding the Kidron Valley, sweeping into the Dead Sea and bringing it to life again.

A beautiful, glowing flame, forming an immense spiral around a thick core, engulfed the city of Jerusalem. This was the Eternal Source of All Power. It roared through the bodies, the souls, of everyone on earth. It seemed comprised of infinitesimal sprites of light. One passed right through Jacob. He had a brief glimpse of an angelic face before it raced off to join the others in the Massive Shaft of Power.

The pulsing, pure, white laser flowed like water—flooding out into the ancient city, through the Kidron Valley and finally out onto the field of Megiddo. The bloodied field glowed as the sacred light blasted over the land.

# CHAPTER
# SEVENTY-ONE

These shall make war with the Lamb,
and the Lamb shall overcome them:
for he is Lord of lords, and King of kings:
and they that are with him are called,
and chosen and faithful.

—Revelation 17:14


A tomb now suffices him for
whom the whole world was not sufficient.

—Epitaph for Alexander the Great

On the battlefield of Megiddo, all was in pandemonium. The pure, white light struck those who still followed the false prophet. Eyes blasted out of their heads. Flesh seared off their bones.

A young officer wearing the crimson colors of the One World realized, almost too late, what was really happening around him. He saw how he, how each one of them, had unwittingly contributed to this unholy alliance with evil itself. He was instantly tormented by guilt. He began to shudder and weep. "God, forgive me for what I have done. Forgive me!" The penitent soldier cried, tripping backwards, flame and exploding earth scattering above him and shredding his body to pieces.

$$\Omega^2$$

On the mountaintop, the Guardian, now huddling near the creature for protection, was suddenly lanced by a shaft of light. The flesh melted off his body like wax, leaving nothing behind but a black shadow, which immediately disintegrated into the air.

David stared up at the incredible array of fireworks before him. It was more blinding, more sensational, than anything Stone or his Guardian had ever conjured up. At the very sight of this light, the massiveness of the creature began to dissipate. Soon, it had mutated into a small, centaurlike creature, with the hooves of a goat and the upper body of a man, the man Stone Alexander. David watched the transformation in amazement. The once formidable monster had caved, fallen to its knees. David looked over at Stone, whose face was ashen.

"You still think you're going to rule the heavens, Stone?" David said grimly, feeling his life's blood ebbing away from his neck wound.

But Stone was still playing the angles—hoping against hope for a way out. Far too late, he begged for mercy, crying out to the heavens, "Jesus Christ, I beg You, forgive me...!"

By way of an answer, Stone saw a shaft of lightning manifest right over his head. To David and the others in the Valley of Jezreel, in Jerusalem and all over the world—the lightning was cleansing and purification itself, offering the hope of peace and redemption after so much chaos and blood.

But Stone saw something else. In the distance, he saw Jesus Christ, larger by far than the Beast he had created, astride a massive white stallion, coming in clouds of glory, accompanied by a host of angels. The vision of his enemy, his immortal foe, made Stone cower in fear. His eyes were blinded by the brightness of the light. He shouted out to the blazing bolt of lightning, "Nazarene! You...are...Lord!"

By way of an answer, the shaft of light split apart the very mountaintop, and an abyss opened beneath Stone. He fell—catching one hand on the edge of the chasm. He scrambled, trying to pull himself up. Desperately grasping for a hold, Stone's eyes pleaded with David for mercy.

"Please, David, pull me up...I beg of you..."

David, left hand clamped over his neck wound, crawled slowly toward the edge of the precipice. He took Stone's hand in his own. Much to his surprise, it was again warm and fleshly. David saw that Stone was hanging on by a mere thread—a root imbedded in the crevice. Stone looked up at him, terror in his eyes.

David looked at Stone disconsolately, still clutching at his hand—knowing full well that in order to complete his mission he must not help Stone.

"David, please—I'm your brother. I love you..."

David was filled with a rush of compassion for this lost soul. How true to Greek tragedy it was, that one who had risen to such heights, who was once far too proud to beg, was now, through his own arrogance, hovering at the door to eternal perdition. And this tragic hero was his brother—and he knew that he had no choice but to let him go.

Without even thinking, David heard himself saying, "I'm sorry, Stone." David then closed his eyes, murmuring, "Thy will be done."

Stone's eyes froze in fear, realizing that those words had sealed his doom. The root that had held on so precariously finally broke off, hurtling the screaming Stone far, far down into the abyss.

David watched in anguish as the earth slowly closed back up, completely covering the cavity that had just swallowed up the body of his brother. But he didn't have to suffer very long. Soon, he was feeling no anguish, no pain, no remorse, no grief. He was crossing over to the other side.

*As his soul began to leave his body, David began to see the entire picture clearly. He had led an important life. A moral life. He had followed his convictions and done what he believed in, right up to the end. He understood that he had played a necessary part in this nasty duel between the two elemental forces of life—darkness and light. He appreciated for the first time how honored he had been to have served that purpose—to have been selected as the one to oppose, and then expose, the devil himself. There were no longer any doubts about the choices he had made. He knew that he was meant to be on that mountaintop, with Stone, at exactly that place and that time. He now understood that this had all been, somehow, preordained, and he felt proud to have been chosen to this office. He had become*

*Fletcher Christian at last, leading his people, if not to a tranquil island, at least face to face with the truth—from which they could then pick up the pieces and start a whole new life. A whole new world. He felt at peace.*

*The sun's rays shone gently down on David, and he basked in the warmth. The sunlight transformed him, and he now felt himself a part of it, a being entirely of light. As his spirit rose, he looked down at his poor, broken body. He felt one with that man, and yet completely free from his pain and suffering. He was moving further and further from the earthly realm, soaring through a world more real than the physical plane, but invisible to all but those who have been saved through their love of God.*

# CHAPTER
# SEVENTY-TWO

Our birth is but a sleep and a forgetting:
The soul that rises with us, our life's star,
        Hath had elsewhere its setting,
            And cometh from afar:
        Not in entire forgetfulness,
        And not in utter nakedness,
But trailing clouds of glory do we come
        From God, who is our home.

                    —William Wordsworth,
                *Ode on Intimations of Immortality*

The dawn sun broke over the eastern skyline to reveal a field filled with men and women of all races and nationalities—only recently at war with each other. But there was no more fighting. The tanks and helicopters seemed to have miraculously disappeared. A sense of renewal, of healing, filled the world with joy. Everyone tended to each other's wounds, sharing their food and water, cooking together over open fires. The bitterness, the hatred, the insanity of the One World seemed to have been washed away by a sea of blood and tears and the glory of the Light. Now, there was nothing but love and the ecstasy of rebirth. The final millennium had begun.

> Behold, I make all things new.

> —Revelation 21:5